Loose
on the
Wind

by
Will H. Hays, Jr.

Printed in the United States of America

printing number

2 3 4 5 6 7 8 9 10

Library of Congress Catalogue
Card Number 89-91466

ISBN-0-9624303-0-7

For my beloved children,
Kathy, Bill and Amy

Acknowledgment

I wish gratefully to acknowledge the assistance and encouragement given to me by some good people during the long haul of getting this novel from my head into print. They include my wife Ginny for her patience during the book's progress and her championship of the result; my son Bill for his unique, invaluable contribution to its final form; Valerie Lyon for her principal research into the Kansas scene of 1875; and a score of other kind generalists and specialists for their help in areas of their interests and mine.

The characters and events in this novel are fictional; and any similarity to or identification with actual living or dead persons or actual events or locales other than those specifically mentioned or generally known historically is neither intended, expressed nor implied.

Will H. Hays, Jr.
Crawfordsville, Indiana—1988

CHAPTER 1

The long, flickering light, dark, light, dark echoing tunnel roared above and around him. He was being shot through a gun barrel too large-bore for its bullet. He was the bullet. White-garbed people were hanging onto him, trying to keep up with the bullet in him that was crushing him like a boulder he was trying to squirm from under, ghostly people masked and capped with only their eyes visible, straining toward the swinging doors ahead, staring into his eyes searching for life—his life, Mattie, for God's sake?—amid tubes and bottles and whining tires.

He seemed to hear his voice. Far away. Dry and hollow. "Mattie?"

Her "Here!" was stricken.

"Love."

"I love you, too, Mark," her face floating into the mist of his remaining awareness, "and you can't leave me."

A youngish male voice was harassed but gentle. "This is as far as you can go, M'am. Let you know as soon as we're able. Tell me his name, please."

"Sergeant Mark Keller."

Blinding light exploded the dimness, seizing him and the gurney and catapulting them into a suddenly stalled, white-tiled, quick-talking glare. Before he drowned in unconsciousness he heard some of the talk. Various voices. Faintly.

"Hell of a good job, Son, plugging that hole. How long?"

"Maybe twenty minutes since we started back."

"Move your hand now, I'll hold the bandage now. Nurse, cut the rest of his shirt off."

"Haven't seen a sucking chest wound since—last night."

"Who'd his wife say he is?"

"A cop. Sergeant Mark Keller."

"Bastard shot him was DOA. Ambulance driver said a drug bust. Neighbor saw it said the other guy shot first, and they'd been friends."

"Chalk one for the cops."

"Not if we can't stop this one's hemorrhage."

"Judas, I remember now, I read about this one. Toughest cop in Manhattan. Lone wolf. Law's the law; they mind or they wish they had. Goddam

1

them! He's got to make it, bless his soul. I'm tired of wading through murdering junkies to get to work."

A tired voice: "Wonder if someone's blessing the DOA's soul?"

"The hell with the DOA, Nurse."

"Maybe the hell with his wife, too, Doctor? Maybe his child?"

"Come ON!"

Come on, come on, come on . . . into the cavern of his dreams and memories, along the restless, cluttered trail of his lifetime with its forlorn beginning and at-hand ending. Some of his heroes, dead and living, waved at his passing: Theodore Roosevelt, Daniel Boone, the wasted point-man of his Vietnam patrol, Abraham Lincoln, Sergeant York, Norman Vincent Peale, Wyatt Earp, the mayor. He stood again on his life's peak where Mattie had said she would marry him, and he stared again with his parents into the abyss where he and they earlier had buried his beloved sister. The cavern's walls whispered Mattie's gentle warning: "Don't forget human nature, Mark; you can't mend the world yourself." The whispering became a muttering and grew to a rattling clangor and subsided abruptly in a hissing, jerking halt riveted by a howl:

"Bancroft!"

CHAPTER 2

It was a changing world when Luther Cain first stepped from the train into Bancroft, Kansas.

Barbed wire was a novelty on the market. Benito Juarez was in control of Mexico. Jean Baptiste Camille Corot had died recently in Paris. The Black Hills gold rush was at its peak west of Deadwood.

There were other things which were true that summer: Ulysses S. Grant was serving the third year of his second term as President of the United States, and the nation still was reeling economically from the Panic of 1873 after two years and still wrestling with the grim effects of the Civil War, including Reconstruction, after ten.

Five years before Luther Cain's coming to Bancroft, the Franco-Prussian War had brought an end to the reign of Napoleon III of France, John Davison Rockefeller had helped organize the Standard Oil Company, and 176 Irish-Americans under General John O'Neill had tried to capture Canada as a base for a further attack on Great Britain. Four years before that summer Gilbert and Sullivan had finished their first musical collaboration—an opera called "Thespis"—and a force of United States Marines had made a raid on Korea because some Koreans had burned an American ship. Retaliation for such an affront in those days was considered a matter of honor. Three years previously Buffalo Bill Cody had opened in Chicago as headliner in Ned Buntline's play, "The Scouts of the Plains," and reportedly had suffered a bad case of stage fright. Two years earlier Mary Baker Eddy had divorced a Swampscott, Massachusetts dentist; the fossil bones of man's ancestral Oreopithecus had been excavated in Italy. The preceding year a devastating grasshopper plague had swept the plains west of the Mississippi River.

Those were some of the things that had happened five years before Luther's arrival in Bancroft. The year after his coming General George Custer and his entire command were to be massacred by the Sioux in the Battle of the Little Big Horn in Montana. There was to be something else in the year ahead: Luther Cain was to overtake his predestination.

3

Often events are known to be important at the time they happen. The importance of other events are recognized later. In the case of Luther's coming to Bancroft, both aspects of this truth occurred in combination. His coming was important to the town and to him at the time he came because the town wanted his help and he wanted the job of helping it in his particular way, which was the way he earned his living. His coming also was learned afterward to have been important to the town and to him without anybody knowing it at the time because it presaged both the town's and his awakening to a neglected tenet of human accord.

That was to be a rude awakening all around.

On the August afternoon when the tall, sinewy, brown-mustachioed man first stepped from the train into the dust of Railroad Street (which paralleled the track on both sides of it) the plains surrounding Bancroft shimmered in the furnace heat of the Kansas sun. He was almost afraid to breathe deeply for fear of searing his lungs. Even the dogs and the little boys, who he knew from his experience in other frontier towns usually gathered about the station at train time, were missing. He guessed that the dogs had fled the heat under boardwalks and wagons and the little boys under the sluggish waters of the creek which the train had crossed east of town. He admired the dogs' good judgment and envied the little boys.

He stood aside to let the other deboarding passengers step past him and shifted his saddle on his shoulder with one hand and got a firmer grip on his bed roll with the other and gazed about carefully under his hat brim at his immediate surroundings as was his occupational habit.

The gray clapboard depot slumping in front of him couldn't yet have been weathered by more than a half-dozen winters but it looked as though it has suffered fifty. A desk and a telegraph set were visible through its open front door. Also through its open door he could see a grill lettered "Tickets and Mail." A dozen men were standing among their carpetbags under the building's wooden awning, putting off until the last moment climbing into the train's two stifling passenger cars. Some of them looked at him briefly, wary of letting their glances show too much curiosity.

At the head of the train the fireman was funneling water into the locomotive's boiler from a stilted tank beside the track and the engineer was complaining loudly to the station agent about having been delayed for three hours on the arbitrary order of a Texas trail boss. The Texan had seen the train's smoke coming in the distance and had sent some riders to halt it so his cattle shouldn't be stampeded. Beyond the water tank sprawled a lumber yard and reared what appeared to be a makeshift grain elevator.

Visible between two cars, on the other side of the track, a dilapidated blacksmith's shop was flanked by a board corral penning a few dusty, tail-switching horses. The waist-up-naked smith worked with casual power at the outdoor forge as though the day were a cool October one. Luther filed a mental picture of him under "useful."

Down the track in the direction from which the train had come there was a bridge over the creek and beyond that a dozen miles the horizon, with nothing of significance in between except a distant dust cloud.

Down the track the way the train was going, far beyond the lumber yard, was another horizon with some clouds above it and nothing between it and Luther that a white man could see from where he stood. Indians probably could see ten thousand years of faded memories—perhaps why they had fought so hard.

He walked to the station door, dropped his bed roll to the boards beneath his boot heels and stood with his saddle on his shoulder, waiting for the train to pull out and the agent to return to the building. When the train jerked away presently he could see the part of the town lying below the track. It wasn't much. Across from the lumber yard there were a couple of acres of stock pens and loading chutes made of planking and railroad ties. Nearer the station, directly opposite him, there was a clutter of unpainted buildings—honkytonks, boarding houses, some small stores, a billiard room, a dance hall, two or three livery stables— the whole divided into quarters by a street running straight south from the track and by one fifty yards below running at right angles to the other. Horses drooped along hitching rails lining the two powdery streets and men walked in and out of the buildings and along and across the streets in groups or singly, noisily or quietly. Mostly quietly in the burning daylight, although Luther knew that after nightfall it should be another story. They were men of types with which he was familiar: muleskinners, bullwhackers, troopers, railroad gandy dancers, gamblers, buffalo hunters, homesteaders, drummers, cowboys. Mostly cowboys.

5

Mostly Texas cowboys.

Luther grunted. His tan eyes darkened a slightly weary shade.

A hundred yards eastward from the jumble of buildings toward the creek hulked a two-story frame house with three horses tied to a rack in front of it. More horses should be tied in front of the house as the day and then the night wore on. A brief trill of female laughter sounded distantly from one of its upstairs windows.

Beyond the house and across the street on the bank of the creek a low ramshackle building with no windows and an adjoining corral oozed smoke from a tin chimney. A slaughter house undoubtedly. The smoke probably meant the butcher was making soap.

Southward from this graceless part of the town out on the sweltering prairie below the track-side clutter several thousand cattle were being held by cowboys from a half-dozen trail-end camps, waiting their turn for shipment to Kansas City or Chicago. The cattle weren't hard to hold on such a hot day, being content temporarily at least to browse on the parched grass. The long drives up from the Brazos and Red and Canadian and Cimarron along the Chisholm and the newer Jones and Plummer Trails gradually had taken most of the wildness out of them.

"Howdy," Luther said to the agent. The short, fat man was approaching him carrying a sack of mail. "Reckon you could tell me where the mayor's office is at?"

The agent tongued his tobacco cud behind his left molars. "With you in a minute." He spat and went inside the station and after a moment came out again without the mail sack but with the cud still bulging his left jowl. "Mayor's office?" His small blue eyes flicked up the rangy length of Luther Cain, from high boots past tooled holster and silver gun butt and white shirt to round-crowned black hat. "You ain't Luther Cain?"

Luther nodded.

"Say now," the agent smiled, putting out his fat hand, "we been looking for you. Name's Ed Sarver—railroad agent, postmaster, and town councilman. Welcome to Bancroft bygod!"

They shook hands.

"Toss your saddle and bed roll in here," Ed gestured through the door, "we'll send someone for them later. I'll not tell you where the mayor's office is at. I'll take you there."

6

"You got your work to do," Luther said. "I'll just go if you'll point the way." He started to reach for his bed roll but Sarver beat him to it.

"I got no work can't wait." The agent-postmaster-councilman stepped into the station, swinging his burden ahead through the door with his knee. "East-bound train come through this morning and west-bound one you rode is the last today. I'll lock up while I'm gone; sort the mail later."

Luther followed him inside and stowed his saddle in the corner where Ed Sarver put his bed roll.

"Yep," Ed said, "at the meeting after Marshal Tucker left I was the one moved we telegraph you about coming. Unanimous it was except for Johnny Newlin; he mixes with that bunch down there." He waved a hand southward. "Don't know how he got hisself elected."

"Much obliged," Luther said.

They went outside, the agent locking the door behind them but forgetting about the open window. Luther didn't call it to his attention.

Ed spat again and waved his hand northward this time. "Other side."

Walking around the station they entered another part of the town: a wide, grassless plaza lined with buildings of various sizes and congested with people, horses, wagons, and piles of building materials and of unloaded merchandise in front of stores. Ed identified some of the buildings and Luther noted the signs on others. Stockmen and Farmers Bank. Guttman's Drug Store. Wagner's Grocery. Doc Bowman's office. Barber Shop. Courthouse. Land office. Shawnee and Longhorn saloons. Berg's Dry Goods. O.K. Outfitters. Farmers Restaurant. Allgood's Leather Store. Butcher Shop. Plains Hotel. Oliver Hardware Co. Tinsley's General Store. Drovers Hotel.

"You'll likely want to stay at the Drovers," Ed said. "Bill Crum, the mayor, he owns it. Been saving a room the last few days figuring you'd be along. Maybe after you get the hang of the town you'll want to move in a boarding house. Mother Swain's the best."

"Coming and going all hours, wouldn't want to bother the lady," Luther said. "Hotel be fine."

"On the east side running north, that's East Street. On the

west side is West Street. Figures, don't it? Yonder at the top of this square running east and west, that's Pacific Street. Up above the square—can't see from here—there's Cottonwood Street and Kansas Avenue and over west is Buffalo. Up there's where the houses is at, where the townsfolk live. About two hundred of them. Houses I mean. About a thousand regular townsfolk, counting kids."

Luther squinted. "Couple of troopers standing over by that picture gallery. And I seen more below the track. Fort Reynolds?"

"Built nine year ago," Ed nodded, "partly to guard the railroaders grading through here. It's east there across Owl Creek. Fact you might say this town growed out of a railroad camp. Then buffalo hides and afterwards the cattle started coming." They stepped around a water pump and trough onto a wooden sidewalk. "Mayor's office here in the courthouse. County sheriff's too. Reckon you'll take over Tucker's. Jail's in the back."

As they mounted the half-dozen steps of the frame structure a small, dark man and a tanned youngster came out of the door. "Afternoon, Solly," Ed greeted the man. "Be proud for you to know this fellow with me." He smiled toward Luther. "Meet Luther Cain. Luther, this here's Solomon Berg and his son, David. Owns Berg's Dry Goods. On the council, too."

The merchant's brows flew up in comprehension. He thrust out his hand. "Real pleasure, Mister Cain!"

Luther gripped the hand. "Howdy, Mister Berg."

"We've all been looking forward to this day." When their hands parted, the small man bent quickly toward his son. "You know who this is, David? The famous Mister Luther Cain, come to keep order for us." He straightened. "Yessir, a real pleasure if I can speak for the town's decent citizens."

The boy's eyes brightened suddenly. "Father," he pointed at Luther's belt, "is that the pistol the people at Kansas City give him for killing Kid Owen?"

Solomon Berg's grin was a bit embarrassed. "I expect that's the one, David."

"Will he be in the bucket brigade?" the boy asked.

Ed Sarver laughed. "Solly got up our volunteer fire brigade, Luther."

Solly looked mildly proud. "And we'd be honored to have you as a member, Mister Cain. In your case we'll let the twenty-five cent monthly dues go and you won't even have to pay dance assessment."

"Have a dance every month," Ed said.

Solly nodded. "Just been talking to the mayor about next month's. He's willing to auction off the turkey but not to judge the baby contest in the afternoon."

"He wants reelected," Ed said.

The merchant shrugged. "Somebody got to do it. Maybe the new marshal?"

Luther raised his hand in silent remonstration.

"Say, Mister Cain," Solly asked, "you don't call a quadrille by any chance?"

Luther grinned. "I'm lucky getting through a dance without breaking somebody's toes."

"Well guess I better get on back to the store now. Once more, Mister Cain, we're mighty glad you come."

"Glad to be here."

"Drop in any time. Want Esther to meet you soon too. Come on, David."

"Can I look at your pistol close next time, Mister Cain?"

"Close as you want, David."

The merchant and his son went down the steps and the new marshal and the station agent climbed up them through the door. "Right busy town," Luther said as they walked past the courtroom with its plank seats and raised bench and drew abreast of a door marked "Mayor." Just beyond it was another door marked "Sheriff" and beyond that an alcove containing a desk and two chairs. The word "Marshal" was painted on the desk. As though to emphasize Luther's remark an eight-mule wagon clattered by outside, the skinner's hawing and popping of his blacksnake whip resounding through the thin-walled building. Luther squinted at some barred cell doors down the hall from the marshal's desk and at a man dozing in a chair tilted against the wall across from them.

"She's a boomer all right," Ed said. "You might say that's the good and bad of it. Good for business and bad for hell-raising. Or good for hell-raising. Depends how you look at it." He turned the mayor's doorknob. "Reckon he's here if Solly just seen him." The door swung inward on the official at his desk. "Yep. Howdy, Bill; it's me and somebody you been wanting to meet."

9

The mayor looked up under his derby, "Afternoon, Ed," and beyond at his friend's companion and stood up, towering above the desk. He reminded Luther of daguerreotypes of Abraham Lincoln. His derby, tilted forward, looked like a hawk on the tip of a pine tree.

"Bill Crum," Ed said, "Luther Cain."

"I'll be damned," the mayor said.

He unlimbered his lank arm and extended it across the desk and Luther stepped forward and shook hands with him. It was a good handshake. Both ways. Both men smiled.

"Howdy," Luther said.

The mayor's long forefinger pointed at a couple of extra chairs. "What say we set and talk?"

Ed pulled the chairs from the wall and all three men sat down.

"Might as well get down to business," Bill Crum continued in his bass voice. "Then if the business turns out all right we can visit."

Luther decided he and the mayor were going to get along in good style.

The town father crossed his legs loosely and leaned back and laced his fingers behind his head, tilting the derby still farther forward. "Hear you know your job and do it good. If we didn't think so we wouldn't telegraphed you." He cleared his throat, indicating the end of that phase of the conversation. "Like we said pay's two hundred dollars a month plus two dollars and fifty cents extra for every arrest. You pick your own deputies."

Luther nodded.

"I hold court every morning but Sunday and you got to appear with ever defendant. Nobody can be jailed more than overnight without coming before me except them arrested on Saturdays; them you can keep 'til Monday morning." His brows arched inquiringly.

Luther nodded again.

"I'll give you a three-dollar-a-week rate at the Drovers on an eight-dollar room if you want to put up there. Over the kitchen. Maybe some hotter this time of year but a damn site warmer in winter."

"He already figured on the hotel," Ed said.

Bill's gaze remained on Luther. "Mister Cain?"

"Fine, Mayor."

Crum unlaced his fingers and uncrossed his legs and leaned forward, shoving his hand across the desk a second time. "We got us a deal."

Luther leaned forward and gripped his hand briefly.

"Call me 'Bill' eh?" the mayor smiled.

Luther returned his smile. "I answer quicker to 'Luther.' "

"Now the business is done, Luther, except for the swearing in—we'll do that in the court room—what you think of our town?"

"He ain't seen much of it yet," Ed said.

"About like any other I reckon. I'll have my hands full. Not that it ain't a nice town."

"It is that. Least could be. Will be, now you're on the job. Lots of good people here. Good family kind of folks with kids and all. Gets along with each other mostly. 'Cept when they's fighting as the preacher says; that's one of his jokes." Bill shook his head. "If it wasn't for these here transients crowding in ever summer we'd be all right. But if it wasn't for them—'specially the Texas cowmen—we'd about go broke I reckon. That's the dilemmy of it." He shook his head again.

"Maybe we can figure that out."

"Sure hope so."

Luther stood up. "And maybe we better get started."

"We'll go in the court room." Bill got to his feet. "Want to get me some witnesses in off the street. Word'll get around faster that way than any. Name 'Luther Cain' ain't unknowed around here. Maybe it'll spook some of them." He paused, looking closely at Luther. "Want to know why Charlie Tucker left?"

Luther shrugged.

"Pretty good man Charlie was," the mayor said. "But not good enough to stand his daughter being raped by a drunk. Him a widower and her seventeen, the apple of his eye. Drunk got away and she got pregnant and then Charlie got drunk. Stayed that way six months. We all felt damn sorry for him, hoped he'd get better. Deputies been doing most of his work. But two weeks ago he put her in a wagon and took off back East somewheres."

Luther stared at the mayor for a moment. "I ain't married," he said quietly.

Ed got to his feet. "I'll be one of them witnesses, Bill."

CHAPTER 3

By Cal Nolan

New York—I've heard it said that every man is many men. One thing I've learned in writing this daily column is not to trust generalities; so I can't say generally about each man being a lot of others. But I do know one man who is at least one other.

This man is a cop in Manhattan named Sergeant Mark Keller, who boasts nearly 20 years on the NYPD—well, not "boasts," being a quiet man—and for my money eminently qualifies as one of "New York's Finest." He is a conscientious public protector and trouble-shooter.

The sergeant has made some enemies along the trail of his dedicated public service—partly because of his fierce dedication to his job—but no one can rightly challenge his integrity. Personally, I think we need more like him. But I've just learned we may lose him.

He's now lying in a hospital, grievously wounded by the bullet of an alleged drug dealer. Incidentally, both the latter's alleged dealing and his hanging out on earth were ended by the sergeant's return fire, according to witnesses.

I've said Sergeant Keller is at least two men. Those two are policeman and husband, public man and private man. I've known him and his wife, Mattie, for about ten years; and before—God forbid!—he's reassigned to a new, farther-off patrol, I want briefly to tell you more about him. And them. And associated people and events . . .

On the evening of his arrival in Bancroft the new marshal sat by a window in the Drovers' crowded dining room next to a summer-cold stove and studied a dog-eared copy of the *Bancroft Republican* in the waning daylight. He had finished the hotel's offering of beef, turnips, corn cake with sorghum molasses, and dried peaches; and as he read the weekly he sipped a second cup of black coffee. Pretty good coffee.

Luther always made it a point to be a regular reader of a town's newspaper. It could be an important source of enlightenment to a man in his line of work, not as much concerning events— by the nature of his job he was apt to learn about those first—as concerning the temper of the community, its attitude toward the marshal and his work and, by implication, the shape of problems to come. Reading between the lines was often more important than reading the lines.

The *Republican* seemed to be a pretty good paper. It was edited and published, Luther noted, by Carl M. Norris, a man whom he should drop around and meet tomorrow. This issue had four pages of news and an insert carrying advertisements of patent medicines, harness, a carload of coal, liniments, fancy button-up shoes, plows, buffalo coats, a bargain in calico at seven cents a yard, and a score of other items. The patented news stories and features from Kansas City dealt with the "Whiskey Ring" trials in Midwestern federal courts, plans for next year's national Centennial in Philadelphia, the high tariff, redemption of greenbacks, a successful Brotherhood of Locomotive Engineers strike in the East, and the Government's offer to buy the Black Hills from the Sioux for six million dollars.

Locally the construction of the new schoolhouse on Kansas Avenue was reported by the paper as "whizzing along." It announced a grange meeting in the Bell Mare Livery Co. barn and a covered-dish supper at the Methodist Church ("Soldiers welcome"). The arrival of a new trail herd from Texas on the plains south of town—two thousand cattle and a dozen cowboys—was heralded as a sign of Bancroft's continuing popularity as a shipping center although it was hoped editorially that shipper Jason T.M. Pickett would caution his men about the local ordinance against discharging firearms inside the city. In a box on the front page the mayor was quoted as saying that Mister Luther Cain, celebrated peace officer, had been contacted by the City Council

13

in regard to filling the marshal's post recently vacated by Charles Tucker and that it was understood Mister Cain was en route to Bancroft to accept it. Further details were promised in the next issue. On the same page there was a vivid account of a fist-and-knife fight involving a dozen customers of the Maverick Saloon south of the depot, which was categorized as the sort of shameful incident—by no means isolated although "perhaps fortunately" not fatal—that the prospective marshal ("See box") would undoubtedly discourage. On the back page Nicodemus Endicott was reported nearly to have choked to death on his jew's-harp in the Shawnee Saloon, a temporary crisis alleviated by music-loving Doctor Roy Bowman who was quoted as saying it was the first time he ever had removed a foreign body from a throat to the tune of "Arkansas Traveler."

"Mister Cain?"

Luther looked up from the newspaper. A fuzzy-lipped youth approached him carrying his saddle and bed roll.

"Mister Sarver told me to fetch these up from the depot." The youngster's eyes were wide with awe. "Want both in your room, Mister Cain, or the saddle in the stable?"

"Ain't seen the stable yet. Both in room fourteen. Just a bit," Luther added as the boy started away; "what's your name?"

"Noble Buck."

"Thanks, Noble."

"Sure, Mister Cain! Just you holler if there's anything else you need. I work at Mister Sarver's ice house back on Pacific by the creek. Just on the other side of the Plains barn and the stage station by the bridge."

Luther nodded. "I seen the building this afternoon."

"Thanks, Mister Cain. Sure been nice meeting you. I shoot pretty good. Not meaning to brag, but I got third in the turkey shoot Fourth of July. My uncle give me a Spencer from the War. My aim just comes natural they say." He hitched up the saddle and bed roll. "You just holler now."

"I'll do that."

The boy went away looking as though he could carry his burden to Denver.

A more resonant voice said "Mister Cain?"

The marshal glanced at a gray-haired, frock-coated man at the next table who was leaning toward him smiling. "I'd about decided that's who you was when the boy called your name. I'm Preacher Howard Smith."

"Howdy, Preacher."

The man arose and brought his coffee cup to Luther's table. The two of them shook hands. "Mind if I set a spell?"

"Make yourself to home."

"Thank you." He sat down across from the marhsal. "Bill Crum told me you was coming. Good to have you in town."

Luther nodded.

"Come by train?"

"That's right."

"Hot as the Hell-fire of eternal damnation, that train."

Luther grinned. "We didn't need to fire the stove, that's the truth."

The preacher's laugh was hearty without either flattery or deprecation. Luther liked him. It was getting so he liked everybody in Bancroft. This disturbed him fleetingly because a marshal couldn't afford to like many people.

"We built us a church up on Cottonwood Street this spring. Before that I rode circuit into Bancroft and held some camp meetings oncet in a while. I'm here all the time now though. Tomorrow night we're putting on a covered-dish spread. Sure hope you can come."

"Maybe I can. Much obliged."

"Our folks will want to meet you. And mighty good eats, I promise you." The preacher's smile seemed to come easily. "Short sermon; I promise you that, too."

"You preach the Bible?"

Howard Smith gazed at him for a moment, considering the question. "I stick right close to it."

"Read back in Kansas City where some Englishman says we come from monkeys. I've met a few men seems to bear that out."

"Believe we've all met a few, Marshal." The preacher's eyes twinkled at this turn of the conversation. "I heard about Darwin's book. Interesting all right. But I'm more interested in where a man's going than where he's been."

Luther's expression remained serious. "Reckon you got to take the Bible whole or not at all. Reckon that's the way I think about most everything."

"From what I hear nobody's apt to complain about the way

15

you think about anything." The preacher's grin was guileless.

Luther drained his coffee cup and set it down. "You figure smarter people than you wrote the Bible, Preacher?"

Howard Smith didn't hesitate. "That I do, Marshal."

"And I figure smarter people than me wrote the law."

"So you take it whole too?"

Luther wiped his mustache with the back of his hand. "Better get back on the street now." Arising he took his hat from a hook on the wall, threw a half-dollar onto the table and called to the woman who had served him, "That includes this feller's coffee." He looked back at the preacher before he started away. "See you tomorrow night if I ain't somewheres else not of my own choosing."

The preacher smiled again and gave him a little salute. "Thank you. You won't regret it. Fried chicken is the ladies' specialty."

A number of heads turned in Luther's direction, interestedly, appraisingly, carefully, as he walked across the dining room and into the lobby. Heads also turned toward him in the lobby, eyes glancing aside from casual conversations about the weather and earnest discussions of politics and railroad rates and around from the lighting of coal-oil lamps and up from the leather sofa at the other end of the room next to the bar doorway and across from the stairway with its newel's imported bronze cupid. The glances weren't conspicuous or prolonged and they weren't commanded by something imperious or startling in Luther's appearance. The word simply had got around the premises that as of late that afternoon the new marshal was a resident of the hotel. And any man, whatever his pursuits, motives, or intentions, whether good, bad, or uncommitted, naturally should want to know what the new marshal looked like. Especially if the new marhsal happened to be Luther Cain. The room was sprinkled with muttered private comments for a moment before earlier conversations were resumed. "Looks about like anybody else don't he?" "Looks different from most of them don't he?" "Looks like a good man." "Looks like a bad man." There was one philosopher in the lobby: "Looks like a lonesome man." And there was a nervous individual who left the room and went into the bar.

Outdoors Luther gazed up at the darkening sky and picked his teeth with the silver toothpick he always carried with him. The afternoon's clouds on the western horizon had moved gradually up into evening thunderheads encroaching on the town far above it. They promised a night's storm, a desperately needed drowning of thirsty grass and crops and a desperately ticklish job for the cowboys left to nightherd the cattle south of the railroad track. The wind was rising. Luther smelled the distance in it, the faraway plains it had swept across, their dust it had embroiled in itself, the acrid sweetness and the coolness and the saving dampness it was bringing. He took a deep breath and exhaled slowly and started walking along the front of the hotel toward the northeast corner of the square as the day's last light faded.

The wide, dark, rutted plaza was less congested than in the afternoon with wagons and their teams of mules and oxen and draft horses. But the hitching rails around it were still crowded with cowponies silhouetted now in reflected lamplight, and the boardwalks fronting its stores and shops and saloons echoed with the shuffling, hollow thumping and scuffing of boots and shoes and moccasins worn by scores of men pushing up and down under shadowy wooden awnings and in and out of glowing doorways, occasionally laughing and calling to one another but mostly talking in ordinary tones. The shrill whinny of a horse mingled with the rumble of thunder and the less celestial tinkle of a piano.

The east side of the plaza along which Luther turned southward was lined mainly with business establishments and professional offices. It had only one saloon. That afternoon Luther had noticed that ladies stayed pretty much on the east side except when they crossed to the Lone Star Cafe or butcher shop. He glanced into some of the windows as he passed them. The blinds of the Stockmen and Farmers Bank were pulled but Guttman's Drug Store was crowded and Wagner's Grocery was selling supplies as fast as three clerks could push them across the counter. The four chairs in Doctor Bowman's waiting room were occupied by three spavined oldsters and a young man with his arm in a bandanna sling. Next door the barber was standing on a milk stool hopefully rubbing liniment on the bald scalp of an otherwise hairy giant seated before him while two waiting customers sprawled on a bench under a sign heralding the advent of Meek's Marvelous Minstrel Show—A Million Laffs. Beyond the barber shop, after each of them had a deep swallow of whiskey, Doctor Rice began pulling a tooth of a buckskin-shirted buffalo hunter, a process collecting a small sidewalk audience. Between the dentist's office and the courthouse the Longhorn Saloon's cherry bar separated a crush of citizenry on one side from the aproned bartender on the other and overlooked several monte, keno, and poker games in progress at tables along the opposite wall. The courthouse was dark now except for the jail at the rear, there being no hearings or civic meetings scheduled for the evening.

Crossing the southeast corner of the square Luther headed between the courthouse and the railroad station toward the part of town which spoiled below the track. He could hear it before he cleared the corner of the station; and as he rounded the building and crossed into South Street its din grated on his ears and temper like a calliope playing "Dixie." The fact he had fought with the 11th Indiana Volunteers under General Lew Wallace and lost a brother at Shiloh had something to do with his feelings; but principally they were rooted in his marshal's respect for his job. His attitude was forged of duty and his duty was clear. The engraved strip of metal glinting on his shirt, pinned there with a flourish by the mayor that afternoon before witnesses, attested to his duty's clarity. Unobtrusively he hitched up his gun belt and walked down South Street with his left thumb hooked beside the belt's gleaming buckle.

Even the horses tied along the street were more skittish than those in the north part of town. Except for the garishly ornate "Portugese" Theater and Saloon the unpainted and false-fronted and shored-up slab-patched buildings were uglier than those above the track. Several of them had sod roofs. One shack had lost its roof altogether, possibly in a windstorm, and had been abandoned. There were no sidewalks. The underfoot mixture of dust and manure and wind-cast garbage ended just short of those door sills where it hadn't been tracked inside. The jumble smelled like an outhouse, Luther thought, although nobody seemed to mind. At least the milling groups ignored the stench as they thronged in and out of the squalid structures, whooping and cursing and guffawing and arguing against a background of piano and banjo and fiddle music which was nearly swamped in the night's uproarious tide.

A lightning flash paled the scores of lamp rays glimmering from doorways and windows up and down the street. The wind was growing stronger. The thunder rumbled louder and then the street was dark again. The marshal stepped out of its shadows into the glowing Portugese. The agent had told him that Johnny

18

Newlin owned this palace of amusement and that Johnny Newlin was the power below the track. Professionally it behooved the marshal to make Johnny Newlin's acquaintance.

The darkness in which Mark Keller found himself was enveloping but not perceptibly threatening—neither jagged nor smooth, loud nor silent, crowded nor empty. Simply it existed, although it did contain movement: a throbbing, like a heartbeat. "Colorless" should have described it in more than one way. At first. Then a faint tint emerged and the throbbing quickened and the face of a young woman glowed, partly from the dawn but partly of its own light. It was a face framed by long, brown hair, first glimpsed by happenstance in company of a smirking man's—on a long-ago patrol, as a matter of fact—a candid, unnecessarily rouged face which ultimately was to become the polestar of Mark's firmament but at the time merely was the tacitly provocative guise of one Mattie O'Sullivan.

The unconscious sergeant's muttered self-reproach at pain he may have caused her later was as inaudible to the surgical team as to himself.

The Portugese was filled with a half-dozen tables at which men were playing cards and drinking quietly in the hubbub about them. Other men were standing two-deep at the bar which ran along one side of the room toward a curtained stage at its far end. A blind man with white hair was playing an upright piano below the proscenium of the small stage. The air was blue with cigar smoke and thick with a mixture of whiskey and sweat and coal oil. A woman came out of a door beside the bar and closed it behind her. She was smoking a cigar and her sallow face was sliced by a purple scar from her left ear to the corner of her mouth. A strand of her long hair hung forward across her left shoulder and down damply between the roots of her breasts which were stuffed into the bodice above her short skirt and button-up shoes. She looked tired as she walked toward two similarly clad but visibly unscarred younger women standing at the bar drinking with a brace of Texas-looking cowboys.

The bartender glanced above his broken nose at the man in the round-crowned black hat, his eyes sagging to the badge on Luther's shirt, narrowing for an instant and jerking up. "Fire and fall back, boys," he said loudly to the customers between him and the peace officer. "Leave the marshal step up for a shot."

The customers squinted around, changed their minds about

objecting and moved aside. Luther stepped into the vacated space. The bartender bent to a shelf beneath the bar, straightened and set a bottle of whiskey and a small glass before the marshal. "Best we got, special for you."

Luther nodded and poured himself a drink and swallowed it. He wiped his mustache. "Good enough."

"Help yourself, Marshal."

"No thanks." He palmed a coin from his pocket and slapped it onto the bar.

"I mean it's on the house," the bartender said.

Luther stared at him. "Where's Johnny Newlin at?"

The bartender shrugged and picked up the coin and took back the bottle. He inclined his head toward the door from which the scarred woman had emerged. "Office yonder."

The marshal turned and walked down the bar and opened the office door unhurriedly without knocking. A thin man sitting at a plank desk in a circle of shaded lamplight looked at the intruder across the shoulder of a woman seated opposite him. Beyond the man and woman was another doorway through which Luther glimpsed a second room with a brass bed and a small table beside it bearing a china pitcher and bowl. A tall wardrobe stood on the bed's other side.

"There's a law agin walking in a man's living quarters without knocking, and I live here," the man frowned.

"What law is that?" the marshal asked.

"Mine." The man's frown was replaced abruptly by a smile. "But I see you're a lawman yourself. So you're welcome." He stood up. "Name's Johnny Newlin, I own this place."

"Luther Cain."

"So I just now figured, Mister Cain." He waved toward the woman who had turned in her chair to face the marshal. "Carrie Shaw. She's one of my girls. That is she works here." His smile tightened slightly. "Smartest of the lot but needs a spanking once in a while."

"Little out of my line," Luther said solemnly. His mouth corners tilted beneath his mustache.

"Glad to know you, Mister Cain," she smiled in return, arising. "Heard about you coming."

She put out her hand and Luther shook it. "Likewise, M'am."

He shook hands briefly with the proprietor. "Nice place you got, Mister Newlin. Hope it stays thataway."

"I see you mean getting right down to business," Newlin said. He turned to Carrie. "Go on back to work now. Just don't loan them saddle-bums no more of my money."

"Not if they don't need it," the woman said and left the room.

The proprietor whispered a curse. Then he returned his attention to Luther.

"Well, Marshal, glad you like the Portugese. Take a chair there."

"Ain't got time to set," Luther said. "Got some town to cover."

Johnny Newlin looked disconcerted. "I figured you'd want to talk a little business."

"What kind?"

The proprietor's face darkened a shade; but he hesitated only a moment. "Like say maybe free drinks, and maybe acquaintance with my girls." He stared into Luther's expressionless eyes and decided he needed to sweeten the pot. "And maybe a cut of the games. That's all right. Whatever's fair."

"For doing what?"

"I'll just answer that direct, Marshal. For not marshaling too heavy like in some of them other towns you been. Heard you marshal pretty heavy. These here herders up from Texas, these hunters, troopers, all the rest of these jaybirds, they don't like having their hurrahing spoilt. When their hurrahing's spoilt they're likely to trade somewheres else, 'specially these Texas men. Where'd I be then? Where'd any of us businessmen be then? Matter of fact where'd Bancroft be, Mister Cain?"

"What makes you figure I'm going to marshal heavier than the law says?" Luther asked calmly.

"I heard about, Marshal."

"That why you didn't vote to hire me, Mister Newlin?" Luther turned toward the door, pausing with his hand on its latch. "You keep your free whiskey and girls and games and I'll keep order, which is what the rest of them hired me to do. That's what I come in here to tell you." He pulled the door open. "I'll say goodnight now." Stepping from the room he closed the door carefully behind him.

Carrie Shaw was waiting just outside the office. "Like to have a drink with me, Marshal?" Her brown hair glinted in the lamp-light and her face didn't look as tired as the scarred woman's. Not yet, Luther thought. It certainly wasn't a fresh face but it wasn't spiritless in its corruption either, almost pretty under its rice powder and lip pomade.

"No thank you, M'am."

"Not even one?"

He shook his head.

"You got something against drinking or against me, which?"

"I got something agin your—" his hesitation was almost un-noticeable—"boss."

"I heard through the door what you told him." She shrugged. "You got your job to do. He's got his. I got mine." Her straight teeth gleamed. "So I'm asking again if you'd like to have a drink."

After a moment he grinned and pointed at the bar. "Changed my mind."

They stepped along the room and Luther motioned over the heads of some customers to the bartender with the broken nose. "Same bottle. Two glasses."

The man got the special bottle from under the bar and handed it and the glasses to the marshal. "Like I said, Marshal, on the house," he winked.

Luther returned his wink exaggeratedly, took one glass and gave it to the woman, kept the other himself, splashed some whis-key into them both, and handed the bottle back to the bartender along with a larger coin this time. "You don't remember too good do you?" He turned to the woman, "Here's looking at you," and swallowed his drink.

"And here's looking at you," she said as she took a sip of hers. "Thanks."

He gazed about them. "Sure would like to have a cut of this place." He grunted appreciatively. "Legal." His glance paused on the stage. "You dance up there too besides drinking with the folks?" The edge had left his voice.

"Sometimes." She seemed to take his amity for granted now. "Like when a troupe comes through and needs us girls to fill in." She looked down at her glass. "That's what I used to do, troupe. Got stranded here last summer. One time I danced for six weeks on a river boat, St. Louis to New Orleans." Her lashes rose. "Seen a lot then."

22

"Reckon you did."

She sighed. "New Orleans like no other place."

"Reckon that's right."

"Just different is all, Mister Cain. Beautiful different. Houses with balconies, shiny big carriages, fancy dresses, live oak trees with moss hanging down." She gazed at him intently. "You know."

Her reliance on his understanding was vaguely appealing. She had called herself a girl. Suddenly he thought of her as one instead of a woman, if there were a difference except for age. He guessed she was over thirty by maybe a couple of years. He shook his head. "Never been there." He set his glass on the bar. "And right now instead of New Orleans I got to get back out to Bancroft. Glad I made your acquaintance."

"Can I call you Luther?"

"If you're pleased to."

"Goodnight, Luther."

"Goodnight," he said and walked out of the Portugese saloon thinking about the way the lamplight glowed on her bare shoulders.

It had begun to rain hard and the street's dust and manure and garbage were turning into a foot-thick quagmire. The storm, however, wasn't dampening the spirits of the night's celebrants. A quivering radiance of lightning unveiled a savage bronc trying to unload its rider into the boggy intersection of South and Jimson Streets and the immediate crash of thunder failed by several decibels to drown the whooping of the sodden crowd lending the horse encouragement. Staying as close to the buildings as possible, lowering his head but not his eyes against the wind and rain, Luther sloshed down to the corner. By the time he got there the bucking horse had succeeded in its aim and had bolted off into the night and the crowd was dragging the mud-covered rider into a saloon for a drink. Luther looked eastward along Jimson Street past several more saloons and a gun shop and a livery stable toward the two-story frame house he had seen from the station that afternoon. Light shone through the rain from every window of the house but it seemed peaceable enough. He looked westward along the street past a billiard hall and several buildings which he judged were rooming houses. Across from the rooming houses the lightning silhouetted another stable. Beyond that he made out the edge of the stockyard. Tomorrow by train time the pens should be full of bellowing, wild-eyed cattle if there were any cattle left on the plains to drive into them after the panicking clatter of the storm. Sensing there was nothing in that direction requiring his attention he dodged into the lee of the darkened Wholesale Exchange Company and began making his way back up South Street toward the track. As he reached the entrance of the Eastern Saloon a shot exploded inside the building and he collided with a hatless man lurching out of it. Luther grabbed the man's arm.

"Hold up," he ordered.

The man swung around and stared at him in the light of the doorway, wind-whipped rain streaking a drawn, pale face with open mouth and terrified eyes.

"Let me go!" the man shouted. "He's after me!"

Luther's grip tightened. "I'm the marshal. Who's after you?"

"Marshal!" The man stopped trying to pull his arm free. He pointed into the doorway. "Arrest him! He tried to kill me!"

Luther shoved him back through the entrance and followed him inside. As he stopped to squint about the room the marshal took off his black hat with his left hand and slapped the rain from it against his thigh and put it on again. The Eastern was crowded with men and women, about ten to one, but none of them was dancing. Some were standing with their backs to the bar. Others were pressed in grinning ranks along the side walls, quiet at the moment except for some thick-tongued mutterings and a soppy belch and a few immediate giggles. Behind the bar hung a cracked mirror, undoubtedly a very prized rarity. It reflected the backs and sides of heads staring at Luther and the pale-faced man standing beside him in the flickering light. The fetid air smelled faintly of gunpowder among other things.

"What's going on?" the marshal asked conversationally.

The heads all turned toward a lanky man leaning with both elbows on the bar, snake-like fingers of one hand dangling a heavy revolver. "I'm Jason T.M. Pickett," he said loudly as though that answered the question.

Luther nodded. He turned to the man whom he'd shoved back into the room. "And what's your name?"

"Harold Koster, Marshal. I'm a drummer for Peeble's Shoes. And I have a citizen's right to a quiet drink."

" 'Fine footware for fashionable females,' " Luther recalled. "I seen your ad in the paper."

Somebody cackled.

"But instead of a drink I get pushed around by ruffians and shot at by that bully!" The pale-faced man pointed at the lanky one. "What kind of town is this?"

"From what I seen of it," the marshal said, "it's a town where a man can get a quiet drink if he wants one up north of the depot. If I was you I'd stay up there."

Somebody cheered drunkenly.

Luther began to walk casually down the length of the hall toward Jason T.M. Pickett. "Now I don't mind most kinds of noise myself. But gunfire inside the city limits does make me jumpy. Besides I understand from the paper we got an ordinance agin it. You read about that ordinance, Mr. Pickett?" He stopped an arm's length away from the man. "You was mentioned, too, as I recall."

The herd owner snorted like one of his bulls. "Ever hear of a Texan reading a paper called *Republican?*" He smiled at the room's burst of laughter. "But I know all about your ordinance, Lawman, and I don't give a damn, drunk or sober. I only shot at that little bastard to run him out of here. If I'd wanted to kill him he'd be dead. And if he don't get out of here quick I'll shoot at him again." The long fingers coiled about the revolver butt and raised its barrel.

"Look out, Jason," a woman screeched, "that's Luther Cain!"

Jason T.M. Pickett, however, didn't hear her out. Luther's gun barrel slammed across the left side of his head just above the ear and he dropped like an axed steer, blood gushing from his temple across his unconscious face.

"Jesus!" somebody muttered.

The marshal stood still for a moment, his revolver ready for a different kind of use. His eyes swept the motionless cowboys in front of him and the rest of the hall in the mirror. Nobody seemed anxious to challenge the ordinance further. Then he walked slowly backward to the doorway and stopped beside the drummer.

"You go over there," he motioned with his gun, "and you get Mister Pickett by the scruff of the neck and you drag him back up here if you ain't too goddam set on that drink."

Harold Koster obeyed briskly although not without consid-

25

erable sweating. When the inert cattleman had been hauled to Luther's feet the marshal holstered his revolver, bent over, heaved the man with a loud grunt onto his shoulder, and straightened. "Get him at the jail tomorrow," he said to the cowboys at the bar.

Turning with his burden he stepped through the doorway into the rain and into the tumultuous legend of Bancroft, Kansas.

"He come to town with the wind didn't he?" the mayor said later to Roy Bowman when he heard about the marshal's first night on the job.

The doctor's words sounded extravagant as soon as he'd said them. "Hope he don't reap the whirlwind."

CHAPTER 4

Carrie Shaw awakened slowly in the after-storm coolness of the bright noon.

It wasn't a shivering coolness because the month was August; and the brightness didn't flood her stingy room at the rear of Lane's boarding house on Jimson Street because it was dimmed by the cloth drawn over its single window; but the day was comfortable and fragrant; and Carrie's awakening was a quiet, lazy, tender discovery of its relief from the stifling summer heat.

Her breasts and belly felt safe against the clean ticking. She opened her eyes and stared under her lashes at the locked door across the room. Then she turned over and stretched, yawning and arching her back and drawing up her long, white legs and pushing her arms overhead beneath her brown hair spilling across the pillow. Relaxing abruptly with a sigh she kicked down the sheet, closed her eyes again and smiled. As she lay motionless except for the slow, gentle pulse of her breathing she wondered why she was smiling. Maybe it was because she didn't have a headache and a cottony tongue. Maybe it was because a bird was singing outside the window.

There had been lots of birds on her parents' farm in Indiana. They used to awaken her with their song there too. Before her father's death she hadn't had headaches. And her smile on awakening then hadn't been something to wonder about, it simply had been part of the new day. Her father had been against frowns. And in favor of whiskey.

Her father also had been against her mother's hatred of men and in favor of fiddle music, funny stories, dolls made of corncobs, and letting his wife have her tantrums in echoing solitude while he and Carrie took long walks in the woods to see how the rabbits were running and the squirrels hoarding and the quail hatching. He wasn't much for work but he was a whole-hearted supporter of happiness for little girls.

After her father had blasted his heart out with a scattergun Carrie had begun to have headaches from time to time. Like the summer she was fifteen and the melancholy haying hand from

Slippery Elm, muttering about the release of them both from their miseries, had surprised her in the barn at milking time and fondled her in a strangely fermenting way. Absently she tucked her knees sideways and reached down and pulled the sheet up to her chin. Later that ancient evening she had voiced her bewilderment at the experience and her mother had knocked her across the kitchen in a fit of rage over having whelped such a wanton daughter. The next night the hand had sneaked back and hissed her out of bed after her mother had gone to sleep; and with deep burning anger tinged with throbbing curiosity she had stolen down to the corn crib with him and there he had made love to her as the moonrays through the slats had corrugated their bodies with light and shadow and her forlorn moans had blended with the hooting of an owl in the barnyard oak. The woman on the bed wasn't smiling now. The next Sunday, her head pounding again, Carrie had told the preacher about her sadness because her father had said that anytime life got too much for her she should turn to a man of God for help. The preacher had turned out to be a man not of God. He had asked her for the sake of total confession and remission of sin to let him see just how the hayer had treated her. Under his ministering hands, swallowing her initial, mortified, chaotic impulse to vomit, she had ended up repeating the whole performance with him in what had become a welter of sacrificial penitence. Then he had told her mother that Carrie had made improper advances to him. And her mother had knocked her down three times in the grove behind the farmhouse.

The next year after her mother had smashed Carrie's scalp open with a piece of cordwood for screaming that she welcomed the passion of men because it made her feel loved, she had run away to Indianapolis and thence to a succession of dismal cities from Indiana to Colorado and from Louisiana to Kansas. No, there was one bright city: New Orleans. As she had told Luther Cain the previous night it was beautiful. In the fifteen—well, eighteen—years since she had run away from home she had got over hating her mother but not over loving men loving her. At least wanting her. That had led to a variety of jobs (as she preferred to call them) all involving showing herself to men in one way or another. They had included among others singing for her meals with a revival group on the streets of Indianapolis, waiting on tables in a men's boarding house in Denver, modeling for a French artist in New Orleans, languishing for a year as the mistress of a rich Illinois farmer, posing as Joan of Arc in a circus tableau, serving countless beans to thousands of Union soldiers in St. Louis, and touring for three seasons with the Paris Variety Company out of Chicago. Her search for consolation also had led to a six-year, childless marriage to a Charleston gambler who had taught her to read books and had bought her pretty clothes when he was winning. When he was losing he hadn't minded sharing her with a demanding creditor to square a debt but he had become irreconcilably jealous when she'd started a rival poker game.

Once undertaken, such an extravagance of loneliness had become very hard to get over. She had settled for the act of love, she supposed, instead of being loved and loving. Until the real thing came along anyway. She kept telling herself.

Luther Cain had said last night that he never had been to New Orleans. But certainly he had been in many of the towns she'd seen. Bound to have, a man like that. She wondered where he had been born. She would ask him the next time she saw him.

Odd in a way how she'd felt friendly with him right off considering he was a figure of authority. He sure had told Johnny Newlin a thing or two. She probably should see him again today. She hoped so.

Her smile returned and she opened her eyes and threw back the ticking and slid out of bed, her body glowing in the room's yellow dimness. Putting on her wrapper she unlocked the door and walked along the narrow hall to the back porch and down its three steps into the sunny backyard with the outhouse at its far end. As she hummed phrases of "Beautiful Dreamer" she mused gratefully that the reason she didn't have a headache and a cottony tongue was that she hadn't been obliged to drink as much as usual the night before. The Texas youngster with the broken arm whom she'd befriended after Luther Cain's visit to the Portugese hadn't been much of a drinker despite his wanting to be.

Returning to the back porch she picked up two buckets set there for the roomers and filled them with water from the rain barrel gaping just beyond the eaves' overhang. The sunlight glistened on the cleanness of her billowing hair; but clean or not she wanted to take a woman's advantage of the night's downpour to wash it in soft water. She balanced the bucketsful back to her room, poured one of them into the hand-painted porcelain basin which Charlie Tucker had given her and the second into the wooden washtub in the corner beside the summer-cold stove. Another round trip to the back porch filled the washtub. Locking the door she took off her wrapper and washed her hair in the basin on the bureau with her imported cake of French soap from Kansas City and then kneeled and rinsed its dripping length in the washtub on the floor. Drying it with a towel which she left twisted around her head like a turban she bathed standing up in the tub, still humming.

After her bath she dragged the tub to the window and bucketed its contents out beneath the curtain. And presently with some daubings of Lundborg's California Water for good measure she was fully dressed in her summer-weave cotton underwear and black cotton stockings and button-up shoes and long-sleeved gingham dress and her hair was combed up into a waterfall like the picture in Godey's Lady's Book. She pulled aside the curtain at the window, took a final glance in the cracked mirror above the bureau, blew herself a kiss, touched the twining violets printed on a greeting card stuck in the mirror's frame, picked up the empty buckets to return them to the back porch, unlocked the door, and left for a leisurely, friend-retarded, lighthearted walk to the Lone Star Cafe under the optimistic sky.

"I feel good," she said to Oscar Lacy who owned the Lone Star. "I'll have some of them eggs you been crowing about."

"How many, Carrie? They're two bits apiece today."

"Who cares about money? I said I feel good. Two, Oscar, sunny side up. And side pork and biscuits and coffee."

"Betchy," he grinned. "Honey with your biscuits?"

"Sure I want some honey—Honey." Her laughter sparkled in the day. "And speaking of sweet things how's Missus Lacy this afternoon?"

"I heard that," Missus Lacy called from the kitchen. "I'm doing fine. How are you, Carrie?"

"Like I told Oscar. I feel good."

The voice from the kitchen became newsy. "Hear about the new marshal last night?"

"One reason I feel good," Carrie replied without thinking. It had just come out. "I don't know why I said that."

"What you say?"

"I met him last night, Missus Lacy." She was blushing faintly.

Oscar grinned. "You ain't getting a crush on him already are you? You're always getting crushes on them handle-barred buckaroos."

"Jealous?"

"You'll have to talk louder," Missus Lacy complained.

"She's blushing," Oscar called.

Carrie grimaced at him and raised her voice. "He come in the Portugese last night, Missus Lacy."

"I mean about his buffaloing Jason Pickett with a pistol barrel in the Eastern."

"I never heard that." Carrie's tone was awed. "Lordy that's something. Jason Pickett."

Oscar shook his head dubiously. "Old Man Pickett didn't like it much when he woke up in jail this morning. And neither did his riders at the mayor's court. Reckon we ain't heard the last of that buffaloing. Hope the marshal can take care of hisself."

Carrie hoped so too. On general principles. She should hope that for anybody who dared buffalo Jason T.M. Pickett. "What day you going to bring my breakfast?"

"Think how good it'll taste the day I do." Oscar walked to the kitchen door. "Sarah, we got a starving maverick wants a couple eggs with pork and biscuits and coffee."

"And don't forget the honey, Honey."

"Couldn't likely do that."

"You two sound like a couple fifteen-year-olds," the voice from the kitchen allowed.

Carrie was depressed for only an instant at the thought of being fifteen again. She had finished ruminating for the day; and there was an exciting prospect ahead: a warning talk with the marshal who might not otherwise realize his jeopardy. It was a citizen's duty to caution a new marshal about potential hazards in his bailiwick. He might not realize how touchy Texas cattle barons were. She had to admit to herself that wasn't a very good excuse—not with a Luther Cain—but at the moment she couldn't think of a better one for talking with him again so soon.

Several hours later at the northeast corner of the square above the railroad track Raymond Davis stepped from the Stockmen and Farmers Bank into the afternoon sunlight, shifted his healing arm to a more comfortable position in its bandanna sling and headed southward toward the depot. In the hip pocket of his reinforced pants was an envelope on which his mother's name and address had been written by an accommodating man in the bank and inside the envelope was a cashier's check for fifty dollars made out to her. He was going down to the post office in the depot to mail it. It was half of what remained from the wages paid to him by Colonel Cole when their herd had reached Bancroft the previous week. He had decided he'd better send the fifty to her before another day passed or there shouldn't be anything left to show for his part in the three months' drive up from Texas, not the way Kansans took a cowboy's money. His mother could use it to buy the second-hand piano she'd had her eye on all spring, the one offered for sale in Missus Dillingham's estate after the widow's death of pneumonia. Missus Dillingham's husband had brought the piano to his ranch from the East somewhere. The cashier's check also should serve in place of a letter. In his twenty years he hadn't learned to write mainly because he'd worked pretty much all the time since his father's death ten years ago at the hands of Sherman's troops near Bentonville.

As Raymond had told the lady at the Portugese last night this summer's trail drive had been his first. He had gone to work for the Santa Clara Ranch the previous fall and liked to think that a hard-riding winter's work for Colonel Cole had caused the owner to choose him as a drover this spring. Of course being a newcomer to the outfit he'd drawn the job of riding the dust-choked, manure-splattered drag of the herd and had been the butt of a score of practical jokes by the old-timers. But he'd kept the lame and weak cattle moving in good shape in his lonesome assignment and even had managed a grin the morning after the night in camp when Indian Jesse had painted up like a Comanche and terrified him awake with a knife at his throat.

It hadn't been an easy summer.

The two-mile-long herd had been raided twice by Indians, once by a hunting party in search of beef in lieu of buffalo meat annihilated by White Men and another time by a war party in search of scalps. The war party had left three of its braves dead in the sun and thanks to the cowboys' Spencers, only Kid McBride dying with his privates slashed off and his stomach gutted and his raw head oozing blood on the hot prairie grass. Both attacks had scattered the cattle for miles and it had taken several days each time to round them up again. It had taken only an hour and a prayer to bury Kid McBride.

Raymond had broken his arm one lightning-scarred day a month ago during a stampede when his horse had stumbled in a hole and pitched him headlong onto the pounding earth. That was a time when he had been glad he was riding drag instead of point or flank. The next morning Ed Johnson, looking for cattle, had found him wandering afoot and had horsebacked him double for five miles on a skittish bronc to the chuck wagon. There the camp cook Tenderloin Smith with a versatility born of long experience had set and splinted his arm. Two days later he'd been riding drag again.

As late as last night Doc Bowman had repeated his amazement that the arm almost had healed, adding it was enough to make a man give up medicine if everybody was going to be a damn doctor.

Raymond reached the depot and passed the envelope through the grill to Ed Sarver.

> . . . I met Sergeant Keller for the first
> time in a Manhattan courtroom one winter
> morning. I was scrounging material for this
> column and he appeared as arresting officer
> at an arraignment in an armed robbery case.
> I remember noting the accused's colorful array
> of abrasions and contusions . . .

Up the plaza the way Raymond Davis had come Luther Cain left the Drovers Hotel. He picked his teeth with his silver toothpick as he sauntered along Pacific Street to the *Republican* building behind the bank and between Watts' law office and the Masonic Lodge.

The marshal was tired. Four hours' sleep wasn't enough for him. He had got to bed at three finally after telling the night clerk to awaken him at seven so he could be in the mayor's court at eight to state his complaint against Jason T.M. Pickett. After the hearing when he'd questioned the early hour Bill Crum had told him it was a matter of expedience: convening at a time when the rowdy element was apt to be asleep made for a more orderly transaction of business since the hearings were open to the public. The previous Bancroft mayor had held his hearings in the early afternoon and had spent more time banging for order than listening to the merits of the cases. Luther could see the sense in that; he remembered the same difficulty in other towns; it was a good idea. That morning however a dozen of Pickett's riders had showed up in a loyally ornery mood evidently considering their jobs more demanding than their hangovers. When one of them had cursed Luther loudly and obscenely the marshal had slapped him sprawling onto a bench and with slitted eyes had ordered the rest to sit beside the bruised man with their hats off like a row of schoolboys. He even hadn't bothered to make an impromptu complaint against the loud-mouth; the disdain in his ignoring of the incident had seemed more effective in dealing with it. Bill Crum had glanced at him inquiringly and he had nodded toward Pickett, and the mayor had taken up the cattleman's violation of Ordinance 14.

"You guilty of shooting off a pistol inside the city limits of Bancroft?" the mayor had asked the defendant.

Pickett had stared hard at Luther from under his bandaged temple. "That ain't all I aim to be guilty of before I quit this stinking town."

"Ten dollars," the mayor had said and thus had ended that morning's town court business.

The marshal now stepped into the front room of the *Republican* building which obviously served as an office. Beyond it he could see two men and a boy standing in the back room beside a press grinning at a sheet of newsprint which the younger man was holding.

"Howdy!" he called.

The younger man looked at him through the doorway, handed the newsprint to the boy and came forward. "Afternoon." His expression was affable and intelligent and there was a crinkle of humor around his brown eyes. "What can I do for you?" Then he saw Luther's badge. "I'm Carl Norris, Marshal."

"Editor of the paper?"

The man smiled. "Last time I heard. You must be Luther Cain."

Luther returned his smile. "Last time I heard."

They shook hands.

"Fine to meet you, Marshal."

"Thought I'd make your acquaintance, Mr. Norris. Read your paper last night. Right good reading."

"Obliged." The editor motioned toward a chair against the wall. "Have a seat." After his visitor had settled down he lowered himself into another chair behind his cluttered desk. "Glad you like the *Republican*, Mister Cain. You're going to be in it this evening."

Luther waited.

"Not the first time ever. I've written about a couple of your doings other places and maybe you saw that item in the last issue about your coming here. But this story's the first since you've been marshal of Bancroft." His smile widened. "And I don't mind telling you I got a kick out of writing it today. Jason Pickett! He's had this town treed for three summers and you put him in his place your first night, not to mention one of his cowboys over at the court this morning. Hell of a funny story."

Luther didn't see the humor in it. He'd done his job as it had presented itself each time. But he smiled politely.

The editor swung in his chair toward the door to the rear room. "Fred! Billy! Come out here!" He turned back to the marshal. "Want my printer and devil to meet you." When his two employees entered he tilted his head toward the visitor. "Fred Martin and Billy Plunkett, meet Mister Luther Cain."

Fred put out his hand. Billy's mouth opened soundlessly. Luther leaned forward and shook hands with each of them.

"Mighty proud to know you, Mister Cain," Fred grinned.

Billy wet his lips with his tongue. "Holy cow," he said presently, "wait 'til I tell Dave Berg and Noble Buck!"

"I met Dave and Noble yesterday," Luther said, leaning back again. "You a friend of theirs?"

"Yesterday!" Billy croaked. "They never told me. But I guess I ain't seen them yet today." He looked somewhat mollified. "Holy cow!"

Carl Norris laughed. "This is quite an event for these boys, Mister Cain."

Luther didn't know what to say so he didn't say anything.

"Yes indeed," the editor augmented. "Quite an event for all of us. You're a famous man."

"Sure are," Fred Martin said.

Billy tongued his lips again. "Heard you killed twenty men."

Luther frowned. "You heard wrong."

"I guess that's Mister Cain's business, Billy," the editor said. "You better get back to work." His admonition included the printer. "We've got a paper to get out this afternoon." When his employees had returned to the press room he looked back at the marshal. "You're news Mister Cain; hope you don't mind." He gestured apologetically. "How many men you killed, that's the public talking and the public's on your side. It's none of their business maybe but they're on your side and they're curious about you."

"I ain't a murderer, Mister Norris."

"But this paper's more interested in your future, the job you're going to do here in Bancroft. That's the part we're going to print."

The marshal squinted at him. "Reckon I'll do whatever the job calls for."

"And part of the paper's job is helping you do yours any way it honestly can."

"Fair enough."

"I'd like to be your friend, Marshal. That fair enough too?"

"Sure," Luther smiled.

"That's fine then."

"Fine with me."

The editor leaned back in his chair. "Now, any statement you want in this week's issue?"

"Only I'm going to enforce the law and play no favorites."

Carl grinned. "Like Jason Pickett?"

"Like anybody breaks it."

"Pickett thinks you went too heavy on him last night. That's the way he's talking around today."

"Didn't go heavy enough maybe if that's the way he's talking."

"Says shooting off a pistol for a little fun isn't cause to bust a man's head."

"That's not why I hit him."

The editor pursed his lips thoughtfully against his touching fingertips. "Self-defense? Think he was going to shoot you?" He reached for a pencil.

Luther shook his head. "If I thought he was trying to I'd have shot him first."

"Did he try to hit you?"

"You might say he tried to hit the ordinance I swore to enforce.

I was defending that in front of a room full of people. If he'd got away with that there wouldn't be no more ordinance."

"Interesting point," Carl said. "What about enforcement through fines?"

"Got to get them in court 'fore you can fine them. Sometimes they don't want to come; sometimes they think they're bigger than court. That's no way to get along."

Carl laughed. "Not with you."

"You figure I was too heavy on Pickett?" the marshal asked casually.

"I didn't see it Luther. But from what you say I don't think you were. Besides I'm not a lawyer. I'm a newspaper man. And you're good copy," the editor added with a smile, "so don't change your ways on my account."

Luther didn't smile. "I don't reckon I'll change my ways without good reason."

"Not with the job you've done in those other towns," the editor conceded. "Tamed some wild ones I know. Looks like you're going to tame this one too. More power to you. We need a strong hand here."

"Do the best I can." Luther tugged on his hat brim and stood up. "Better be moving on. Tell the boys yonder I'm glad I met them. You, too."

"Same here, Luther. Drop in any time. And read the *Republican* tonight."

"I'll do that."

On Pacific Street again the westerly breeze whispered warmly in the marshal's ears and the sun felt good on his shoulders. Yesterday's oppressiveness had lifted. As he walked across the stage station beyond the Plains Hotel's stable and corrals he thought about taking a mid-afternoon nap in anticipation of the long night; but he shunned the thought in view of the looking around he ought to do before nightfall. After the first few days he should know generally what he was up against in Bancroft and what he wasn't up against and when he couldn't spare some time for himself and when he could. In the meantime it was necessary to continue finding out as much as possible about the routine and layout and significant people of the town. Such items of information as much as his gun and fists and brain were tools of his job. The law was his job's pattern and lawbreakers were its raw material to be molded to the pattern by use of the tools.

That morning in the mayor's court he had met two of the deputy marshals, Lafe Jackman and Big John McAlister, and had asked them to tell the third, Little John Brock, to meet him at the stage station when the coach arrived from the north. A few minutes' conversation with Lafe and Big John had satisfied him of their probable competence and he'd invited them to stay on their jobs. Now he was interested in having a conversation with Little John. He hoped it should pan out the same way. It should be a good thing to have experienced men to back him up who already were familiar with the town. They could get acquainted with him and his methods as they went along; and if they didn't like the deal they could fold out later.

He sat down on a bench on the porch of the dusty clapboard building beside two men and a woman who evidently intended riding the stage south. The men were taking turns talking lightly to the woman, reassuring her about the trip and explaining that Nick Caldwell, the driver for the next leg, undoubtedly was the best hand with a six-horse team west of the Missouri River. Maybe in the whole West. Luther gathered she was a bride-to-be on the way to meet her groom who'd staked a land claim down on the Cimarron and had sent for her. Apparently she'd last seen him in Omaha six months ago and was facing not only the isolated homestead but her forthcoming marriage with some trepidation. Her soft young cheeks were flushed with a fever of mixed emotions but her smile was hopeful. The marshal admired her and felt sorry for her at the same time. Life on the prairie had tested some strong men and women to the limit. Love anywhere however seemed to have a strength of its own doubling that of lovers, although the other side of that coin he'd learned the hard way was that such doubled strength could mean doubled grief at love's loss. Anyhow the young woman probably should have safe conduct to the threshold of her future if the two men's sympathetic smiles prophesied anything at all. And they were right about Nick Caldwell; Luther had heard through the frontier grapevine about his driving skill.

Inside the building the marshal could hear another southbound passenger complaining to the manager that his shoe case had got rain-soaked on the last trip. "And that's a hell of a way to run a stage line!" the voice concluded loudly. The manager might have been replying to a child: "Sorry your samples got wet last month, Mister Koster. This time we'll wrap your case in a tarp and have Nick Caldwell hold it on his lap." The salesman's voice grew even louder: "And I don't appreciate your sarcasm; that's no way to talk to a member of the traveling public."

The doorway spewed the man whom Luther had rescued in the Eastern the previous night.

"Afternoon," the marshal grinned.

"Mister Cain, can't you do something about people insulting people? I have a citizen's right to a quiet trip but instead . . ."

"Mister Koster," Luther interrupted, "for a man who values quiet so high I've noticed you sure make a lot of noise."

One of the men on the bench laughed.

"Well!" the salesman sputtered, swinging coldly toward the coach clattering across the bridge at the east end of Pacific Street. "This town is a nest of ruffians!"

A stagecoach's arrival, like a train's, was always a crowd-getter. Now children ran and adults strode or sauntered from all directions to share Luther's scrutiny of the snorting and hawing and rattling and mud-slinging onrush. For the rest of the crowd it was an achievement in itself; there always was the chance compounded of various chances like Indian attack and wreck and holdup and runaway that the stage shouldn't arrive at all. For waiting relatives and friends this made the event intimately suspenseful and for others at least dramatic. But for a marshal there was an additional possibility to make it important on an official basis: a troublemaker might alight among the passengers. Little John Brock knew this from experience also and settled on the bench beside Luther as the manager stepped from the station and opened the coach's door.

"I'm John Brock," the deputy said cheerfully to the marshal.

"Howdy, John. Luther Cain." They shook hands.

"Big John give me your message. I been to Plainville in a buckboard fetching a prisoner. Just got back."

"Any trouble with him?"

"He's a her. Pearl Vollie. Stabbed her sister Tuesday night over their Uncle Vince." Little John laughed. "Takes all kinds. County attorney says we need Vince for a witness but can't figure where he run off to."

"Sometimes women is more trouble than men in a buckboard," Luther grinned.

"We got along all right. Pearl's seventy-five."

Luther's grin widened. He gazed under his hat brim at the newcomers stepping into the damp street. "Know any of them passengers?"

"Hearts Ferris yonder. He's a gambler and a slick man with the ladies but no trouble much. I'd say the rest was drummers and the like."

The marshal returned his glance to the small, ewe-necked deputy. "See Colonel Cole shipped the rest of his herd east today."

"Found him a second buyer who'd pay his price," Little John nodded. "As I come past the yard they was loading the last of them. Been at it since daylight. About forty cars looked like."

"Forty-two some feller told me."

The deputy chuckled. "Some feller didn't have much to do. I didn't count, I had my hands full with Pearl."

"Not too full to hear about the price," Luther said, "and learn how long they been working and make a good guess about the cars."

Little John shrugged.

"Want to go on being deputy?"

"Fine with me."

"Reckon I'll head down to the railroad depot," the marshal yawned, standing up. "Figgering on going to that church supper tonight, John?"

"Not tonight."

"I might go if nothing comes up. I'll be there for a while if you boys want me later."

"Sure." The small man looked after the big one and spat contentedly. "Sure, Marshal, we'll set on the lid."

CHAPTER 5

The sergeant was jerked from the hospital rack and flung upward across the city and plunged down among his neighbors at that never-forgotten block party where he'd seen Mattie O'Sullivan for the second time and talked with her for the first. She had moved into his neighborhood (no one seemingly knew from where) while he'd been overseas. He had thought block parties had vanished with his childhood but the people up and down the street hadn't admitted that. He'd been glad they hadn't, despite—or maybe because of—his post Vietnam funk mixed with his rookie-cop jitters. He'd needed a break from his workaday hassle. Mainly he'd been glad because it had allowed his talking and eating hot dogs and looking at the building-squeezed moon with the new girl on the block—new to him anyhow if not to a staring, vaguely hostile stud wearing elevator shoes. He and Mattie had talked about several things, among others his new job and her qualms about its risks, her own bookkeeping job for the elevator-shod stud's pawnshop around the corner, her opinion that most people were basically good and Mark's that some were, the fact that she was his junior by a half-dozen years, and what a nice evening it had been.

Abruptly in near pain and borne on an icy stench, the sergeant was wrenched back to his jeopardy.

As the sun abandoned it to the night, Bancroft—the "Queen of the Plains" according the *Republican*'s banner—put on her sequined dress and started out for the evening's fling. She seemed to be in a festive mood, Luther noted as he walked northward on East Street toward Cottonwood. But he knew that a man couldn't tell for sure with these frontier girls; she might end up with blood on her skirts before dawn. With her left hand she was pouring drinks around the plaza and below the track and with her right she was cooking fried chicken at the Methodist Church. She was ambidextrous that way which was what made an affair with her an interesting thing. Also a pretty dangerous thing.

Luther wasn't entirely sure what he was doing in Bancroft or why he continued marshaling. Maybe marshaling meant more to him than making a living. Maybe he enjoyed gun muzzles. Hell! He wasn't usually much for thinking such thoughts. A glimpse

41

of—what was her name? (he pretended)—Carrie Shaw's bare shoulders in the yellow lamplight of the Portugese glowed in his mind for an instant. And at the same instant the breeze wafted the scent of frying chicken to his nostrils. Whether or not a man liked fried chicken was something he could be sure about, he grinned in the darkness, like say rain wetting things. Or loneliness needing company. His grin disappeared.

As he turned up the three front steps into the church he heard the remainder of the grace: "Bless this food to our use and thus to Thy service." He stopped in the open doorway and took off his hat as the Reverend Howard Smith continued: "And also bless our new marshal who's just now entered here among us tonight. We know he's got a hard job ahead of him with the Godless element of this sometimes Babylon and we know he'll do it fine. Amen!"

The roomful of people looked around at Luther as the preacher walked toward him.

"Welcome, Mister Cain. Glad to have you. The ladies is just about to serve the best vittles you ever bit your teeth into."

All of the ladies and most of the men in the room smiled.

"This is Luther Cain, Folks," the preacher said to them. "Let's make him feel welcome."

There was a flurry of clapping, generally gratuitous but here and there specifically dutiful on the theory that forthcoming helpings might depend on participation. "Howdy, Marshal; welcome, Marshal," echoed from a couple of quarters.

"Howdy," the marshal nodded, his weathered cheeks reddening slightly.

A half-dozen of the ladies turned to filling the quickly forming food line's tin plates from crocks burdening a table at one side of the kerosene-lit room. The bench-pews had been pulled aside.

"Come and get it, Marshal," Howard Smith said, "before the soldiers eat it all. They's always the hungriest."

"All right."

The Reverend got the marshal a knife and fork and installed him at the end of the shuffling line and went back to the front door to greet other arrivals. Luther turned to a man and woman who had taken their places behind him.

"Evening," he said.

"Evening, Marshal," the man smiled. "I'm Orville Allgood and this here's my wife, Louella."

The marshal shook hands with them.

"Hope you like our town, Mister Cain," the woman said. "It's not all the Babylon Preacher Smith makes out."

"Maybe he ain't all serious when he says that, M'am."

She nodded. "That's part of why we like him here. Got kind of a wit about him."

"Some preachers is all down in the mouth," her husband agreed. "Not Howard; he'll pull him a joke now and then."

"Like the day he shot off a buffalo gun in church," she recalled, "to wake up Grandpa Titus."

Orville also obviously recalled the incident with relish. "When the old man lands on his bench again Howard quotes the Psalms at him: 'The voice of thunder was in Heaven, the lightnings lit the world; the earth trembled and shook.' And he says, 'You hadn't ought to sleep so much, Grandpa, you wouldn't be so jumpy when the Lord hollers at you.'"

Luther joined in the laughter of the surrounding group. The line continued shuffling forward.

"Read about last night in today's paper, Mister Cain," the man ahead of him said. "That was pretty comical too. Old Pickett learnt his lesson all right."

The second man forward added: "'Low he's a sorehead today in more ways than one."

Again the group laughed. Luther didn't join in this time. He reached the lower end of the table, picked up a tin cup and plate and held out the plate. "Thank you," he said to the freckled-face plump woman who ladled him some mashed potatoes. "Them look mighty good. Don't know how long since I tasted mashed potatoes."

"I fix them all the time out to my homestead, Mister Cain," she said. Then she blushed and giggled like a schoolgirl. "Lots of ladies around here do."

"What Widder Schultz means," Orville Allgood said, "is drop by, Marshal, and she'll fix you some more."

"Pshaw!" The woman touched her flushed face with her free hand.

The marshal's moustache tilted. "Reckon I'll do that, Missus Schultz, if I'm invited."

"You won't be sorry neither," Orville said. "She's the best cook in the county—next to my wife."

"How you know that?" The man ahead of Luther craned past the marshal at Missus Allgood. "Best keep an eye on him, Louella."

43

Louella smiled confidently. Widow Schultz went into another spasm of giggling. "Go on with you!" Tears squeezed from under her lowered lashes; and in the flickering light Luther couldn't tell whether they budded altogether from her laughter.

"I mean I've eat after her here at church before," Orville expounded.

Missus Allgood waved down the men. "You leave Bertha alone now and let her serve the best mashed potatoes in this county including mine."

The freckled-face plump woman opened her eyes and smiled at her champion. She spooned some potatoes onto Orville's plate. "There, you lucky man."

The line moved forward another step.

"You folks live up around here?" the marshal asked the Allgoods.

Orville nodded. "Kansas Avenue. A block east next to the crick."

"Orville's in the leather business," his wife said. "Any time you're needing a bridle, saddle, belt, anything like that, drop in to his shop. On Pacific."

Her husband grunted. "Don't have to buy advertising, Marshal."

"I'll sure remember," Luther said. "I seen your sign."

A frail woman put three pieces of chicken on his plate, each as plump in its way as Bertha Schultz. "Eat hearty, Marshall. Gravy?"

"Be fine."

She turned to the next server. "Gravy for the marshal, Chloe."

"Gravy coming up," Chloe whispered.

"Indian busted Chloe's Adam's apple with a war club," the man ahead of Luther explained.

The woman shrugged. "Can't talk so good," she whispered, "but my husband says he don't mind."

The marshal squinted and grinned slightly in commiseration. He turned to the man as Chloe dipped some gravy onto his potatoes. "You in business here too?"

"Homestead about four mile south. Name's Northcutt. Main business right now is keeping them Texas cattle out of my crops."

The man beyond Northcutt paused as he started away from the table. "You going to do something about that, Mister Cain?"

"Sounds like the sheriff's job," Luther said. "But I'll say something to the herd owners I see."

The man laughed shortly. "They may listen at that. Anyhow Pickett's likely to listen now. The sonofabitch! Sorry ladies, forgot where I was." He departed with his food.

One of the servers filled Luther's coffee cup.

"Len's boy got beat up yesterday by some cowboys," Northcutt explained. "For shooting one of Pickett's cows."

Chloe's Adam's apple and now Len's boy; Northcutt seemed to be the evening's explainer.

"Shooting cows ain't legal," Luther pointed out.

"Neither's tromping down Len's crops."

"That why his boy shot the cow?"

"Yep."

Luther frowned. "Much trouble like that here?"

"Nothing new about it. Sod-busters ain't popular with trail drivers and trail drivers ain't popular with us."

"Can your grange treaty that with them?"

"Can't treaty with them that don't want to."

One of the ladies called out pleasantly, "Keep things moving up there, Mister Northcutt."

The farmer and the marshal stepped away from the table holding their full plates and cups.

"And cowmen say their cattle got as much right to the grass as our plows has."

Luther shook his head. "Not according to the law they ain't. The grass on your homestead is your'n."

"They say they can't tell where our land begins at."

"Reckon they can tell where your crops begins at."

"Say they can't drive a big bunch of cows that careful. Bound to be herd-leavers," Northcutt probably quoted some cattleman. Luther reflected that at least the cattleman had taken the time to argue; must have been from northern Texas. "But I heard about that barbed wire somebody invented," the farmer continued. "Going to order me some of that and fence my land. That ought to stop them bygod." If God was good to a certain sod-buster, Luther reflected further. The farmer concluded: "Hope it cuts the hell out of them critters."

There was a gentle commotion near the front door. Luther glanced toward it and saw a trooper salute and bow with a flourish

45

to a woman stepping into the crowded room. The soldier was smiling. "If it ain't the flower of the prairie!" he greeted her loudly.

"Howdy, Carrie," another trooper grinned. "Have some fried chicken."

Howard Smith was standing behind her with a pleased expression. He gestured toward the table. "Good evening, Carrie. Step over there and help yourself." His voice rose meaningfully. "We're glad to have you with us, Sister."

Luther had recognized her at once although she was dressed differently than when he had seen her last. He'd been right in thinking the night before that she should be prettier without makeup. She seemed younger-looking. Less dissolute. At least in these surroundings.

The momentary distraction of the room ended and the general conversation resumed and only a couple of the ladies looked less pleased than their minister or at any rate disconcerted. Most of the men appeared delighted although Luther guessed that some of them didn't know her.

"Wonder who the lady is?" Northcutt verified the marshal's guess. "Them soldiers knows her."

"Preacher Smith knows her too looks like," Luther said. "Believe I do myself."

That seemed endorsement enough for the farmer. "Yep must be somebody new the preacher's working on to join up. Worker for the Lord he is."

Somebody across the room motioned for Northcutt to join him.

"Eat with Cal Hubbard and me?" Northcutt asked.

"Thank you just the same; believe I'll eat outdoors. Kind of warm in here."

"See you later, Mister Cain."

The marshal walked toward the front door, intercepting Carrie Shaw on the way. She looked at him and her eyes spoke to him immediately but her tongue waited until he acknowledged her presence.

"Evening, Carrie," he said quietly.

She smiled. "How are you tonight, Marshal?"

"Hungry. Thought I'd go outdoors and eat. Cooler out there."

Her smile widened. "Think I'll eat outdoors too. Mind if I do?"

He started again toward the door. "Ain't for me to mind even if I did. Which I don't."

46

"I see you got some chicken, Mister Cain," the preacher grinned as he detained Luther once more. "Hope you like it."

"Can't miss I reckon."

"And I see you know Carrie Shaw yonder. Put in a good word for the Lord will you? Can't miss there either."

Luther shrugged noncommittally. "Maybe I ain't the one to do that."

"I'd say it wouldn't do no harm." Howard raised his hand to forestall the marshal's further disclaimer. "Just preaching the Bible, Mister Cain. 'Feed my lambs,' Jesus told Peter. I figure that means wherever you find them."

Outside among the overflow of people from the church Luther found a window-lit space in the side yard and sat down cross-legged, resting his plate between his knees and his coffee cup on the ground. The food was as good as Howard Smith had promised. He greeted a couple next to him—the Blaines who lived on Buffalo Street and had been new to Bancroft the previous summer—and talked with them for a few minutes about the district school house which was being built on the opposite corner. Mister Blaine seemed vaguely familiar and it turned out he was the barber whom Luther had seen the previous night rubbing liniment on the customer's scalp. He also was a part-time carpenter who worked on the school house for three hours every morning. When the marshal complimented him on the building's appearance he looked pleased and pretended not to notice Missus Blaine's arm-pat of wifely pride. They had two children, one of whom was deaf and dumb Mister Blaine volunteered apparently in anticipation of Luther's finding it out from somebody else. Luther had the feeling it was one of the first things he told all new acquaintances.

"Likely make him that much smarter," the marshal said, "keeping up with other kids that don't have no trouble."

The Blaines glanced at each other.

"Here you are." Carrie Shaw's voice smiled in the shadows.

The marshal looked up at her and started to his feet.

"Don't get up," she said, "you'll spill your food." She settled quickly on the ground beside him with her plate and cup.

"Get your dress dirty," he said.

"No there's some grass here." She looked expectantly at the couple beyond him. "Hello."

47

"These here's the Blaines," the marshal said. "Miss Shaw."

"Pleased to know you," Missus Blaine smiled.

Mister Blaine nodded pleasantly. "Haven't I seen you someplace?"

"You done some carpenter work down at the Portugese last week," Carrie reminded him. "I was sewing on a lady's hat in the back room."

"Sure," he nodded again after an instant's hestitation. "Sure I remember." He returned his attention closely to his last bite of chicken.

"You a seamstress, Miss Shaw?" Missus Blaine asked.

Carrie shook her head. "I'm just pretty good at sewing. Doing it for a friend. One of the other girls that works there." She seemed to straighten sitting in the dimness.

There was a swallow of silence.

The marshal cleared his throat. "Right handsome place." He recalled Johnny Newlin's facetious smile. The hair at the nape of his neck crawled with a surge of anger briefly and unaccountably.

"Well," Missus Blaine said, "I'm glad to know somebody's good at sewing. I'm sure not."

Very faintly Luther heard Carrie exhale.

Missus Blaine glanced at her husband. "You about finished, Lester? Guess maybe we better get back to our young'ns if you are." She looked at the marshal. "And speaking of the young'ns again, Mister Cain, thanks for your kind words about little Tim. Kind words has a way of helping." As she arose with Mister Blaine she turned to Carrie. "Miss Shaw, would you help me with a dress I want to make sometime?"

"Glad to any time, Missus Blaine."

"Good night to you both," her husband said.

Luther spoke unreservedly: "Proud to make your acquaintance, Folks."

For a few minutes after the Blaines had taken their empty plates into the church the marshal and the woman from the Portugese ate in silence.

"A few nice people in this town," the woman said then.

The marshal looked at the way the light from the window kindled her hair. "Along with the other kind you likely know a lot of."

Her eyes rose to meet his. "Luther, let's talk about how good this chicken tastes and what a nice night it is out."

He chewed quietly for a moment before nodding.

"And how glad I am I come here," she smiled. "I was supposed to go to work at sundown but I wanted to come here before I went." Her lashes lowered as she took another bite. "Fried chicken reminds me of Indiana."

He didn't say anything.

"That's where I was born. Or did I tell you? Where was you born, Luther?"

"Indiana."

"No fooling!" she laughed delightedly. "Where abouts?"

"On the Wabash near Terre Haute."

"Near Vincennes for me! Well what do you know? We was practically neighbors."

"Few years between," Luther said.

"Come on you're not that old. How old are you anyhow?"

"Forty near as I can figure."

"I'm thirty-three," she blurted honestly. "I mean I may not look that old but I am." She pressed her fork against her smile. "Not that forty's old. I don't mean that."

"I was seven years old when you was born."

"I like a man to be older." She took a sip of coffee to cover her fluster. "That is I mean if I liked a man I'd like him to be older."

"You like me?" Luther thought he must have been hypnotized by the word "like."

Carrie gazed at him for an instant before replying. And as he was about to speak again she said "Sure" with conviction.

He changed the subject. "How you know Preacher Smith?"

"Surprised?"

"Well not exactly . . ."

"I was just teasing, Luther. I met him in Berg's Dry Goods a while back and we got to talking and he invited me to come here whenever I wanted. I used to not like preachers."

The marshal tried to make amends. "He only invited me yesterday."

"Yesterday was your first day in town." Her tone was teasing again. Then abruptly it became solemn. "Look at that," she pointed upward. "Ain't that a sight to see?"

He gazed overhead. The rising moon glowed like a hearth coal, wreathed in a smoke of summer smells. He had looked like that at eternity a number of times. Usually it had been a flashier

49

view compressed in the muzzle of a .44 pointed at him, the ordeal of its threat numbed a little by his own exertion, its smell a black-powder pungency. Tonight its guise was benevolent and bloodless.

"Real peaceable," he nodded.

"Wonder what's on the other side of the moon, Luther?"

"Reckon we'll never know."

"Maybe after we're dead."

"Hope that won't be for a while." He felt oddly depressed for an instant. "Thought we was going to talk about fried chicken."

She smiled. "And what a nice night it is out. The moon's part of the nice night." She drained her cup and put her half-emptied plate aside. "Walk me as far as the railroad?"

"Ain't going to finish your food?"

She shook her head. "I had enough."

"Why only to the railroad?"

"Well I thought maybe—." She seemed to be studying the hem of her dress. "You know. Your job and all."

"I got a lot to do below the railroad." He swallowed the rest of his coffee, picked up her plate, stacked it on his, and stood up. "Bring your cup inside and I'll walk you all the way down."

Her teeth gleamed in the moonlight. "Whatever you say."

After they had carried their utensils into the church and told Howard Smith goodnight they started southward along East Street together.

Her starched skirt brushed against the butt of his gun in its holster.

"Walk on my left," he told her, pausing for a moment to let her cross in front of him.

"You got to think about things like that all the time don't you?"

He didn't reply.

"I'd be scared to be a marshal." She looked up at him soberly. "Ain't you ever, Luther?"

"Can't afford it much."

"I'd always think what could happen."

"Can't afford not to do that."

She didn't return his quick smile. Her tone was concerned. "Oscar Lacy says old man Pickett feels pretty riled about your buffaloing him last night."

"Who's Oscar Lacy?"

50

"Owns the Lone Star Cafe. You want to be careful of Pickett. He's mean enough natural without being riled. Could even come gunning for you the way he's talking."

"Or send somebody," the marshal amended, "while he goes on talking." Then he nodded. "I heard what he's saying today. Talkers like him ain't usually doers."

"He's a doer, Luther. I seen him. Killed a Yankee hunter in the Portugese last summer for spitting in his Texas face. Maybe that deserved a fist," she said bitterly, "but not five bullets and four of them in a corpse. Said he was saving his other gun for any goddam marshal come around objecting."

"Charlie Tucker come around?"

"Charlie's wife just died and he'd took her body to Missouri on the train and by the time he got back Pickett was headed south. While Charlie was gone his deputies arrested Pickett all right and there was a trial if you could call it that. Johnny Newlin and his bartender and some Texans swore it was did in self-defense. But I seen it and it wasn't. Only I was too scared to say so."

"How long after Charlie's wife died did his little girl have her trouble?"

"About six months." Carrie's voice softened. "He held up 'til then but that broke him. After that he wasn't no good at his job."

"So the mayor told me. You liked Charlie I reckon. Know him pretty well?"

"He was a good man."

"So the mayor told me. Know him pretty well?"

"He was good to me."

"Johnny Newlin good to you?"

"Johnny never hurt me. I work for him and he pays me."

"You like working for him?"

"I don't know."

"You like working in his place?"

"I don't know, Luther."

"How'd you start there?"

"I told you our troupe got stranded."

"I mean all them men?"

She gazed at him uncertainly. Luther was afraid for a moment she wasn't going to answer and suddenly he was angry at himself for asking the question. He blew softly through his clenched teeth. *Women.*

51

When she did reply her voice sounded small. "I had to work somewhere."

"The hell with it," he apologized.

"How does anyone know why they're where?"

"All right."

She forced confidence into her tone. "A girl does what she knows best."

He took an audible breath. "All right, Carrie."

"All right yourself," she laughed abruptly. "I only meant a bar girl's got to bar and a dancer's got to dance and a singer's got to sing. Just like a marshal's got to marshal."

He felt color seep into his face. He was thankful for the darkness. "You sing too?"

"Not very good but them rawhides can't tell the difference by midnight. Sometimes I get them to sing along with me and drown me out. Come in the place later and see for yourself."

He grinned. "If I didn't have to get some sleep tonight I would."

"It ain't so bad it'll give you nightmares. Don't be a sissy."

His grin spread into a chuckle. "Maybe I'll come by before I turn in."

Women could bamboozle a man if a man didn't watch himself.

He pulled her back from the path of a trotting horse at the Shawnee corner and they crossed Pacific Street and continued along the square's east side. The wooden sidewalk was thronged with the night's above-the-track population, resident and transient; and without seeming to Luther kept his eyes moving over the crowd's faces and actions, thinking about his job with one part of his mind and about the woman beside him with another.

He had cultivated the knack of thinking about two things at once. He could divide his mind into separate, independently functioning halves, one half impersonal, the other personal, and always keep his duty apart from his susceptibilities although not necessarily from all emotion. For instance, he could feel anger while performing his duty but his performance wasn't controlled or even much affected by anger. That was the way a marshal had to be able to be, he'd decided a long time ago, and that was the way he intended to keep things. He didn't know why the matter had cropped up in his thoughts but he certainly wasn't going to argue with himself about it. There was no reason why such things should change; they were a set pattern with him, a very efficient pattern not subject to challenge. He didn't know who wanted to challenge it. Hell, he was thinking in circles and to no damn purpose.

"A penny for your thoughts."

He shook his head.

"Why the frown? They worth a nickle maybe?"

Big John McAlister was approaching them. "Evening, John," Luther nodded, relieved by the distraction. "How's things?"

"Pretty fair. More drunks than yesterday; Colonel Cole paid off the last of his waddies today. But so far only noise." The deputy smiled and winked at the woman. "Hello, Carrie. How's my girl?"

She flicked him lightly on his chest with her forefinger. "Extra good. How's my boy?"

"Pining for you. Luther trying to beat my time?"

"I ain't engaged to you yet you know."

"That's the trouble with a girl everybody likes; never sure where you stand."

"You just stand aside, Big John, and we'll be on our way. We been to the church supper," she smiled with an inflection of pride, "and now I'm going down to add to the noise you spoke of."

"Bound to get noisier when you walk in there. Happier. I can hear 'em now." The deputy made a display of nudging the marshal. "Got your hands full, Luther."

The marshal's grin was affable. "So I noticed."

"Well goodnight, Carrie," Big John touched his hat brim. "See you later, Luther."

The marshal and the woman left the deputy and started past the dark railroad station and across the moon-brushed rails into South Street.

"I want to thank you for letting me eat with you tonight." Carrie looked up at his face. "And for walking me to work."

"I didn't let you eat with me. I asked you to. Quit talking thataway. It don't befit you."

She laughed. "I did just come out and set beside you without even a by-your-leave."

"I asked you inside the church and you know it."

"That what you done, Luther?"

"Sure, I told you I was eating outdoors where it was cooler."

"I'm glad you told me that."

"Why not?" His tone had taken on a slight edge. "It was hot in there."

"Yes," she murmured still gazing at him. "I felt it too. The heat."

"What else but the heat?"

"Nothing." her voice dropped to a whisper. "Them things never really happen."

"What don't?"

"Nothing."

As they walked along South Street they were submerged in its flood of noises and smells and jostling humanity. The nightly resurgence of the summer-long celebration was under its raucous way. A buffalo skinner in greasy buckskin with a knife hanging at the back of his neck on a thong staggered past them alone.

"Whew!" Carrie held her nose. "He's a ripe one. No wonder he's by hisself."

Three men riding along the street in the shadows yelled and waved at the woman and she returned their greetings.

"You're right popular," the marshal said.

"I'm glad. I like being liked. Most everybody does."

"Depends on who." Luther's light touch guided her into Jimson.

"Who cares as long as they wave and smile and even tip their hats sometimes." She smiled. "Not many of them tip their hats. Only Big John. And the preacher."

"I don't mean Big John and the preacher. I mean some of them that comes in here." They paused at the entrance of the Portugese. Two cowboys lurched out of the doorway without noticing them. "Trash like them."

She looked after the cowboys.

"Maybe they're not trash. Maybe they're nice as a kid I met in here last night."

"They're drunks and saddle-bums. Your friend Newlin called them that."

"Maybe they had a long ride like this kid did. Three months in the saddle's a long, hard time. I guess they get a long thirst and they drink hard to make up."

"What kid?"

She smiled at her mental picture of Raymond Davis seated at a table stretching his third drink out for half an hour. "Then there's others don't drink very hard; they only want to. Reckon to prove something." She shrugged. "Just a boy a long ways from home and with a busted arm to boot. I felt sorry for him." She put her hand on the marshal's bicep. It felt like a tree burl. "Speaking of a drink, want to buy me one?"

Her touch seemed to heighten his inexplicable annoyance. He wanted her to keep her fingers there and take them away at the same time. She took them away and his arm felt both deserted and secure again. "You go on to your customers. I got some things to see about."

"All right. Maybe later."

"Goodnight, Carrie."

"You ain't coming in later?"

He frowned down the street toward an outbreak of rebel yells. "I don't know. Got to get some sleep if I can."

"I'm sorry. I mean I hope you get some sleep. If you're that sleepy."

He glanced at her.

"I mean I don't blame you," she added with a guileless smile. She turned toward the doorway. "Thank you again for a very nice time, Luther. First regular beauing I had in years." She stepped into the saloon. The swinging doors squeaked on their hinges behind the stem of her straight, narrow back with its blossom of brown hair.

"You're welcome," he grunted inwardly. He tugged down his hat brim and headed at a calm pace toward the shouting. His thoughts weren't as calm as his stride but he forced them into an order of action concerning the ruckus ahead. Maybe no action would be called for. Shouting was harmless. But rebel yells had been known to swell into gunfire as in the somewhat more earnest ruckus between the States. The bullet he had taken at Fort Donelson ached momentarily in his left leg although it had passed on through at the time. A law officer came to know instinctively which noises meant trouble and which ones didn't. There didn't seem to be the probability here but there was a possibility that bore looking into. And he was in a mood to assume the possibility.

Long ago, dream-like, Mark tossed the warm pigeon upward into acrobatic flight as the younger kids surrounding him beside the coop on the roof applauded their champion with their grimy hands.

He pushed into the group in front of the Maverick Saloon for a close appraisal and was almost hit by an arcing fist. He took another step forward in the dimness and seized each of the fighters by the neck and slammed their heads together. One of them sagged to his knees and the other bellowed with frustration.

"Leave me go, goddamit! I'll kill the bastard!"

Luther shoved his fingers inside the standing man's shirt collar and twisted it tight against his larynx muffling further protest to a squeak. "You ain't going to kill nobody." The fallen man struggled to arise and Luther jerked him up with a rough hand under the shoulder.

"Leave 'em fight!" The spectator's yell started a chorus of complaints. "What the hell you doing, you sonofabitch?" The encircling group began to constrict threateningly. The marshal released the combatants and stepped back and suddenly his gun glinted in the doorway's light. There were those in the second rank who didn't see it. "Get your ass out of here!" The inner ring stopped moving forward abruptly. "Leave me through," a young voice in the rear shouted, "Teach the bastard manners!" The circle burst apart and a cowboy with his arm in a sling stumbled into the center. "What you doing my pardner Jesse?" He peered into the face of one of the fighters. "You right, Jesse? Best pardner in a world. Best fighter!"

"Shut up," Indian Jesse muttered, "he's got a gun on you."

The cowboy swung unhearingly toward the marshal. "Jesse wants to fight Mustang you let him. None a your business!"

"You're drunk." Luther looked at the sling. "And you got a busted arm. I think I heard about you. Go on back to your mama's teat."

Jesse spat a mouthful of blood. His eyes were on Luther. "Raymond don't know you're a lawman."

"Can't talk to me thataway!" Raymond railed at the marshal. "Damn bastard!" He drew back his unfettered fist.

"I'll talk to you this way," Luther said as he struck the cowboy across the mouth with the back of his left hand. Raymond's wobbly knees gave away and he sat down hard on the dark ground holding his mouth and staring dazedly upward at the marshal. Luther's voice was tired. "Any more cussing you want to do?"

Raymond continued to stare upward at the marshal.

"Him with a busted arm!" Mustang Johnson muttered.

"D-d-didn't need to kn-n-nock him down!" someone stuttered.

Luther supposed the stuttering usually drew laughter from a crowd. It didn't tonight.

A whispered oath embittered the sour night further. The lawman realized it was he who'd cursed this time. "Clear out of here," he said loudly, motioning with his gun. He glanced at the young man on the ground. "All but him."

"Leave the kid be."

The kid moved his hand from his mouth. "All right, Tenderloin, is all right."

"Clear out, I said, or I'll jail the bunch of you!"

The group disassembled raggedly into the Maverick's doorway. When its last grumbling member had gone inside the marshal holstered his revolver and helped Raymond to his feet. His helping hand wasn't lenient but it didn't jerk the boy up.

"You all right?"

The cowboy nodded sullenly.

"Let me give you some advice, Son, whether you're sober enough to hear it or not. Don't butt in your elder's business. And drink with your friends all you want but don't do it to prove nothing." Luther squinted in apparent thoughtfulness. "There's something else: if you want a girl get one as young as you, then you won't get over your head." He glanced at the youngster's bandanna sling. "Too bad about your busted arm."

Raymond spoke quietly after a moment. "Near healed."

The marshal pushed the cowboy on his way. It wasn't an unfriendly push. Then he turned back along Jimson Street with a sour feeling in his gut that he may have looked like a bully to the kid. Bullies had roiled him ever since his brother Elijah had been bloodied by one defending him when he was a kid himself. He was glad Carrie hadn't seen the last few minutes' rumpus.

Funny she'd come from the banks of the Wabash too.

"Hey, Mister Cain!"

He stopped and looked around. Noble Buck was trotting toward him waving a piece of paper in the night air. "This here's yours!" The boy took several deep breaths when he reached him. "Plumb out of wind."

"What you doing down here this time of night?"

Noble handed him an envelope. "Must have fell out of your pocket at the church. I et there after you. Thought it might be official business, Mister Cain."

Luther recognized the envelope. It bore his return address and contained a boot order he'd penciled on the train and hadn't got around to mailing since his arrival.

"Thanks, Noble. But you don't want to come down here at night."

Noble wiped his nose on his shirt sleeve. "Is it official business, Mister Cain?"

"I wouldn't call it that exactly."

The boy looked disappointed.

"But it's pretty important," Luther admitted.

The boy looked proud.

"Who was it you said give you that Spencer from the War?"

"Uncle Vince."

"Why don't you live with him?"

"He left town for Dodge City Tuesday night in a hurry. Anyhow I sleep in that shack behind the ice house. 'Pretty important' huh?"

Luther nodded. "Why did your Uncle Vince leave town?"

"Didn't want to get mixed in that stabbing maybe."

"Dodge City?" The marshal's sudden hunch seemed incredible but he decided to play it. "You got any cousins, Noble?"

"Sure. Old Cousin Pearl. She stabbed Cousin Opal. Cousin Opal ain't quite so old."

"Pearl Vollie?"

"Yep."

Luther grinned inwardly. He cleared his throat and laid his hand on the boy's shoulder. "Noble you know the prosecutor wants to talk to your Uncle Vince only he didn't know where he's at?"

The boy swung his head slowly from side to side. "Why he's over there to Dodge like I said."

"Needs him as a witness. I want you to tell the prosecutor what you just told me. Reckon you can come down to the courthouse tomorrow and help us," Luther paused "with some official business?"

"Gee whiz, Mister Cain!"

The marshal dropped his hand. "Get back on cross the track now and I'll see you in the morning."

The boy started off at a trot. "Remember, Mister Cain," he called over his shoulder, "you just holler whenever you need me!" He turned and came back a few steps. "And don't forget I shoot

58

good like I told you." He turned forward again and disappeared into the shadows.

The fatigue of Luther's four hours' sleep in thirty-six hit him behind the eyes like a hammer. He pinched the bridge of his nose and saw a red kaleidoscopic vision of a brown-haired woman astride a wild horse led by a smiling preacher whose mouth dripped blood and whose broken hand held a smoking revolver.

He decided that Big John and Little John and Lafe had to take over for the rest of the night.

Entering the community life of Bancroft was a good deal like catching onto a moving train.

With forty-two cars.

CHAPTER 6

The last week of August anticipating September's caresses and October's exhilaration and winter's exertions slipped into Bancroft as a virginal bride does into bed: hopefully but apprehensively.

Aside from the changes of seasons nobody knew exactly what to expect; there was simply a faint uneasiness in the air.

The days were still hot and it was strange to think that within three full moons at least one blizzard was certain to be a thing of the past. A Great Plains blizzard always brought death—another certainty based on past experience—and it also was strange to think about who consequently would be dead then who was alive now. But that conjecture wasn't what lent the town its subtle melancholy. There was something less predictable and defined.

Jake Barlow at his forge across from the depot glanced at the wheeling skies and frowned for no reason and went back to work on a plowshare without singing to himself.

Johnny Newlin didn't know at what hour Jason Pickett and his cowboys should hit the Portugese again in their sullen rounds that Wednesday but he knew they were bound to come in as they prowled among the below-track honkytonks.

Solly Berg suspected that his wife and some neighbors were planning a surprise party for him on his birthday the following Friday. Deep inside his heart his suspicion made him feel good. So all right he was too nice a fellow as Carrie Shaw had told him one time; but that was the way God and history had made him and he couldn't change now. He was glad Esther and his neighbors thought enough of him to give him a surprise birthday party. (Maybe they should invite Luther Cain. *There* was a man.)

Doc Bowman let his cards lie face-down on the table until all five of them had been dealt him. He liked the suspense of waiting until the whole truth was available and then the catharsis of finding it out all at once. Seated at the doctor's left in the quiet back room of Guttman's Drug Store Carl Norris looked with a good newsman's impatient curiosity at each of his cards as it was dealt. At Doc's right County Attorney Jim Watts not only looked at each of his cards as it was dealt but made a noncommittal remark about ıt as he put it into its sequential place in his hand

and mind. Mayor Bill Crum—"house" dealer today by arrangement with druggist-gambler Harry Guttman—dealt in the way he mayored: honestly, with a show of indifference but aware of everything of significance around him.

"How many cards?" the mayor asked after he had opened and the others had stayed.

"I'll stand pat," the lawyer said. "Bird in the hand's worth two in the bush."

"One." Doc Bowman replaced his discard with the new card dealt him by the mayor, grinned, shrugged and tossed his hand onto the table.

The dealer brushed the end of his thumb across his tongue and eyed Carl Norris.

"I'll see three," the editor said. Typically he still didn't look satisfied after he'd glanced at his three new ones.

The mayor discarded two cards and dealt himself an exchange. "I'll take them two Jim left in the bush."

Jim Watts bet five dollars. Carl Norris called him of course. And Bill Crum raised the bet five.

The lawyer's eyes clouded at the mayor's disregard of logic. "Up five again," he said somewhat testily, shoving more chips into the pot.

The editor sighed and folded.

The mayor matched the lawyer's raise. "Call."

They spread their hands. Jim Watts had a straight and Bill Crum a full house. The doctor and the editor smiled over their good sense in getting out. Bill didn't smile; it didn't seem polite among friends; instead he grunted "When the hell you going to learn to play poker as good as you practice law?"

"Speaking of the law around here," Doc Bowman chuckled, "I heard a funny story this morning. Recall last week when Luther Cain buffaloed Pickett?"

The mayor raked in the pot and the others nodded.

"Pickett's been brooding about it ever since and yesterday got tanked up in the Portugese and sent a kid to tell Luther he wanted to see him for a peace talk. Waited there with a rifle so when Luther stepped in the door he had him covered. You know what Luther said?"

The mayor began to deal another hand as the others gazed at the doctor.

"He said, 'Mister Pickett, your pants are unbuttoned.' And

Pickett being the dandy he is, which Luther heard about, forgot and looked down at his pants and when he looked up again Luther's pistol was pointing right square between his eyes."

The mayor slapped the table with a whoop of laughter. "That's the damn funniest thing I heard in six weeks."

The hoots of the lawyer and editor echoed the mayor's delight.

"That isn't all," the physician continued. "Luther jerked the rifle away from Pickett and gave it to the kid. Said, 'Here, Noble'—that was the kid's name—'Mister Pickett wants you to have this rifle for running his errand; it'll take the place of your wore-out Spencer.' Then he turned around and walked out with the kid following him like he was God; and Pickett stood there turning blue. For once that Texas sonofabitch couldn't say a word."

"Yessir," the mayor said again, "funniest damn thing in six weeks."

County Attorney Watts looked reflective. "Kid must have been that red-headed Buck one delivers ice. Lived in that shack back of the ice house."

The doctor nodded. "Still lives back there."

"No he don't, Doc. Luther Cain came up to me in the courthouse Monday morning and introduced himself—I hadn't met him yet—and he had this Noble Buck with him. Luther'd heard from Little John Brock I needed Vince Simpson as a witness against Pearl Vollie and he'd found out the kid knew where Vince was. But after we got that straightened out Luther had something else. Wanted to talk about the kid living in that shack. Said he didn't think it was a good idea. Handed me twenty dollars to give Mother Swain for a month's room and board and asked me to see Noble moved over there. Wanted to make it sound official, make sure the kid did move."

Carl Norris grinned. "He's going to make good copy."

"Supposed to be such a hard case." Doc Bowman picked up all of his cards at once.

"He is, Doc," the mayor said softly, "and don't you forget it. We didn't hire him without knowing all about him. When Kid Owen in Kansas City went for his gun Luther shot him smack in the face instead of the stomach where it's quicker. Kid Owen used to pride himself a lot on his good looks." His glance prodded Jim Watts' opening bet.

"Five bucks," Jim said.

Doc tossed in five. "Stay for a while."

Carl stayed for five too. "Last winter I wrote about the time in Abilene he faced down six men with that one gun of his. And he never even drew it."

"Drew his reputation," the doctor surmised. "Sure he's tough. I'm glad he's around."

The county attorney smiled. "Makes prosecuting safer, too. Like doctoring and newspapering and mayoring."

"Nobody'd shoot you, Jim," Doc muttered, "you're too bad a poker player to waste."

The mayor looked at the lawyer. "That's the truth. I'm staying for five. How many you want?"

"One."

Bill dealt the card to him. "Trying for a straight or a flush this time out?" He shifted his glance to the doctor.

"Three cards. I wonder if a man ever knows all about another man."

The mayor dealt three to Doc. "I meant we knowed all about his marshaling." His glance continued to the newspaperman. "Carl?"

"I've got to look at every one I can." The editor dropped three cards and picked up three newly dealt ones and looked at them and then across them at the doctor. "Interesting question. Can't ever know a whole man. That it?"

"Every whole man's divided into parts," Doc said, "and those are divided into parts on down. Some of them nobody else knows about; and some of them the man himself don't even know. That's what I've come to anyhow."

Bill Crum dealt to himself. "Dealer takes a couple."

Doc checked the bet to Carl and the newspaperman checked it to Bill and the mayor checked it to Jim with a sly look: "Going to bet on your openers?"

"One thing I bet," Jim said, "is Luther Cain knows more about himself than most men. Not because he's smarter. Just because he's not that complicated. Strikes me as a plain, tough lawman first, last and always. Now that's just from talking with him a couple times and hearing about him."

"Going to bet your openers?" the mayor repeated.

"Two dollars."

"Two's a crazy kind of bet," the mayor frowned impatiently.

"You opened for five. And if you're bluffing you ought to bluff bigger and if you made your straight or flush you ought to ride it harder."

"You teaching me poker?"

"Guess I might as well stay at that rate," Doc Bowman smiled, tossing in two chips. "All I'm saying is everybody's complicated. Can't count on anybody being plain one thing or another." He squinted. "Be interesting to know what made Luther the way he is."

"Call," the editor said, pushing in two chips. "Bound to be interesting watching Luther Cain tame this town is what I'm saying and I'm going to have a good time writing about it."

Bill Crum thumbed-and-forefingered his derby from his forehead and with the same thumb and forefinger set twelve chips in the center of the table. He stared at the lawyer. "Maybe another time I wouldn't raise after checking but my patience is run out. Up ten." Anticipating Jim's surrender he almost laid down his cards.

"Now right there's something that isn't a good time." Jim Watts shook his head ruefully. "Cost me ten dollars to call that raise won't it, Bill?"

"Ten's just right."

"Yep looks like I got myself in a fix here."

"Looks that way."

"But I guess I got to keep you honest." Jim counted out ten dollars and contributed them to the cause of learning poker.

"Fold," Doc said unequivocally.

Carl tossed his cards down. "Me too for Pete's sake."

Bill spread his hand showing three handsome aces, a ten and a four.

"Four queens—" Jim displayed the evidence—"and a little duece." He began to sweep in the pot. "How you reckon that duece got in there?"

The mayor muttered something unintelligible.

Outdoors the slanting sunlight gleamed on Luther Cain's silver gun butt as he stepped into Orville Allgood's leather store to buy a birthday present for Solly Berg.

CHAPTER 7

As Mayor of the City of New York, I'm proud to address you this morning. We're gathered here to honor certain members of the City's Police Department. The first of those is an officer whose courageous action on the night of August twelfth, nineteen hundred seventy, was in the highest tradition of "New York's Finest." His partner having become suddenly sick earlier, this officer singlehandedly confronted more than a dozen armed members of a marauding street gang whose leader had just fired at an innocent tourist and was aiming to fire again. With the barrel of his sidearm, the officer knocked the leader senseless, probably saving the tourist's life. Dispersing the rest of the gang with the threat of his still un-fired weapon, he manhandled the unconscious hooligan—ah, offender—into his squad car and drove him to the precinct and saw him booked before resuming his patrol. Later that night, still singlehandedly, he rescued an alleged prostitute from a beating in progress by her alleged pimp, took the female to the hospital and the pimp to the precinct lockup. The hospital emergency-room personnel reported that his quick transportation of her there probably saved the female's life—his second life-saving act of the shift. By these brave and efficient actions he brought credit, not only to himself but to the Department and the City. In recognition thereof it is my privilege to award to Patrolman Mark Keller, along with my congratulations, this Certificate of Honorable Mention for Outstanding Performance of Duty. I might add it's the third such award in nine months for this rookie officer who came to our Department as a decorated Vietnam veteran . . .

Friday dawned as cool and elegant as a Boston heiress, but by noon Bancroft was hot again and women's dresses clung damply to their backs and coursings of sweat tickled men's chests and armpits under their shirts.

After a midday sandwich at the Lone Star Cafe, Solly Berg stopped in the Schmidt Brothers two-man cigar factory for a box of their ropey, black stogies. The cigars were a birthday present from Solly to himself and he mentioned the fact to Gus Schmidt.

"Gluckwunsche zum geburtstag," Gus beamed at him across a long table piled with tobacco, "many happy returns." He cleared a space of moist-leaf wrappers and twisted filler and took the box of stogies back from Solly and set it down. Then he called to his brother across the room, "One of our new Lola Montezes, Fritz!"

Fritz picked up an ornate box and brought it to the table and handed it to Gus, smiling, holding out his other hand to their customer. "Happy birthday."

Solly shook his hand. "Thank you, Fritz."

"Ya," Gus said, placing the box of Lola Montez Superbas on top of the stogies with obvious pride, "these much better tobacco. And see how the new label in the light shines?"

"Very pretty," Solly complimented them both.

Gus nodded. "New labels just from Chicago special."

The three of them gazed at the red and gilt lithograph of the beautiful actress. Solly sighed.

"Schone ya," Gus agreed.

"Wunderbar," Fritz breathed.

Shaking off his trance Gus lifted the fancy box and handed it to Solly. "For you, mein freund, on your birthday. Free from Gus and Fritz. First Lola Montezes out of this factory going. Schmidt Brothers' new cigar."

Solly was pleased. "I'm honored. Thank you very, very much. I'm sure they're fine; your cigars have always been."

Gus threw up his hands. "Nein!" He pointed at the box which Solly was now holding with great care. "But those—ah! Those our masterpiece ist!"

"Yessir mighty fine," Solly could only repeat.

The little ceremony completed, Gus wiped an eye-corner with a knuckle and grinned broadly. "What other presents today you get?"

Solly managed a grin. "My wife and son didn't say anything this morning. But that's all right. They're trying to fool me, there'll be presents tonight all right." His chuckle sounded almost convinced. "A surprise."

"Sure," Gus nodded.

"Oh sure," Fritz said.

"Unless they didn't remember," Gus qualified the brothers' assurances. "Sometimes people don't remember." He shrugged. "Myself I wouldn't mind, I got too many birthdays already."

"Oh I won't mind either if they've forgotten. I couldn't blame Esther and David, not such darlings." Solly looked suddenly thoughtful. "Maybe because of Yom Kippur they decided no party.

But I think they haven't forgotten. No." He waggled his finger at the Schmidt Brothers. "You watch tonight."

"We watch," Gus and Fritz said in unison.

At Mother Swain's boarding house Noble Buck finished his noon meal of side pork, pickled cabbage, and cornbread and left the crowded table on the back porch with a shy nod to the landlady standing in the kitchen doorway.

"Had enough, Noble?" she asked. "Carrying that ice all day got to eat enough."

"Yessum."

Fred Martin spoke through a forkful of cabbage. "Reckon that ice feels pretty good on your back a hot day like this."

"Yessir."

"You going to get strong carrying that ice," Ralph Cox said. Ralph clerked in Berg's Dry Goods and was five feet tall. "Next to Blacksmith Barlow you going to grow up the strongest man in town."

"Don't know about that," Noble said.

Mother Swain nodded. "That's why he's got to eat."

"He come to the right place," Howard Smith said.

The landlady affected a curtsy. "Thank you, Preacher, compliment accepted."

"Got to get back to work," Noble said. He left the porch.

"Nice boy," Mother Swain smiled after him.

Ralph Cox nodded. "Friend of young David Berg."

Fred Martin swallowed his mouthful of cabbage. "Him and Billy Plunkett's good friends too. Billy's our devil down to the newspaper. Noble stops in there oncet in a while on his rounds."

"Them three goes fishing together," the dry goods clerk said.

"And the other day," the printer grinned, "they was talking about maybe the new marshal going with them sometime. There'd be a sight; Luther Cain fishing for bluegills alongside three boys."

"I can see that," the preacher said. "Luther was at our church supper and I talked with him a few other times too. He's different from what you'd think. I believe he's got his gentle side; his work hides it."

"Heard about that church supper," Fred said, "how he got friendly with that Carrie girl. She there, Preacher, that true?"

Howard squinted at him. "I invited her."

"I like her too. Most everybody does." The printer shrugged. "Just wondering."

"Even women do," Ralph Cox said, "if they'd admit it."

"I admit it," Mother Swain said from the doorway. "And I never met Luther Cain but I like him too by hearsay what with sending Noble over here with Jim Watts. If Mister Cain and Carrie wants to get friendly that's all right."

Howard Smith smiled. "I wouldn't hardly say they was friendly that way. But you're a good woman, Mother."

She waved disparagingly. "I'm past fifty, I'm too old for romance myself. I get my tingles out of looking, 'though some men ain't worth looking at."

The men at the table laughed. At the end farthest from the kitchen door Jeb Hill pushed back his plate, belched and stood up. "You ain't too old to cook good."

"Or look good to me," Wyoming Nye allowed. Wyoming owned and tended bar in the Shawnee and the disappearing meal before them was his breakfast.

"You got a good eye, Wyoming," the preacher said.

Instead of going directly back to work Noble Buck had climbed the stairs and walked along the hall to the rear second-floor room of the boarding house. Now he was standing in the middle of his room looking around and smiling. He did this private savoring of his recent, miraculous affluence at least twice a day. It gave him a feeling of confidence and of belonging. The air was hot and smelled of manure from Bollinger's Stable but inside these four walls it was his air and its stove-heat in the wintertime would be his and that sure would beat the snowy cross-drafts of the shack behind the ice house. Back of his eyes he thanked Luther Cain and Jim Watts and Mother Swain and for good measure Preacher Smith who by association might have had something to do with his good fortune. Then he turned around and went along the hall and down the stairs and outside to his ice wagon which was dripping a damp outline of its bed in Pacific Street's dust.

"Haw!" he called contentedly to Shag as he took up the reins.

Around the corner, down the plaza and across the track Jake Barlow looked up from his anvil to answer Ed Sarver's question. "What I allow about the Injun trouble up north? I allow there's more trouble coming up there. Just hope it don't spread back down here to Kansas."

Ed frowned. "Ain't we got enough trouble already: Texas cowmen running head-on agin sod-busting nesters, townsfolks wanting Texas business and law and order at the same time, damn Texans shipping from somewheres else if we don't lick their boots?" His tone was supplicant as though Jake Barlow could dispel Bancroft's adversity by a sweep of his great arms.

"Administration in Washington can't make up its mind," the blacksmith said; "it don't know what the hell it's doing."

"Didn't reckon you was a Democrat, Jake."

"I'm as good a Republican as you. But I done my share of Injun fighting under Carrington and I done my share of fighting with my late wife too—God rest her soul—and I found out Injuns and women is alike one way; you got to treat them tomorrow the same as today or it mixes them up bygod. The Government just don't savvy redskins."

"If they anything like women," Ed smiled, "it's no wonder."

Jake gestured with his five-pound hammer as though it were a twig. "After dealing the Injuns hell-fire and brimstone the Government switches around six, seven years ago and hands them the Powder River country and the Black Hills and asks them pretty please to stick to them places and white men to stay out. Then what's it do next?"

"What's it do next?" Ed asked obligingly

"It sends Custer into them Hills to see if it's true there's gold been found there and it sure is."

"Judas," Ed said unbelievingly.

"Now anytime you reckon you can tell cowmen to stay off that Powder River grass and prospectors away from that Black Hills gold you sure gone soft in the head. So what's bound to happen?"

Ed almost hated to ask: "What's bound to happen?"

"Well bygod you watch. One way or another it spells a big fight."

" 'Big fight' eh?"

"Them Injuns got a bad heart and they been raiding and killing already and that's give the soldiers a bad heart too."

Ed squinted ruefully. "Just hope it don't spread down in Kansas like you said. We already done our Injun fighting."

The blacksmith hunched his naked shoulders in a huge gesture of frustration. "All that blood I seen wasted, on both sides. Like the goddam War Between the States." He rubbed his hamlike hand over his face and snapped the sweat into the litter of iron and wood around him.

Ed deliberated on Jake's articulated thoughts for a moment. "Judas!" he muttered again. "You do a lot of thinking about things don't you?"

"Some I reckon," the blacksmith shrugged. "Smithing takes a heap of back but not much mind. So I give my mind over to studying about one thing and another."

"What you think about Luther Cain, Jake?"

The blacksmith looked reflective.

"Ain't that a fine thing we done?" Ed prodded him. "For the town?"

"You fellers on the council hired yourself a famous marshal all right," Jake agreed. "And I reckon he didn't get famous without knowing his job."

"He's hard," Ed nodded, accepting his friend's remark as a compliment. "Just what this town needs."

"Hope he ain't too hard."

Ed was amazed. "How can a fellow be too hard for a job like that? Charlie Tucker wasn't hard enough. That's why the job broke him."

"I mean a lawman's got to remember he's dealing with humans and he's got to remember he's a human hisself." The blacksmith was measuring his words. "That's what I mean by 'too hard.'" He raised his hand against Ed's remonstrance. "I know to stand up agin a bunch like that"—he motioned southward— "you got to be gun-hard all right. And you can't let nothing get under your skin too much like Charlie done his wife's dying and his little girl getting ruint. But I reckon a lawman's bound to have human feelings inside him like everybody else including that bunch down there; and if he figures he don't have such feelings and they don't neither, then them feelings is apt to throw him like a bronc when they go to bucking."

Ed mulled this concept. "Don't know, Jake," he said finally. "You're maybe saying Luther don't know his own self good. But he sure as hell knows the likes of them," he duplicated Jake's southward gesture, "else he wouldn't be alive today."

70

The blacksmith tonged a piece of red-hot strap metal from the forge to the anvil. "Hell I don't know no more about Luther Cain than you, not as much. I only talked to him a couple times. And I liked him, I ain't saying I didn't. Bygod, he's going to put a crimp in anybody breaks the law. And that's what this town needs, like you said. He cached a shotgun in my shed here the other day and I aim to help him however I can."

"But what?" Ed asked.

"No 'buts.' Reckon I do too much studying sometimes. And too much talking." Jake slammed his hammer down on the piece of metal. "And too much crepe-hanging."

Ed laughed. "You're just sore at the Government today, Jake."

"Sure that's right. I'm sore at the goddam Government."

Northward on East Street in Wagner's Grocery Missus Blaine, wife of barber and part-time carpenter Lester Blaine, paid the proprietor two dollars and fifty cents for a twenty-pound sack of sugar and turned toward the door and collided with Carrie Shaw. The younger woman had come into the store to buy some coffee to boil on the cook stove which Everett Lane had set up that week on the back porch of his rooming house on Jimson Street for the convenience of his paying guests. The stove had been Carrie's idea to compensate in part for the lack of a full kitchen. Everett had promised to move it into the hall when winter came and to vent a flue for it to the outdoors. Without meaning to look a gift horse in the mouth Carrie wished he should set up a small heating stove in the outhouse, too.

"Afternoon, Miss Shaw," Missus Blaine nodded.

"Missus Blaine," Carrie smiled.

"About that dress I mentioned at the church supper. I wasn't fooling about needing help with it if you want to."

"I wasn't fooling about helping you either, Missus Blaine."

"Could I call you 'Carrie?' "

"Be glad if you did."

"I'd be glad if you called me 'Ruth.' You think maybe we could start that dress pretty soon, Carrie, so I could wear it to the fire brigade ball this month?"

"Any afternoon is fine with me."

"You sure?"

"Sure. You got the material?"

"Eight yards of silk from my sister in St. Louis."

"Silk!" Carrie breathed. "What you doing this afternoon?"

Ruth Blaine's eyes lighted. She glanced down at the sack of sugar in her arms. "Taking this home." She looked up tentatively. "That's all today 'til I start supper for the young'uns and get dressed for a surprise party at Esther Berg's. Already done my chores."

"Mind if I walk home with you for a while? I got a while myself. We could start on the pattern this afternoon."

Missus Blaine looked uncertain.

"Unless you rather not."

The older woman's lips trembled with excitement. Suddenly they weren't older-looking lips. "Guess I rather do that than anything!"

Carrie laughed. "I'll get my coffee I come for and be with you in a minute, Ruth."

CHAPTER 8

. . . When this columnist once asked Sergeant Keller why he'd chosen a police career, his answer was about as forthright as they come: "Because I thought I'd be good at it." And after a hairy car chase and shoot-out later, when we wanted to know why he stayed on such a dangerous, depressing job, our notes quote him as saying: "It's not as dangerous as 'Nam. Besides, I'm not responsible why I do it, just how; in a way I don't have to think, only act; so it's not depressing either." We've been thinking that over since then, especially in the light of more recent events . . .

Eastward across Owl Creek the casually regimented afternoon of Fort Reynolds was disordered abruptly by a shrill, angry whinny and the shriek of nails being jerked from tortured planks. This racket was followed by the crack of splintering wood and a thudding of shod hooves on sun-baked clay and a Comanche warwhoop mingled with shouted curses.

"That stallion," Colonel Evans gritted, "that big red bastard! I told Sergeant Sullivan it was an outlaw." The post commander—a gaunt, graying man with gnarled hands—got up from his desk and strode to a rear window of the headquarters building. "But Sergeant Sullivan fancies himself a better bronc peeler than artilleryman. And he may be just that, wanting to stick to a muzzleloader. Come and look at this."

Luther Cain arose and stepped behind the officer and peered across his shoulder at the commotion outside. A powerful, snorting sorrel was fish-tailing across the cavalry yard in a frenzy of rage with the obvious intent of murdering its hatless, flapping-legged rider. As the colonel and the marshal watched, one frowning and the other grinning, the huge animal reared and wrenched backward in a vicious attempt to mash the soldier under its toppling weight; but the soldier sprang from its withers as it fell and scrambled clear of the thrashing heap of horseflesh and sprinted for the refuge of a doorway and of a contemplative chew of tobacco while he studied his next tactic.

The post commander turned back toward his desk. "That's the hammerheaded outlaw the sergeant's decided is going to haul the off-side of his beloved muzzleloader around. He might as well stand in front of his cannon and light its damn fuse."

Luther resumed the visitor's chair. "He ain't a bad rider but he's got a bad horse there for sure."

"He'll agree with the first part of that but not the last." Colonel Evans sat down again behind his desk. "Sergeant Sullivan is a damn stubborn Irish fool."

"I don't know about a fool, Colonel, but I'd call him an optimist."

The officer laughed briefly. "That at least." He squared some dispatches in front of him on the desk and leaned back. "Well, Mister Cain, we were talking about off-duty troopers. You said they haven't been giving you trouble in town and you don't want them to."

"Since I been in Bancroft they ain't been mixed up in nothing serious. Drunk now and then and a scuffle or two like comes natural. And maybe they been suckered by some gamblers and women and done a spit of hollering about that. Course I try to watch out for them plays. But then being suckered is natural too at least for soldiers." Luther's quick grin was replaced by a squint. "Thing I don't want in Bancroft is like back at Riverland. Four soldiers and five Texas cowboys killed in a battle over who won the late War. And I don't reckon you want that kind of doings."

"Hardly. That didn't do Colonel Allen's promotion chances any good. It didn't do those nine men any good either I'll have to say. Any suggestions, Mister Cain, about an ounce of prevention?"

"I'd say a pound of soldiers, Colonel. That's what I come over here to talk about. If you detail a couple men ever night to patrol the town and keep an eye on their own kind I wouldn't have to bother with the troopers."

"You're not asking me to assign this detail to you are you? I'm afraid I'd wonder about my authority to do that."

Luther shook his head. "I wouldn't have no authority over your men. And they wouldn't be nothing official as far as civilians is concerned. But we'd keep track of what each other was doing, work with each other watching for trouble. And preventing it."

The colonel pressed the tips of his knobby fingers together and stared at the marshal across them. "Sounds reasonable, Mister Cain."

"It'd help my job, Colonel, and it'd help keep any fracas from cropping up between the Army and civilians. That comes under your job too I reckon."

"You give your job a good deal of thought don't you, Marshal?"

"Thinking about it is part of it."

"All right it's agreed." The post commander leaned forward. "Are you by any chance a reading man?"

"Do some book reading oncet in a while when I can. That is besides a newspaper. A newspaper's bound to be reading for me; learn a lot of information out of it about things going on around a town."

Colonel Evans stood up. "It's important to be informed." He walked toward a single shelf of books next to a map of Kansas on the wall. "Not only about what's going on, which in my work we call 'intelligence,' but about how to deal with the given situation in terms of action. We call that 'strategy' and 'tactics.' " He paused in front of the shelf and pointed a long finger at the marshal like a school teacher—a good school teacher, Luther grinned inwardly. "You're a man of action, Mister Cain, just as I am. Your job requires it as mine does. And from what I've heard yours is effective action. Had you ever thought of yourself on the order of a military officer?"

"No," Luther confessed. "I was a noncom in the War. I liked it that way."

"You're an officer in the war against lawlessness now whether you like it or not. I assume you do like it or you wouldn't be doing it."

Luther's mind flicked back to his Sunday evening thoughts as he had walked toward the Methodist Church wondering why he continued marshaling. He hadn't resolved anything about it then and didn't now. "Maybe I don't know why I keep doing it."

"Why did you start?"

The marshal frowned, not at the colonel's asking the question but at its difficult implications. Somehow he felt obliged to answer it as honestly as he could. He didn't know whether or not his answer held the whole truth but he was sure it was partly true: "Maybe because I do it good."

"There's satisfaction in that certainly."

"And maybe partly . . ." Luther broke off. This sort of self-appraisal wasn't easy. He couldn't understand why he wanted to try a little harder.

The post commander waited silently.

"It makes me feel free. I don't have to pass the laws. I only enforce them. Like in the Army. I only had to do what smarter men figured out."

"You're a smart man, Mister Cain. Why do you think the men who make the laws are smarter than you?"

"Making the laws is their job," Luther said sharply, "enforcing them is mine. I can't do everything. No man can."

"I didn't mean to press you, Sir. I'm just curious about what makes people tick; it's a fault of mine. But I'm only curious that way about people I consider worthwhile, people who have something to offer to their time and place."

"That's all right." Luther's voice had lost its sharpness.

"You obviously have great respect for the law, Marshal."

"I like to see it enforced. I like order and peace. I don't know why people want to break the law to each other's hurt when all they got to do is get along."

The colonel nodded. "Yes, Mister Cain, it makes a person angry sometimes to rediscover human frailty. But I'm afraid it's here to stay." He took a thin volume from the shelf. "To get back to what I started to say: as a law officer you at least have to think about strategy and tactics involved in law enforcement don't you? In the same way an army officer has to think about those things in his larger-scale battles." He walked back toward the marshal holding out the book. "Certain basic principles of warfare have been developed over the centuries by great warriors. Here's a compilation by a French general of Napoleon's quotes on the subject. I've heard that Stonewall Jackson always carried a copy in his haversack during the War. You might be interested in reading it." He handed the volume to the marshal. It was entitled "Military Maxims of Napoleon" and apparently had been read many times judging by the thumb prints and candle wax which Luther noticed on its pages as he leafed through them. "It's not a moral treatise, it's a technical manual. And it occurred to me that some of its techniques might be adapted to marshaling." The army officer smiled. "For cues on the moral aspects of your job you'll have to look elsewhere." His smile seemed faintly sad.

"Much obliged, Colonel. That's right kind of you." Luther closed the book and stood up. "And right now reckon I best be going. I've took enough of your time." This strangely deep-talking man made him a little uncomfortable for some reason. But the marshal was attracted to him at the same time. Elijah Cain, Luther's older brother, had talked that way sometimes when they were younger before Elijah was killed at Shiloh. "I'll see you get the book back directly." He shifted the volume to his left hand away from the silver gun butt poised in its holster.

The colonel's intuition absorbed the gesture and he sighed. "I was hoping before you leave you'd allow me to show you around the post. We've a pretty small garrison now—not much activity in this area—but this used to be an important fort, you know. The stockade still shows marks of a siege a few years back."

"Got a while," Luther said after a moment's hesitation. "Fine with me." He pulled down the brim of his hat.

"After you," the colonel smiled toward the door.

The commander of Fort Reynolds and the marshal of Bancroft spent an hour inspecting all of the Fort's buildings and facilities. They pursed their lips and nodded at the horses and mules in the stables and walked around a few of the animals which the commander ordered a private to trot out and they tasted some cornbread which the bakers were baking and drank some water from the storage tank and chatted briefly with a soldier in the three-cot hospital and shoved their noses into some hay to find out whether it was molding and stood to one side—the colonel returning salutes—as a squad marched out of the main gate with shovels on their shoulders to repair a rain-washed road and again a few minutes later as a mounted company rattled into the fort from a training sortie. Finally they climbed to the parapet for a look at the town from the highest point in the area. When they had finished the pleasant tour and were about to part company the men shook hands. Luther leaned down from his saddle and Colonel Evans squinted up in the afternoon sunlight.

"Mighty nice meeting you, Colonel. Much obliged."

"You're welcome, Mister Cain. Come back when you can. I'll

77

send the first patrol over this evening and have them look you up."

The marshal straightened and saluted and the post commander returned his salute smartly as the rider swung his horse into a trot toward the bridge at the east end of Pacific Street half a mile down the creek.

CHAPTER 9

The patient's fouled lung gusted its thin, baleful sob of guilt-grief for the thousandth time as his sister's battered ghost scudded across his soul from the day of their youth and their love and his failure to lock his departing door against the neighborhood's skulking maniac.

The surgeon's voice was calm but brisk: "Patient's getting light, Doctor. Anesthetic."

The briefly shallowing pit lost its bottom again . .

Late that afternoon while Luther changed his clothes in room 14 of the Drovers Hotel to go to Esther's surprise party for Solly, he thought about his boyhood in Indiana. He hadn't attended a surprise party since his youth. He ordinarily didn't let his mind glance back much beyond the War but when he did the smoldering memory of a ghastly December night always seemed to catch fire in his brain no matter how hard or casually he tried to look around it. The ancient agony of it made him wince now. Inevitably he went on thinking about it as he dressed.

It seemed he could smell the wheaty perfume of his cousin's hair and feel the caress of her breath on his cheek as she leaned close to whisper a confidence or laugh at something or ask him a question in innocent embarrassment over some perplexity of life. He was twenty and she was sixteen when she came to live with them on the farm beside the Wabash after her parents' death of typhoid fever. He already knew something of the world learned from a summer with Barnes Brothers Circus and a job on a Wabash River flatboat and a fall at a Terre Haute sawmill and four months as night clerk of a Terre Haute hotel; and she counted on his knowledge as a bulwark against her own bewildering inexperience. It made him feel protective toward her, a feeling he didn't recognize for what it was until awareness of its torment became inescapable.

He was sure her legs were the prettiest things he'd ever seen not counting her auburn hair of course and her cameo face and swan's neck and ivory shoulders and graceful arms and firm breasts and slender waist and curving hips. It hurt him almost as much as it did her when she broke one of those legs in two places in a fall from the barn. He suffered with her as she lay in feverish agony, often delirious, during the days immediately following the accident wishing he could do her hurting and crying and shivering. But all he could do was press wet cloths to her forehead and hold her hand and gently force her to eat beef broth which his praying mother brewed on the kitchen stove over a wood fire stoked by his father. Then during her aching weeks of immobilization after the breaks began to heal he spent all the time he could spare from his chores talking with her and reading awkwardly to her and even laughing with her when she felt like laughing to counter the pain.

There was a law of the church to which his parents belonged—whether of God or man he wasn't sure—which said that cousins must not be in love. When he realized he was in love with her he spent a lot of time tossing at night on his bed in the room next to hers. Occasionally when she moaned in her sleep he got up quietly and stood in her open doorway watching her averted, moonlit face half-buried in its dark bower of hair. And sometimes he thought things which he evidently oughtn't, things mingled of proscribed love and hopeless desire and rash, blissful taking. His desire for her one night was so great that he got dressed and saddled the black filly and galloped it wildly in the darkness for two miles not caring whether or not the animal fell, not even thinking about that. The sure-footed filly didn't fall, however and he didn't tell anyone about his ride which didn't mean the girl in her bed beside the window didn't hear him go and come back as she muffled her sobs in her pillow or that he didn't hear her sobbing and grit his teeth in his own misery.

On the hideous night in December when he saddled the filly again and rode down to Miss Mamie's place to return a book they'd finished and to borrow another one, his parents already had gone in the buggy to a school meeting and he hesitated about leaving his cousin alone for two hours although she told him she should be fine and urged him to go. He put a pitcher of water and a tin cup beside her bed and raised the wick of her lamp and shoved more logs into the small heating stove in her room. Then he shrugged into his sheepskin coat, put on his coonskin cap and departed with a wave. From outside he saw her leaning sideways in bed against the window peering at him between cupped hands. He waved and she returned his wave with a gay smile.

That was the last time he saw her alive.

He saw the distant red glow in the sky the moment he left Miss Mamie's and flung himself onto the filly like a crazy man frightening her into a dead run which he didn't let her slacken until they reached Otter Creek again and she had to slow down to lunge across its four-foot depth. For the rest of the ride she gave him everything she had but it was a longer way than any horse could go at full speed; and as she alternately trotted and loped along breathing the cold air in racked gasps he stared ahead in a hell of mounting despair fighting against searing images on the bloody horizon, praying with all his might, hoping until beads of hope burst from his temples and oozed down his numbed face.

When finally he reached the farm he found what couldn't be and what had to be and what should forever be in his nightmares. His parents and a few neighbors had arrived ahead of him and were standing before the embers like grotesque shapes of death blood-red on one side and black on the other. As he rode up to them they turned their faces from the red of the fire to the blackness and told him in brief, soft, terrible words what he had to know and what he didn't want to know. "Reckon she couldn't get out. We knowed it wasn't you in there because of her size."

It! Oh God. Oh God.

As soon as dawn came his father sitting in front of a neighbor's fireplace mentioned a fact of which he hadn't spoken during the night. "Son, I had all the money we own hid in that house. It ain't important like your cousin but it's gone too."

"We'll find it maybe," Luther sighed tonelessly. After a moment he aroused himself. "Come on."

They went back to the ashes of Luther's impossible love and found the half-melted iron kettle in which his father had hidden the gold coins. The coins were gone.

"Got to thinking last night," the stooped man muttered. "Got to thinking it might been somebody broke in for the money. I got drunk last week and told about it." He gazed sadly at his son. "Rheumatism near killing me."

Luther swung toward him. "Told who?"

"Don't remember who. Just telling."

They never found the thief who perhaps had upset the lamp beside her bed in struggling with Luther's cousin whose lonely, hampered courage the lawbreaker must have misjudged. They did find signs of a man's waiting in a thicket nearby and of his stealthy approach and hurried retreat to and from the house—or what had been the house—but his tracks disappeared on the shale of a ravine back of the barn and a day-long search failed to rediscover them ahead of an obliterating snow storm.

His tracks never were to disappear from the back of Luther Cain's mind.

Leaving the Drovers the marshal walked to Solly's house by way of the Farmers Restaurant where Little John Brock had said he always ate supper. The deputy just had sat down to an uncommon steak which seemed half as large as he was.

"I'm on my way to Solly's, John. If a pair of soldiers comes looking for me tell them I'll be down later. Colonel Evans is sending them across ever night to walk patrol."

"Liked your idea?"

Luther nodded. "Pretty good man."

"That he is."

When he knocked on the Berg's door it was opened by the lady of the house. Her cheeks were flushed with pleasure and she brushed back an errant strand of gray hair from her temple.

"Mister Cain it's so nice you came. Ever since I talked to you Wednesday I thought now something's going to come up to keep him away from Solomon's party. But it didn't."

"No M'am."

"Come in, come in. The rest are already here and Solomon will be here any minute. He's going to be so surprised."

The marshal took off his hat and stepped through the doorway. "Yes M'am." He handed her the belt which he'd had Orville Allgood wrap in white paper. "For him."

"David'll hide it with the other presents." She passed the package on to her son. "Everybody's being so nice." She closed the door behind Luther. "The others are all in the kitchen; you just go on in and David and I'll wait out here."

The marshal unbuckled his gun belt.

"And take that and your hat, too, so he won't see them."

82

The boy's eyes were wide. "Can I look at your gun closer after while, Mister Cain?"

"Go on with you now, David, hide Mister Cain's nice present." She pushed the marshal gently toward a door across the room. "The kitchen's in there. Solomon's going to be here any minute. Oh I'm so flustered. I'm . . ."

A footstep on the porch interrupted her. Luther grinned, strode to the kitchen doorway, ducked through it and closed the door softly behind him. A crowded semicircle of men and women stood grinning at him in the dusk filtering through a window. He recognized most of them: Doc Bowman, Jim Watts, Mother Swain, Carl Norris, Ed and Abby Sarver, Bill Crum, Lester and Ruth Blaine, Ralph Cox, Howard Smith, Gus and Fritz Schmidt, and several others. He waved at them and jabbed a silencing forefinger toward the front room. They heard Solly come in the house and Esther ask him after he'd kissed her cheek to go look at the new curtains in the kitchen. A moment later he was in the center of a laughing, back-slapping group and mopping his eyes with a calico handkerchief and repeating in a smiling mumble "You shouldn't be so kind to me, you shouldn't be so kind, please, Friends, not so kind . . ."

"What the hell, Solly, a man ain't twenty-one every day."

"Lester, watch your language."

"Solly, how you feel, you old goat?"

"Many happy returns, Solly."

"Gluckwunsche zum geburtstag, once more."

"Are you surprised, Father?"

"All these nice friends love you, Solomon."

And so it went shifting back into the front room and progressing through the opening of presents, reminiscent of everybody's childhood in the suspense of giving and receiving, and through a babble of hilarity gradually calming and on outdoors to a shadowy candlelit table of cornucopian extravagance, even including white biscuits, under a dark cottonwood tree and finally into a relaxed aftermath of conversations segregated according to sex.

"How's the children, Ruth?"

"Both had the stomach misery, Mother, but they're over it now."

And across the yard: "Seen you riding back from the Fort today, Luther. They say anything about fixing that wash-out on the Plainville road?"

"They're working on it."

"Talk to Colonel Evans?" Howard Smith asked.

The marshal nodded.

"Interesting man."

Luther nodded again.

"He comes to church once in a while." The preacher leaned back and looked at the stars. "Don't really like soldiering but he's good at it. Told me his father was a general. That's why he went in the army."

Luther remembered the post commander's obscure curiosity about why he had started marshaling.

"You gentlemen just don't know," Solly sighed, "how much I enjoy this surprise party. You just don't know."

The sound of running feet surged around the corner of the house followed by the feet themselves of Noble Buck and Billy Plunkett.

"Mister Cain," Noble panted. He took a labored breath.

"Jack Bennett's in town," Billy blew through his teeth. "Down to the Portugese!"

Noble exhaled. "Drinking whiskey."

"And waiting for you," Billy gasped.

They completed their message in unison: "Miss Carrie sent us."

"I told you to stay away from down there," Luther frowned.

They shook their heads. "We was at the railroad station," Noble said. "Miss Carrie come up and said to warn you."

"That Jack's a bad one," Billy appended to their report.

The marshal turned to Bill Crum. "Who's Jack Bennett?"

"The boy's right," the mayor said, "he is a bad one. Comes over from Dodge ever so often looking for a fight."

"Wanted down in Texas, I heard," Carl Norris said.

Luther shifted his glance to the newspaperman. "Why don't they come up from Texas and take him back?"

Doc Bowman laughed sourly. "Reckon they don't want him back."

"Better look into it." Luther stood up. "Don't let it trouble your birthday, Solly."

David Berg's eyes were even wider now. "You going down there, Mr. Cain?"

"Never you mind, David," his father said, adding softly, "I'm so sorry Jack Bennett came to Bancroft tonight, Luther."

"Are you going?" Noble said breathlessly.

"If he's waiting for me I better oblige him."

"You're going!" Billy's tone was awed.

"Now you boys stay here," Solly told them. "Mr. Cain don't want you down there."

Luther shook hands with Solly. "It's been a nice party." His voice was tranquil and his movements had become almost lethargic. He turned to David. "My hat and gun in the kitchen, Son?"

Solly shivered. He was glad he wasn't either the man at the Portugese or Luther Cain. He couldn't understand what could possess anyone to issue such a challenge or accept it so casually. Deliberate violence always had been a mystery to him. Bennett was a mysterious stranger in all ways, Luther in this way at least. What spurred their different pursuits of a shared fury?

As David darted into the house the marshal walked to the group of quickly silent women. Even Mother Swain's worldliness had failed her; she couldn't voice her apprehension either. "Best be going now, Missus Berg," he smiled. "I thank you."

"You're welcome, Mister Cain. Please be coming back more often." The hostess swallowed and raised her voice. "It made Solomon very proud."

"Here!" The front door slammed and David ran toward the marshal. "Your gun and hat." He shoved them into Luther's hands, staring in fascination at the silver, candlelit butt in the holster.

"I'll drift down there with you," Bill Crum said. "Doc, you and Carl and Jim round up Brock and Jackman and McAlister if they ain't already down there." He looked at the young messengers. "You boys see the deputies?"

The marshal raised his hand. "I'll want to handle this myself." He lowered his hand and put on his hat and buckled on his gun belt. "Bennett ain't waiting for them."

"Mygod, Luther, it wouldn't hurt none for them to be around."

"And I don't want you fellers around neither," the marshal added.

"We're sure as hell going!" The mayor glanced at Esther Berg. "Sorry, Ma'am, but Bennett's the one busted up your party."

"You're damn right and I'm going with them," Lester Blaine said.

"Watch your language, Lester." To his wife's credit she didn't discourage him otherwise.

Luther's stare hardened on Bill Crum. His voice was suddenly wintry in the warm night. "You're the mayor, you can fire me and go to marshaling yourself. But if you ain't going to fire me then you," he gazed around, "and all the rest of you is going to stay at this birthday party like you had some manners."

There was a deep-breathing silence.

Howard Smith broke it: "I feel like cussing too, Lester, but Mr. Cain's right. He's good enough marshal for me."

"Didn't mean it that way," Lester said quietly.

The mayor flushed in the shadows. "Hell no."

Doc Bowman nodded. "I don't need any extra patients tonight."

Luther turned and walked alone toward the street. Even the youngsters didn't try to follow him. In the squinting group behind him Jim Watts grunted a curse about a man's own way of doing things.

CHAPTER 10

. . . When we asked Mattie Keller what it was like being married to "New York's toughest cop," she told the column she wouldn't know, she was married to the town's nicest husband. "Besides," she said, "for every thug that hates him there are six kids that love him. He's kind of the Pied Piper of our neighborhood."

Come to think of it, the Pied Piper of Hamelin also was a couple of men in one— if we remember the story correctly. . .

Jack Bennett also had his own way of doing things. And of looking at them before, during, and after doing them. As he leaned against the Portugese's bar it was before he was going to undertake what Jason T. M. Pickett had hired him to do; and as he saw the job ahead he rightly was going to kill Luther Cain with all the acquired skill and natural hate he had brought with him from Texas and his boyhood, which were considerable. He had become skillful, that is to say fast and accurate, with a pistol through dedicated and frequent target practice and a share of blooding experience during the last ten of his twenty-two years. The self-feeding hate churning his existence was the main reason he had striven so hard for expertness with his gun. Shooting people without being shot first or in return had provided a temporarily satisfactory way of relieving his hate-ache pending the day when terrifyingly but orgiastically he was going to shoot his father. The widower had begun whipping him every day instead of every week before Jack had run away from the bastard's house for good on his twelfth birthday. He had planned to take his closest friend with him but his old man had shot the collie the night before. The faces of men Jack himself had shot since then had been his father's, the face of aversion, of hostility, several times of malevolent authority. Everything he'd heard about Luther Cain gave the lawman such a face. He also had heard that Cain's talent with a gun was as awesome as the man was pitiless. The nearing gunslinger sure wasn't going to come by any pity from him; and as for who slung his gun fastest Jack could only reckon the next few minutes were going to see some mighty fast slinging. Somebody was about to end up dead. He hoped he wasn't; he liked to think of spending Pickett's money. But if the sonofabitch Cain killed him it was better than dying in bed. Unless it was one of Nell's. A man had to die sooner or later. Whether he had lived or not.

South Street was its usual raucous self as Luther strode along its glowing border of ramshackle buildings in the direction of Jimson Street and the Portugese Saloon. Ahead through the crowd he saw Carrie Shaw pushing toward him. Her hurrying legs and fluttering skirt and taut bodice and strained face and sweptback hair all heightened the effect of her urgency. She was breathing rapidly when she reached him and brought him to a halt with an outstretched hand. Her fingers were tight on his forearm.

"Seen you coming, Luther. Been standing at the corner. The boys tell you?"

He looked down solemnly at her agitation. Warmth replaced the bleakness of his eyes for a moment. It had been a long time since anyone had seemed concerned about his hide.

It occurred to him that he was concerned about this woman's well-being, too. He sucked in his breath. Well for godssake. That was rattlebrained. Now was no time to be rattlebrained. His eyes chilled again.

"He's still in there and talking ugly, Luther." She glanced behind the marshal. "Where's Big John or somebody?"

"Busy."

"You ain't going in alone."

He shrugged off her hand. "I ain't going in with nobody. Especially you. You stay out here."

"Luther, he's drinking all right but that don't slow him any. I seen him in town this summer. Only way Charlie Tucker jailed him was making him sick. Bartender put something in his whiskey."

"Charlie was sick hisself this summer."

When the marshal began walking on again the woman knew further dissuasion was useless. "Luther," she asked as she trotted along beside him, "you like me any at all?"

He didn't seem to hear her question.

"You like me any, Luther?"

This time he did. "Sure I like you. Stay back!" *Goddam!*

She slowed her pace and fell behind him and as the space between them widened she called after him, "Me too, Luther!"

A drunken muleskinner in the dark street mimicked her: " 'Me too, Luther!' "

Somebody laughed uproariously above the cadence of the piano from the Portugese. A horse whinnied. Carrie touched her face with both hands and cried without making a sound or shedding a tear.

An instant after Luther Cain stepped into the Portugese a hush began settling over its throng and in another instant the flickering room was blanketed by silence except for Jack Bennett's breaching rasp.

"Goddam quiet must mean we got company!" The shaggy-haired, sallow-faced man turned slowly from the bar. Luther saw that he was probably in his middle-twenties. One of his eyes stared grotesquely at the ceiling and the other stabbed straight across the intervening space into the marshal's face as though it had disembodied impact. Moisture of its strain made it glitter like a rattlesnake's. "And goddam if we ain't got company!" the youth laughed without a hint of humor.

A shiver of unreasoning hate crawled up Luther's spine and it made him angry at himself and his anger made his voice icy. "You go by the name of Bennett?"

"That's right, Marshal. You the marshal ain't you, judging by that tin hanging onto you?"

"I heard you want to see me."

"I heard you like hitting folks over the head. I heard you like to do that."

"Pickett hire you?" Luther asked matter-of-factly.

"What makes you think I ain't working on my own, Marshal? For the pleasure of it."

"You like your work, Bennett?"

"Now that's something I sure do. Yessir, I sure do."

"Then why don't you start working?"

The scraping of a chair accented the moment's silence.

"Right now," Luther added, "you sonofabitch."

Bennett's good eye blinked almost imperceptibly. Otherwise he didn't move.

"I asked why don't you make your play you yellow-livered, cross-eyed sonofabitch!"

The young man's lips parted slowly. His words echoed in the room like a knell. "I'll make my play when I'm goddam ready." The slight color it had possessed had drained from his face. "And I'll be goddam ready—now!" he ended in a bellow, bending his knees and jerking his gun.

The slug from Luther's exploding weapon raised Bennett upright again and slammed him backward half-way across the bar. His abruptly red-gushing face bubbled toward the rafters, his outflung arms twitched and collapsed upward as his legs crumbled and let his senseless bulk slide into a dead, distorted coil on the floor, all before one of the bartenders could finish saying "Christamightyjesusgodinheaven!"

Smoke hung like a pall between the marshal and the body of the lawbreaker.

"I seen it now," somebody whispered hoarsely.

The purple hole where Bennett's wall-eye had lived drained its crimson onto the floor's planks.

"Christamighty," Mayor Crum was to remark the next evening during a poker session in Guttman's back room, "he sure is hell on faces ain't he?" "Lucky shot maybe?" Carl Norris was to wonder. And from Doc Bowman: "I doubt it." And from Jim Watts: "It sure wasn't lucky for Bennett."

This bloody evening however the resurging talk was less dispassionate and at least in one instance less ambiguous. The half-door of the Portugese swung inward on the mounting hubbub and Carrie Shaw ran to the marshal, seeming at the last moment to force her hands from touching him, her eyes shimmering with anxiety. "I watched through the window; I can't stand this, Luther, you can't kill me like this again!"

He grasped both her wrists with his left hand and stared at her through slit lids. "You can't work here no more." He pushed her away and turned back to the harvest of his private cultivation. "Stand off!" he shouted, motioning with his revolver. "Leave him be for the undertaker." He glared about the room. "But take a good look. And remember."

The hubbub dropped to a buzz of guarded comment.

"And you get the undertaker," the marshal pointed at the

proprietor; "you do that little chore so next time you'll mind what Texans you cater to."

To say Johnny Newlin looked unhappy is a compendium of his expression. His face was astringent with unwillingness. But he went.

"Damn!" old man Cy Blix muttered. Cy's job was sweeping out the Portugese every morning. Tomorrow morning he was going to have to mop as well.

The blind piano player asked a question softly of the scarred woman who had lit a fresh cigar and she answered him with a word and he turned to the keyboard and began playing a galop. The room's buzz of comment became less guarded and under duress of the music swelled gradually almost to normal volume. The night's two bartenders—somewhat shakily—began pouring drinks again for some of the drunker customers. One of the rice-powdered girls whose jobs included serving drinks at the tables vomited into a spittoon and was led through a back hall door by another girl. Luther had holstered his gun and now was standing near the entrance of the saloon gazing impassively under his hat brim at the occupants who were carefully avoiding his eyes.

Carrie wasn't one of those who weren't looking at him. Sensing he didn't consider his job on the premises finished yet she hadn't attempted to speak to him again but she was looking at his face closely, partly in order to study its cliff hung with a wiry moustache and partly to avoid looking at the corpse on the floor. His seeming composure lent her the strength to quell her verging hysteria but at the same time it frightened her. She had seen violence but somehow it never had been so swift and ferocious and absolute. She thought about what she had called out to Luther in her anguish and her heart pounded. She thought about his reply and her heart pounded harder. In the glacial moment his "Sure I like you" had echoed warmth; a living man had breathed under the shroud.

For his part Luther's thoughts weren't as composed as his appearance; and they weren't confined to the routine of removing Jack Bennett's body. As he waited for the arrival of the undertaker and probably of his alerted deputies he freed a portion of his thoughts to the recollection of what Carrie had said to him and what he had said to her and how he'd felt about it in those orgastic moments before and after Bennett had sprawled onto the floor. He didn't know what to make of those things exactly. They seemed to bear out his inkling in the street outside, the fleeting moment of amazement that this woman meant something to him. He glanced at her and found her staring at him with her lips parted as though to ask a question, of herself maybe, and felt the question in his own mind grow more demanding. He looked away quickly. *What the hell?* If she didn't mean something to him why should he look away quickly, why should he care where she worked? Bygod! For an instant Luther Cain felt the hollow ache of uncertainty; it was an unaccustomed feeling and it rattled him. He growled under his breath.

"Marshal Cain?"

With a surge of relief he swung toward the voice. A soldier dropped one hand from a perfunctory salute, pulling his glance from the body on the floor. Beside the first soldier a second one was gazing at Luther numbly. They both were young but weathered by their profession. The marshal's eyes swept their sleeves.

"Yes, Corporal?"

"I'm Black, and this is Blue."

Luther squinted at their grave faces and curbed his smile. "Howdy, Corporal Black." He shook hands with each of them. "Private Blue."

"Colonel Evans ordered us to report to you for instructions." The corporal's glance strayed again to Bennett's corpse. "If you're busy now, sir, we can wait."

The comment, its grotesque respite from his disconcertion, drove Luther's smile into the open. Indeed he felt like laughing. "That's what I'm doing now. Waiting."

Corporal Black cleared his throat. "Yessir. For the undertaker."

Private Blue swallowed. "Yessir."

"You recruits?"

"We been out here a month," the corporal said.

The private nodded. "We can handle this patrol all right."

"Reckon the colonel wouldn't detailed you if you couldn't." The marshal's face reassumed its coolness. "Main thing you remember is not let nothing take your mind off your job." His jaw muscles flicked under his cheeks. "The rest is plain common sense."

"Yessir," Corporal Black said.

"Yessir," Private Blue agreed.

Both troopers appeared to feel better about their assignment. The marshal told them quietly where his shotgun and ammunition caches were and cautioned them against revealing this information and was telling them the names of his deputies when Lafe Jackman and Big John McAlister walked in.

"Here's two of them." Luther said, making the introductions. "The other's Little John Brock." At that moment the third deputy arrived. "And this is him."

After the troopers had departed to walk the streets of Bancroft, Little John lighted a cigar and brought up the subject of the corpse which was spreading its eight quarts of gore in front of the bar. "I remember the last time we turned Jack out of jail he said it was the last time he'd be in it and I laughed at him." The deputy drew on the stogie. "Looks like he's got the laugh on me," he exhaled the smoke.

"Me and Big John was up to the Bell Mare barn, Luther," Lafe said. "We come as soon as we heard. Somebody stole some harness."

"No need to come," the marshal thanked them.

"I was in the damn privy," Little John shrugged. "Had to wait a minute or two."

Carrie couldn't fathom their chuckles from her chair twenty feet away. She'd had to sit down because of lightheadedness and as she sat there she wondered whether she could ever fathom herself and her passions let alone the enigma of men. Especially the transcendent riddle of Luther Cain. And her abrupt, mysterious preoccupation with that.

"Well, boys," she heard him say, "one of you stay around here for the hearse. I aim to walk Miss Shaw yonder to her rooming house."

"Hello, Carrie," Big John called. "Didn't see you setting there."

"She does look a mite peaked," Little John said.

Jake smiled. "But more'n a mite pretty tonight."

"Needs to get the hell out of here a while."

The marshal's words were deliberate and loud and unequivocal. "Bygod she needs to get out of here for good." And he looked straight into her eyes as he spoke.

After a moment she sighed and stood up slowly.

Then she fainted.

"Hell's fire, Luther," Big John grunted as they jumped toward her, "you scared her half to death."

Little John had seen the way she'd returned Luther's gaze. "The hell you say," he grinned.

CHAPTER 11

Even in the sergeant's anesthesia his captain's rasp grated: "Okay, good job, you're a good man but do you have to go so heavy every goddam time? Cool it some, I'm telling you."

Sometimes captains were like women, bragging on a man's knack and cramping it. And women sure could be aggravating. Yes even Mattie every now and then. Bless her. Women could get a man jealous of other men without their ever really looking at one, just by being womanly. Of course that was the man's fault but it still was riling—at himself anyhow. Women and captains, both of them could be aggravating as hell.

On the other hand no lawman could afford to be riled or aggravated.

Not if he wanted to do his job right.

And stay alive.

In the middle of the following week in the middle of Pacific Street in his unvarnished way the mayor suggested a holiday for the marshal of Bancroft:

"Why don't you take the goddam day off?"

"I don't need the day off."

"Like hell you don't."

"Little John . . ." the marshal began.

"And Big John and Jake can mind the town while you catch some sleep. You're getting crotchety. Or was you just acting unnatural polite before?"

Luther stared at Bill Crum.

The mayor patted him on the shoulder and towered on under his derby toward the courthouse.

An hour later lying on his bed in the Drovers Hotel with his boots off the marshal stared at the ceiling and thought about being crotchety and decided it had been his fault for letting Johnny Newlin get under his skin at the coroner's inquest Saturday. What otherwise should have been a routine signing of Jack Bennett's death certificate and a prompt verdict of justifiable homicide had been cluttered by the Portugese's proprietor's harangue about damage to his property and interference with the trade of his establishment by an agent of the municipality. The property damage

95

had turned out to be the shattering of three bottles of whiskey by Bennett's flailing arms and the trade interference a matter of making some Texans feel unappreciated in the Portugese Saloon. Coroner Roy Bowman had appeared to take Johnny's remarks in his stride but their implication had riled Luther. The fact Bennett had tried his ordinary best to kill the agent of the municipality hadn't seemed to be as important to Newlin as keeping the Portugese's customers happy. Damn that cow shit to hell. On the other hand the marshal now realized he needn't have got so riled about the affair. Usually he shouldn't have even when the grinning Doc unofficially had conditioned his exoneration of the marshal, with a wink at Luther, on the city's paying for the spilled whiskey. Maybe the coroner's winking at principle for the sake of appeasement had churned Luther's spleen further; still he oughtn't to have let it bother him. Certainly not let it show to the obvious pleasure of the tin-horn saloon keeper-politician.

There had been something else in his craw since the previous Friday night.

But the marshal didn't know for sure what it was.

Maybe he needed sleep as the mayor had said.

But he wasn't sleepy.

He got up and put on his boots and hat and gun belt and walked downstairs past the newel cupid and across the crowded lobby and outdoors onto the railed veranda. Half a dozen men including Howard Smith were tilted in chairs against the wall passing the time of day.

"Howdy, Mister Cain," the preacher smiled. "We was talking about you."

The marshal's frown was involuntary. "That right?"

"We was wondering where you come from."

The skin of Luther's forehead relaxed. "Wabash country, Indiana."

"See?" the preacher said to the others. "It was the way he said 'cow' the other day." He exaggerated the marshal's Hoosier accent: " 'Keeyow.' "

All of them including Luther chuckled. The marshal hadn't chuckled since Friday night.

"Looks like a delegation," one of the loungers pointed at three approaching youngsters, "to a fishing convention."

Noble Buck, David Berg and Billy Plunkett paused before

96

the veranda's single step with willow fishing poles on their shoulders.

"How they biting, boys?"

"That's what we aim to find out." Billy toed the dirt of Pacific Street.

David glanced at the marshal apologetically. "If you're not too busy."

Noble explained, "Would you maybe like to go with us, Mister Cain?" His gaze was deferential but not subservient. "We went by the courthouse and Mayor Crum said you might be up here. Said you'd took the afternoon off."

"He said that?"

"Said you might be asleep but you might not."

Luther nodded solemnly.

"We figured on finding out."

"I'd judge he's awake," Howard Smith said, " 'less he talks in his sleep."

One of the other men embellished the preacher's judgment: "Or sleeps standing up like a 'keeyow.' "

The marshal's expressionless gaze swept over the loungers and returned to the youngsters. "Think maybe it's a little windy around here for fishing, Boys."

Billy glanced at the sky in private confusion.

"There ain't much of a wind," David pointed out politely.

Noble smiled in sudden, tentative rapport. "Not where we're going."

The seated men laughed.

"Well that sounds like a good place to go," Luther said. "Only trouble I ain't got no pole."

"We'll cut you one," David assured him. "There's some willows up there."

Billy's eyes came abruptly alight. "Right where we cut ours."

"It's only about a mile up the creek," Noble said. "The beaver pond there's plumb full of bluegills and catfish."

The marshal tugged down his hat brim. "Warrant I'll catch some?"

"Sure!" "Yessir!" "Gee whiz!"

"Why stand here talking about it when I could be doing that?"

Howard Smith smiled after the departing commotion. "Puts you in mind of the Pied Piper."

"He's pied all right," another of the company muttered, "walking a mile in the heat of the day."

"I'd say it was a forced march," a man in a battered Union cap said.

A baldheaded man opined no one could force Luther Cain to do anything he wasn't a mind to.

"I had the feeling he was a mind to go fishing today," the preacher allowed, "but for himself, not bluegills."

Preacher Smith came close to the truth. Luther suddenly had welcomed not only an unguarded outing with youngsters who had no bone to pick but the chance for some fresh-air musing on a stifled sentiment. He wanted to haul that in on an unhurried line and look it over. He might or might not throw it back.

CHAPTER 12

Mark's psyche, prodded by scalpels and probes, tumbled through long-ago alleys scrawled with graffiti and strewn with garbage toward a flame less searing painfully than glowing with the hope of relief from an old pain, of contentment in a new love (could it be?) and a newly meaningful life which Mattie and his job might bring him, were his and her varying attitudes reconcilable and their bemusement verifiably love. As for their differing concerns about some things, he'd submitted his young know-how as shielding him from police work's risks, and she'd acceded to his brash demand by changing jobs from the creep's pawnshop to a market. For him, at least, dealing with their more intimate feelings had been thornier. When he'd used that word in groping for an explanation of his quandary she'd laughed and said roses were her favorite flower.

"I swear he just grinned, Doctor."

A mile above Bancroft on the bank of Owl Creek's pond the marshal leaned back and yawned and closed his eyes, resting his head on his interlaced fingers and propping his fishing pole on his elevated knees with its hemp string dangling unscrutinized in the muddy water. The boys were slightly disconcerted by his casual disregard of the bottle-cork bobber but they didn't mention it even among themselves; they were too glad to have him along as their companion dozing there like a friendly lion ready to spring awesomely awake in their defense against various imagined hazards. It was a stirring, almost smothering thing to have the famous Luther Cain as a fishing partner. For days their hearts and tongues should be crowded with pride. Both young and old people should stare at them with exhilarating respect.

Actually Luther wasn't dozing as much as daydreaming. Maybe it was the company of the boys, all boys being chronic daydreamers. His daydreams weren't disquieting at first; they followed a balmy trail blazed by the warmth of the sun and the stroke of the breeze and the musk of the creek and the hum of insects.

He let his mind wander over the terrain of his present job and found it almost as smoothly rolling as the prairie about him.

99

The pay and room and board all were first rate. Bancroft's residents mostly were sociable and cooperative and sincere in wanting a peaceful town. Its transients didn't count, their breaches of the peace being normal grist for a marshal's mill. Here and there Luther's thoughts came across outcroppings of local opposition such as Johnny Newlin's mercenary malice and the quandary of a few honest businessmen about Texas trade; but for the most part the citizens seemed committed to backing his attack on lawlessness. And he intended to attack that in the only way he knew: without quarter or question. Some people made laws and some people broke them and Luther Cain earned his living repairing them. It was a community triangle and he was paid for drawing the final side of it.

His ruminations topped a rise abruptly and came face to face with the wraith of Carrie Shaw hovering over the plains like smoke from a smoldering campfire. Like all of mankind's campfires its embers signified the vicinity of either friend or foe, tranquility or trouble, good or evil.

He was gratified Carrie had quit her job at the Portugese and started sewing. Sewing was a hell of a lot better for any woman than working for Johnny Newlin and associating with the trash in the Portugese. For the moment he managed to ignore the past implications in her case of "working" and "associating." Instead he thought about the meaning of "sewing" relative to Carrie's present and future: her grubstaking by Lester Blaine at Ruth Blaine's behest involving Lester's promise to see her financially through at least the first weeks of her new venture; her promoting of an extra chair for her room from Everett Lane so her customers could sit down if, as she'd worried aloud to Luther, any nice customers should come to Jimson Street; her yawning adjustment to the early-morning sunlight and to seven o'clock breakfast at the Lone Star; her quick, imaginative fingers which had sent three of Missus Blaine's friends happily back to their lightened chores in the two days since she'd been Open for Business; the prospective delight of other housewives who should read her advertisement in the *Republican;* the fact that making hats and dresses for respectable ladies was a damn decent proposition, a hell of an improvement over working in the Portugese and associating with its scum.

Again he forced his mind away from her past. What the hell

did her past have to do with her present and future, the things which interested him? He shook his head on his clasped fingers. "Interested!" What the hell did that mean?

The boys who heard him mutter the word glanced at him. They didn't know what it meant either.

His reflections found him walking Carrie home from the Portugese under the stars the previous Friday night. The two of them hadn't been able to see much of the stars in Jimson Street's glow but when they had crossed South Street toward Lane's rooming house and the stock pens beyond it they'd been able to make out the Big Dipper. The first words either of them had spoken since leaving the saloon had been Carrie's, "Look, Luther, the Big Dipper." Her voice hadn't been very steady. His hadn't been as steady as usual. "That's it all right."

The unsteadiness of his voice hadn't had anything to do with the violence they'd left behind them. "The reason I don't want you working in the Portugese is it ain't a good place for a woman to be working."

"Yes, Marshal."

He had stared at her. "I ain't joshing."

"No, Luther," she had apologized, swallowing her faint smile.

He had felt her hand slide under his left arm. "Not for no decent woman."

"I want to be decent."

"Why else you think I care?"

Her fingers had tightened. "Only where I work?"

"Sure where you work. And what you work at, bygod."

"Why, Luther?"

" 'Why' what?"

"Why you care what I do?"

"Hell . . . !" the marshal was at a loss.

"Why'd you say you like me as you were going in the Portugese?"

"Why'd you ask me?"

"What did you mean when you said you did?"

"What did you think I meant?"

She'd taken a deep, soft breath. "You're sure not a man to duck a fight but you're ducking my questions."

"Well, don't ask so many damn questions."

"They're all one question, Luther."

He realized what she had said had been true; he'd been ducking her one question. "One too many for me I 'low."

"It was the way you looked when you said it. Maybe I didn't have the right to hope more than 'like' but I hoped it anyhow. I reckon I need someone to more than like me," her tone had been sad, "the way I do you."

His strange timidity had rattled him. "Don't know what you're saying."

"I'm saying I think I could be in love with you, Luther, even already."

Her words had hung in the night air for an instant like the stars except warm instead of cold and distant.

"Hell, Carrie."

"Would it be hell? Couldn't you understand at all?"

"I didn't mean that. I just don't know . . . " He'd broken off in his unaccustomed confusion.

"If you could maybe fall in love with me, too?"

"No!"

"You couldn't?"

"I mean that's not what I said."

"You could?"

"Goddammit."

"Yes, Luther?"

"I just don't know if I can put up with it."

" 'Can?' 'It?' "

"Could put up with all that." Red night sky streaked his brain. "I just don't know . . . the hell with it."

Her voice abruptly had lowered and gone flat. "You don't know if you could afford to. That what you mean?"

"What the hell you mean now?"

"You the marshal, me a saloon girl."

"Don't talk thataway, I told you oncet!"

They had reached Lane's. He had stared down at her eyes and mouth and bare shoulders in the lamplight of the house's hall. The cool night had seemed hot.

Suddenly she had stretched up on her toes and kissed his lips and her voice had regained its buoyancy. "Thanks for beauing me home, Luther. I'm getting to like it." Then her gaze had turned serious but not sad for a final moment. "You go fishing or something and think about me. I'm not going back to the Portugese,

Luther. But I can't pretend I haven't been there and I don't want you to. You think about whether that's enough." She had turned and run along the hall towards her room.

The marshal opened his eyes and looked at the three boys.

"Hi, Mister Cain!" Noble waved from six feet away.

"You got a nibble a while ago," Billy said from beyond Noble, "but I reckon you figured he wasn't worth hooking."

"Else he would hooked him," David frowned at Billy.

Luther smiled at them absently and closed his eyes again.

So he had gone fishing as it turned out and now, as she had requested, he was thinking about whether Carrie Shaw's present and future were more important than her past, whether her never going back to the Portugese was enough.

Why was it something he had to decide?

I'm saying I think I could be in love with you, Luther, his mind heard her say once more, even already.

"Hell!" The coals of a killing house glowed behind his eyes.

The boys glanced back at him and this time shrugged their shoulders at each other and smiled knowingly although they still didn't know what his muttering meant except probably it was about something important. Some official business.

Whether or not it should be hell depended on a lot of things. To Carrie he had denied meaning it could be hell but he had recognized the possibility it might be. Wasn't that what had made him tongue-tied in the starlit night, made him feel rattlebrained when she'd asked him whether he could fall in love with her as earlier he had felt rattlebrained for an instant before going into the Portugese?

He grunted in amazement.

Was it because he . . . ?

He couldn't be in love with her, for godsake! He'd met her only a little while ago; he'd talked with her at the Portugese the night he'd arrived and at the church supper the next night and maybe six or seven times since then in the Portugese and on the streets including last Friday night when he'd killed Jack Bennett and had seen her home afterward. He couldn't be in love with her. Not like twenty years ago.

It was hell, surely. And not because she was or anyhow used to be a saloon girl and he was the marshal.

Goddam that Johnny Newlin. And that trash in his saloon.

Even the likes of that kid with the broken arm who didn't know how to drink. No, not that kid whose name Luther had learned was Raymond Davis; he maybe wasn't trash; he just had sat and drunk with Carrie. So she'd said.

It might be hell but its fire was sweet-hot and its heat seared him sweetly in the goddammdest places like in his belly and at the nape of his neck and under his hat and through the middle of his chest and in his conscience which was of a highly individualized sort. Sometimes its flames scorched his being like lightning and the rest of the time flickered slowly but steadily at his peace of mind, singeing his craw.

Before his mind's eye Carrie's indecent dress burned off and she stood briefly in the starlight with nothing but her long brown hair veiling her passion and provoking his.

His fishing pole stirred between his legs.

Those were no thoughts to tolerate in the company of kids.

He sat up quickly and grabbed the pole which was bending urgently toward another nibble and gave it a vigorous heave.

"Hey, Marshal, you got one!"

"A bite!"

"Hook it!"

He jerked the fish out of the brown water in a silver arc onto the bank.

He couldn't see it clearly as it flopped in the tall grass.

But felt like a "keeper."

Damned if it didn't.

But was it?

CHAPTER 13

. . . Interviewing Mark Keller, one becomes convinced of his dedication to law enforcement, indeed credits a fellow officer's testimony that the sergeant tracks his job with the single-mindedness of a hungry tiger. We've heard from several lawbreakers and even a solid citizen or two that his approach to straying from the straight and narrow is downright unfriendly. Mattie O'Sullivan Keller, however, a romantic as well as lovely lady, has told us with her Irish grin a somewhat different story. Although her husband may seem to equate, or to think others equate, affability with leniency and always to be sternly calm and collected, such isn't invariably the case. For instance, back in their courting days, his first blurting out that he loved her was obviously scarier for him than breaking into the midst of a bank robbery . . .

During September the marshal of Bancroft, perhaps stimulated as Doc Bowman opined by the fine weather, chalked up more arrests than his predecessor had made in the previous half-year. Deputies Brock, McAlister and Jackman made some plays of their own of course and assisted their principal in others and the nightly patrol from Fort Reynolds accounted for its quota of chastened troopers; but mainly this record-breaking assault on civil disobedience was a one-man operation. Luther Cain was just plain unfriendly when it came to lawbreakers.

All this caused Mayor Crum to miss a good deal of fresh air and sunlight. As he said one evening to Jim Watts in the back room of Guttman's, "I'm getting callus-assed from setting in that goddam court all morning." And it presented Carl Norris with the happy dilemma of squeezing both increased news and indispensible advertisements into the unexpandable *Republican*.

"Newsprint on the frontier is worth its weight in greenbacks," he grinned, "but so is Luther Cain."

The county sheriff wasn't so cheerful about it. "He's a hard man," he grumbled to the turnkey at the common jail. "Out in the county we try to get along with folks instead of whopping them over the ear." Of course the sheriff depended on election by those non-whopped folks.

It was true however that the marshal seemed to take particular satisfaction in humiliating offenders with his revolver—especially the mouthy ones below the track—instead of shooting them with it. Down there some of the rasher transients began referring to him as "Buffalo" Cain when they were sure he was well above the track.

During the month, the marshal also set some kind of record in getting acquainted with Bancroft's permanent residents. The majority of them returned his respect and, where guardedly proffered, his friendship. Without exception the young boys of the town were his partisans, summoned to his heroic colors by the trumpetings of Noble Buck, David Berg and Billy Plunkett and their own awe. And even Spot, a half-wild mongrel which had come from nowhere and had slunk everywhere around Bancroft for six months dodging stray shots in an endless search for a master, finally found one in the marshal and quit growling at everybody.

Luther occasionally sat in on poker games in Guttman's back room with Mayor Crum, Doc Bowman, Jim Watts, and Carl Norris and won his share of amiable arguments and hard money. Sometimes he bucked the faro tiger in the Longhorn Saloon on the east side and in the Shawnee Saloon on the north side of the plaza. He dropped into another church supper. He killed a bat in Missus Berg's kitchen when Solly and David were in Plainville overnight trying to collect an overdue receivable. Notwithstanding his earlier disclaimer, he did a pretty fair job of dancing at the September fire brigade ball, enchanting a dozen ladies including Missus Blaine in her new silk dress. He helped Jake Barlow unload twenty kegs of horseshoe nails in five minutes from the afternoon westbound and then lost his half of the trainmen's payoff on a cock fight the next day. Shoving his revolver inside his boot-top he sat in the Methodist Church through an hour-long sermon (shortened by Howard Smith that Sunday in deference to the marshal's duties) and, after shaking hands with the congregation at the preacher's invitation, left for the Bell Mare Livery Company corral to referee a prize fight between Kansas champ Mickey Malone and local challenger Virgil Bayliss. He made a shorter speech than the Gettysburg Address but an equally fine one according to Mother Swain following Bill Crum's oration on the day they hung the bell in the new schoolhouse, saying simply he thought the mayor had said everything appropriate to such an occasion except one: "I reckon it's time we adjourned this meeting." He paid two more months' rent on Noble Buck's room. He came down with a three-day attack of the ague. Drawing on his farm background he gave Herman Northcutt some good advice about relieving impacted milk cows. He learned from Lafe Jackman that Big John McAlister had saved Lafe's life once by splitting a Comanche's skull with a Conestoga singletree, from Big John that Lafe had been a killer in a packing plant back East before taking up a different sort of killing under General Meade and from both of them that all anybody knew about Little John Brock was what Luther had found out: he was a five-feet-nine giant in a fight and enjoyed that particular activity almost as much as he did eating beefsteak.

Bill Crum told Carl Norris privately one day of his decision not to run for mayor next year, office-holding on top of his hotel and poker interests having become "a pain in the ass," and said he thought Luther Cain could be elected easily if the marshal should be a candidate. "This camp could do a hell of a lot worse only don't tell that scalawag I said so or he'll be wanting a raise."

All this half-reluctant, half-disposed socializing by Luther posed a vaguely disturbing dilemma for him. Ironically despite his instinct to remain apart from it for the sake of better marshaling he was becoming enmeshed in the town's society in part because he marshaled so well. It seemed obscurely that most of Bancroft's citizens had begun horning in on his own pride in his job and making him feel they felt safer because of him. They seemed to be developing a sort of proprietary interest in him which he found irksome. He didn't know why he found it irksome. He felt obligated in some way and responsible to them instead of for them. It seemed to have something to do with curtailing his freedom to pursue his work for his reasons rather than theirs. But he didn't know why his reasons and theirs weren't the same or that they weren't. And he found himself mildly liking the sensation of popularity.

The tightest thread of his involvement in the variegated tapestry of the town was sewn by Carrie Shaw, a seamstress of natural skill in patterns of romance as well as dresses. There was a seemingly unconscious sureness of her needle as it stitched a message of ardor in his guts—or in his heart or mind or wherever the hell but it felt like his guts to him the way it pricked him awake sometimes at night with a dry, hot taste in his mouth. It riled him to think he couldn't think what he really thought at those times about the desirable seamstress who used to be a desirable saloon girl. It made him damn mad. Then the echo of her sunny laughter or the image of a soft, sweet glance would fill his mind and he wouldn't be angry anymore at all. He would fall asleep again with a grin hovering under his moustache and the next day saunter down to Jimson Street to have a cup of coffee with her and see how things were going in her cluttered room at Lane's which also was her shop.

Usually things were going pretty well these days.

One bright noon when he dropped in however her face was clouded with discouragement.

"What's the matter?"

She shook her head, tears budding in her eyes.

"What's   "

"This goods!" She flicked her hand over some material on her knees. "It won't gather right."

"I asked what's the matter."

She inhaled and exhaled wearily. "You'll know soon enough."

"How will I know?"

"Oh Luther." She stood up and let the material slide to the floor and stepped across it contritely into his arms. He hardly heard her muffled words. "Maybe you were right."

"About what?"

She shook her head against his chest.

His mouth searched downward and found hers and kissed it for the fourth time in their acquaintance—once after a church supper and three times after as many goodnights at her bedroom door. For every kindling time he'd kissed it he had imagined its

108

luscious warmth a dozen times. What most recently had been her eager lips were tense now.

"Right about what?" he repeated after a moment.

"Luther, I love you."

"I'm proud you do." He said it quickly, somehow feeling it was necessary to cover imagined embarrassment on her part; but she obviously wasn't embarrassed, she was preoccupied with her concern. Maybe that left him the embarrassed one. Not as much embarrassed as surprised. Dammit maybe excited. What the hell, not much doubt about that.

"But maybe I hadn't ought to love you, you hadn't ought to be proud."

He frowned. Then abruptly warmth flooded him and his frown was shoved aside by a smile. He bent to kiss her again.

"No, Luther." She slipped her fingers between their mouths, her eyes glistening. "I'm trying to tell you if you'd listen."

"Reckon maybe," the words surged over his awkward tongue, "I love you, too." It was the first time he had said it aloud and it came close to stunning him.

It didn't seem to stun her. "I know, Luther. But maybe you hadn't ought to, that's what I'm trying to say. Not the way they're talking."

He stared at her, shaking his head. (I know, Luther, she had said.) He licked his lips. "Talking?"

"Some of them in the Portugese. And even some others that don't mean no harm, not really; but they're laughing about it all the same." Her eyes showed how much this defamation of him wounded her. "At you, Luther, not me. They're tired of laughing at me. But you're someone they need to dirty."

His body stiffened. Very gently he took her arms from his shoulders, squeezing her hands briefly and depositing them against her hips at each side. Then he hooked his thumbs slowly in his gun belt and eased it up an inch. His gesture struck her as somehow, had she known the words, enchanting and ominous at the same time.

"Newlin?" he said.

"Him, too, I guess. But mostly them Texans. Not all of them, mostly Enos Dowling."

" 'Laughing?' " His voice held no inflection.

109

"Mostly at you, Luther. That's why this won't work." Her eyes flashed. "Nobody's going to laugh at you! I ain't going to be the reason for you putting up with that, I ain't going to be their dirt for them."

He patted her cheek tenderly with one palm. Then he turned toward the open door of the room.

Her voice became apprehensive. "Where you going?"

"Back to work."

She grasped his arm. "Don't play their game, Luther."

Carefully he disengaged her fingers. His cold gaze warmed for only an instant's benevolent locking with hers. "Nobody's going to laugh at us very long, Carrie, don't you fret about it."

He left her wishing with half her pounding heart she never had met him and with the other half she never should lose him. Most of all she wished she'd met him years ago on a summer day in Indiana; and in a sense she had although she didn't realize it.

CHAPTER 14

The captain's reproof was as acrid as the sergeant's dream. "I told you before, you got to try to cool it some. Now you're getting the Civil Liberties Union down on the commissioner and him down on me. He's for you, for all cops, and so's the mayor; but you got to be for them. They got problems, too."

Theirs didn't include being shot at.

The next night in the Eastern Saloon the marshal got into another fracas. The trouble started when he spotted the cowboy there whom he and his deputies suspected of having stolen a five hundred-dollar thoroughbred from the Bell Mare Livery Company barn on the night Luther had killed Jack Bennett. Big John McAlister was with the marshal in the saloon when the suspect, wearing a gun, entered with a girl and limped to the bar and asked for two whiskies. The lawmen hadn't seen him in town since the day before the theft and that had combined with the description of a witness unknown to him to increase their suspicion; but apparently he now deemed the crime old enough to make Bancroft's whiskey and a certain South-Street girl safe again. As safe as whiskey and a South-Street girl could be.

The marshal nudged his deputy. "Ain't that our Bell Mare horse-stealing varmint?"

Big John squinted across the room. "Might be."

"Reckon we'll ask him."

They moved toward the bar.

Among the Eastern's other customers was Tenderloin Smith, trail cook for Colonel Cole. At the end of the summer's drive Tenderloin had stayed over in Bancroft and taken a job cooking for Oscar Lacy. Oscar had wanted to give Missus Lacy a vacation from the Lone Star's kitchen and Tenderloin had agreed to fill in at the cafe until Colonel Cole came back through town from Chicago on his way home to Texas and picked up Tenderloin. That made it handy for everybody. The Colonel had gone to Chicago on the train with his cattle and while there had invested in a new packing plant with a syndicate of big-city moneymen as a way of rounding out his cattle empire. It was understood he was due back any day now.

The cook was enjoying a few drinks at the bar alongside the evening's newcomers. As a matter of fact he was a little drunk. He was celebrating the colonel's imminent return. They had been youths together in Virginia and then down on the Brazos which was why the cattle king continued looking out for his old friend after striking it rich, so to speak.

With his deputy slightly behind his left elbow Luther stopped about six feet from the suspect and spoke to him softly. "You with the bowlegs, turn around real slow and keep your hand off your gun."

The cowboy gulped his mouthful of whiskey and stared at the bartender as though the latter's eyes might mirror the speaker as clearly as the glass behind the bar. In a way they did; they looked scared. Slowly the man swung around to face the marshal, his gaze widening at sight of the badge on Luther's shirt. His girl giggled. He said nothing and was careful to keep his hands unoffending.

"What's your name?"

"You're handsome," the girl said.

Luther didn't take his eyes off her companion.

Pushing herself unsteadily from the bar she slid one of her feet in the marshal's direction. "You know you're handsome, Honey?"

"You're drunk," Big John grunted at her. "Vamoose."

"Not talking to you," she told the deputy. Her giggle faded into a pout. "Talking to him."

Big John reached forward and seized her arm and pulled her around behind him. "Stay back here."

"I asked you a question," Luther reminded the cowboy.

"Don't know it's any your business, but it's Enos Dowling."

The marshal's jaw muscles tightened.

"You get them bowlegs riding thoroughbreds, Enos Dowling?"

"Don't know what you're talking about."

"One particular fine bay, black mane and tail?"

"Don't know what you're talking about."

"Sounds to me you do," Luther told him. "You get that limp saying 'no' too fast?"

112

"Was born lame!"

"In the head?"

The girl giggled again, looking around Big John at the marshal. "You're funny too!"

"Go to hell," the suspect muttered, shifting his glance expediently to the disloyal harlot.

"Me or her?" Luther asked him.

"Limping ain't funny."

"I'll tell you where you and me are both going: up to the jail." The marshal jerked his head toward the door.

"What you taking me to jail for?"

"We aim to find that out right soon. Get to limping!"

The girl's hoot of merriment brought a flush to the cowboy's face. "Goddam you!"

"With him in jail," she snickered "we can get to know each other real good, Marshal," her hand snaking past Big John's arm to Luther's ribs "—Honey."

"That's enough." The deputy brushed her hand aside.

"Real good," she emphasized.

Dowling's fury spewed over the girl and the marshal alike. "Goddam you to hell!"

"I said get along," Luther repeated.

"You can't shit on me!"

"You shit on the man owned that horse."

"Don't know what horse you talking about."

"One you stole."

"You can't prove I stole no horse."

"Why else you hollering like a caught horse thief?"

Big John frowned. "Ain't you going to take his gun, Luther?"

"He's too yellow to use it."

The girl's laughter was a derisive confirmation of the insult. Down the bar beyond the group Tenderloin Smith hiccuped and delivered himself of a thick-tongued observation: "Looks to me like somebody's riding somebody's ass unnecessary."

The deputy glanced at the cook. "Keep it to yourself, Tenderloin."

At that moment in his raging torment Dowling dropped one surprisingly quick hand to his holster an instant before the marshal's revolver exploded with an ear-splitting roar. The bullet tore through the outer flesh of the cowboy's right shoulder and successively carried away half of the cook's right ear and buried itself in the wall at the end of the room.

Dowling spun on his heels and fell and Tenderloin, his hiccups gone, dazedly raised his hand to the side of his head and pulled it away and stared at its wet redness.

The reverberating air stank of black-powder smoke.

"Mygod," Big John said hoarsely. "Luther . . ."

Luther shook his head as he replaced his gun. "It's his shoulder. Doc can nurse it in jail." He stepped over the writhing form on the floor toward the stunned cook. "Didn't aim to nick you too, Tenderloin," he said quietly.

"Christamighty!" Tenderloin muttered.

With careful fingers the marshal turned the cook's head sideways and inspected his wound. "That's a hell of a tore ear; sorry. We'll get you to the doc right quick."

" 'Hell of a tore ear,' " Tenderloin repeated numbly.

The pale bartender looked apprehensive. "That waddie went after his gun first, Marshal." He pointed nervously at Dowling who had struggled in shock to a half-sitting position gripping his bleeding shoulder. "Yessir I seen that much." He seemed anxious to establish amicable relations with the marshal. "I'll swear to that any time. And I reckon he stole that horse too. Yessir."

"You just swear to what you seen" Big John muttered.

"You do that," Luther agreed mildly. " 'Yessir.' And we'll handle the horse stealing."

"Anything you say, Mister Cain."

Luther turned to his deputy. "Better stay around here, John, while I take Tenderloin up to Doc Bowman's. I'll send Doc's rig back for Dowling." He looked down at the moaning cowboy. "While I'm gone he can study about that bay."

"He's bleeding pretty good."

"I seen a lot worse at Fort Donelson." The marshal motioned to one of the Eastern's score of silent customers. "You with your mouth open shove your palm hard agin that wound and keep it there." Taking Tenderloin's arm he pushed their way through the crowd to the door.

"Jumping Jesus!" somebody said behind him.

Two mornings later when Dowling, his shirt hanging loosely over his bandaged shoulder, appeared wanly before Bill Crum in the courtroom the mayor questioned Earl Chester, owner of the Bell Mare Livery Company and of the missing thoroughbred, and Wayne Gambill, Earl's stable boy who had caught a glimpse of the bowlegged horse thief limping ahead of the bay out of its stall, and the suspect himself; and then he bound the cowboy over to the circuit court and set his bond at five hundred dollars. Dowling didn't have the five hundred on him or in prospect so Bill sent him back to jail to await trial. "The doc can look after your shoulder better there anyhow and the food ain't the worst in the territory . . . quite."

That afternoon in his office with what he thought was the day's official business behind him the mayor received a distinguished, gray-bearded, azure-eyed visitor. It developed that Colonel Avery Cole had arrived in town an hour previously on the west-bound train and had sought out Tenderloin Smith and heard the story first-hand from his old friend about the demolished ear.

"It's a hell of an ear, Mayor," the colonel affirmed, "just like Tenderloin said. They just don't come any more homely. And it's a hell of a town where a man can't have a lonesome drink without losing an ear to a marshal's stray bullet."

Bill Crum thumbed back his derby and scratched his forehead ruefully. "Luther's mighty sorry about that, Colonel."

"I didn't trail my herd all the way up here from the Santa Clara Ranch to get my cook's ear shot off."

The mayor sensed which way the wind was blowing. "We want you to keep bringing them up to Bancroft, Colonel. We don't much care any more where Pickett ships his at but we like your trade. That winging Tenderloin was an accident."

"I surely hope so. But I talked to some men on the way over here and the story goes Cain didn't need to shoot at Dowling."

"Dowling tried to draw on him."

"After he was bullied into it."

"A lawman's got a lot of troubles in this town, Colonel. He just can't let nobody get ahead of him including no horse thief. Else he'd end up behind everbody. Like Charlie Tucker."

"Charlie Tucker didn't wing any bystanders." The cattleman leaned forward in his chair. "But that's not the point. Tenderloin got hit by a bullet that needn't been fired the way I hear. Sure a lawman's got troubles. He's got to keep the peace. That's his job. But aggravating people don't make for peace."

115

"Maybe depends on who them people is."

"I'll say it this way: aggravating the wrong people for the wrong reasons."

"Meaning you?"

"Meaning anybody don't see eye-to-eye with Luther Cain." The colonel leaned back. "Tenderloin didn't lose that ear a couple nights ago because he got in the way of a peacemaking bullet; he lost it because Cain was warlike against a cowboy he decided stole a horse."

"You been way a month, Colonel. You don't know what Luther's had to put up with."

"I watched him some before I left. He's warlike inside"—the visitor tapped his own chest—"and taking it out on people. Or else he just don't give a damn about people, about anything but keeping the peace. What he calls the 'peace.' Either way that don't make for a good lawman."

"I'll have to say I never seen a better one." Bill Crum felt the tug of obscure truth in the colonel's assertion however. "I tell you he's getting this town slowed to a standstill. The cowboys is scared to hell of him."

"Scared means hate. You better slow your marshal, Mayor, before he gets in bad trouble himself. That's all I'm saying right now." The visitor stood up. "Speaking of Pickett, you know where he is?"

"A few of his outfit's still here, what hasn't drifted back to Texas. I hear Pickett went to Kansas City to spend some of his cattle money." The mayor grinned faintly. "That was right after Bennett's play didn't pan out. But he's back now I reckon."

"Who's Bennett?"

"Jack Bennett. A no-good bastard thought he could jerk a gun with Luther Cain. We figured Pickett hired him to kill Luther. Couldn't prove nothing."

"Tried to go against Cain?"

"Buried out west of town." Bill got to his feet, his frown returning. "If there's something to what you said about the marshal he'll know it when I tell him. If I tell him. If there ain't nothing to it he'll know that too. Reckon I'll leave the deciding up to him." He put out his hand and the cattleman shook it. "Wouldn't want to lose your shipping, Colonel, but wouldn't want to lose Luther neither."

116

Their hands parted. "Coming in here was my own idea, Mayor."

"Didn't figure you for no errand boy."

"Looks like we all got our troubles. Tenderloin's might be eased some if the town paid for his doctoring anyhow."

"Sure. It'll do that."

For most of the afternoon the mayor considered whether or not to tell the marshal about the cattleman's visit and finally determined such was his duty to both Luther and his own conscience. He was not going to make a reprimand or a warning of it. He merely was going to quote his visitor's remarks. As he had told the colonel it should be up to Luther to assess their relevance. He was pretty sure Luther wasn't going to take them too seriously but maybe seriously enough.

He found the marshal in the Drovers dining room eating supper and reading the *Republican*. He sat down opposite him and ordered only a cup of coffee.

"Ain't eating tonight, Bill, or can't stomach your own food?"

"Ain't hungry just yet." The mayor shoved back his derby which he always either was shoving back or tilting forward. "Had me a caller this afternoon."

Luther sensed that curiosity was expected of him. "What he call about?"

"I'll just tell you what he said. I don't know if it was any of his business."

The marshal forked a piece of meat into his mouth. "Who?" he asked through the bite.

"Colonel Cole. He got back today."

Luther nodded as he chewed silently, his face expressionless.

"He seen Tenderloin's ear and come over to talk about it. Didn't like it. I told him we was sorry it happened."

The marshal lowered his fork. "Why didn't he talk to me?"

"Don't know." Bill's hesitation was an instant too prolonged. "Maybe I was handy."

Luther laid his fork carefully on his plate. "What else he say?"

The mayor sighed. "You didn't need to shoot at Dowling." He raised his hand. "I told him Dowling drawed on you. But he was sore about Tenderloin and wasn't making much sense maybe."

117

Bill lowered his hand to the table again. "Said he heard you rankled Dowling into drawing."

The marshal's eyes narrowed to slits. "You tell him Dowling's a horse thief?"

"I told him you couldn't afford to let no troublemaker get ahead of you including no horse thief; your job was hard enough already."

Luther stared at his friend, waiting for him to continue.

The mayor cleared his throat. "But he said you aggravated folks where you didn't have to because you was riled about something. Goddam, Luther, I didn't say that; I ain't got no complaint about how you marshal."

"You didn't say it, just thought it?"

"Whoa, now!"

It seemed to Bill that the marshal relaxed somewhat. With private relief the mayor did also.

Luther shrugged almost imperceptibly. "You're paying the fiddler, Bill. It's up to you to call the tune. I'll play or not."

As simply as that the problem, if one really existed, was back in Bill Crum's lap. And on his conscience. "Yeah, Luther, sure." The waitress brought his coffee and he took a mouthful and sputtered it back into the cup. "Hell's fire and painted ladies, that's hot!" His tongue felt branded. "I like your tune fine bygod, just don't bust your bow scraping too hard. That's all I'm thinking. The dance ain't worth it."

"Ain't upholding the law worth it?"

"Oh goddam hell yes, Luther; but your hide's worth something, too."

"I aim to keep my hide and the peace both." The marshal's gaze was unblinking. "If you got no objections."

"Damnation no, Luther."

"But if Colonel Cole has? Or Johnny Newlin?"

"The colonel means all right and his shipping's good for the town but without no law there wouldn't be no town. And as for Newlin he can go plumb to hell in a buckboard and I'd not turn in my saddle to see."

"Cole talked about his shipping?"

"He was sore over Tenderloin. He's all right."

"Sure," the marshal nodded stiffly. "Sure he's all right."

"Take it easy, Luther."

118

"You said that before. Don't bust my bow scraping too hard. Keep the dance happy."

The mayor's grin was still a little apprehensive. "You ain't going to bust it. Too many folks favor the way you scrape."

"Including you?"

"Including me."

The mayor didn't often temporize. He didn't consider he had just now. After all a man's friends counted for more than his foes. And any foe of law and order was in opposition to Bill Crum, as to Luther Cain, by virtue of Bill's office if not of his wholehearted dedication. Probably Colonel Cole didn't qualify wittingly as such an opponent but Johnny Newlin sure as hell did.

So the mayor had temporized.

CHAPTER 15

. . . The startlingly hot tide hissing up the sand tugged at Mark's feet, nearly unbalancing him. Mattie strained away from his arms in momentary panic and as quickly relaxed into his safekeeping. The surf rumbled like a truck passing far below.

The eastern sky was bleeding from the slash of dawn the next morning as Luther left the shadowy courthouse and the night's brooding work—the vigilant rounds and the study of Wells Fargo and Santa Fe reward circulars and the crude printing of a note to Sheriff Light about a cattle rustling rumor—and walked out into the coolness of the welling day with his adoptive mongrel at his heels. Usually he didn't stay this late on the job but his seething stomach and a dozen nightlong cups of coffee had thwarted sleepiness. He assumed his tired scuffing boots should take him to his room in the Drovers Hotel; instead he found them turning southward across the railroad track and down South Street and out Jimson Street to the pinkening facade of Lane's rooming house. In the stillness of Bancroft's very early morning he stopped and stared at the closed front door. Then breathing audibly although there was no one but the dog to hear his pain he strode across the dust to the door and opened it and moved softly along the hall to Carrie's room. His faint rap followed by another brought a murmur from beyond the panel and a hiss of bedclothes and a scrape of a bolt. A sliver of open doorway exposed a drowsy, startlingly child-like portion of Carrie's face and tousled hair and immediately widened with her gaze to let him step forward.

"Luther," she whispered.

Inside her room he shoved the door shut behind him with his heel and rebolted it and took off his hat with an awkward flourish. "Good morning," he managed to smile under his moustache.

She couldn't remember ever having seen him nervous before. Perhaps it was an illusion of the creeping light. She flicked up her tumbling hair with the back of her hand and slid her tongue across her lips. "Something wrong?"

"Just wanted to say 'good morning.' "

"Well good morning," she smiled uncertainly, pulling her calico wrapper closer at her throat with absent fingers. She laid her other hand on his arm and stretched upward briefly to kiss his lips and then gestured toward the room's two chairs. "Sit down, Honey, and I'll brew us some coffee on the hall stove."

"Had my fill of coffee last night." His tone was a shade less warm than his smile. "Call me anything but 'Honey.' Been meaning to say that."

She looked slightly confused. "Why sure, Luther. Whatever you want."

"I want to kiss you again."

"All right." She stepped into his arms. When she drew away from him after a moment her opening eyes were shadowed with concern. "What is it, Hon—Luther?"

"What's what?"

"Something's the matter."

"With that kiss?"

"I liked that fine, Dear."

"And I like 'Dear' better."

"I'll remember."

"I been called 'Honey' in some mighty low-down honkytonks."

Her cheeks colored minutely. "Let's set down, Luther, and talk over what's on your mind." She led him to one of the chairs and seated herself in the other opposite him, touching her hair again. "Just caught a glimpse of me in the mirror. Wish I'd knowed you was coming, I'd looked better."

"You're a sight right out of a picture hanging in a St. Louis hotel lobby, Carrie. Prettiest picture I ever seen. A woman with hair like yours setting in a dress like the one you got on looking out a window."

This time her flush sprang from pleasure. "Thank you, Dear," she smiled, glancing down at her draped knees. "This ain't a dress, it's a wrapper I put on when I answered the door. To cover me."

"I know."

Her smile faded in unfamiliar embarrassment.

"I could tell when I put my arms around you there wasn't nothing but skin under it." He arched his brows in elaborate admonition. "Be sure you don't answer other men's knocks without asking who it is." He wished he hadn't attempted the jest; her eyes hinted it had stung her; then perversely he wanted to sting

121

her again. "Hope you don't answer other men's knocks noway no more." He wanted to club himself with a wagon spoke when he saw the mist come into her eyes. "Reckon I'm tired, Carrie. Had a hard night. And I got to get back to the courthouse in three hours."

"I can see you're tired," she blinked. "Would you want to lay down on the bed here?"

His glance narrowed infinitesimally.

"Take a nap here, Luther? It's time I was getting dressed anyhow."

"They hire a man to keep order and then cuss him if he does. I'm on my way to the hotel from the courthouse."

She let the non sequitur pass. "You won't be bothered here by nobody."

"You ain't 'nobody,' Carrie. You're a sight for sore eyes. And mine's sore. More ways than one."

She swallowed. "I'll be going out for breakfast."

"I don't complain being bothered by you. It's others."

"I knowed there was something the matter, Luther. Who cussed you?"

"Not actual," he muttered. "But when Bill Crum ain't sure . . ." He broke off. "The hell with it." His grin was forced as he stood up and tossed his hat onto the bureau. "I don't need no nap, I only need to be with you."

She remained seated and gazed up at him. "I been hearing about your shooting with Dowling. You ain't told me about it since then, so I know it was over me. You oughtn't to fight over me, Luther. Not with him or nobody."

"He had it coming."

"I told you I was scared things wouldn't work out for us."

"The hell with that too!" His hand trembled slightly as he laid it on her shoulder. "Carrie, my run-in with Dowling didn't have nothing to do with you. He's a horse thief."

"You don't need to fight everbody in the world, Luther."

"Now *you* telling me?"

She covered his hand with hers. "And for sure you don't need to fight over me. You got yourself enough."

He squatted onto his haunches beside her and took her face between his palms. "I need to kiss you."

"Oh, Luther." As she twisted sideways to slip her arms around his neck the top of her wrapper fell open. She didn't seem aware of it. "I need to kiss you too!"

His hands seized her along with his lips. He moved one hand gently to cup her freed breast.

After a moment she pulled back her head with a soft moan. "Luther, you never did this before, we kissed but you never did this."

"I wanted to before." He lowered his head to kiss her nipple, her breast nesting in his rich moustache.

Her whisper was urgent. "You really love me, Luther?"

"Yes." He hadn't equivocated this time.

"It won't work unless you really love me."

"Damn you yes! The hell with everbody else; the hell with Dowling and Newlin . . ."

"See?" She pushed suddenly at his hands, trying to struggle from his arms. "It just won't work." Tears flooded her eyes. "You cuss when you love me, you cuss the way you said they did, you cuss because loving me brings you trouble with them."

She might as well have been struggling against a grizzly. He arose from his haunches and pulled her up with him and his mouth smothered her moan. Abruptly in the red dawn she clung to him in a convulsive, frenzied returning of his passion; then she wrenched her lips from his and sucked in a breath.

"No, Luther, don't do me this way, don't . . ."

"Yes!" he gritted.

She braced herself. "This ain't the way I want it to be; you got to understand." She began to sob. "This ain't the way I want you, not mad."

"I ain't mad at you."

"You're mad at what I was."

"What's past is done, you said. Dammit!"

"It's done all right but you don't believe it, not yet. Maybe you never will. Maybe they won't never let you. I can't rub out the past, Luther, and neither can you. But I love you and I'm looking to what's ahead. And you got to love me the same way or it ain't never going to work for you and me. Even then maybe never."

With a sickening, guilty surge the violence seemed to drain out of him—"I'm sorry, Carrie"—and to be replaced by a wave of painful tenderness. "I didn't aim to make you cry." His arms became gentle with remorse and protectiveness. "I don't want to rub out nothing but making you cry just now; I don't want to do nothing but love you the way you said." He squinted at her upturned face, his clumsy tongue groping for words to make her believe what he was too confused about to be fully sure of himself. "I reckon I been riled and ornery and took it out on you this morning. But not because I wanted to." He was sure about one thing: "I only want our love to ride out everything."

She sniffed at her tears and almost smiled. "I need you to kiss me again, Luther. Quick."

He did that. Tenderly and lovingly. Then he grinned at her and released her except for one hand and led her to the bureau. Picking up his hat he lifted her fingers to his lips in an old-world gesture of courtliness that brought a tinge to her cheeks. Carrie never had felt so loved or valued or secure. Her smile glowed with gratitude.

"Thank you, dear Luther."

He put on his hat—"Get some breakfast!"—and turned toward the door—"See you later"—and slid back the bolt and left her standing in her dawn-red room listening to his waning tread in the hall.

"Thank you," she whispered again.

> *. . . His captain told us that a character who tried to frame Sergeant Keller a few years ago ended up in a frame himself—on the post office wall, "and I can probably get you a print for your paper, if you like."*

It was a good hour before the marshal of Bancroft, as tired as he was, finally fell asleep in his own room at the Drovers Hotel. It was a good thing he didn't know what Johnny Newlin was up to at the time or he might have taken longer.

"So they say you got to get up early in the morning to skin Luther Cain," the Portugese's proprietor said matter-of-factly to the group in his office; "so all right we're up early and we're going to skin the sonofabitch raw."

"This is the earliest I been up since I come off the trail." Jason T.M. Pickett looked worn out. "I got to get back to Texas, I'm getting too old for this high life."

"Ivy Painter'll age any man before his time," Texan Latigo Eyler recalled from experience.

Johnny frowned. "Mister Pickett didn't get up early and I didn't put up five hundred dollars to bail out Enos so we could jaw about Ivy Painter." His tone assumed a certain pride. "Even if she is one of my best."

Mustang Johnson smiled. "Heard you lost your best one to the marshal, Johnny."

"You keep Carrie out of this, goddam you." Johnny's face reddened. "You hear me?"

"Sure, Johnny, sure. No offense."

Jason T.M. Pickett yawned. "Let's get down to business so I can get some sleep."

The proprietor turned to the cattle shipper. "Sure, Mister Pickett, we'll get down to business." Then he addressed the group at large. "I been figuring how to get shud of that sonofabitch for good and I got an idea."

"I'd fancy being the one to shoot him," a cowboy leaning against the closed door said. "The bastard slapped me in front of everyone when I was over to Crum's court with Mister Pickett last month."

"You wouldn't stand a chance, Duke," Pickett said flatly.

"Reckon we could hire Champ Bayliss to whip him good before we shoot him?" Indian Jesse's dark face brightened a bit. "For openers?"

Pickett looked at the half-breed. "Where's your boss stand on this, Jesse?" He turned back to Newlin. "You talked to Avery Cole about this, Johnny?"

The Portugese's proprietor shook his head. "He ain't that sore. And anyhow the fewer knows the better."

"He sure as hell was sore about Tenderloin's ear," Indian Jesse said. "But he ain't one to shoot nobody hisself 'less it's a cattle rustler."

"Well who's going to do the shooting?" Pickett asked Newlin.

Johnny leaned back in his chair and smiled. "Nobody."

"Nobody! What the hell you got us here for?"

"To get shud of him like I said, skin his hide."

Pickett looked skeptical. "You mean with a knife for chrissake?"

"In a face-up fight he'd kill anybody," Johnny judged, "and

125

if we bushwhacked him we'd be throwed out of Bancroft. Or hung."

Indian Jesse sluiced a mouthful of tobacco juice into the spittoon. "Who's to say we'd get found out?"

"We don't need to take that chance. All we need to make this a friendly town again is him leaving for good without nobody the wiser we done it."

"You just going to walk up and tell him to get out?" Latigo scoffed.

"Townsfolks is going to do that."

Duke snorted. "Why they going to do that?"

"Because they don't want a goddam road agent for a marshal."

Jason T.M. Pickett leaned forward in the moment's silence squinting at Newlin. "What you got in mind?"

What Johnny had in mind was a plan as hackneyed and theatrical as it was also in his opinion likely to work. As the Stockmen and Farmers Bank's temporarily biggest depositor Pickett should make a drunken spectacle of withdrawing his money in cash, telling Bank owner Clay Gibson he was riding the stage north to Omaha before going back to Texas. Drovers Hotel chore-girl and former Portugese trollop Hortense Bass, who owed her ex-boss a favor, should steal the marshal's silver toothpick while he was taking his weekly bath and pass it to Drovers roomer Jason Pickett before the Texan checked out. When the stage carrying Pickett and Mustang Johnson was about five miles outside Bancroft two masked highwaymen, Indian Jesse and Duke, should hold it up and relieve the cattleman of his poke, one of them calling the other "Luther" in the process; and after running the unhitched stage team off into the night they should ride away in the direction of Bancroft with their swag. The passengers and driver undoubtedly should mill around in the moonlight talking about the holdup. Pickett and Mustang should mention incidentally one of the robbers' use of the name "Luther." At about that time in the light of a match to his cigar Mustang should note the glint of a certain silver toothpick on the ground beside Pickett's boot heel where no one should have seen the Texas rancher drop it.

"And then things is going to commence looking goddam bad for Luther Cain," Newlin concluded.

Latigo's stare was dubious. "What if Hortense talks about it?"

"She knows she'd wind up in Owl Crick," Johnny said, "Same as anyone here who did." His glance swept the gathering. "That's right?"

Latigo's frown was replaced by a grin. "About right at that." The group mulled Newlin's plan silently for a moment.

Jason T.M. Pickett cleared his throat. "When Cain's supposed to be out there holding up the stage, what about folks seeing him here in town?"

"That's where Latigo and Enos come in. About dusk Latigo's going to tell Cain he just seen Enos high-tailing out of town on another horse that don't belong to him . . ."

"What you mean, 'another'?" Dowling's interruption was indignant. "I ain't admitted stealing . . ."

"Keep your shirt on, Enos. I'm only saying Cain thinks you stole it. And when Latigo tells him you jumped bail on somebody else's horse again he's going to start after you pronto, sheriff or not and coming dark or not. That'll take him out of town a couple hours 'til he meets you coming back from Ellsville."

"I don't know about meeting the sonofabitch out there in the dark, Johnny," Dowling frowned, touching his bandaged shoulder absently.

"But you're headed back. Tell him you been to Ellsville for a change of scenery; he can't do nothing. But you tell the folks in Bancroft you never seen him at all."

"Goddam," Dowling grunted, "shoulder's mighty sore for riding yet "

"Only way I figure we can get him out of town. You yellow like I heard he called you?"

"Goddam!"

Johnny smiled. "Didn't think so." He turned to Eyler. "And you tell the folks you didn't see him neither, Latigo. That's two words against one." He looked at the Texas cattle baron, his pride showing again. "Well, Mister Pickett, how's all this set with you? Pretty good plan?"

"One thing you ain't covered." The cattleman frowned at Jesse and Duke. "You two going to remember who my cash belongs to, bygod?" His brows relaxed at their earnest nods. "All right. I reckon it's a pretty good plan." His creeping smile answered Johnny's. "Bygod, if it don't land Cain in his own jail it sure as hell ought to run him out of marshaling."

"Anyhow out of Bancroft," Newlin chuckled, "after I get through raising hell about it at the town board meeting Monday night."

Duke grinned. "Slick as a goddam Tammany politician, Johnny."

In the dimness of room 14 of the Drovers Hotel Luther Cain muttered in his sleep and rolled to the other side of his creaking brass bed.

Down the hall a man's hoarse demand stifled a woman's giggle.

Outside Noble Buck and his horse Shag wagoned a load of ice along Pacific Street.

CHAPTER 16

On Monday night in the courtroom the council meeting, ordinarily attracting an audience of a few merchants, three or four householders and a boozy loafer or two along with turnkey Hale Meese, spilled into the hall with its press of noisy spectators. After several futile demands for order, Mayor Crum took the minute book from Clerk Billy Custer and banged it on the long table. Even then it was a while before the gathering which included a group of boys on the back row quieted down.

"And anybody don't stay quiet," Bill reinforced his injunction, glaring at the crowd from his presiding chair at the head of the table, "is going to get throwed out."

A southern drawl at the rear of the lamp-lit room disputed him: "You ain't going to throw nobody out; this here's a public meeting."

"What you fixing to do about Luther Cain?" another Texas voice hooted.

Bill tilted his derby forward with a deliberate thumb. "Far as citizens of Bancroft is concerned this here's a public meeting all right. But far as out-of-towners is concerned it's public just as long as I say so." He stared at the Texas delegation. "Speaking of Luther Cain, he'll see my say-so goes. We got plenty room in the calaboose tonight."

From his seat half-way along the table council member Newlin addressed the audience suavely. "Naturally we're glad to have our out-of-town visitors with us. Bancroft's always been a friendly town—" he cleared his throat—"up to lately. But I agree with the mayor we got to stay quiet so we can get down to business."

Somebody snickered.

Johnny's expression remained righteous.

The first order of business was consideration of an ordinance sponsored by the Bancroft Ladies Betterment League (the title had caused Doc Bowman once to ask gallantly how the ladies could be better) requiring all saloons to close for three hours on Sunday mornings. The proprietor of the Portugese Theater and Saloon with a glance at editor Carl Norris's scratching pencil moved its

129

adoption. "I always favor Bancroft's good church-going ladies.' On a second by Ed Sarver—"I always do what my wife tells me"— it was passed unanimously.

"Who says this ain't a woman's world?" the mayor asked the ceiling, ordering the clerk to record the ordinance in the minute book for his later signature. "And the ladies will ask the marshal to remind us of that right often I don't doubt."

Next on the agenda was council member Bert Oliver's request that the town repair the sidewalk in front of his hardware store. "Planks all rotted out and I lost three customers through there already. Not one's been seen since and my business can't stand that kind of drain."

The audience's laughter, inhibited considerably by nervous awareness of impending matters, was limited to the first four rows; the rear half of the courtroom wasn't in a laughing mood. After some discussion by the council concerning the cost of the repairs and, with attorney Jim Watts' counsel, of the town's legal liability member Solly Berg suggested a compromise: Bert should pay for the labor involved and the town for the materials. This was agreed by all concerned, including Bert who was a reasonable man as also noted by Carl Norris for the *Republican.*

The repair of Pacific Street sidewalk out of the way, the council took up the replotting of the cemetery west of town which had grown too small, the dispersion of the square's cluttering horse-and-wagon jam which had grown too large, and an informal apprisal of the last quarter's mercantile receipts which had stood pat. All this consumed an hour to the mounting suspense of the civic-minded half of the audience and the irritation of the didn't-give-a-damn half.

"Well," Bill Crum said regarding the summer's business stalemate, "least the town ain't losing ground. Maybe we're not plumb out of the last couple years' depression but we ain't going downhill, what with cattle drives still coming up."

A cowboy standing in the doorway called out, "You ain't going to have no more cattle coming up if you keep Luther Cain on your payroll!"

"Well," the mayor said, "I reckon our session's over for tonight." He arose. "Meeting adjourned."

"Wait a minute now," Johnny Newlin objected. "Set down, Bill, we got one more thing to come before us."

"Damn right we do," the man in the doorway added loudly.

Bill stared at him. "What you mean 'we'? When was you elected?"

"Just the same," Johnny interceded, "there's a matter of unfinished business I want to bring up for the good of the town. And I sure was elected if you recall."

The mayor sighed and sat down. "All right. But I aim to have order while we're doing it."

"That's right," Johnny said mildly, glancing toward the doorway. "You remember that, Duke." His gaze swept over the audience and returned to the mayor. "This matter of unfinished business is hard for me to bring up being it makes the town look bad, but so many folks mentioned it to me I can't do nothing else and do my elected job." He took a weary breath—"I'm talking about what happened Saturday night"—and swung slowly toward the marshal standing in the flickering light at one side of the room near its front.

For an instant all the assembly's eyes spiked Luther to the wall, a number hesitantly, some apologetically, others viciously. Then they pulled out the collective skewer and stabbed at the speaker again.

"It's a sad day when a good town like Bancroft comes under a cloud of disgrace—" Johnny's words became measured dramatically—"when a fine visitor who's brung us a lot of business, Mister Jason T.M. Pickett, gets robbed of his money right under our nose like the whole town's heard about last couple days." His gaze sought out the cattleman among the spectators. "We sure are sorry that happened, Mr. Pickett." As a mutter ran through the crowd his voice quickened and rose with indignation. "And making it all the worse is when that unfriendly cloud called 'robbery' is blowed over the town by somebody they trusted."

Jim Watts spoke from his seat in the audience: "This is not the place to try a law case."

"That's right," Bill Crum said to Newlin, "this ain't the place to try no case even if there was one."

The Portugese's proprietor looked at the lawyer. "You saying stage robbery is no law case? With witnesses and all? You not going to prosecute?"

"Jim said," the mayor pointed out, "this ain't the place. This here's a council meeting. What the hell you up to?"

"As county attorney," Jim said, "I'll file against anybody I think committed a crime. Based on reasonable evidence, naturally."

Johnny's lips curled in a sneer. "Lawyer talk. You heard the story going around: one of them calling the other 'Luther' and Mustang finding Cain's toothpick out there and Cain missing from town while the holdup's going on. All that told by witnesses. What else you call 'reasonable evidence,' for godssake?"

In the third row a spectator whispered to another, "Johnny's got guts all right." They both were looking at the marshal's baleful stare.

"Or maybe you're too friendly with him," Newlin added just loudly enough to be heard.

Jim Watts blanched. "What you mean . . . ?"

"I'm not knowing about the law," Solomon Berg interrupted the prosecutor. His tone was abashed at his own temerity. "But I'm wondering how many 'Luthers' in the world there are and how we can know whose toothpick it was and why we must believe Mister Cain was at a place he says he wasn't."

Johnny looked hard at his fellow councilman. "You add up a 'Luther' that's Cain's build plus a silver toothpick he can't show now plus nobody seeing him a couple hours that night—him the marshal always walks the streets—and then if you ain't got a stage-robbing sum you sure as hell got a peculiar lawman."

"I never believed them, Mister Cain!" Noble Buck shouted from the back row.

"Me neither!" Billy Plunkett and David Berg confirmed together.

"Bygod we do," another, hoarser voice growled from the same direction, triggering an accusing chorus. "And you goddam kids be quiet."

At the marshal's feet his dog growled.

Bill grabbed the minute book again and stood up and slammed it onto the table with all his lofty strength. "That ain't the goddam point! Now shut up or I'll throw ever one of you in jail for disturbing the peace!"

"The mayor and Jim Watts is right," Johnny Newlin said. He got to his feet beside Bill and raised both arms in an imperious gesture which somehow induced relative silence. "The point here ain't to bring Luther Cain to law for robbing Mister Pickett's money; that's for Mister Watts and the judge. But what we can do tonight is slow a marshal who's got too big for his goddam britches."

At Johnny's use of "slow" Bill Crum glanced disappointedly at Colonel Cole in the audience. The gray-bearded cattle shipper shook his head almost imperceptibly in denial of complicity in this public accusation. Instinctively the mayor believed him, at the same time recalling the colonel's earlier warning.

"Let's both set down again, Johnny," Bill said in an effort to salvage some common sense from the developments. "Let's be reasonable here now."

"That's what the hell I'm saying," Newlin smiled. He lowered himself into his chair after Bill had retaken his. "It's up to Jim Watts to do his duty but it's up to the council to protect the good name of Bancroft by lifting Cain's badge while the law runs its course. That's what's reasonable."

"A man's innocent 'til he's proved guilty," Ed Sarver reminded the council and the room.

Bert Oliver nodded. "Anybody can claim anybody's a stage robber. That's no reason to lift his badge before nothing's proved."

"If a man's innocent," Johnny contended patiently, "he'd turn in his badge voluntary with all that evidence against him. He'd figure folks would wonder about his marshaling under a cloud."

"That's like pleading guilty," Ed said.

Newlin shook his head. "He wouldn't want to go on marshaling with folks taking him for a stage robber. And we wouldn't want to let him, us being elected to serve the folks of this town."

"What if he ain't guilty, Johnny?" Ed Sarver persisted.

"That'd make me look a fool all right, if he's got the gall to stay around and take that chance. All I'm doing is guarding the good name of Bancroft."

"That all?" the mayor's brows were skeptical.

"Scared of your duty now, Mayor, or him?"

Bill's brows pinched into a scowl. "You want to watch yourself, Johnny."

In the moment's tense silence a number of the people in the room shifted their glances to the marshal. Those gazes from the rear except Noble's and Billy's and David's were openly hostile; among the others some were dubious and some seemingly embarrassed by Luther's shadowy reticence. His mongrel growled again softly. Everybody looked back at the council as Bert Oliver spoke.

"You mean suspend him temporary?"

Johnny shrugged. "You know a better way to do your duty Bert? Ought to make it permanent I vote."

"I know a better way." Luther Cain's voice jolted the proceedings like a pistol shot. Almost listlessly he stepped across the short distance from the wall to the somewhat brighter glow of the chimneyed coal-oil chandelier; but his tone was a long way from listless. He gazed at the assemblage from under his round-crowned black hat. "I want all you folks to know I sure do admire the public spiritness of the council."

"Now wait a spell, Luther," Bill Crum said, reddening.

"Especial Johnny Newlin." The peace officer glanced at the mayor. "I aim to do the talking a while now." He looked toward the rear rows of spectators. "I want you all to know how much I appreciate you backing me up in front of our," he spat the phrase, "out-of-town visitors yonder. All excepting those kids back there. Makes a hired lawman feel mighty good. Anyhow a peculiar one like me. Makes him know why he was hired; because everybody trusted him to do his job right."

Bill took a quick retrospective glance at his misgivings. A finger crept toward his uncomfortable collar. "Now it ain't . . ."

"You can't talk us out of our duty!" the Portugese's proprietor interrupted stridently.

Solly's frown was painful. "We're knowing you do your job right, Mister Cain."

Bert swallowed. "Sure."

Johnny struggled from his seat. "You don't own the goddam town, Cain!"

"Set down you bastard," Luther suddenly gusted, taking a step toward his accuser.

Johnny slumped back into his chair. His face was livid. "It's our business suffers not yours; your only business is hitting folks over the head and shooting them." He appealed to the audience. "You fellows back there ain't that right?"

"You're goddam right!" Jason T.M. Pickett bellowed.

Several cowboys shouted their profane agreement.

The mayor whacked the table with the minute book for the third time.

Luther's tone returned to an ominous flatness as he stared at Newlin. "I got another business you overlooked, Johnny, and that's keeping anybody like you from trying to run mine."

"I'll run you out, we'll run you out of town."

The marshal's forefinger leveled directly at Newlin's eyes. "That's what you figured to do all right, stampede the town. But you forgot somebody might have the guts to turn the herd."

"What the hell you talking about?"

"We wasn't going to let him stampede us, Luther," the mayor said earnestly; "but you wouldn't want this story about you going on neither."

The marshal seemed almost to smile. "I got a little story of my own to tell now Johnny's took enough rope to hang hisself." He looked across the heads of the crowd toward the rear of the room. "Come up here, Hortense."

CHAPTER 17

The chore-woman of the Drovers Hotel arose from her inconspic-
uous seat and moved forward down the boot-cluttered aisle, her
middle-aged face sallow in the lamplight. She looked frightened;
but a faint, determined smile quivered on her lips. A buzz of mingled curiosity and disconcertion went through the audience.

"Right up here," Luther pointed to a spot directly under the
chandelier. "And turn around so everybody can see you."

The woman did as she was told, clearing her throat.

"What's your name," the marshal asked her, "in case anybody
don't know?"

"Hortense Bass."

"You're chore-woman at the Drovers, ain't you?"

She nodded.

"And last fall you used to work at the Portugese?"

She nodded again.

Johnny Newlin had paled. His eyes flicked toward the spectators and returned to the other members of the council and then
to the marshal. "What's she doing here?" His voice was agitated.
"She's out of order." He looked at the mayor. "You said this was
a council meeting. Not a trial you said."

"What the hell you complaining about? You started it."

"And I'm the one aims to finish it." Luther turned to Newlin.
"You're going to look like that fool all right, Johnny, and there
ain't a goddam thing you can do about it."

The saloon keeper started to his feet. "I ain't got to sit here
and listen to lies!"

"Not if you don't want to get hit over the head. That's my
business you said."

"You threatening me?"

"Same as you been doing me all night. Right now you're going
to set there and listen real good." Luther's glare shoved him down
again muttering an obscenity. The marshal turned back to the
woman. "Go ahead."

Hortense licked her dry lips.

"Tell them what you done for Johnny, Hortense."

136

She inhaled nervously. "He done some things for me. I ain't saying he didn't. When I got sick he talked Mister Crum into my job at the Drovers."

Knowing the nature of her sickness Doc Bowman in the second row shuddered again at her employment by a public hostelry. He had tried to dissuade Bill from hiring her but his friend had filed a creditor's protest about the poor old biddy starving to death which was the sort of whimsy that had molded their friendship. Someday surely they'd have state health laws for godssake. Doc at least could hope.

"And Johnny loaned me a hundred dollars once," she continued. "I liked working for him. He was fair." Her dull eyes became duller and she licked her lips again. "But I also liked somebody started in the Portugese about a year ago. Liked her real good same as you would a daughter." Her chin began to tremble.

"You ain't answering my question," Luther frowned not unkindly. "What did Johnny Newlin tell you to do Saturday noon?"

"Yes I am answering, Mister Cain. I'm telling you why I done it and then why I told you I done it. I owed it to Johnny like he said. But I didn't owe him hurting the girl, not when she's got out of the Portugese and doing nice work, kind of work she ought to be doing." Hortense's voice lowered. "Not when she's fell in love." The woman's gaze became supplicant. "She's so happy, Mister Cain. You got to never hurt her."

The marshal's jaw dropped for an instant.

"Shut up, Hortense!" Johnny yelled at her.

Luther swung toward the Portugese's proprietor savagely and silently and Johnny quailed from him and the marshal returned his attention quickly to the woman. In the back of the room Mustang Johnson and Enos Dowling and Latigo Eyler got up quietly and left. Indian Jesse's expression was impassive. Duke Grimes looked confused. Jason T.M. Pickett's face had grown more florid and his glance was blazing on Newlin.

In his disconcertion Luther seemed to notice none of these things. "What you mean, Hortense?"

"When I seen they was making it look like you was a stage robber I knowed how much it'd hurt that girl. Sure she ain't my girl natural but she is in here like I said." She touched her thin bosom with a shaking finger. "I told you about Johnny getting me to steal that silver toothpick because I want her to go on being happy. Even if they throw me dead in the crick like Johnny said I want her to do that." The woman sighed without artifice. "I'm sick anyhow. Maybe I'd feel better in the crick."

Bill Crum couldn't help himself: "What girl?"

"Why, Carrie Shaw, Mayor."

"You didn't tell me a reason," Luther muttered. "You only told me what you done and what it looked like they was doing. 'Lowed you hated Johnny, Hortense."

"No, Marshal, I like him."

"She's lying!" Newlin said in a strangling voice.

The marshal ignored him. "Johnny said he'd kill you if you told?"

Hortense shrugged. "Somebody would. But he never done nothing bad to me." She looked at the Portugese's proprietor. "You ain't really going to kill me are you, Johnny? You got to understand I couldn't let you hurt nobody sweet as Carrie."

Newlin ground his jaws together without speaking. Saliva flecked the corners of his mouth.

"He ain't going to kill you," Luther said very slowly. His words hung in the sweat-stench of the air like small thunderheads. He turned toward the spectators. "Everybody in this room take a good look at this woman and take a good listen to what I'm saying. If anything happens to Hortense Bass I'll know who done it. I'll know who to come after. And I'll come after him 'til one of us is dead." He turned back to Johnny Newlin. "And you'll be first if you're that much a fool. I see we're missing a few of your cronies; you make sure to pass along that word. You understand?"

Johnny looked as though there wasn't much doubt of it.

"Now bygod," the mayor said, "this here meeting's adjourned for sure." This time he didn't have to pound his point home with the minute book.

Luther took Hortense's arm and walked wordlessly with her to the door.

"Yessir, Marshal," Carl Norris whispered happily to himself, "yes indeed!"

Preacher Smith winked at Noble Buck.

Noble and Billy and David grinned.

At the back of the room attorney Jim Watts smiled tolerantly at the ceiling, his eyes not altogether amused.

CHAPTER 18

The humming-buzzing continued, sometimes harmonious, more often discordant. The deathly specter lunged at Mark Keller and veered away, deflected as much by his stubbornness as by the virtuosity surrounding him. The stark room in which his body lay was far from his dream's haunts at the moment; those, sliding over one another, held the tired faces of his parents, a happy girl's tragic annihilation, newspaper city rooms, a rare moonlit street on a memorable night, sullen courtrooms, loaded buses hissing into the city's terminal unloading city problems, a lightning flash, thunder crashing. Mattie's eyes were lifted to his, their sweet moisture quenching an old fire. The blare of a siren crushed her murmuring "I'm so proud of you but I'm afraid for you too, please take care of yourself—and of others." And when he'd asked about "others" she'd looked uncertain herself and said that "Human beings can make mistakes without being bad." And he'd said that "Bad is bad and good is good."

"Can't see what's laming him," Noble said as much to himself as to Solly. "Don't reckon it amounts to a whole lot, only enough he favors it some I noticed." The fourteen-year-old iceman facing toward the ancient horse's rear had clamped Shag's raised left-front hoof between his bent knees and was scraping dirt from it with a stick. The gelding's traces rattled as he swung his head around stiffly to nip at the boy's available buttocks, the denim of those patched with flour sacking. Noble slapped the animal's muzzle with the stick without looking backward or straightening. "Goldang it, Shag, quit that." After a few more moments of scraping for a rock or other evidence of the morning's small (hopefully) problem, Noble let the hoof fall, stood upright and shrugged around the horse's rump at the merchant-volunteer fireman. "Nothing as I can see, Mister Berg. Not a daggone thing." He sounded encouraged and discouraged at the same time.

Solly by both nature and interest felt obliged to comment; but he recognized the need for tact. "He's a fine horse, Noble, very dependable. Yes indeed." He cleared his throat. "How old is he? Getting along in years is he?"

"Nick Caldwell when he come through the other day I asked

139

him to look in Shag's mouth. About thirty, Nick said. I didn't figure him that old. I mean I don't." Noble spoke to himself again: "I mean I hope not."

"Don't worry, Noble, the old fellow's not quite ready for the bone-yard yet." Solly realized at Noble's almost imperceptible wince that his tact had failed him momentarily. He thought he might make amends; he thumbed over his shoulder at the firehouse double-doors. "Old Maude in there isn't any colt you know and Cricket's right behind her. And those two are the best team of any fire brigade in Kansas. They pull that water wagon like it was feathers, you saw so yourself when us members of the Prairie Hawks," his voice became resonant with pride, "fought the Longhorn fire last spring."

Noble remembered very well the April night when the saloon had begun smoking and flickering ominously and threatening the whole east side of the plaza with its evil orange grin visible through its door. Like what quickly had become the fifty other citizens of irrelevant sexes and ages supplementing the regular brigade in two parallel, facing lines he had helped hand-pass the wagon's stiff leather buckets between its water vats and the saloon's flames. Women and children mostly had formed the return empty-bucket line, men passing along the filled buckets and the regular Prairie Hawks manning the ends of both lines, dipping up water and starting it along at one end and throwing it onto the searing fire and starting the empties back at the other. The flames, although less belligerent, still hadn't been entirely exhausted when the vats had bottomed out which had required a galloping trip up past the firehouse and east on Pacific Street to Owl Creek—brigade members and their buckets hanging onto every hold the wagon had offered—for a frenzied and only partial refill. In the wagon's absence other members had redeployed the lines between the saloon and a succession of former whiskey barrels filled with water which the brigade maintained around the plaza and it was Noble's extra job to keep full. By good fortune the interim wetting had kept the fire at bay until the returned wagon's dousing had killed it for good. Also for good generally the adult male firefighters and a number of plain fire watchers thereupon had adjourned to the Shawnee Saloon to wet their parched whistles, the Longhorn still having been very much a part of the scenery but too smokey for already stinging eyes.

140

"You fellers done a fine job on that fire all right, Mister Berg."

"Lot of people did; I remember you passing those buckets along like they were red-hot, Noble. You're a husky boy for your age; you may be big enough to join the Prairie Hawks yourself one of these days. Guess it's manhandling that ice. But I was talking more about our horses that night, how they might have some age on them like yours there maybe but still plenty of chutzpah."

Noble looked quizzical.

"Get-up-and-go," Solly grinned. "No, my young friend, don't sell us oldtimers short now."

"You're not old, Mister Berg."

"Older than—" he pointed—"what you say his name is?"

"Shag."

"Older than Shag. Some days I feel older than Methuselah like when it's my turn to come down here early like this to feed the team and clean their stalls and then go work in my own store twelve hours. I'm a little sore-footed myself by the time I get home some days. But that doesn't mean I'm ready for the bone-yard either, in a manner of speaking."

The youngster returned the merchant-volunteer fireman's broadening grin. "Well I better be on my way, Mister Berg; it's my day for the east side and all south of the track. Sure been nice talking to you though. I want to say that." The iceman climbed onto the wagon's seat and gathered its reins. "Well thanks again and 'bye now." He waved to the merchant-volunteer fireman and turned to his horse—"Git-up, Shag!"—and continued into his day.

His day had started as usual at five o'clock with a quick arising at the combined insistence of neighborhood roosters and his distended bladder and had been urged on by Mother Swain's corn cakes, molasses, milk from the cow she kept out back, and coffee brewed to the thick blackness Howard Smith likened to Hell at midnight and Wyoming Nye (not in Mother's presence) said was stronger than the goddam bust-skull whiskey he served out-of-favor customers at the Shawnee. Before leaving his room the second time to go down to breakfast—his first having been to visit the outhouse beside the cow shed not far from the well, a typical juxtaposition which gave Doc Bowman the shudders—Noble had pulled from under his bed the carbine Marshal Cain had jerked away from Jason Pickett in the Portugese and turned over to him. Since the day of that gift he hadn't taken the saddle-gun out of his room for fear its former owner should reclaim it on sight; and it was now his most prized possession not only because it was a Winchester '73 but because Luther Cain had given it to him.

A personal gift from Luther Cain was like one from President Grant or Abraham Lincoln or Noble's former teacher's heroine, Victoria C. Woodhull, 1872 Presidential candidate of the Equal Rights Party whose non-election day was spent in jail. Incidentally Miss Haniford's—his former teacher's—occasional lectures on subjects not covered by McGuffey's Readers had included (along with Victoria Woodhull's daring espousal of such things as abolition of the death penalty and easing of divorce laws and universal government and birth control) her own belief in the virtue of total honesty; and his recollection of Miss Haniford's teaching that morning again had caused Noble to reflect briefly on how he had come to possess the Winchester. Dishonestly? By unlawful taking? Even by "robbery?" Whose robbery? Not Noble's, he simply had held out his hands when the gun had been shoved into them by Marshal Cain. But equally surely the lawman wasn't a robber; he had proved that in the council meeting the other night; he was a lawman and lawmen enforced the law, not broke it. He was Luther Cain. Noble had shaken his head in minute frustration. It had been a little too much for him so early in the morning. He had returned the rifle to its cache and headed for the back porch. One thing though: he was going to do his best to hang onto the— *his*—Winchester and win next July Fourth's turkey shoot with it; and he would go on from there to win shoot after shoot until he had qualified for the Grand International Rifle Match like last September's out East when the Americans had whipped the Irishmen. He had read about last year's in the *Police Gazette*. Maybe he'd have to take along a Sharp's buffalo gun too; some of the distances were up to a thousand yards, too far for a carbine.

After breakfast he had walked eastward on Pacific Street, crossed West and continued in the slanting sunlight along the north side of the plaza past the Drover's and Allgood's Leathers and Berg's Dry Goods and the Farmer's Restaurant—the only establishment already open—and Tinsley's General Store and the Shawnee and, crossing East Street, past the fire house and undertaker's and Gopher Hole Saloon and Plains Hotel and stage station to the ice house where daily his career began and ended.

He had known this day was going to be an early fall scorcher;

142

the sun's low yellowing rays had buffeted his chin and chest below hat's shade like a sirocco. He had taken his time leading Shag from his stall and harnessing him to the wagon and backing that against the elevated ice-house doorway and floor, sweeping the straw from the next ice-tier, chipping out various-size chunks of his merchandise—cut from Owl Creek's pond last winter—tonging those into the wagon bed, throwing a bleached tarpaulin over the load, dipping half a dozen wooden buckets into the creek and hanging them on the wagon's sides, climbing aboard the outfit, and with a "Git-up, Shag, gee, boy!" starting along Pacific on his rounds.

The time he had taken doing all this hadn't been a measure of its thought; the routine long ago had become rote; so he had thought some more about his Winchester and the marshal and shooting matches and the astounding good fortune of his friendship with Luther Cain—his and David's and Billy's friendship with the marshal but mostly his he felt somehow—and how scary it was at the same time to hear about the marshal's several run-ins with several bad people, none of whom except for Mister Newlin had Noble known personally. Actually Mister Newlin had been friendly to Noble when they had met almost every other day as the iceman had made his deliveries to the Portugese and Noble had wondered why the saloon-keeper hadn't wanted to be friendly with the marshal as well. It had seemed to him anybody in his right mind would want to be friendly with Luther Cain. He had recalled pleasantly seeing Miss Carrie Shaw and Marshal Cain a few times walking together and talking in obvious friendship. He liked Miss Shaw, too. She had the nicest smile he'd ever seen, in fact she was the nicest lady altogether. He had ignored what a former school friend—not David or Billy—had smirked once about her, something the boy had overheard his father tell another man.

At this point in his thinking Noble had pulled up Shag in front of the Plains and made his delivery there; and when they had continued on past the still-somnolent Gopher Hole and the drawn blinds of the undertaker's he had noticed the horse's slight limp for the first time and had reined in at the fire station to inspect Shag's hoof and talk with Mister Berg about that and what had turned out to be several other things. Mister Berg was quite a talker but very friendly. Noble sure appreciated friendly people

143

like Mister Berg and Marshal Cain and Miss Shaw and Mister Newlin and Mayor Crum. The mayor always spoke to Noble as they passed on the street although usually unsmilingly; the mayor didn't seem to be a smiling man most of the time as undertaker Dale Darling didn't either.

After topping off the evaporation of the East Street corner fire barrel with one of his water buckets and stopping at the Shawnee Saloon where teen-age Snowball Lee was emptying spittoons across the board sidewalk into the street and at the Farmer's Restaurant whose maw breathed grease fumes into the gradually tainting day, Noble guided Shag around the Drover's corner to the two-story building's kitchen door. When he shouldered a hundred-pound ice block into the room, staggering under its weight, he found Luther Cain standing beside the stove drinking an after-breakfast cup of coffee and talking with Teddy Quillin who had decided last fall to trade a chuck wagon for a hotel and had gone to cooking for the Drover's. The cook stepped over Luther's sprawled mongrel and went into a stone-walled, ventilated closet to open its ice chest. The marshal drained his cup and gave the iceman a hand with the block, gripping one of the tongs' handles.

"Thanks, Marshal," Noble grunted. "Ever bit helps."

"Even if you could've handled it yourself."

The iceman grinned. "Even if." He slammed the chest shut.

"Many these hundred-pounders in a day, Noble?"

"Besides this place only the Plains and Farmer's and Lone Star and butcher shop ever-other day. Rest of my customers takes mostly fifties and twenty-fives. When the weather ain't so hot not even that many."

"Sounds enough to me."

"Well I better be going, Mister Cain. Thanks again. You too, Mister Quillin."

Teddy nodded as he latched the closet door behind them.

The marshal picked up his hat. "Which way you going from here?"

"Over to Wagner's Grocery and down the east side to the Longhorn and then across the track." Noble's eyes widened suddenly. "Want a ride, Marshal?"

"Only going to the courthouse but figured I might."

The iceman couldn't believe it almost. He crossed the kitchen

144

quickly and held open the door to the outside. "Right thisaway. Shag and me don't have riders much, only David Berg and Billy Plunkett and the like. We'd be mighty pleased. 'Course them boys hang onto the back step but you'll set up front with me."

A few minutes later Noble had brimmed the fire barrel at the hotel corner and he and his two passengers—the dog had jumped onto the seat between them—were creaking behind Shag across the plaza's north side toward Wagner's. The grocery was the second building down the east side from Pacific below the Stockmen and Farmers Bank and Guttman's Drug Store; and just beyond it at mid-block Doc Bowman's office and Lester Blaine's barber shop leaned together in mutual support as their owners had been known to do on rare occasions like after last fall's grange picnic.

There had been good reason then for Doc and Lester to commiserate mutually. Along with their friend Cal Hubbard they had lost to the grasshopper plague all that was left of the drought-stunted corn crop they'd helped that good farmer finance. Cal being a teetotaler they had felt obliged to drink for his misery too. Although they'd taken their chances Cal had said over and over he was going to repay them; indeed he had managed already to make a payment on what he insisted was due each of them from the sale of buffalo hides he'd fetched back from a two-week hunt farther west; and they were reconciled that the balance should follow eventually. They were just glad, all three of them, that he hadn't mortgaged his farm to the bank which should have had to foreclose because of the scores of defaults axing debtors and bankers alike during those desperate months a year ago. Things had been bad with all farmers and local stockmen throughout Kansas and still were not good, just maybe a little better. Early in the current spring the eggs left by last summer's insect swarms had hatched and again there was an attack but not as bad. The Texans had managed to trail their great herds up to the Kansas railheads and load them quickly enough onto east-bound trains to avoid the worst of the drought and grasshopper troubles—if compounding those to some extent for some farmers, at least bringing dollars into railroad-town economies. And although hampered by a statutory requirement of county officials' endorsement the railroad's free transportation for relief supplies had helped a little the previous year as also had, and to a diminishing degree still did, locally organized relief efforts. During the winter the War Department had issued army surplus blankets and clothing to the frontier's destitute and near-frozen rural population; but a lot of the intended beneficiaries hadn't got a glimpse much less a feel of those items, "bureaucracy being ever thus" as Carl Norris had put it in an editorial. Early in the new year the federal Department of Agriculture had distributed carloads of free seed for spring planting and the Kansas legislature had appropriated funds for a state relief committee which had worked mainly through local organizations which also mainly had got into internecine feuds, again to the *Republican*'s editorial disgust.

Not many scars of those slowly fading bad times were visible about the plaza however—only a few unrepaired wooden sidewalks and a sagging roof or two and through the Shawnee's morning-wide door some ragged sleepers on its benches (Wyoming Nye had been very poor himself once) as Noble Buck and Luther Cain and Luther's dog jounced across the wide, rutted, dusty space. Noble never had felt more proud, the lolling-tongued Spot more befriended, and Luther, at least for the moment he indulged himself, more content even while realizing contentment for him was risky. The iceman glanced sideways under his yellow straw hat at the marshal's profile under the latter's round-crowned black one to relish Luther's presence once more but not before the lawman's eyes had resumed their customary vigilance.

"Nice day all right ain't it, Marshal?"

"Mite warm for fall."

Noble ran a thumb under his leather shoulder pad. "Yep I was saying to myself going to be a scorcher."

The marshal touched the youth's arm. "Hold up a spell."

Noble pulled on Shag's reins. "Whoa."

"Morning, Doc," Luther called to the physician emerging from his office. "Supposed to be going to work not quitting this time of day."

"Two of you look like Don Quixote and Sancho," the physician called back "with that ass between you."

"Beats a horse's ass."

"Noble," Doc called earnestly, "don't you give a damn who you're seen with?"

The iceman hadn't been involved previously in such witty not to say exalted repartee; but he gave it a try, remembering the

146

physician's patient Latigo Eyler. "Least I choose my company good."

Doc reflected for a moment. "But I swear I'd take care of any cowboy came along you know. Hippocratic oath."

Noble grinned at his passenger. "I swear by my company."

Luther's eyes crinkled above his moustache. "Throw in your hand, Doc, you lost the pot." He elbowed the boy. "Move on. We got stylisher folks to talk to, Noble. And I'll have to say I like yours."

Buoyed by the marshal's sanction and the physician's laughter Noble slapped the reins on Shag's rump in a daze of felicity. Four buildings farther just past the Longhorn he let the lawman off at the courthouse. He would check the adjacent saloon's ice needs on his return trip. "Thanks for riding with me, Marshal."

"Other way around, Son. Keep that in mind." Luther's moustache tilted as he nodded toward the wagon's load. "And keep cool."

It was in harmony with his day when the iceman met Carrie Shaw a few minutes later in front of Jake Barlow's smithy where he'd reined up after crossing the track into South Street. As usual meeting her tightened his chest and thickened his tongue. "Good morning, M'am," he managed, jumping down from his wagon. "Howdy, Mister Barlow." He guessed the two friends had been passing the time of day as Carrie paused on her way to the plaza and Jake waited for his forge to heat up. She returned Noble's greeting amiably as always. So did Jake in his less outgoing manner. Noble told the blacksmith about Shag's limp showing up that morning and while the big, leather-aproned man took a look at the horse's left-front hoof and ran a talented hand over the animal's leg and shoulder the iceman groped for words to keep Carrie from walking on her way. An interesting news item didn't spring to mind; neither did a witticism notwithstanding his recent practice. He exhaled an "Ah" without a finish as Eddie Foy might have put it. That comedian had appeared on the Portugese stage last spring. Noble felt like a comedian who wasn't getting any laughs. He tried again. "Ah . . . I was wondering if you'd want a piece of ice, Miss Shaw."

Carrie's smile held no hint of teasing. "Why thank you, Noble, I sure would on such a warm morning."

The surprise of her assent immobilized him for a moment. Then he hurried around to the wagon's tailgate, picked up a handsize chip and brought it to her.

She started to accept it and then hesitated. "Wait, it'll be so cold." She dipped into the pocket of her muslin dress, pulled out a hankerchief, wrapped that around the bottom of the piece of ice, and took it from him. "There. Thank you."

"You're welcome, M'am." He tried to swallow the small commotion in his throat. "Glad to. Any time. You bet. Ah . . ." He sounded as though he were about to gargle but nothing else escaped his fluster and apparently wasn't going to without help.

Carrie came to his rescue. "Cools a body down."

He didn't know about her body (except for its grace) but it didn't cool his down any; he hadn't passed his fourteenth year among mortals without encountering passion and the impact of her particular aura was a lot to cope with. Carrie, of course, was aware enough to have sensed not only his fever but something of its cause. Her rescue attempt had failed. She seemed obliged to try once more.

"You happen to see Ruth Blaine as you come down here, Noble?"

This time it worked. He found his voice, more loudly in fact than necessary. "No, M'am, this ain't the Blaines' day for ice and I didn't run into her on the street neither." He lowered his voice with some effort. "Ah but if I see her on the way back I'll tell her you asked. I'll sure do that." He seemed to be making up for lost talk-time. "I seen Marshal Cain though. Give him a ride in my wagon, him and his dog. Took him to the courthouse. We talked to Doc Bowman on the way. Doc sure is a joker." He chuckled at the recollection. "We traded jokes back and to. Marshal Cain said . . ."

"Your horse might have sprang his shoulder," the blacksmith interrupted, "if it ain't plain old-age rheumatism. Nothing to fret about; couple days' time and some liniment ought to bring him out of it I judge."

The morning's second reference to Shag's advanced years didn't make Noble feel better than the first but the optimistic prognosis cheered him. He didn't need much cheering because talking with Luther Cain and Carrie Shaw in one day had exhilarated him already to the point of euphoria.

148

"I sure thank you for taking a look at him, Mister Barlow."
He reached earnestly for his pants' pocket. "How much I owe you?"

"That'll be about forty dollars, Noble. I can add it to your tally."

"Forty . . . ?" The youth actually had paled under his tan for an instant before wits returned. "Oh sure, just add it to my hundred." He shrugged at the woman. "Got to pay high for the best."

Carrie laughed. "That's what I always used to say."

Noble's joining laughter was faintly shaky but he felt if she wasn't embarrassed he had no right to be. His extended hand was engulfed by the blacksmith's. "Like I said, Mister Barlow, I thank you for your help but I'd feel better paying something for it."

"You keep asking me and I'll let you." Jake dropped the iceman's hand. "Learn to quit when you winning, Son."

"Like I done," Carrie smiled.

There was every reason for her happy mood to persist. It was a lovely day; the ice she held was pleasant on her tongue; neither Jake Barlow nor Noble Buck were personifications of trouble as far as she was concerned, past, present, or future. Things were good. She was on her way to a good breakfast at the Lone Star and after that to a good visit with Ruth Blaine about a good dress she was going to make for a good friend of her friend.

Noble couldn't miss the woman's high spirits; he was glad for those and attributed them to her normally friendly nature which surely was at least half their story. If the story had other chapters those were fine with him too. Climbing back onto his wagon he tossed to her and the smith a good-bye salute as he'd seen troopers at the fort do and clucked Shag into motion down and across South Street toward the Eastern.

The previous day on the plaza Max Coleman had requested an increase in the saloon's usual twenty-five pounds of ice to a hundred in honor as well as accommodation of the beer shipment he'd got from Kansas City on the morning train. Ten kegs Mister Coleman had said; liquid manna which according to station agent Ed Sarver hadn't flowed also over Johnny Newlin's Portugese for some reason. Johnny of course had fired off a telegram to the beer distributor about his shortage, the betrayal of his longtime patronage, and had been telegraphed in return to take the matter up with the obvious miscreant: the railroad or more particularly its train crew because everybody knew train crews liked beer and didn't like frontier-town riffraff, especially Portugese-drunken cowboys who shot out their engines' headlights and fist-fought their brakemen and clogged their tracks with cattle.

Mister Newlin had showed guts as well as gall in appealing to Marshal Cain about the matter, Noble had heard, but the marshal had said beer theft wasn't his line, he specialized in stagecoach robbery. This was reported to have frustrated Mister Newlin so much that he had become momentarily as rigid as a tombstone and no more able than one to talk and then had stalked out of the courthouse on legs as stiff as a spavined horse's. Noble hoped he felt better today; usually he was a pleasant man to visit although his inexplicable hostility toward Marshal Cain had put a crimp in Noble's regard for him, had sort of put Noble in the middle it might be said.

When the iceman finished wrestling the hundred-pounder into the bin behind the Eastern's bar, to be ice-picked later by the bartender into a cooling cache for the beer, and admiring the polishing job Mister Coleman was giving the imported mirror and agreeing with the proprietor that General Grant wasn't as bad a a president as a few malcontents claimed, he hawed Shag around the corner's Wholesale Exchange Company and pulled on past the gun shop to a halt in front of the Portugese. The establishment's owner was standing outside its swinging half-doors explaining loudly to some early customers, as Noble overheard climbing to the ground, why his saloon wasn't going to be pushing beer across its bar that morning as the Eastern was.

Clearly Johnny Newlin didn't relish the admission. "The goddam railroad drank it! But I've got a shipment coming, Boys."

Noble walked around to the rear of the wagon. "Morning, Mister Newlin," he called from its tail-step. "Only twenty-five today?"

Welcoming the distraction if not its phrasing the saloonkeeper called back he wanted "a goddam hundred!" and strode from his critics across to the iceman, lowering his voice to the security of Noble's discretion. "I meant twenty-five 'til I get my beer, then the hundred."

"Sure, Mister Newlin, I understand."

"Max got a hundred I reckon," Johnny muttered

150

"Yep, the Eastern was lucky." The youth began picking loose the twenty-five-pound order. "Not having his beer stole the way you done." He nodded for emphasis. "You was just plain unlucky."

"You're a savvy kid."

"Yessir." The iceman tonged the freed block toward his belly, noted with a glance that Mister Newlin's friends were dispersing and heaved it onto his leathered shoulder. "Best get this inside 'fore it melts."

The proprietor followed the boy into the saloon and watched him stow his delivery in the large zinc-lined icebox, one of the Portugese's more exotic trappings although not quite on a par with the Eastern's mirror in Johnny's secret, covetous opinion.

Without Max Coleman knowing it Johnny had been sneaking up on that mirror for a good while; maybe one of these days he could get Max drunk enough to play draw poker for it against the icebox. Johnny prided himself on his draw poker but of late had laid low about that particular talent in view of the game's possibility. Max probably should demand considerable boot with the icebox because he prized the mirror so highly and had come by it so hard, having ridden with it from New Orleans up the Mississippi and Missouri by riverboat and across a good deal of Kansas by the new train; but Johnny knew Max also had a mighty hankering for the Portugese's zinc-lined icebox—not exactly an inconsequential item itself—and a high regard for his own poker skill. The key was getting him drunk or at least staying more sober than he; and Max was no dunce when it came to shenanigans. One of these days Johnny should get the job done and thereafter be the owner of both the mirror and the zinc-lined icebox; and then the only thing lacking his consummate proprietorship of his business and of his being should be Carrie's waking from her aberrant dream.

Carrie wasn't cut to a sewing pattern; she wasn't meant for a sonofabitching marshal; she was what she was: the best goddam cowboy teaser in his stable. And goddammit more than that, as he had come paradoxically and astoundingly and painfully to recognize of late, she had dropped some sort of loop over his emotions, tangling his preconceptions with emergent reality, his lust with affection to say the very least and mixing the hell out of him especially since she'd been showing up places like church suppers and Prairie Hawks dances with that strutting bastard.

151

"Well, Mister Newlin, hope your beer comes in by day after tomorrow." Noble slammed the icebox door. "See you then." He put out his hand and the saloonkeeper shook it. "Hope this nice weather holds out."

"Nice and hot?" Johnny smiled faintly. "Good for the ice business."

"Betchy." The iceman moved in the direction of the doorway, paused and looked back at his customer. "Being it's so hot you wouldn't want a piece of ice to suck on like I give Miss Shaw while ago?"

The image of Carrie's open wet lips disconcerted the proprietor only for an instant. "Hell no." He cleared his throat. "What's in the icebox is fine." He raised a hand briefly. "Much obliged."

"I'm much obliged for you business, Mister Newlin."

"Seen Carrie Shaw a while ago did you? Take some ice there?"

"Ain't been past Lane's yet. Seen her on South Street headed for the Lone Star I reckon. Eats breakfast there I noticed. Sure a nice lady." Pride seeped into Noble's voice. "I run into lot of friends on my rounds. Like her and you and Mister Barlow this morning. And Marshal Cain, give him a ride to the courthouse. And Doc Bowman." The boy's tone turned confidential for a sentence. "I kind of hope something comes of Marshal Cain and Miss Shaw. And Mister Berg showed me . . ."

"I hope Carrie Shaw's got more goddam sense than mixing with that road agent!"

Noble had forgotten temporarily about the trumped-up robbery. He wished he hadn't mentioned Luther Cain. At the same time he was amazed and offended by the saloonkeeper's continued pretense of the marshal's outlawry. The charge had been repudiated publicly and now he must do it privately. "What road agent is that, Mister Newlin?"

"The one trying to take over this town, the one told Hortense Bass he'd kill her if she didn't lie for him . . ."

"It was the other way around," Noble wedged into Johnny's irate indictment.

". . . the one so goddam mean he makes a rattlesnake look good-natured and got a lot of folks thinking he's a lawman instead of lawbreaker, the one got some poison in him makes him a hater I'm telling you, that's the one!"

The iceman saw the odds of his easing the standoff between

Mister Newlin and Marshal Cain weren't in his favor so he decided to fold out of the game at least for the time being. "Reckon you're entitled to your slant but I can't see it thataway." He headed for the swinging doors again. "Best be going now."

As Noble stepped across the threshold he almost stumbled. He had been shaken more than he wanted to admit by the proprietor's diatribe. It was mostly lies. Mostly? All lies, first that accusation about the marshal threatening Hortense Bass and then all the rest of it. Why should Hortense Bass fear Luther Cain when they both felt the way they clearly did about Miss Shaw? Hortense and Miss Shaw and Marshal Cain were friends. Johnny Newlin was the unfriendly one, that seemed plain even if he'd never been unfriendly to Noble. The iceman's head throbbed as he climbed onto his seat and slapped the reins on Shag's rump. Probably coming out from the dim saloon into the glaring sunlight had given him his headache.

From the Portugese he reined the horse and wagon in a big u-turn back along Jimson and across the bottom of South Street to the Maverick Saloon where, as at the Shawnee on Pacific Street above the track, the day's activity hadn't got much beyond another youngster's listless sweeping up and emptying spittoons. There were two drinkers at the bar and one customer from the previous night asleep in his chair at a poker table, head fallen on his folded arms, but no call for ice from the bartender. Noble considered it wasn't as classy a place as the Portugese despite its heavy nighttime play when the Texas cowboys were in town. Ice wasn't among its priorities.

"Don't take no wooden nickles, Bobby," he cautioned the sweeper-emptier as he got back onto his wagon seat.

"Found a dollar this morning," Bobby confided hoarsely behind a cupped palm, glancing backward for an instant, "on the floor next to one of the tables."

"The one where that waddy's passed out?"

Bobby's forefinger flew to his lips. "He ain't passed out, just sleeping; might wake up for lordssake."

"Didn't drop off his table I reckon?"

Bobby grimaced and ducked his shoulders. "Quiet for lordssake, Noble."

After the iceman had left a ten-pounder each at Everett Lane's and another rooming house on Jimson Street—both owners and most of their tenants had been introduced to iced tea by traveler Carrie Shaw—he backtracked Shag and the wagon up across the railroad to the plaza, delivered a twenty-fiver and some comments about the morning's heat to the Longhorn's day bartender and short-cut through a rutted alley between the saloon and Doctor Rice's dental and eyeglasses office to the houses ranging eastward toward Owl Creek. By the time he had brought his welcome service to all of those it was almost noontime judging by the pounding sun. Gratefully he turned Shag and himself back to Bolinger's Stable and Mother Swain's next-door dining table.

Following Shag's hay and maybe his own pork roast and plenty of water for them both he should head his horse and him-self—not really reluctantly because they both pretty much liked their jobs—northeastward with their enjoyment into that part of the town's sprawl of homes where they had a good many friends, as they did in just about every other part. And there were a num-ber of fire barrels up there to fill besides.

No two ways about it, Noble Buck had an important job to do and a spate of important friends like Marshal Cain and Miss Shaw and Mister Berg and Mister Newlin and Doctor Bowman and Mayor Crum and some not so important but good all right like David Berg and Billy Plunkett and Uncle Vince and Mother Swain. And Shag.

After all that's what life was all about.

He had a good life all right.

Mighty.

He was at that precise point in his reflections when he fell off his wagon seat dead.

Noble hadn't heard the shot but Luther Cain had as he was walking down the steps of the courthouse toward his noon meal at the Drovers. And he saw Noble fall sideways the six feet to the dusty ground, yellow straw hat bouncing off at the impact, old horse lurching a couple of steps forward in surprise. He sprinted across half the plaza toward the hideously still boy. The shot's sound had echoed up from below the railroad; a Sharps rifle shot the marshal's experience told him. Doc Bowman now running from another direction had heard a nightmarish thunderclap after a cloudless bolt. Carrie Shaw's startlement back at her sewing had needle-pricked her thumb. Jake Barlow earlier had seen two buckskinned men staggering eastward arm in arm across the bottom of South Street, one of them carrying a rifle, and had thought it was a mite soon in the day even for buffalo hunters to be drunk; and Johnny Newlin had heard what turned out to be the same two make a shooting bet in the Portugese.

The iceman had lost the bet.

Luther and Doc reached Noble's body in their same gusting breath. The physician knelt beside it and put two fingers against the throat's carotid artery and with the other hand jerked open the shirt. Leaning down he put his ear to the white naked chest, leaving his fingers on the artery. After a moment while Luther stared at the obscenity Doc straightened on his knees, dropped his hand from the artery and with his other gently turned the shattered side of the young head away from the sun and gathering flies into the hot, receiving dust.

"Gone. My God, Luther, he's gone."

"Sonofabitchinbastardshithell." The marshal's nearly inaudible snarl seemed to drip like acid from beneath his moustache. The tendons of his neck whipped into relief as he swung his stare southward. Resolve which had seemed hammered from him by disbelief the past few minutes hardened almost visibly. "Come from down yonder," he rumbled. "Going down there."

Doc got to his feet, turning his attention to the people trotting and walking fast from all directions toward the plaza's dreadful tableau. "Nothing to do, Folks. It's Noble Buck. Shot dead." He pointed at one of the converging group. "Get Dale Darling, Wyoming."

"Who the hell want to do a thing like that, Marshal?" someone asked himself and the group and the lawman's back moving away above long-striding legs.

"Reckon the marshal's heading to find out," someone else said.

"Plain can't understand it."

"It's not for understanding," a woman's voice shrilled; "it's this town, this terrible prairie; oh I saw them kill him, I saw him fall; this wind and dust and mud and grasshoppers and nobody out there to talk to, nobody in town but twice a year to visit and then it's fighting and shooting . . ."

"Now, Mother, you're upset, this has upset you." Her huge, weathered husband laid his arm tenderly across her shoulders like an oxen yoke. She was relatively huge herself with child. "We'll keep going home now; wagon's loaded beside the Drovers with the kids in it waiting for us, we'll go on home. Can't help this poor boy."

"Dirt floor, dirt wall," she began to sob, "no window, soot faster than I can clean," her voice rising almost to a shriek, "sick cow!"

"I'm building us a lumber house, Abigail." His mortified glance locked with Doc's for an instant across Noble's body. "Be done by snow I promise; and got medicine in the wagon for Ol' Bess."

The physician spoke upward into the homesteader's vulnerable gaze. "You're way out of town, Mister, come past my office over there, pick up something calming for the lady." Somehow he managed to smile at the trembling woman. "I'll be along soon as we're done here." He turned to the rest of the pressing crowd. "Stand back, Folks, nothing to do here. Please go about your business. Undertaker's on his way, let him get through here, don't hold things up, they're bad enough already." His eyes suddenly flashed with rage which everybody seemed to recognize wasn't directed at any of them. "Goddammit, move!"

Sadly they began to do his bidding.

CHAPTER 19

"You missed it, you lost, you owe me, Red."

"Hell I do. We going up there look at it bygod. You'll see I hit."

"Want Portugese Red first. Bet my pick and I pick Red. Soft little filly. You owe me Red goddammit."

"Don't owe no Red. I hit it. Anyhow Red ain't little; fat as a fresh cow's udder."

"Never hit it. Goddam thing still there. She ain't fat, more featherbed."

"Natural a sunspot on a post's still there you bastard, only won't be there don't we go look quick. Sun don't stand still."

"All right we go look."

"Allons. We go."

"But after Red, I done told you six times. And don't give me that foreigner talk. Talk American."

"Goddammit ain't going be no Red if I hit it, can't you get that in your thick skull? Tell you one more time . . ."

"Shit you hit it."

"Shit I didn't."

"We betting again for godssake?"

"We already bet for godsake. Never seen nobody damner dumb. Dumber damn. Hell with it. Tell you once more. Attention: you claimed my Sharps ain't true when you busted yours and went to mine, claimed that's why you never got as many hides this time out. I said this morning you ain't the shot as 'fore you got old-age blind. Goddam mad you got; bet I couldn't hit nothing with it neither and being horny said loser pays for a go at Portugese Red . . ."

"Soft little filly. Ain't neither fat."

". . . and you seen that bitty white spot on a freight-yard post yonder and I hit the sonofabitch, I'll show when we go there now. Being sunspot it maybe moved already; ain't buying if I hit where it was at when I squeezed off the round."

" 'Squeezed' hell, pawed off."

"Never pawed no trigger. Best rifle shot Second Louisiana Brigade."

"Best shit Rebel army. Don't know why they give you them goddam medals."

"Ain't arguing, just ain't paying bygod. Not 'fore you show me where I missed which I didn't. Nosiree you bastard. I hit."

Johnny Newlin's voice intruded on the dialogue from his saloon's doorway. "Whatever you hit, Frenchy, you'd favor me shooting on down the street. Hell of a headache." He pinched the bridge of his nose. "And if you don't know it there's a ordinance against shooting in town. I don't give a damn except for my headache but the mayor does. And that sonofabitching marshal."

Neither of the buffalo hunters appeared startled by the dire specter which suddenly, motionlessly was present beside the Portugese twenty feet from them and thirty from its proprietor but Johnny involuntarily sucked in his breath and took a slow step backward. The sound which seemed to the saloonkeeper lingeringly and far away to emerge then from the apparition was like a knell; to the buffalo hunters it was the vicious snap of a bear trap they'd heard in another time and place, almost sobering them.

"Stand where you be, Newlin." Luther Cain's face was tornadic. Then his stare lashed back at the man holding the Sharps. "And you drop it."

Johnny sensed that Frenchy's hesitation before letting the rifle fall had brought him within a hair's breath of extinction. "He's drunk, goddammit, Marshal. Both of them. They was only target-shooting, meaning no harm." Johnny realized that for the first time in a long while he was scared and he didn't know why; it almost were as though the two hunters' obscure jeopardy also were his and maybe others'. Unaccountably Carrie's image threaded through his mind for an instant. "Shooting in town sure, fine them for that, that ought to teach the loud bastards, ought to be enough. Right? Right, Marshal?"

Luther didn't take his eyes off the buffalo hunters. His exhalation was like a snake's hiss. "Shitting your pants, Johnny?"

"You just looked funny is all, Marshal. Your face . . ."

" 'Funny?' " The lawman grimaced balefully. "Ain't seen nothing funny lately." His grimace faded into a squint which reminded Frenchy, fast regaining perception, of someone sighting down a rifle barrel at him.

Frenchy's more slowly sobering friend elbowed him. "Looks like sonofabitch got a burr under his saddle." He addressed the marshal directly. "Pissed off about shooting in town, Lawman? Well don't fret your ass; partner here can't hit nothing, not even," pointing northward, "post yonder for chrissake."

Luther's voice was slab-flat. His eyes were locked with Frenchy's. "Shoot up thataway bit ago did you?"

The hunter pulled his stare from the marshal's and turned it on his friend. "Hell yes and hit the goddam sunspot on the goddam post. We go up there now I show you."

"Missed the goddam post clean," his friend said.

Luther's chained rage sundered with a ferocity Johnny Newlin likened at the next afternoon's inquest to a killer cyclone. "Never watched a thing to beat it," the saloonkeeper testified, "he was onto them jaybirds so fast spitting and hitting I could hardly see it."

"'Spitting?'" Doc Bowman, presiding as coroner, asked for clarification.

"Manner of speaking. Cussing and saying all them things."

"What things?"

"Like 'I'll show you what you hit: not a goddam post, a fourteen-year-old boy.' And other things."

"What other things?"

"Called them 'cowshit slobberjawed drunken trash' if I remember."

Doc cleared his throat. "Didn't mean cuss words. I meant did he say anything about arresting Frenchy—the dead man—anything like that?"

"Not as I remember."

"Did Frenchy make any kind of play against the marshal?"

"Not as I saw. Partner did draw a knife. Now listen I want to say something right here: I feel as bad as everybody else about Noble Buck getting killed yesterday. That kid and me were friends the same as him and lot of other people." The Portugese's proprietor, seated at one side of the table, looked around the silent courtroom. "The crowd here shows how many friends he had. And I want it plain I'm answering Doc's questions with what I saw and heard and nothing else, no hard feelings against the marshal, nothing but being sad about Noble getting killed however that happened and doing my duty as a citizen." Doc noted that not a skeptical eyebrow was lifted throughout the room. The saloon-keeper looked back at the physician-coroner. "Just wanted to say it."

"All right, Johnny. We heard it." Doc shifted in his chair at the table's head. "Let me get this straight again: you said Marshal Cain lit into those two when all Frenchy Lesueur did was admit he shot at a post up this direction which he claimed he hit and his partner Pat Tharp claimed he missed. And something about a knife."

Johnny nodded. "Lit into them like I never saw no one lit into before. Kicked Pat double in a heap so his knife flew over in the next county and had Frenchy bleeding from the nose and mouth and ears all three before knocking him stone cold, dead cold it turned out."

"Fractured skull," the coroner particularized for his lay audience. "Since we know what killed him the only other thing we got to find out is if a crime might have been done but not by who. If there wasn't we're done." He raised his eyebrows at the county attorney seated opposite him for confirmation.

Jim Watts spoke decisively. "But if it looks like there was a crime I'll bring it to book. Naturally I can't use your finding a while ago that Noble's death was by a third party; from all I heard Noble's likeliest killer is dead." Jim glanced somberly at Luther Cain leaning against a side wall. "But I guess his killer's killer isn't. It's the facts of Frenchy's death you're finding out now, Doc, as you said. I'll do whatever's my job when the time comes."

No one in the room signaled a doubt of it.

Doc returned his attention to the saloonkeeper. "Johnny, you mentioned Pat Tharp drawing a knife on the marshal. He draw it before or after the marshal hit anybody?"

The Portugese's owner didn't answer immediately. It was evident a number of things were tumbling through his lowered head. Of all the courtroom's watchers maybe only Carrie guessed that one of those things was Noble's image. He looked up and spoke slowly. "I think Pat drew his knife after Cain hit Frenchy. But everything happened so fast I can't swear to it."

The coroner frowned. "If you can't swear to it I guess the county attorney couldn't use it." He looked inquiringly at Watts.

Jim nodded. "Reasonable doubt. Of course this isn't a trial

160

you understand; regular rules of evidence don't hold as much. And you're only finding out how, not who."

Doc hummed for a moment, staring at the ceiling. Then he looked at the buffalo hunter sitting across from Newlin. "Pat, you gave me the idea little bit ago you didn't draw your knife until the marshal took after Frenchy. How could the marshal kick you and the knife away like Johnny said if he was taking after Frenchy?"

The buckskinned man's expression turned quizzical, then confused. "I only know what I done. I told you what I done."

"From what we heard you were pretty drunk. That bear on what you could swear to?"

"Hold my whiskey good as any man, I'll swear to that."

"Swear you didn't try to knife Marshal Cain?"

"Goddam right I tried to knife him. He was taking after my partner I told you."

"Knifing's against the law except to save a life," Jim Watts interjected. "Pardon, Doc, can I ask him a question even if this is your inquest?"

The coroner waved his assent.

"Pat, I understand you didn't draw your knife in your own defense but Frenchy's. The marshal wearing a gun?" He glanced briefly at the doctor. "This is going a little beyond the inquest."

"Hell, I don't recollect," Pat said. "Reckon so. Always does."

"I saw it in his belt," Johnny Newlin confirmed. "Wondered why he didn't take them in with it instead of fist-fighting."

"One more question?" the county attorney requested of the coroner.

"Go ahead."

If Marshal Cain meant to kill your partner, Pat, he could have shot him. Why did you think Frenchy's life was in danger?"

"Don't know for chrissake." The hunter squared his shoulders belligerently. "Frenchy didn't have no chance against that big sonofabitch and neither would I without my knife."

"Who hit who first?" the coroner asked.

"Cain did."

"Sure of that?"

"That's the way I seen it."

"Can you swear that's the way it happened?"

The county attorney leaned forward intently, assuming Doc's

continuing leave. "In a trial? Under oath, Pat? I'd have to be damned certain of it."

"Well I ain't goddam certain maybe. But I recollect it that away."

Jim leaned back.

Doc looked at Luther Cain against the wall. "Anything more you want to say, Marshal?"

The lawman shook his head. "Said my piece. That's my job: keep the peace."

If anyone noticed the inadvertent play on words there was no evidence of it.

The coroner sat quietly regarding his folded hands on the table top. After a moment he looked up. "Jim, what's the legal word for killing without a crime?" He thought he knew the answer but maybe not everyone in the audience did.

" 'Justifiable homicide' might be one. 'Accident' might be one."

"Looks like this might be one or the other of those. What you think?"

The county attorney let out his breath slowly. "Not enough evidence of intent, not even who was defending who." He seemed to be talking mainly to himself. "Only one trial juror needs to have his doubts. I can see more would." He shook his head and shrugged his shoulders. "And Noble Buck was well liked around here. Irrelevant of course. Legally."

Doc had been staring at his friend. "All right I guess all said and done it's my party." His gaze swept the room. "Anybody want to decide this for me?"

Nobody spoke up.

The coroner hit the table with his palm. "Accident! Inquest adjourned."

The half-dozen Texas cowboys who had sat at the back of the courtroom throughout the proceedings in uncharacteristic silence remained silent as they arose and filed out with a few other transients ahead of the townspeople. They knew when they were outnumbered. It wasn't that all the townspeople were convinced "beyond a reasonable doubt" that justice had been done or at least an appropriate compromise with the devil reached. Perhaps most of them did in view of their yearning for law and order; but what they'd heard during the afternoon left some of them uneasy for reasons difficult for them to articulate or even understand.

162

CHAPTER 20

Carrie Shaw was one of the vaguely uneasy townspeople and so was Howard Smith and perhaps it was by chance or perhaps her instinct they found their paths crossing at the corner of Pacific and East Streets an hour after the inquest.

"Headed my way, Carrie? Going up to the church."

She nodded. "Taking this dress to Missus Allgood. I go right past there to Kansas Avenue."

"No reason not to walk together."

The faintest hint of disconcertion crossed her face although she spoke lightly. "Not if you don't mind being seen alone with a working girl, Preacher."

His smile was disarming. "Not a girl in your line of work." He touched the fabric folded over her arm. "Pretty cloth. And I'll allow a pretty dress."

"Hope Missus Allgood likes it. Thank you." She responded to his gesture that they resume moving up the dusty street. He walked between her and the infrequent neighborhood buggy and wagon and cowpony traffic but it still was necessary for her to step over occasional horse-droppings, and his hand under her elbow helped. She began to feel more comfortable, not content by any means given her sense of Luther's ordeal but somehow not quite as insecure as three minutes ago and certainly not as an hour previously. "I seen you at the inquest."

He nodded. "I did you, too."

"What . . . ?" Her tongue couldn't deal with the rest of her uncertainty.

"What I think about it?"

"Not so much it . . ." Again definition failed her.

"What they said Luther did?" He decided to go one further step in his effort to help her and suddenly he realized to help himself understand what had happened yesterday and today. "Are you like I am, Carrie, maybe wondering what truly happened? I saw his look when he headed down to Jimson Street."

"No!" She cried, stopping and seizing the preacher's arm, pulling him up short. "He liked that boy but he'd never kill in

163

cold blood no matter what or who, I'm telling you he wouldn't, I know him too well." It hit her like a rifle bullet that although she knew a good deal about Luther Cain—they'd had some long talks lately—she didn't know everything about him, even things a lot of friends and lovers knew absolutely about each other. And they weren't even complete lovers. Yet. "Maybe we ain't been acquainted for long, far as time goes, but I'm telling you: never!" Tears budded in her eyes.

Howard Smith's tone was gentle. "Sure, Carrie, just sometimes a man has all he can stand." He motioned them on again. "Speaking of what you're working at nowadays I'm glad about that and I'm glad about you and the marshal being friends."

His mentioning the two things in conjunction didn't escape her. She sniffed away her eyes' mist. "I'd been wanting to quit that other a good while, it wasn't just Luther. But I owed Johnny Newlin a lot. And I don't mean money. He was a friend to me when I needed it bad. I know Luther and him don't hit it off, especially after that crazy stage robbery Johnny tried to rig which if you ask me Pickett put him up to. But I still like him for old times' sake; far as I'm concerned we're still friends unless he does something else crazy to hurt Luther, then we're through." Abruptly she drew in her breath and fell silent in mortification. She hadn't revealed these many thoughts about her and Luther previously to anybody, maybe even to herself she realized in wonderment.

The preacher appeared not to have noticed her fluster. "I think he really didn't try to hurt Luther at the inquest."

"I seen that too." Her confidence emerged tentatively. "He liked Noble Buck more than he don't like Luther."

"Good way to say it." Howard smiled at a thought. "I also think Johnny and Luther not hitting it off could be over you, Carrie."

"Johnny's had all of me he's getting." She swallowed, flushing. "All of my time."

He was careful not to heighten her embarrassment by letting his smile die abruptly.

They had arrived at the intersection of East and Cottonwood Streets. The Methodist Church was on its northwest corner and the one-room schoolhouse on its northeast.

"Too much of a hurry to stop for a minute?" He waved casually toward the church's open doorway. "Like to show you something we just got. Think you'll be interested."

Inside she followed him down the single aisle and onto the platform and stepped with him behind the pulpit as he beckoned her to do. He picked up the large Bible lying open there, closed it carefully and handed it to her.

"When you heard me preach last Sunday did you notice that? Beautiful, eh?"

She looked down at the book again. "Couldn't see it over the pulpit." Her fingers caressed its leather cover. "Yes it is."

"Didn't have the cowhide on it then; been commencing to come apart for a while."

"Sure pretty now."

"Orville Allgood put that cover on this week at his leather shop. Took him couple days. Didn't cost the church a cent."

"That's real nice of him," she smiled. "They're nice folks both of them."

"Yes they are but it wasn't his idea."

Her raised eyebrows politely asked whose it was.

"Luther Cain hired him to do it. Then Luther give this to us as a present." Howard grinned. "What you think about that? Told me things was bad enough but if the Bible wore out he wouldn't have a snowball's chance in Hell. Exact words."

Her eyes misted again. She touched a lash with a quick forefinger. "Preacher, you ever noticed you can't tell what on earth he's going to do next?" She shook her head wryly, her smile mirroring Howard's. "Maybe that's his ace in *my* deck."

"Depends on the particulars I'd say. Buck him in his job, jump the law reservation, a body can be real sure what he's going to do. Other things you might be meaning I don't know about; you're the one got to decide whether to play in his game or not, what the stakes are for you." He patted her shoulder encouragingly. "But I know I like the man and it's easy to see you do too. Maybe more'n a smidgen. And from things he said times we talked I got the feeling it runs both ways. Not that we talked about you right out, understand."

She was only mildly surprised by her own reaction. "I don't mind you two talking about me; we been talking about him after all." Since first meeting Howard Smith weeks ago in Berg's Dry Goods she gradually had come almost to feel at ease with the preacher. From the beginning of their acquaintance somehow she had been able to carry on a conversation with him without wanting to puke—the only such preacher since her teen-age defilement by one—and for this moment she didn't want their communication to end. "I need to talk some more."

"Let's sit down and talk some more then." He led her to the front pew and when they were seated leaned forward with his elbows on his knees, head turned toward her, and waited for her to continue.

"Did you talk to Luther after the inquest?"

He shook his head once. "No. Carl Norris was asking him questions for the newspaper and then he took off with Big John somewheres."

"I didn't get to neither." Her tone was melancholy. "I feel sorry for him some way. I know that's like feeling sorry for a grizzly but they is already loners."

"And Luther's not?"

"Not by choice maybe."

"He chose his line of work."

"Or else it chose him, kind of because he's good at it, not because he likes it." She sighed. "I know what that means. Kind of a trap."

He was intrigued by her discernment and afraid anything he might say should cloud it so he remained silent.

"When you wondered while ago what truly happened yesterday I was only saying he couldn't out-and-out murder nobody. Shoot in self-defense and maybe kill, he done that several times in different places I heard. Part of his job. I was with him one time. Jack Bennett. Scared me to death." She shivered. "But maybe that don't rule out something bothering him. I can understand it."

"Like feeling trapped the way you said," the preacher mused, "and being mad about it. Doc Bowman told me once a man can be mad without knowing why, without even knowing it at all. Makes a man ornery. Not meaning Luther is ornery."

"Or a woman," Carrie smiled ruefully. "Maybe I was that way once. I was pretty ornery."

"You couldn't be mean-ornery, Carrie, it's not in you. We all do wrong-ornery things. The trick is not to keep on." He returned her smile. "That's where my deal commences. You're in my game

166

now and anybody sitting in can talk about whatever they need to any time." His expression resumed its serious attentiveness without a hint of pressing her.

She decided as far as she was concerned this man could be a hell of a friend. To both her and Luther. She needed to continue talking. "Luther told me couple nights ago about when he was a kid in Indiana something very sad happened."

"His cousin dying?"

She was relieved the preacher knew; it was miserable even to recall let alone retell Luther's aching words; but again she was surprised, if not so mildly this time, that the man apparently made of granite had shared with Howard Smith a fragile confidence she'd assumed was a secret yield of her and Luther's passion.

Howard sensed why she may have paused. "We had some pretty weighty talks a few times lately, Luther and me. I started them for his same lonesomeness you spoke of, sort of eased into things, didn't know how he'd take to it. First time he shied off. But funny thing next time he was the one drifted around to it, wanted to talk about why some humans act devilish when there's no call to, when maybe they don't even want to, 'including me sometimes' he said so low I near didn't hear it, but mostly I reckon he meant the likes of Bennett."

Carrie recalled another hostile face. "And Enos Dowling."

"Course he might have been talking more about himself than I got then. When he told me about his cousin dying he cussed mean."

"Like it was his fault. Done the same when he told me. Looked right at me when he done it, too, almost like he was cussing me." She brushed the absurdity out of the air as she had at the time. "He couldn't help her dying."

"Must have loved her a sight."

"Sure it's sad"—Carrie's tone was faintly resentful—"but it ain't a reason to be mad at hisself."

"Nor others," Howard said, "and sure not you." He straightened on the pew, pushing the small of his back, arching it briefly to get a kink out. He grinned at her. "Yep more'n a smidgen I allow. Just don't neither of you figure you got it easy and you may make it in spite of old debts and young ghosts and the Dowlings hanging around. And keep your sense of humor."

"Luther don't have too much of that."

"Maybe he'll grow into one given time." The preacher looked depressed for an instant. "If he gives himself time." His expression relaxed again. "We'll all try to help him. Last couple days haven't been very humorous for anybody. But we'll stick together. We'll do all right."

Her face held a great deal of sweetness. "You preached a beautiful funeral for Noble Buck this morning, Preacher. Everbody said so. Everbody thanks you. Including Luther and me. And Frenchy's was fine, too."

"There's lots of good people in Bancroft including Luther and you." He laughed. "Liking my preaching just goes to prove it."

She smiled. "Could I ask you one more thing?"

"Whatever you want I told you."

"Couple times you mentioned me and Luther liking each other, maybe more than liking which is true at least with me and I'm pretty sure with him. Hell—sorry, Preacher—I'll say it: loving each other."

He nodded matter-of-factly.

"See what I'm wondering is how that could be. Maybe if it even could be." Her tone was disbelieving. "Without dragging this out, you believe in love at first sight?" A blush threatened her cheeks. "Well maybe second sight?"

"I believe anything can happen with folks. 'Love at first sight' is about what happened with me and my wife. God rest her soul."

"Didn't know you was ever married."

"Good while ago. Happy too. She was a true angel. Died of cancer before I come out here. Partly why I come. After her there wasn't much left back East for me."

"I'm sorry. Glad you're here, though," she added, "and that you had her for the time."

"Thank you. Appreciate your saying that." He cleared his throat. "Carrie, want to tell me any more about you and Luther?"

"Well we only got acquainted maybe couple months ago you know. At your church supper right after he come to town. I'll never forget that church supper." Her voice became solemn. "Preacher Smith, something happened to me that night, started happening anyhow. Maybe then for him too. I never knowed what being happy was before but scared at the same time like I was going to fall in a well of happiness and drown. When he asked me to quit John-

168

ny's Portugese I never give it a second thought, like something I been waiting for; but quitting didn't all of a sudden make everything fine all the time. Sometimes I feel in his mind I can't never quit, he'll always remember, man and lawman. Other times it's like nothing about me counts before we crossed trails, only . . ." She struggled to find meaning as well as expression. "Something keeps him reined up like he wants to run but his bit hurts too bad, keeps him back from me, from us."

"A body can love somebody without the other feeling the same. Maybe he just don't . . ."

"I know he feels it, I know it! I can tell the way he held and kissed me the other night." She looked defiant. "You was married, you know what I'm talking about. And I know from different kinds of holding and kissing I had to put up with, different as night and day." Her brief defiance melted into reasonableness. "I know I ain't a prize. But I ain't a pig neither and not just the outside of me. I got a brain and feelings. And they tell me and I'm telling you Luther likes me a whole lot. Loves me! Same as I do him no matter how short a while we've knowed each other. But he's got some kind of hobble on. He claims it ain't where I been in my life, that's past; and I think he means it or wants to bad enough to make it come true if it ain't already. I just don't know what the hell—sorry again, dammit—I mean . . ." She looked at the ceiling.

"Dammit, go on," Howard grinned. "Let me ask you a question: is it all hunch with you, this hobble, or did he say or do something to give you that way of thinking?"

Her eyes were reflective only for an instant; it was clear the memory was close to her mind's surface. "Right in the middle of almost making love night before last when he seen me home—I said 'almost,' Preacher—he pulled up short and begin talking fast like he had to let it out; and that's the time he told me about his cousin dying and about some robber. And if you don't think that was a bad time to tell me about another woman, cousin or not, dead or not, you got another think coming."

Howard nodded soberly but his eyes glinted with amusement. "Reckon so."

" 'Specially with that cussing," she added.

"Which wasn't at you, Carrie." His eyes' humor faded abruptly. "Nor at me the other time. Just at the pain."

169

A frightening thought crossed her mind. "You don't reckon he's married? Got a wife somewhere? That couldn't be it could it?"

"Reckon it could; like I said anything could happen. But someway I'd bet against it. He'd tell you."

"I hope not: him having a wife." She felt better. "Sure he'd tell me." Another thought occurred to her. "If he is hamstrung by anything why wouldn't he tell me that too?" She offered an answer to herself: "So maybe he ain't hamstrung and it's all in my mind." She felt better still.

"Or else he don't know it himself," the preacher said slowly, squinting at the notion.

Her better feeling reverted to quandary.

Howard stared past her out a window. "I call to mind another thing Doc said once: 'A man grows up in the shape of his boyhood.' Luther told me he was twenty when his cousin died. That's not much more'n a boy."

"Ain't sure I'm following you."

"I'm not sure I'm leading anywhere." He sat silently for a moment before returning his gaze to the woman. "I was thinking about his cussing because of hurting and being terrible mad over what happened to his cousin when he was twenty and she was sixteen and," hurrying past the fact for Carrie's sake, "he was crazy about her and also maybe taking on its fault and that other thing Doc said about being riled coming out ornery sometimes and Luther himself saying he might act devilish once in a while for no call." He snorted. "Reckon I just led us into a bramble bush. And scratched my thinking cap off."

She wasn't ready to abandon her astounding dialogue with this new friend. "Maybe I'll have to think like Doc about one thing: bad early times makes for bad later ones." She took a deep breath. "Could have been what happened to me. Listen, Preacher, I don't know why but I got to tell you something I never talked to no one about since it happened including Luther. The reason I didn't is I couldn't, not didn't want to exactly. Like unpainting a barn. But talking this way all of a sudden I got to. If you'll hear it. Maybe partly it's you're a preacher. Talking to a preacher about a preacher maybe'll get it out of me so I'll make Luther a good wife for sure if he'll have me, if he'll ever let me get that close." Tears more of excitement than distress were running down her cheeks. "I don't know why I'm crying. Jesus!"

"Jesus is hearing it."

She told him in simple, straightforward words about the simultaneous desecration of her and of the Hoosier church eighteen years ago and while she was at it about running away a year later to pursue the extravagant fantasies which had brought her to this place and moment and question. "You reckon maybe I kept on running away all these years with nobody after me?"

His mind was still grappling with an eighteen-year-old image. "You were fifteen!" He shuddered. "Why don't you hate me?" He glanced Heavenward. "Jesus, hear us both, help us both, forgive us all." He looked back at the woman and spoke after a moment, frowning. "Carrie, I don't know if this makes sense but do you know what just come to me that you got to do?"

She shook her head, brushing her cheeks with the back of one hand.

"Besides forgiving me and forgiving yourself you got to forgive that no-good preacher in Indiana a long time ago. If there's a way you can do that then I got a idea he can never chase you again." A little smile broke through his face's cloud. "Old Doc never said those bad things had to last forever."

"Don't know as I can do that. Not you, nothing to forgive you for, only to like." She shrugged. "Me, what I done can't be undid so I'll try to forget it." She sighed. "But that old devil . . . well I sure would like to forget him too, Preacher. And if forgiving is forgetting reckon I got to try." Slowly she gathered up the dress material she'd laid on the pew and arose. "Missus Allgood's going to wonder whatever happened to me." Her still-moist eyes met Howard Smith's squarely. "But she'd understand if I told her what good's happened here." She extended her hand. "I thank you for talking to me."

He enclosed her fingers gently in his. "It was a privilege."

That night as she lay naked in the warm, dark disquiet of her bed watching behind closed lids the kaleidoscope of the day— its sadnesses and surprises and truths and enigmas—Carrie's shifting glimpses of Luther swooped her senses like a garden swing from high to low, from happiness to dejection, from damp lust to chilling fear. She tried to seize for respite on Preacher Smith's sanity and on her own new views of herself and her—what was he?—lover, future husband (neither being realities now and maybe never), man she loved (yes, yes), man who loved her (yes?); but her grasp failed for a moment and she continued sailing up and down between exultation and chagrin. She didn't want Luther to change a bit and she did want him to change a little bit, an inconsistency of want she realized but couldn't articulate although probably Howard and Doc and even Luther should have called it typically female in their typically male benightedness. She exulted in the man's manliness, his signified ardor for her, his strength, his determination to do his job without fear or favor; she was chagrined by the austerity of his manliness, the hesitancy of his ardor's practice, the seeming ferocity of his strength, the occasional imtemperance of his job's conduct. Thinking of his two guises made her uneasy, vaguely frightened; to want this virtuous man so much made the thought of losing him a nightmare, to lose him by an excess of his virtue made the nightmare hideous. She moaned softly in her discomposure and a comforting hand crept without will to a nipple and stomach velvet and wetness and almost at once into motionless sleep with the rest of her weary being.

Incredibly over the uproar of burning walls and floors in the midblock ahead and through winter-closed squad-car windows Mark Keller had heard a scream for help, and against the red incineration of the tenement he'd seen a horse gallop across the avenue from one alley into the darkness of another, its rider tilted forward, raised in the stirrups, forearms at the animal's neck, wide-brimmed round-crowned hat low against the wind.

Mark had been tired, hadn't slept for eighteen hours. He'd jerked his head to shake off the impossible sound and sight. His partner had noticed his spasm and even in their hurry had asked him whether anything were wrong. He'd grunted a denial and of course hadn't mentioned the fleeting, wide-awake dream. Or whatever the hell . . .

The surgeon bending over the patient's opened chest muttered to the anesthetist, "What'd he say? Not waking up, is he?"

" 'Kansas,' sounded like. No, plenty of time, I think."

"Probably never been west of the Hudson. But I don't want him going anywhere right now; better give him some more."

CHAPTER 21

The acrid smell of gunsmoke writhed slowly like a snake into her dreams; the faraway popping and crackling of revolvers and rifles nudged her eardrums; the smell became a stink and the sounds drew nearer as though their perpetrators were riding through the night toward her bed in her room of Lane's boarding house. A shout of her name brought her upright, her heart pounding, her throat stinging and eyes streaming from the smoke filling the room. "Carrie!" Everett's shout again of her name jerked her head about, her blurred vision in the red-flickering dimness flowing with the gagging smoke from under the door toward the open window offering her numbed senses barely a moment's chance to save her. Her brain demanded her legs to swing floorward, arms to push upward, lungs to stop sucking death inward, whole white vulnerable body to lunge at the distant opening this side of which gaped oblivion.

Faintly from the plaza amid Bancroft's less ominous sounds the tolling of the fire house's alarm bell drifted to the south and very soon more loudly was echoed by the bell of the Prairie Hawks' wagon itself as its team bounced it across the railroad track and plunged with it down South Street and swerved into Jimson and clattered to a halt beside Lane's boarding inferno. At the same moment galloping out of the night from below the stock pens Luther Cain and Big John McAllister swung themselves from their blowing horses before the animals had slid on their haunches almost into the wagon and ran, spur-jingles muffled by the flames' roar, toward the back of the house.

Several minutes earlier as he and Big John had been riding across the dark plain toward Bancroft's yellow lights talking about Herman Strauss's threat to kill his estranged wife Laverne who worked part-time at the Lone Star Cafe—they had visited the reclusive man in his dugout to talk him out of it—Luther had noticed a small reddish glow in what had seemed to be the vicinity of the stock pens at the town's southwest edge. During the past twenty years he had seen many fires bloody the far edges of many nights—camp-fires, brush fires, artillery barrages, Indian-raid kindlings—and always if perhaps waningly over time knife-twists of memory had harrowed his gut. It had been the same tonight. He had raised in his stirrups and leaned forward against his saddle's swells as though staring more intently ahead should make the darkness lighter, the source of the burning more visible. When he had broken off their conversation his deputy's attention had followed his. Both of them had heard the feeble calling of the bells.

"Bygod, John, it's getting bigger." Luther's throat had tightened. "Ain't that about where them houses is?"

"Could be the haystack in the pens."

"Or one of them houses." The marshal had said another word half-aloud: "Lane's!"

Simultaneously they had spurred their horses into dead runs.

As they had pounded across the shadowy prairie toward doom Luther's head had thundered in time with the hooves. No no not again, Hell no not again, God, no, not again . . . !

Reaching the back of the house they found Everett Lane and Carrie Shaw lying side by side in the crimson yard where he must have dragged her beyond the searing heat. Everett was vomiting from exertion and smoke and Carrie's hair was smoking. As Luther squatted beside her he pulled off his shirt and covered her naked torso and reached up and grabbed a bucket from the hands of a running Prairie Hawk and poured its water over her head. Big John bent down and turned Everett's head sideways to prevent his vomit from choking him. When Carrie stirred and moaned Luther slipped one arm under her shoulders and lifted her against his chest, his brain still echoing with hoofbeats—never ought to loved again, couldn't ever lose again—over the shouting of firefighters and crackling of flames. She strained upward weakly with returning consciousness, eyes coming into focus, tongue brushing cracked lips trembling in her effort to speak as she gazed at him.

Verbalization came to both of them at the identical instant with its different interpretations: "Carrie, I can't stand no more of this," and "Luther, I didn't burn up," they said aloud together.

She tried to laugh and he tried to smile.

He spoke again. "You all right? I want you to be all right!"

She nodded only a little uncertainly. "I'm glad you do. I sure hope I am—we are."

Big John's grin was unequivocal. "Everett here's feeling better. Looks like everybody might come around."

"Carrie," Everett said hoarsely, "next time we make ice tea in my new boarding house, for godssake, let's put out the goddam fire afterward!"

Solly Berg paused in his rush past them. "All boarders safe, Marshal, thank God. Hotter'n Sinai's devouring fire. See you later."

"Thank God," Howard Smith said, "for saving all us boarders of the world." He stepped forward through the night's curtain. "Like I was saying to someone just this afternoon: He forgives us as we forgive others—and ourselves."

Carrie smiled up at the preacher.

Luther stared up at him expressionlessly.

With a great crash and soaring of sparks the roof of Lane's boarding house caved in.

Carl Norris noted down another legend of the town.

CHAPTER 22

. . . A column on Mark Keller is in some ways an essay on duality. We're writing not only about both a public man and a private one, but also about his own and other people's perceptions of each of those. The public man is hated by lawbreakers and esteemed—hero-worshipped in kids' cases—by law-abiders. The private man is warm and shielding to some people and remote, although usually politely so, to others. Perhaps most intriguing in this regard are what we suspect to be his twofold perceptions of himself: a confident man and a troubled one . . .

Low threatening clouds had heaved themselves above the rim of the plains beyond the west end of Pacific Street as Carl alternately had stared through the *Republican*'s window at them and down at the notes spread on the top of his desk, trying to write a rational story of Bancroft's bizarre happenings of yesterday and the day before.

The reminders and images of his jottings were like fragments of an explosion scattered over his mind's landscape. It was hard to assemble their implications. He had talked with people who had seen some of the two days' events and he had witnessed others himself and generally he had a fairly clear picture of what had happened but not altogether a clear one of why. That is if a person thought of "why" as the latent rather than patent cause. There wasn't room for doubt either way why Noble Buck had died: as he had sat on his wagon in the plaza his brain had been shattered by a bullet carelessly fired from Jimson Street at a post by the drunken Frenchy Lesueur. Patently Frenchy in turn had died from a fractured skull in a fist fight with Luther Cain whose job it had been to find and arrest Noble's killer, the fracas having started when the marshal had gone down to Jimson Street in pursuit of his job. Exactly how it had started and some of its other details hadn't emerged from the inquest. Carl had a hunch that somewhere in those uncertainties lurked the latent cause of Frenchy's death.

Patently Carrie Shaw had been rescued gallantly from a roasting death by Everett Lane—Carl should stress Everett's gallantry in his story—and had been held by Luther Cain's defending arms close to the fortress of his chest in what, despite that imagery's sureness and safety, Carl had sensed had been Luther's quandary and Carrie's risk. Carl had another hunch that the marshal's and the new seamstress's embrace was relevant latently to the town's recent turmoil.

He decided such obscure ruminations were not appropriate to this news story no matter how piquing of his newsman's curiosity. He also decided he didn't have to write the story immediately. He stuffed his pencil into his vest pocket, yelled to Fred and Billy he was leaving for a while, got to his feet, and went out to peddle some advertising.

After their boss had left the building Fred Martin and Billy Plunkett continued working for a while on Friday's issue and a couple of job-printing projects. In setting type for an editorial Fred had difficulty reading a word of Carl's handwriting even after two years of practice and his fingers hung for several minutes over the type box as he tried to decipher it. Then he realized two words were run together and as his setting worked out he put "horse's" at the line's end and "ass" at the next one's beginning. Finishing the editorial he set an article about a meeting the previous Saturday in Missus Lester Blain's home of the Sunflower Sewing Circle at which Miss Carrie Shaw had been inducted as the newest member of that "lodge of lovely ladies." (This caused the printer to predict to his devil that Lila Haniford surely should be descending on their editor this Saturday over that alliteration if not his cussing in print.) Billy meanwhile rolled ink on the type block Fred had set for a flier announcing a Prairie Hawks bake sale and cranked it back and forth against the newsprint cylinder of the second-hand portable army press, predecessor of the *Republican*'s present main one which was stationary, larger and better hand-levered but, as Carl often said, didn't guarantee a better newspaper. He had told Miss Haniford among other citizens that the guaranties of journalistic quality were "gumption and guts." Her response at the time hadn't been recorded.

When the Sewing Circle article had been set and the contracted five hundred bake-sale fliers had been run off the printer and his devil went into the office to rest for a few minutes and smoke their pipes, there being no chairs in the press room. Fred sat on the front room's bench under its gun rack and Billy on its bunk against the facing side-wall, the cold stove partly between them not preventing their seeing each other around its belly. Carl's desk and chair and a couple of visitors' chairs occupied the entire opposite end of the room.

"Where the hell'd he go?" Fred puffed through a cloud of smoke.

"Said this morning he still had Guttman's copy to get."

"He finish those articles about Noble's shooting and the Lane fire?"

Billy's face looked drawn suddenly. "I don't know." He stared at the floor. "I'll sure miss Noble. Dave Berg will too." He sucked on his pipe and exhaled a blue plume.

"What tobacco you smoking?"

" 'Pro Bono Publico.' "

"How long you been smoking that?"

"Since Noble give me a tin for my birthday."

"Forget how old you are, Billy. Fifteen now?"

"Fourteen."

"Well it's hard to lose a partner at any age." Fred set down his pipe, reached under the bench for a hidden key, stood up, stepped to the corner cabinet, and unlocked it. Taking out the crock of whiskey he kept there—and was happy to share with Carl when rarely the editor wanted a nip while working—he pulled its cob, took a swig, palmed the cob back, returned the jug to its shelf, locked the cabinet, resumed his seat, re-hid the key, and picked up his pipe. "Yep. Lost my dog last year you know. Fourteen like you. Except that's old for a dog. Best damn friend I ever had, not counting Carl Norris."

"Reckon I'm your friend, Mister Martin."

"Been working for Carl two years, longest I ever stayed on any paper. Sober most of the time too." The printer seemed belatedly to hear his devil's comment. "Sure I know you're my friend." He pulled on his pipe. "I wasn't too acquainted with Noble. Just when he came by here a couple times and waving at him on his ice rounds. Seemed like a nice boy."

178

"Sure was. Him and me had some great times. And Dave."

"Damn shame what happened. Least the marshal got his killer." Fred whistled through his teeth at the debacle. "Got him good."

"Three of us'd go fishing with Marshal Cain. Noble liked that. Them was good times."

"You boys would go fishing with Luther Cain?"

Billy nodded, drawing on his pipe and squinting as he blew the smoke out slowly. "Yep." He was aware of the printer's sharpened interest and proud because of it, not as much for his sake as Noble's. His friend had been a friend of the marshal who had killed out of that friendship. Anyhow so Billy viewed it. "Up to the beaver pond."

"You never talked about that."

Billy wasn't sure why he had felt the fishing might have ceased if he talked about it. He didn't attempt an explanation.

"I only spoke with Marshal Cain a few times," Fred said. "Right after he came to town when you and I met him in here. Remember? And when he's dropped in on Carl a few times. And on the street once in a while. Just 'howdy' acquaintances. Like to know him better though, way you boys do."

Billy had to be honest. "Going fishing with him and knowing him is two different things, Mister Martin. Noble thought that."

"I've heard he's kind of a hard man to know."

"Well he's not much of a talker and that's no lie."

"Man in his line of work has to listen more'n he talks."

"Reckon he does at that."

"Waddie in the Longhorn yesterday claimed he's got a mean streak. I don't believe it myself." The printer grinned. "Fishermen aren't mean folks, not those fishes with kids anyhow."

The devil tried to return the printer's grin. " 'Specially when the kids ain't mean."

Fred nodded. "I sure got to get better acquainted . . ."

Luther Cain stepped through the open office door from Pacific Street, ducking his black hat under the lintel, looking in turn at the man, the boy, the empty desk, and back at the boy. "Howdy, Billy."

"Well I'll be damned," Fred Martin said as Luther's eyes went to him again. "Just talking about you, Marshal."

Luther didn't comment.

Fred took the bull by the horns. "Yessir, I was saying I hope we get better acquainted."

The marshal's tilting moustache as Billy knew from experience sheltered a faint smile. "No time like the present they say."

"Well now that's right, Marshal. It sure is yes indeed." Self-consciousness tangled Fred's tongue. "How's things every going? I mean . . ."

The devil took the printer off the hook (not the first time, friendship being a two-way trail). "Howdy, Marshal. Something we can do for you?"

"Looking for Carl but I see he ain't here."

"Believe he went over to the drug store about Harry's ad, Marshal." Fred had regained some of his composure. "Back soon I guess." He half-arose and moved sideways on the bench. "Glad for you to have a seat."

Billy was pleasantly surprised when the marshal accepted the invitation by stepping to the bench and sitting down, thumbing back his hat and crossing his denimed, booted legs. Luther usually stayed on the move in town. Fred was both pleased by the lawman's waiting and apprehensive Carl might not return soon, belying his guess. Both the *Republican*'s employees noticed the marshal's badly bruised knuckles but of course didn't mention those.

"Yessir," Fred hedged a bit, "ought to be back soon but you never can tell for sure about old Carl."

"Carl's a busy man."

"That's right, Marshal, what with stories and ads and circulation and taking care of his egg business."

"How many laying hens he got out back nowadays?"

"Forty-seven," Billy answered for the printer. "Had forty-eight yesterday but lost another one last night to a coyote been coming in town. Setting a trap tonight. One of my jobs is collecting eggs, Marshal; you let me know any time you want a few extras. I remember from Noble you board at the Drovers . . ." He broke off, swallowing at his confusion and regret at having mentioned their friend.

Luther nodded. He stared at the boy's lowered face brushed by smoke drifting up from the pipe cupped in both his young hands.

"Guess we all been busy lately," the printer dared, "including you Marshal." He plunged on. "I got to say it, we're for you. I'm saying Billy and me and most of the town. Maybe it was too bad the Frenchman died but the boy died, too, and that sure deserved paying for."

"You couldn't help how hard you hit him," Billy affirmed, "in the middle of a fight. You whipped him for Noble. He got what he give."

Fred's nod stressed the point. "Damn right."

Luther's eyes which had softened as he had gazed at Billy became expressionless along with his voice. "Reckon I wished he hadn't fired off that round in town." He shook his head. "Feller ought to knowed better. Goddammit agin the law." Abruptly he uncrossed his legs and stood up, pulling his hat forward to his brow and resettling his gunbelt around his waist. "I'll go look for Carl at Guttman's. Don't want him to get away. Rain's coming anyway and need to get a slicker at the fire house."

Billy and Fred got to their feet, each extending his right hand. "Sorry you can't stay but we're glad you came by, Marshal," the printer said. "Sure are," his devil emphasized. The lawman shook each's hand in turn. "Appreciate you letting me set a spell, Billy, Fred."

When Luther Cain's frame had vacated the narrow front doorway the printer stepped to the stove, forefingered open its iron maw and knocked out his pipe against it so the ashes fell inside, leaving it opened for Billy. "That man's got his work cut out. But he'll handle it. And I've got another hour's worth myself and you've got yourself some sweeping to do and the paper's insides from Kansas City to pick up at the station. Then I'm heading for Mother Swain's supper table and you can go home or your girl's or wherever the hell you're going."

"Ain't got a girl." Billy knocked out his own pipe in the stove. "Left me for a corset salesman." It was his first attempt at lightness since Noble's black death. The marshal's visit had seemed to make things better. A little.

Fred laughed and threw his arm across the boy's shoulders as they walked to the rear room.

Around the corner on East Street in Guttman's Drug Store just below the Stockmen and Farmers Bank, the *Republican*'s editor folded the ad's layout on which he and the proprietor had agreed and put it into his pocket.

181

"Second page," Harry Guttman reiterated, "above the fold."

"And block letters." Carl paused as he started to turn away. "You playing with us tomorrow night, Harry, or just Crum and Watts and Bowman and me? Five makes a better game."

"Like to but Hearts Ferris is back in town playing at the Longhorn. Joe Larkin says he had a few complaints and don't want bad talk about his saloon, never mind worse trouble. Asked me to sit in some this week and watch Hearts. That's between you and me."

"Well us amateurs in your back room have to get along best we can looks like."

"Deputizing you to take my house cut out of the pots."

Carl realized the druggist was only half-joking. "Sure, Harry, you can trust me. Just like Joe trusts Hearts."

"You want an extra hand how about Ed Sarver? He heard about our games and said he'd like to sit in when there's an empty chair. You can get some of that post office money."

"And railroad and ice-house. He either works for or owns damn near everything."

"And the town council's budget while you're at it."

"Not with Bill Crum sitting there. Too damn honest."

Again the editor paused as he was about to start away. "Speaking of honest government, Harry, did Bill Crum tell you his idea of Luther Cain running for mayor next year?"

The druggist looked bemused. "Hell! Don't Cain think he's got enough headaches already?" His smile was slightly tight. "Besides handing out a passel of them?"

"Don't know if Bill mentioned it to the marshal yet."

"Idea he'd hold down both jobs?"

"Likely couldn't one man be town judge and town marshal both. But the council could hire us another marshal."

"Another Luther Cain? Where'd we get one of them if we wanted to?"

"One of a kind all right." Carl almost asked what Harry had meant by "if we wanted to" but decided the phrase hadn't significance. "Sure put the fear of God in our summer visitors."

"The rowdies among those I'm interested in getting religion, the rest buy merchandise. But I'll have to say he's done what we hired him to do: enforced the law. As he sees it anyhow."

Again the editor was nudged by a small doubt about the

druggist's intent and again he let it ride for lack of rope to tie it down. "Of course the mayor's job doesn't pay what Luther makes as marshal so I don't know why he'd want it either."

"Even if he was to get elected."

"Not much doubt about that is there, Harry?"

"Maybe not."

"My paper would support him."

Harry smiled more with his mouth than his eyes. "Your paper supported the herd law. Can't say everybody went along on that."

The editor returned the druggist's smile without its reservation. "Still supports it. Be sure to read my editorial day after tomorrow."

"I read all your editorials, my friend, agree with them or not. Just had a thought," he added: "you newspaper like you play poker, Carl. Know that? Draw different cards from what you're dealt, never satisfied the way things are."

Carl cocked his head thoughtfully. "You might be right, Harry. But hell maybe that's how newspapering's supposed to be."

The darkening late afternoon indoors and out was brightened for an instant by a lightning flash and for the next deafened by a cannon clap of thunder rattling its structures and spooking its horses and making its humans flinch. And for the third instant the drug store's doorway was filled by Marshal Cain's entry.

"There comes the storm, boys," the proprietor illuminated the obvious.

"Just made it, Luther," Carl said. "But got your slicker I see. Always ready."

"Entrance to rival the ghost of Hamlet's father, Marshal Cain," customer Lila Haniford noted from back down the single aisle. "How much is this talc, Mister Guttman?" She held up a box.

"Fifteen cents. Remember though it's the best you can buy."

" 'Vanity, thy name is woman.' I hear you say that? If so it's a misquote." The teacher put the powder into her gingham skirt's pocket. "Add it to my bill, please? Come Thanksgiving and the start of school I'll be rolling in all those wages—anyway those pumpkins and apples and turnips—and I'll be in to settle with you. Meantime, Mister Guttman, I appreciate your courtesy."

The druggist bowed. "And meantime, Miss Haniford, I appreciate your business."

She smiled and turned toward the marshal. "Speaking of appreciation I want to take this chance, Luther Cain, to thank you for your kindness to Noble Buck." Her smile disappeared. "Mother Swain told me you got him out of that shack into her boarding house. Noble was a good boy and a bright one and I was fond of him. I wish he could have stayed in school a few years longer." She paused for a moment. "I wish he could have stayed anywhere longer." She squared her shoulders. "I don't abide killing anytime for any reason. I want you to understand that. But I'm not judging you, I don't know anything about that Frenchy business, and I do abide kindness. I want to thank you for your kindness to that fine boy."

Luther had taken off his hat when she had started addressing him. He looked down at it now in his hands, not in embarrassment or affected modesty but while choosing the words best to convey his meaning, to let her know its importance to him. Then he looked up. "Thank you, M'am. For myself I'd like to say I don't aim to kill nobody. It happens." He was staring at her intently. "Mostly people try to kill me. Sometimes they kill or hurt other people or try to. And it happens. I don't start out my mornings looking to harm nobody but only to do the job I'm paid by you and the rest to do which is enforce the law. But what happens happens. I reckon it's going to keep on happening as long as the town wants the law enforced and the few wants to break it." For Luther Cain it had been a long speech so he ended it without regret although with a nearly inaudible sigh. Trying to explain what theretofore he'd thought had been self-explanatory had wearied him.

"Amen," Carl Norris said.

Harry Guttman felt he'd had his say earlier.

"Your job's far from easy, Marshal," the teacher said, "and we wish you the best." She started toward the front of the store. "Good to see you, Carl."

"Same to you, Lila, always. But you'll get soaked if you leave now. Look out the window and listen to it on the roof. May be last big rain of the season but it's a gully washer."

She turned at the doorway. "Much as I admire the company here I can't stay. It's my week eating at Blaines' and Ruth sets an early table. Her two boys starve by five you know."

"Well at least let me get you an umbrella." The druggist went behind a counter and brought out one. "Left here, not claimed." He carried it to her. "Bring it back next time you're in."

"I'll go along with you," the editor invited himself. "Have to stop back at the paper a while."

"Trouble with that is we're going in different directions." She accepted the umbrella—"Thank you, Mister Guttman"—looked for a moment at Carl—"Don't drown in this dreary damnable deluge"—stepped outdoors with a laugh, opened the umbrella, and hurried westward under the streaming sky.

"I hate puns," the druggist frowned.

The editor was grinning after the teacher. "It wasn't a pun, Harry, it was an alliteration. Gets it from me. Up to now she hated them."

"Illiterate is right."

"Keep that up and she'll hate you."

Luther's moustache tilted. "Can't say about you, Harry, but sure no hate in her look at a certain newspaper editor we know."

Carl frowned. "What are you talking about?"

" 'Low she's took a shine to you."

Carl was dumbfounded and surprisingly pleased. "Never noticed that."

"Times I count on noticing things others don't."

"I noticed it too," the druggist smiled. "Thought she was a smart woman." He transferred his smile to the marshal. "Just like I noticed Miss Carrie Shaw look at you a time or two at church suppers and places."

Luther reddened slightly.

"Never thought I'd see Luther Cain come close to blushing, Harry." The editor was relieved at the diversion which gave him time to start absorbing the notion of Lila's fancy. "But you can't say he and Carrie aren't smart to like each other. Luther, glad she got out of that fire safe last night."

The druggist started toward the rear of the store. "Well you ladies' men can stand there and moon, I'm closing."

The marshal raised his hand. "Before you do that, Harry, will you get me one of your poisons for this rattlesnake in my belly? Biting like hell last day or two."

"See the doc?"

"Tomorrow maybe if your dose don't cure it."

"Whereabouts it hurts?"

Luther pointed above his belt buckle.

"Not down low on the right side?"

"No."

"I'll fix you a little laudanum for pain. Only don't make a habit of it; comes from opium."

"Hell I ain't a Chinaman."

"And see Doc."

"Hell yes," the marshal grinned, "Pappy."

When the druggist had gone to fill the order the lawman turned his stare on the editor. "Carl, I want to ask you a favor. The boys at the paper said I could likely track you down here."

"Luther Cain tracking me gets my undivided attention. What can I do for you?"

"It's about Carrie Shaw. You know the lady we was speaking of. I seen you at the fire last night . . ."

"Luther, I knew Carrie before you came to town." With a lifted hand he apologized for his interruption. "She is all right, isn't she? I got there while you and Big John were looking after her and Everett."

"Fine. Throat sore some. And her chest from coughing. And tired. Got a room at the Drovers and Ruth Blaine's been over couple times to keep her company. Brung her some clothes from Berg's."

"Good." The editor waited for the marshal to continue.

"Well I know Friday's paper will say something about the fire." Luther cleared his throat. "Along with other things happened you already asked me about. Reckon that's what a newspaper's for, telling the news."

It intrigued Carl that twice within two minutes he had witnessed the stoical Luther Cain in the clutches of flusters. Evidently the lawman's coolness was overrated at least on occasion. Of course generalities were to be indulged at considerable risk. Under certain circumstances possibly fatal risk. "Yes, Luther, been writing or trying to this afternoon on several of those stories: Everett's fire and Noble and the inquest. Hell of a lot of things happened this week. I've still got tomorrow though; paper doesn't go to press until the next morning. But a lot of writing to do yet." Suddenly he realized he had prolonged his reply to delay Luther's asking him to skirt the edge of Frenchy Lesueur's death. He stopped talking and waited again uncomfortably.

"Well, Carl, what I was going to ask . . ." The marshal broke off and started over. "About the fire I reckon you'll tell how Everett pulled Carrie out the back window."

The editor nodded. "Saved her life."

"Sure did. Sure glad you going to tell about that. Fine thing he done."

The newsman's private relief that Frenchy didn't seem to be the subject of the marshal's appeal was chafed by curiosity. What was the man trying to say? "What the hell you trying to say, Luther?"

The lawman lowered his voice as Harry Guttman started up the aisle toward them carrying a small bottle. "Last night you was there, Carl, you seen when Everett got Carrie out she was . . . she didn't have no clothes on." His jaw muscles twitched. "You reckon that's part of the news you got to tell?"

The editor knew it was important not to smile despite his surge of warmth toward this reputedly imperturbable lawman. "Not at all, Luther, nothing to do with the story." He brushed his mouth with his hand. "As they say in my line of work it has no news value."

"I'm much obliged to you, Carl."

The druggist frowned at them both. "As they say in my line of work when it's time to go home it's time to go home. Rain or shine." He handed the laudanum to Luther. "Watch you don't sit on that, you'll need it worse than you do now. Damn new glass bottles they've started using back East won't last out here."

CHAPTER 23

. . . Bless me, Father, for I have sinned. It has been over a month since my last confession. Since then I've made love with a man who's not my husband. Yet. A fine man, Mark is—he is—and we love each other. We're not angels but we found each other. We were alone and kissing goodnight, Father, and it happened to us like we couldn't help it. He was upset— things in his job—and mad and mixed up. Maybe afraid. No he's not afraid of anything. I don't know. And I was worried for him, needed to bolster him up. But we're going to be married, Father. If God forgives us I know we are. And happy! I'm sorry. I'm glad what's happening to us but I'm sorry what happened that night. Oughtn't I be? Yes I ought. I'm sorry. I hope you understand. I hope God does! . . .

Half a dozen hours and two shallow swallows of laudanum following his drugstore visit, both Luther's stomachache and his nightly rounds were behind him for the time being and before him about a foot was the closed door of Carrie's hotel room. As he had crossed the muddy plaza in the after-storm moonlight he had counted the dark second-story windows along to the yellow-glowing one he'd fixed as hers that afternoon. Either she still was awake or had fallen asleep with her coal-oil lamp burning. Whichever the case he'd felt obliged as he had walked toward his own room along the Drovers' upstairs hall to see to her welfare. His upraised sore knuckles fell lightly against the pine panel, even lightly making him wince. As he cradled those in his other palm he heard Carrie's bare feet touch the floor and come softly toward him. Somehow he felt them approach, even saw them with their proud arches and delicately gripping toes. A knot formed in his stomach but a long way from painfully. "Who is it?" he heard her ask quietly. He whispered "Me" and then elaborated more audibly: "Luther." Unaccountably he shook his head as the door opened on her nightgowned form.

"Come in, Dear, glad to see you. Why are you shaking your head?" Since he didn't know he didn't reply and accommodatingly she dropped the line of inquiry, her eyes blinking with amusement.

She closed the door when he'd stepped inside. "All right, if you don't like that one here's another: why don't you kiss me?"

To that question he responded still wordlessly but by tossing his hat onto the rumpled bed and enfolding her in his arms like a found child although there was nothing childlike about the heat which caught between them. His urgency seemed to penetrate her whole being, all the frustration and tumult and dread of his recent days to pour into her; and she was their ready vessel welcoming his need while still half-frightened by her own nightmares. The fire which nearly had killed her the previous night, the ambiguities of yesterday's inquest and her talk with Howard Smith, the pall of Noble's death and the storm of Frenchy's the day before in which double tragedy Luther had played his role, all these miseries suddenly inflamed them with a sense of sharing, of interdependence such as Carrie only had dared foresee and Luther until now had feared. Neither of them gave this happening conscious thought as they held each other. Their refuge was too demanding, rational or not. She didn't exult in it or doubt it and he didn't accept it or reject it; her perplexity and his wariness might or might not return but for the moment they let their mutual reliance happen because there seemed no other course.

Presently with another bristly kiss and almost a rib-crushing hug he dropped his arms, turned and stepped to the small bureau, unbuckled his gun belt, folded it next to the full water pitcher sitting in its bowl, and stood facing away from her. "Get in bed."

She realized his voice's hoarseness wasn't from last night's smoke. "Yes, Dear." And the huskiness of her own wasn't from the smoke either.

"Nightshirt's too damn thin."

She grinned safely out of his sight, padded past the bedside table and its flickering lamp and climbed between the muslin sheets, pulling the top one to her throat and leaning against the propped-up pillow. "Sorry about the nightgown, I wasn't expecting company; but I'm glad you're here." Her grin widened. "To tell the truth I may not have been expecting but I was hoping."

He turned toward her. "To tell the truth I sure wasn't finding fault, just saying a fact: it's a mighty pretty outfit."

"Thank you, Luther. It's thin because the nights are still not too chilly. In the wintertime before too long I'll go to flannel."

189

"Just like you're a mighty pretty woman. And in a thin nightshirt you make a man warm summer or winter."

"Making you warm, Dear, makes me a warm and happy woman. But a pretty one I doubt." She stretched an arm from under the sheet toward him, its hand waiting for his. "Come here, I want to kiss you again. Then I want to talk."

His boot heels struck four measured times on the pine floor boards and he pushed his hat out of the way on the bed and sat down next to her and took her offered hand as her other one touched his cheek.

"Luther, I love you." Her eyes moistened.

His eyes didn't moisten the way hers did and women's often do when they speak of loving but held hers with the dry, hot intensity of men's at such times. "Looks like I love you, too, don't it?"

She returned his smile. "Talked yourself into it?"

His response to that was letting go both her hands and gripping her shoulders and pulling her to him, seizing her lips with his and pressing her against his chest until her murmuring into his mouth became a happily desperate whisper for air.

She pulled away after a moment. "My, that was a kiss all right."

His glance grazed her breasts under her nightgown's voile as she leaned against the pillow a little dazedly. A mist of sweat glinted on his forehead. "What was it you wanted to talk about, Carrie?"

She took a deep, quiet breath and let it out before answering him. Both her hands held one of his. Her eyes scanned his face with more tenderness than he ever had seen in them. They pulled his mind backward to an Indiana farm. Quickly he lowered his eyes from them to her slightly open mouth and again quickly to his own denimed knee.

"You look tired, Luther Week's been a heller ain't it?"

"No taffy pull."

"So, so sorry about Noble Buck."

"Damn shame. Never hurt nobody. Law-abiding all his goddam short life."

"To think I was talking to him at Jake Barlow's a little while before he was dead. He give me an ice chip to suck on. He was so proud you rode on his wagon that morning, Luther." She smiled sadly at the image. "You and Spot setting up there with him riding across the plaza and hollering at Doc Bowman. You was a hero to him. You know I got the idea he liked me too? You know something else?" She waited until Luther looked at her. "I got the idea he liked us if you know what I mean." Her gaze required a response of him.

"I reckon I know what you mean."

"You figure he liked us being together?"

"He never said." Luther sighed, an unusual thing for him. "But I reckon he did, Carrie. And if you want to know it Carl Norris about said the same thing in Guttman's this afternoon."

"Like Preacher Smith done to me yesterday. See, I ain't the only one."

His grimace was almost forlornly humorous. "Like the whole town for godssake."

"Town's got all kinds of things to talk about these days." She lifted his hand to her face and brushed it with her lips and held it against her cheek, her eyes solemn. "I want to ask you something." She inhaled a breath of courage. "A few folks, not many just a few, is still wondering why you lit into Frenchy so terrible hard. They don't excuse him but . . ."

"Because the sonofabitch shot a kid!" He pulled his hand away from hers. "Ain't that enough? Goddam them! And it was my job to try arresting him."

Carrie hadn't made it this far down her thirty-three-year trail without nerve. "They only say he didn't mean to shoot him. It was reckless. And it don't make Noble less dead. But it wasn't a-purpose. They're wondering why you didn't only arrest him instead of beat him." Abashedly she realized Luther might guess "they" included her. "Nobody's saying your job is easy or you ain't good at it, Honey . . . I mean Dear." Relief flooded her that apparently he hadn't noticed her slip. "I know it's hard and you're good at it. And I hated what Frenchy done and I was never madder at nobody in my life."

"The inquest proved Pat Tharp had a knife and him and Frenchy fought me and Frenchy got killed in the fighting. 'Accident' Doc ruled. Goddam right I was mad! Like you and everybody else. But Doc ruled what it was: 'Accident.' And that ought to be the goddam end of it." He stared at her. "Ain't it with you?"

She took his hand in hers again and he didn't resist her nestling it against her warm throat. "Yes, Luther." Her return gaze was as steady as his. "It only scared me—for you—to hear them tell how you fought. I'm glad I didn't see it. Your job scares me. Even if it brung us together it scares me. Luther, let me ask you something: you like doing it?"

"It's a job, Carrie. Doing what I know, what I do good like you said. I reckon I like it all right. I never thought."

"I hope I can get used to it, Dear. I'll try. I hope you can get used to me trying and let me keep on."

The tilt of his head and his smile under his moustache were almost sad. "Don't know as I'd want you to quit."

"Luther, I want to ask you one more thing but I don't want you to get mad all over again. Mostly at me I don't. Please don't."

He wasn't exactly wary, more curious. "What?"

With her heart quickening she risked it: "Remember you told me about your cousin back in Indiana and that terrible fire?"

He tensed and nodded.

"Last night in Everett's yard when he just saved me from burning and you was holding me you looked kind of scared yourself only mixed with mad. You cussed like when you told me about that other fire." Their gazes were fused. Hers begged for understanding. "Is maybe there something inside you keeps you mad, Luther?"

He waited, jaws tight, sensing she wasn't finished.

"Preacher Smith said maybe there is. You was hurt once you know. Being so awful mad at Frenchy, was maybe that already there like dynamite and Frenchy killing Noble set it off?"

"No, goddammit!"

Absurdly she had heard an instant's fear in his voice. "Please don't be mad at me." She rushed on, seized by the notion it was now or never. "And you shying from me lot of times, could it be mixed up with that? Luther, listen to me: am I your cousin some way? Was I her in the fire last night?"

"Hell no!" His upper body lunged frighteningly toward her, arms going around her, jerking her against him, their eyes inches apart. "You're you, Carrie, goddammit to hell!" Before his mouth crushed hers his stare speared into her brain. "And don't you forget it!"

Gradually under his gentling lips and arms and hands her fright dissolved into the returning passion which swirled up through her being, filling it once more with a need to exorcise the ghosts of past evil and past infatuation and embrace the present's goodness and love with her entire body and mind and soul. Slowly and wonderingly and with great tenderness as their whispers rustled the room's stillness and the lamplight nudged its shadows they undressed each other. Their caresses found the most salient strengths and deepest recesses of their beings as their dependency became less uncertain.

"I love you, Carrie, bygod I do."

"I love you too, Luther."

Outside the room Ruth Blaine, smiling fondly at the indistinguishable, recognized whisperings beyond the door where she had stood for just an instant, tiptoed back along the hall toward the stairway, content in the vast safety of her recently endangered friend whom she'd come to tell goodnight.

> . . . *During my interview with the assistant district attorney, he recalled very clearly a late night's talk some years ago with then-Corporal Keller. "You don't forget much about any talk with that man," he told me.*
>
> *They had finished going over the officer's report of his nabbing an accused rapist and murderer who was "a vicious s.o.b. we'd been after for a year before the corporal's good arrest nailed down a solid case for us." The attorney told Keller he'd heard that the officer seldom missed but was glad this time for only the hood's shoulder wound so the State could see him sent up, on which Keller commented that he'd hit the scumbag where he'd aimed so he could "spit in his face through the bars" himself.*
>
> *In answer to the lawyer's question, the policeman said he'd considered college and law school after Vietnam, because he'd wanted to be on the law's side ever since, as a youngster, seeing a "good neighborhood cop wasted by a bad (unprintable)," but he hadn't been able to afford it and anyhow had got*

married. Also, he'd been reminded by a cop friend about police pensions and that the work still was in the law. When the attorney said the work was in fact the cutting edge, the very point of the law, Keller recalled that a buddy of his had "bought it on the point of a reconnaissance patrol," although before they'd moved out the soldier had quoted Bob Hope that "Only the lead dog has a change of scenery."

When their conversation switched to their families at the lawyer's asking whether he had any children, Mark said not yet but that he and his wife were going to keep trying until they did, because they both wanted them and Mattie was bound to be the "best mother this side of Mary."

Incidentally, Mark said that Mattie and he hadn't been childhood sweethearts, as had the attorney and his wife, adding with what the lawyer recalls as odd vehemence that he wished they had been; and then the policeman apologized for his outburst, saying he was just tired, especially of (unprintable) troublemakers like the one he'd shot—maybe too accurately—in the shoulder. And when the attorney thanked the officer again for his help to the city and to law and order generally, warning him with a grin that if he wasn't careful he "might end up a damn legend," Mark Keller's jaws visibly tightened but his muttered reply was drowned by a passing fire truck's screamed outrage at a blaze somewhere . . .

CHAPTER 24

Ruth Blaine awakened at about the same time as the Bolinger Stable's equine boarders did in the next block and as Carl Norris's roosters began crowing at the dawn another couple of blocks east of Pacific Street. It was another early-October mid-week day or at least apt to be when the sun had followed its red glow up over the eastern rim of the plains' great wheel. She had slept well last night in Lester's good arms. Now he had left their bed to go out into the back yard's half-light to milk their cow while she stole a few sensuous moments longer thinking of their love-making in the night and recedingly, mistily of ancient days when happiness had been found in girlhood dreams and devotions and doings. She smiled to herself thinking of that whimsical Carl Norris writing a feature article about her life: "The Travels and Trials of Ruth Chandler Blaine" or "From Crawfordsville to Bancroft with Considerable Bustle" (the latter not really doing him justice).

Although her existence had begun at her birth in the booming Indiana land-office village on Sugar Creek where her father had owned Chandler's General Store and Tannery her own mortality and everybody else's hadn't dawned on her until her thirteenth birthday when, in hideous observance of the event, her mother had died of cancer. During the next five years, however, her mere existence and the cloud of its mortality gradually had fused into bright, throbbing life.

She had absorbed what the local public school had to offer and had supplemented that at her father's insistence and appreciable expense by a year at the town's private school for young ladies in the "Canby Girls' " home. Concurrently with her formal education she'd learned some things good and bad about human nature male and female; she'd been courted and spurned by schoolboys and by students of local Wabash College and had enjoyed close friendships with some girls and suffered enmity of others. In this kaleidoscope of living there had been images of church services and family reunions and parades of Mexican War veterans and funerals and weddings, of cheering at rallies for Taylor and Pierce, of missing her mother, of mourning and laughing and cooking and washing dishes with her father and helping him on Saturdays in his store, reading "Uncle Tom's Cabin," hearing the names Webster and Calhoun and Clay and Douglas in arguments over slavery and free soil and Bleeding Kansas, talking excitedly about townsman Jim Marshall's discovery of California gold at Sutter's Mill and county boy Ezra Meeker's guiding wagon trains to Oregon, and of waiting with all other Crawfordsville girls for whatever acceptable Crawfordsville boy should ask her to marry him.

Then suddenly her life had seemed to come into focus, to stabilize on one image: the twenty-eight-year-old personification of her fantasy, the face and form which now after twenty years were only slightly older and just had left her bed warmed with nearly the same vitality as surged from him on that cold December afternoon. He had reached Crawfordsville—later he'd said from Kentucky along the Ohio and Wabash Rivers and Sugar Creek—during the week before Christmas and she first had become aware of him the day after he'd got there. He had stopped on the other side of the counter in her father's store and stared at her until she'd blushed and instead of asking about the goods piled between them had said, "I hope Santa Claus is good to you too because I'm sure going to be." With that he'd winked at her, reached across the counter and patted her hot cheek, asked if there were a bank in town, and when she'd pointed in the direction of the Elston & Lane one he had headed for the front of the store, calling back before stepping into the winter's bluster, "I'll see you soon, Young Lady."

And he had, the next day in fact. And the day after that. And the next one. And everyday until her father had given her hand in marriage to Lester Blaine twelve months from the week the young man had stepped into the store.

On both the local and national scenes the year before their marriage and the one after it had been mighty eventful. Lester hadn't been in town and courting her for more than two months when her father had overcome initial wariness about the young man's honorable intentions and concurrently had found his youthful energy and ideas just the ticket for a business hard-pressed by booming competition, especially when its proprietor's own energy had been waning with a secretly tired heart. The proprietor had taken on first an employee and then a partner and

196

then a son-in-law. After her and Lester's marriage the store's name had been changed to Chandler's and Blaine's Commercial Mart with the addition of a distillery and a lumber yard to its general merchandising and tanning activities. The expansion certainly had been in keeping with Crawfordsville's and indeed the nation's pulsing growth commercially and geographically.

Locally the variety of small proprietorships—slaughtering, meat packing, hat making, grain and wood milling, coopering, distilling—had been enlarging into evidently sturdy little industries some of whose products had been shipped over ancient waterways and new railroads as far as New Orleans, St. Louis, Chicago, even New York. Nationally almost the entire decade of the 'fifties had been a mingling of overland westward thrusting, explosive industrial development and strident clamor about slavery. Kansas, Nebraska, and Missouri particularly and often literally had become battlegrounds of abolitionists and pro-slavers but the whole country—Congress, state and territorial governments, businesses, people generally—had been seized by a sort of moral-social-economic hysteria.

Things had been moving too fast in too many directions not to crash. And one of the early Crawfordsville victims of the inevitable economic panic of 1857 and its depression had been Chandler's and Blaine's Commercial Mart. Ruth remembered with a sharp pang as she lay now in their bed twenty years after that awful morning when Lester almost had staggered home from a night of sweating with her father over the partnership's books and told her the business was ruined and when an hour later Doctor Mary Hoover had arrived to say her father was dead of a heart attack.

During those winter months Lester had salvaged what little he could of the Mart's financial remnants and one day in the spring, abruptly, even urgently, he had come home with word from a former customer about an opportunity in Springfield, Illinois and that he would start for there the next morning to look into it. A letter from him a month later had said he couldn't leave the launching of his new undertaking to return for her but as soon as possible she was to sell her father's farm where they had been living since the latter's death, bring the money and come to his arms. Rather breathlessly, with mingling melancholy and excitement, she had done as he'd asked and left her home town behind for good. His new venture had turned out to be a combined barber shop and feed store, paid for over time with the farm-sale proceeds and its own earnings. Along with their gracious house which he had built with natural carpentry skill, sharpened as the job had progressed, his gradually succeeding enterprise had nurtured their blending into Springfield's comprehensive life for the time they'd called that community home. One of her fondest memories of those eight years was their friendship with the towering, exquisitely homely local lawyer whom they'd seen elected sixteenth President of the United States. Her two worst memories were of Abe Lincoln's assassination and of Lester's two-year, nightmarish absence after the 1863 draft law had scooped him into the Union Army (although he hadn't resisted going when he'd been called).

As long as she'd known him her beloved husband had thrived on challenges. Maybe mostly that had been his reason for wanting to move to St. Louis the year after Appomattox. He had become familiar with the city during the war; it had been the headquarters of the Union Army's western operations and he'd been stationed there for several weeks before being sent down to the seige of Vicksburg and from there with General Grant to other battles farther east. And when he had been mustered out and found his barber shop-feed store in a state of blight, which he'd assured Ruth of course hadn't been her fault but circumstances', he also had assured her of the Mississippi River boom town's best bet for them both. Seeing his heart had been set on it and remembering after all that he never had let her down she had taken a deep breath and sighed and said she'd move again. She had felt a little more secure the next year however when laughingly she'd told some of her new St. Louis friends she'd noticed construction had begun on a bridge back across the river to Illinois.

Seven years later—years of politically naive, scandal-mutilated Grant Presidency, chaotic post-war "Reconstruction," further rash industrial venturing and frontier-pushing, laborious birth of Blaine's Furniture Company and belatedly of George and handicapped Tim Blaine—another economic panic and its severe depression had sunk its challenging arrows into Lester's mettle and Ruth's loyalty, killing the Company and almost their spirits. The year 1873 had been to their and everybody else's minds an awful one. But on a grim night the next year they had looked at each other across the supper table and gripped hands and touched the children lovingly and Lester calmly had proposed moving not only to a new place but a new way of life about which he had been talking with some visiting cattlemen who'd been there and might decide to go back for good. They'd told him about an almost new but thriving little town in western Kansas of all places. Nothing easy about life there, he had learned, but surely no more frustrating than theirs had been up to then; and according to his acquaintances the horizons of the area's opportunities had been as wide as its fertile plains.

Naturally (she grinned now in the dawn at the word's aptness) they had moved again, hopefully but by no means certainly for the last time. And now they were settled in their Bancroft home which her husband had built like their Springfield one with touches of those in Crawfordsville and St. Louis but with the addition of a shed for the milk cow they hadn't needed before. Lester's carpentry was in demand; he had an interest in their friend Carrie Shaw's seamstress business; he was having talks with Ed Sarver and Oscar Lacy about some kind of food service for railroad passengers; and they had made friends all over town, including the mayor and the marshal at one end of the civic rainbow and Jimson Street's Nell at the other.

CHAPTER 25

Through the murky vapor engulfing him Mark Keller gazed back across the summers turning to falls and to winters and to springs and to summers all over again: Veterans Day marches, high school class reunions, Christmas trees adorned, steaks grilled outdoors and suspects indoors, firecrackers, laughs, a few tears, shooting for practice and for real, working up to 27-day vacations, seeing some good movies and more lousy ones, bowling, talking over old times at the Lodge, trying to talk sense into an erring friend's head, making married love, loving being married, doing a good cop's job by giving crime no quarter and asking none. Most days simply had unrolled, others had unraveled, a few had come apart at the seams but had been sewn up again quickly if sometimes with Mattie's advice. Promotions had come along untrammeled by internal or external politics, given his record and scary probity, until in his sergeancy he'd reach his goal just short of an unwanted desk job. Along the way the mayor had presented to him a rare Medal of Honor and a couple more Certificates of Honorable Mention for Outstanding Performance of Duty.

The lightning of angels flashed again and he seemed to feel a shock and hear a gasp.

Standing at the window of his Drovers room in the morning's first light, tucking his shirt into his trousers Luther Cain saw a man hurry from the narrow space between the Lone Star Cafe and the Schmidt Brothers cigar factory and trot southward across the shadowy corner of the plaza. The figure quickly crossed the railroad track between the depot and the Bell Mare Livery Stable and disappeared past the rear of Jake Barlow's smithy into the warren of honky-tonks, rooming houses and corrals beyond. Everything about the little drama demanded Luther's investigation. Buckling on his gun belt he stepped to the room's door, unbolted it, pulled it open, and strode along the hall to the stairway. He already wore his hat; as with cow-punchers, troopers, and ingrained outdoorsmen generally it had been the first thing he had put on after awakening, followed by his boots, those items having to do respectively with weather and either cactus or rattlesnakes. By the time he had stalked the apparition's way across the plaza and past the rear of the smithy and the side of the Maverick and had emerged into Jimson Street all that remained of it were an echo of hoofbeats and a dust-veiled dwindling of a horse and rider southwestward toward Plainville.

Realizing of course that only his hunch painted the horseman's leaving town as flight and anyhow that the rider already was out of the marshal's legal jurisdiction Luther ignored his itch to light after the man immediately on a horse from a nearby stable. Instead he walked back up to the cigar factory and cafe and between those to the rear yard common to all businesses on the plaza's west side. As soon as he saw the ajar back door of the Schmidts' establishment he figured his lawman's hunch hadn't bluffed him out of the pot and the next instant when he heard the urgency in Gus's muffled voice he was damn sure it hadn't. Reaching the door in three strides he stood sideways with his left shoulder against its jamb and his right hand drawing his gun. With the side of his foot he gave the door a shove inward, his gaze slanting inside with it. Holstering his gun he stepped inside and quickly crossed the small room to help Gus haul the dazed, mumbling Fritz upright. There was a small puddle of blood on the floor and a smear on Fritz's cheek obviously from lying in it and Luther saw a crimson trickle now on the nape of the man's neck from what likely had been a blow to the back of his head.

"We'd ought to set him down 'til Doc sees him." The marshal nodded toward a bench along a table littered with tobacco trimmings. "What the hell happened?"

"On the floor when downstairs later I came," Gus panted as they half-carried the reeling man to the bench and lowered him onto it, his brother pushing him back gently against the table. "Someone he surprised. A little noise earlier I didn't bother." The cigar maker thumbed Luther's attention to an up-tilted floorboard in a corner, his expression doubly galled. "Fritz and money both." He shook his fist at the outrage. "Him for this I'll fix, bastard I'll get."

"Right now you get Oscar Lacy next door; likely he just opened. Tell him to fetch Doc Bowman. Also Big John at the town hall to roust out the sheriff. I'll help your brother."

As Gus headed for the door Luther stooped to peer at Fritz's eyes and shift him more comfortably against the table. Then he straightened and looked around the cluttered room and reckoned

Gus had inferred things about right: the thief must have learned of the Schmidts' old-country way of hiding money under the factory's floor but hadn't counted on one of them coming downstairs from their living quarters so early, had hid quickly, hit Fritz from behind, got the money sack from under the board, stuffed it under his coat, and vamoosed. Luther knew in which direction the sonofabitch had vamoosed, however, and even an hour's start on a fast horse in that country didn't amount to a whole lot; hiding places were as scarce as polar bears in Dixie and man and horse had to sleep and eat and the county's good trackers included Luther Cain. The thing the marshal didn't know yet was how the goddam bully might have learned about the money.

As Fritz groaned and leaned forward from the table, elbows finding his knees and hands propping his head, Sarah Lacy rustled through the open door carrying a splashing-over basin of water and some cloths. "Mercysakes, Fritz, Oscar told me you got bumped on the head. He's went for Doc Bowman. Morning, Marshal." She came to a breathless, purposeful halt beside the men. "Going to clean you up some while he's coming." She set the basin and cloths on the table, craned down frowning at the wound, her fingers delicately pushing aside some strands of hair. Then she dipped one of the cloths into the water, squeezed it out, dabbed it carefully about the oozing cut, pressing it there for a moment, and repeated the procedure with another cloth. Finally she mopped the blood off Fritz's cheek and neck. He bore all this silently and it appeared gratefully, wincing a few times in his obvious grogginess. Luther watched it with his eyes but not with his mind; his thoughts were out on the prairie southwest of town running down some unknown goddam sonofabitching thief who'd bushwhacked an old man who was a friend of his and of a lot of other folks. Unknown the bastard might be now but not for long.

"Sarah," the marshal thought aloud, "if whoever done this didn't stumble over the money, if he knowed ahead of time it was here somebody had to tell him." He looked down at the cigar maker. "Fritz, you hearing me?"

Fritz nodded painfully. "Our money somebody stole."

"That's right. You or Gus tell anybody your money was here?"

The cigar maker raised his eyes to the lawman; they were dull but comprehending; slowly with a sad smile he shifted them to Sarah without speaking.

"They told Oscar," the woman said for him, "in case something

202

happened to the two of them. And Oscar told me." Abruptly another recollection was vivid on her face. "And when Oscar told me somebody heard him. He never meant for that to happen."

"Who heard him?"

"Laverne Strauss, Marshal. The part-time girl here."

Luther squinted. "Husband Herman lives out toward Plainville." It was a statement.

"They're not together, don't get along; she lives down here in the rooming house between the Maverick and where Lane's burned."

"Don't get along is a fact. Big John and me rode out to slow him down the night of the fire." The marshal seemed to be speaking more to himself than to Sarah. "But that don't mean she ain't talked to him."

"Not about the Schmidts' money she wouldn't," Sarah defended her part-time employee, "she's no gossip."

Luther continued to address his line of thinking. "When folks hates each other no telling what they'll talk about."

Gus stepped through the door with Doc Bowman in tow. "Doc down with one of Nell's girls. Oscar the sheriff is finding."

The physician grinned as he crossed the room to Gus's brother. "One of Nell's girls with a bellyache. Morning, Sarah, Luther. Well, Fritz, I hear you been tangling with a damn robber."

"Ya," Fritz muttered.

Doc set down his saddlebags and examined the cigar maker's wound. "I see somebody washed it."

"Hope I did right, Doctor."

"Just right, Sarah." The physician looked closely into Fritz's eyes, asked him what day it was and whether he felt sick at his stomach and set about repairing his damaged scalp with whiskey, scissors, acid, needle, and catgut. "You'll be fine," he assured his patient and the others in the room when he'd finished, "but you sure better rest a couple days, Fritz. That was a hell of a mean hit on the head." He looked at the marshal. "Find what it was done with?"

"Nothing the bastard left here. His pistol I reckon."

"Must have been the butt. Very little harder Fritz would have a fractured skull. Maybe worse if that wouldn't been enough."

"My brother almost killed?" Gus gritted. "Schweinehund I get; him instead I kill."

"Getting him's my job, Gus." The lawman's tone now was

emotionless. "You take care of Fritz." At that moment Sheriff Light ducked into the room behind Oscar. The officer was as tall but not as lean as Luther, a pleasant-appearing, sandy-haired man. Probably in his sixties Luther had guessed on first meeting him. Hard to tell exactly with men who spent much of their time outdoors. The marshal had come to like him as their paths had crossed almost daily in the town hall although they'd had little communication officially beyond helpful exchanges of information. "Thanks for coming, Roscoe," the marshal greeted him. "Got a mixed town-county matter here I 'low. I'd thank you for your help."

"You got it." The county lawman greeted Sarah, Doc and the Schmidt brothers and turned back to his town counterpart. "What you aiming at?"

The marshal related the morning's facts and then approached his interpretation of them carefully, retracing his reasoning as much to validate it for himself as for the sheriff. "Gus and Fritz told Oscar and no one else about the money." He looked at the brothers in turn for confirmation and when each had nodded he looked at Oscar. "And you only told Sarah. But Laverne heard you do it." The Lone Star proprietor nodded and the marshal spoke to the room generally. "So Laverne was the only one knowed about the money besides the Schmidt boys and the Lacys here, that is 'til she must have told somebody. And that somebody's likely the thief; he wouldn't likely let nobody else in on such a find. Course I'm ruling out Laverne herself because it was a man's walk I seen leaving here this morning."

"And I'm ruling out me," Oscar said seriously. "We was in our kitchen fixing to open when he must have been in here. Jesus. Wish I'd heard the sonofabitch."

Luther's eyes narrowed on him. "Reckon he's the kind of sonofabitch I'm glad you didn't hear. Only difference between him and a killer is he just forgot to hit hard enough. And I already ruled you out, Oscar; town can't spare your cooking. How soon Laverne coming in?"

"Not coming today," the proprietor said, "or the rest of the week. Went to Dodge to visit her sister."

The marshal looked at the sheriff. "Can't wait that long to find out who she told. The thief could be out of the county before dark; need to get on his trail. And I 'low we got something to go on besides his tracks and the direction he headed, that being Laverne could have said something to Herman about the cache. Don't know why she would; maybe they got to arguing over something like why he don't make money the way Gus and Fritz does. Him and her raises holy hell with each other ever time they meet. Everbody knows that."

Oscar's nod was emphatic. "Including in the Lone Star time or two."

"And if I don't miss my guess a mile, Roscoe, we ride for Herman's dugout and we won't be far off the goddam robber's trail."

"Let's get to riding."

CHAPTER 26

After a half-hour's steady trotting—the fastest way to cover a lot of ground—the lawmen's unwinded horses had brought them almost half-way to Herman Strauss's sod lair. There hadn't been much talking between the men; even with experienced riders trotting isn't a gait for conversation; in fact anything above a fast walk tends to limit exchanges to necessities and what these riders needed was to get where they were going and do whatever should be called for when they got there. The sheriff did have one question for the marshal however.

"Luther, I don't know if you'll count it any my business but I heard Bill Crum say yesterday about you running for mayor next time."

"No truth to it, Roscoe. Damn scalawag was full of redeye."

"Sorry to hear it. You'd a-made a good one."

Luther glanced across the space between their horses. His expression was not as indifferent as his tone. "Most folks got to vote for a man to elect him. Reckon that lets me out nowadays."

"Ain't the way I hear it." For a fleeting instant Roscoe looked uncomfortable. "Well if you ain't set on it I been thinking maybe I might give it a whirl. Getting too goddam old to traipse over the county. And Bones would step in my boots. And Guttman offered me to come in his drug store to help with the pay."

"Well go to it. I ain't."

With another half-hour's riding behind them and Herman's dugout a few minutes ahead over a low rise the two men lifted themselves at the same time in their stirrups and squinted at a thick brown hump in the grass a hundred yards before them. As a horse's head reared out of the hump whinnying and their mounts whinnied in response they reined to a walk, glances flicking over the prairie, free hands touching their guns, and heeled their animals warily forward until they stood looking down at a sweat-and-dust-caked bay gelding with wild eyes and jagged piece of leg bone protruding through its bloody hide.

"Goddam," Luther said quietly

Roscoe pointed at a small mound of turned earth a dozen feet away. "Yonder."

Luther looked briefly at the sign of a prairie-dog hole and back at its victim. "Bastard just let him lay, saddle, bridle and all." Then he scanned the ground ahead of the tortured horse and nodded toward it. "Bay ain't the only one hurt."

The sheriff's gaze followed the marshal's along the scuffed dirt and mashed grass up the gradually sloping terrain. "Limped hisself over the hill."

"Not too slow though. Ain't too bad off. Not as bad as he might get."

Roscoe smiled a little. "Just hungry maybe; wanted to get home for dinner. Reckon he'll like our jail food?"

Luther didn't reply. "We got to do something about this horse. The shot'll be a warning." He nodded toward the rise.

"Horses whinnying already has been." The sheriff lay his hand on his rifle in its saddle scabbard. "Want me . . .?"

"It's my cowshitting job," the marshal muttered.

They both realized Luther's anger wasn't aimed at the sheriff. He thumbed his Colt's horseback thong off its hammer, pulled the weapon deliberately from its holster—"Set tight"—and fired. The sheriff's horse and his flung up their heads, shied sideways and stood trembling. The gelding's head oozed a bubbling red sluice and flopped back onto the ground, its legs scrabbling the dust briefly and stilling. "Goddam."

"Always hate to see that."

Luther slid his gun into its holster. "Sonofabitch killed him." He prodded his mount with his spurs. "Bygod, let's go."

A short watchful lope later the two lawmen stood wide apart. beside their horses a hundred feet in front of Herman Strauss's home. The sod shanty was half-buried in the hillside. Each man held his horse's reins in the crook of his elbow and his rifle slightly forward in both hands. The marshal glanced at the sheriff and Roscoe took his cue.

"Herman," the county official shouted, "come on out. It's Roscoe Light and Luther Cain. Want to talk to you." He added an after-thought: "And don't start nothing, you ain't got a chance."

"I'm coming, goddam you," a hoarse voice called from inside

the house, "and I know who the hell you are for chrissake. I seen you ride up like you hankered to get shot." The voice added something indistinguishable and Herman pushed aside the buffalo-hide curtain which he hadn't yet replaced for the winter with a wooden door and stepped blinking into the sunlight. Nervousness seemed to heighten his belligerence. "What the hell you want?"

"Little matter back in town of clubbing Fritz Schmidt and stealing his money," the marshal said loudly. "You know anything about that, Herman? You been in town this morning?"

"Hell no I ain't."

The sheriff raised his chin toward the house's sheltering hill. "How come that horse laying over the rise yonder with his leg broke?"

A darker shadow of fear scudded across the homesteader's face. "That ain't . . ." He broke off, his eyes abruptly twitching from side to side in their sockets, his mouth distending.

"You like leaving a broke-leg horse laying thataway?" Luther's tone was acid. "Hurting where he fell?"

Herman's eyes continued their weird movements, his grimace stretching. "Ain't done nothing," he gusted; "get off my place, leave me be."

"What the hell's the trouble with you?" Roscoe demanded.

The marshal was staring hard at their quarry. "He's a sonofabitch is his trouble."

Luther began walking slowly forward, casually raising his rifle a couple of inches. The sheriff moved with him. Their horses followed. There seemed to be a slight frown under the county lawman's hat brim but it could have been a squint. His town partner's face was expressionless.

Herman's expression had turned desperate.

"Luther?" Roscoe shammed joviality without looking at the marshal. "You reckon our friend here's going inside and bring us out something? Like maybe any extry money laying around?"

"Don't 'low it's a good idea, Roscoe, not with that pistol lumping under his shirt. Might forget what he went for and shoot us through the goddam window."

"Well I'll be damned if I noticed that lump."

Luther's stare hadn't wavered from Herman. "So I'll just mosey in myself after he lays down his pistol mighty easy and you . . ."

Suddenly with a shout the homesteader flung himself at the ground and rolled toward the marshal clawing at his shirt and screeching like an attacking redskin. There was no hesitation in the reflex of Luther's finger on the trigger of his carbine. A shattering explosion and a blur of his hand jerking the rifle's lever forward and back melded into his rifle's second ear-splitting blast and the combined echo of the two shots drowned Herman's tearing cough and Roscoe's "No!" and almost his "Look out!" and then the obscenities pouring from the house's window ahead of a blast from its interior and another from Luther's rifle into its window and the dusky face beyond. On the ground Herman's mouth and nose poured out his blood and his eyes rolled upward under his lids and stayed there, his throat gurgling. Dropping his reins and running to the house and levering another bullet from his rifle's magazine into its barrel the marshal jumped over the homesteader and plunged past the buffalo-hide door curtain and found inside on the dirt floor with its face a welter of red the corpse of the man they'd ridden out to find. The money sack Gus had described was on the table and the homesteader's burned flapjacks were in a frying pan on the hot stove. As the past few seconds' implications dawned on Luther he turned slowly to try speaking of them to the sheriff—"Goddam, Roscoe, it wasn't Herman—" but no one stood behind him. "Roscoe!" He pushed outward past the buffalo hide. "Where the hell are you?"

The sheriff lay on his back twenty feet from Herman. Luther ran to the fallen man and kneeled at his side. Roscoe's eyes were open.

"Where he get you, Roscoe?" His answer was under his palm resting on the sheriff's chest. He turned his wet fingers upward and stared at them and back at Roscoe's ashen face.

The sheriff's lips barely moved. "Where it counts, Luther," he whispered. "Herman tried to warn . . ." Then Roscoe died.

All alone Luther looked into the sun and took a deep breath and opened his mouth and yelled until the hill and the sod house and all of Kansas surely heard him and winced.

CHAPTER 27

Roping the homesteader's horse in the corral a short blizzard-distance from the dugout and hitching Herman's and Indian Jesse's corpses onto it and loading Roscoe's heavy body across the saddle of the sheriff's roan which had stood loyally throughout the chaos and stringing together the remuda of death for the trail back to Bancroft were by far the hardest things Luther had done since helping shovel dirt onto his cousin's coffin twenty years earlier. His head ached with the violence of Jake Barlow's hammer every hoof-step of the journey over the rise and past the dead horse and across the plains; the shimmer of the day drove lances into his eyes despite the shadow of his black hat's pulled-down brim. He hadn't had a drink of water since they'd left town and his throat was dust-lined but he couldn't reach for the canteen tied to his saddle horn next to the money sack because Roscoe hadn't had a drink either and maybe Herman hadn't and he owed more than that to the sheriff and the sodbuster. "Goddam! Sonofabitchgoddamtohell!" Carrie Shaw's face swam across his mind's flood; her arms reached out to him before the vision sank under his pain but he wasn't a man to let pain take control of him. He would tell her so tonight, he would tell her whatever needed telling. He would tell her of his need for her. He was very tired of being alone. Why hadn't that sonofabitching pilgrim shouted the half-breed was inside? Rolling eyeballs thataway didn't give the sign; Luther and Roscoe hadn't read it anyhow. Poor sonofabitch should be alive now. Luther hadn't killed him, he had killed himself. And Roscoe should be alive so he could run for mayor. Questions jabbed the back of his mind: why had the lawmen matched surliness with lawlessness; but what the hell had been Herman's right to act surly and mix up people? He shook his head and a deep shade like sorrow enveloped him in the bright sunlight as he trailed his burden the long miles to Bancroft.

For Luther Cain the afternoon passed like a nightmare. When he reached the edge of town a procession of adults and children began to form and grow quietly at first and then noisily behind his own and the two other burdened horses until it became a grotesque parade with himself as grand marshal. By the time the ludicrous pageant reached the funeral parlor next to the fire station by way of Jimson and South Streets and the plaza, Undertaker Darling had learned of its approach and was standing solemnly in Pacific Street before his establishment waiting to step into his important role. Mayor Crum, who had been told by them of the marshal's and sheriff's mission that morning and just had watched from the city hall steps its enigmatic return across the plaza, pushed through the crowd—"Goddammit, folks, this ain't a circus, go about your business!"—to help the lawman and the mortician and the abruptly appearing Doc Bowman untie and manhandle indoors the bloody, not-yet-stiffening corpses of Herman and Roscoe and Indian Jesse. Leaving the dead men with the only mortal who could do anything further for them the city officials gruffly dispersed the remaining gawkers; and after Bill had vomited and Luther had swallowed some bitter saliva they left the horses in David Berg's offered care and walked to the city hall. The physician walked with them. None of them spoke on the way. In the mayor's office with the door closed Luther Cain and Bill Crum looked at each other for a moment and Doc Bowman looked out of the window.

The silence was broken by the mayor. "What in the goddam hell happened, Marshal?"

Luther's moustache moved slightly but everything else about him—eyes, hands, frame, emotions—seemed as inanimate as stone. "I shot Herman. Twice. Thought he was drawing on me. Injun Jesse bushwhacked Roscoe. I gunned Jesse."

"Whew," Doc exhaled.

"Luther, you said you thought Herman was drawing on you. You wasn't sure?"

"I figured he was the one stole the Schmidt boys' money."

Bill realized he had to be careful. "You was pretty damn sure, else you wouldn't took after him, you and Roscoe."

"Turned out I was wrong."

"So was Roscoe I reckon."

"Roscoe backed my play."

The mayor offered the marshal another tack. "Right when it happened why did you think Herman was drawing on you?"

"Jumped at me outside his house pawing his shirt."

"Sure. I can see that."

"Turned out he was trying to get away from Injun Jesse inside . . ."

"Could had a gun in his shirt."

". . . and trying to warn us. If I hadn't figured he'd stole the money I might not have shot him."

"Goddam, Luther, you can't let everybody take shots at you and then ask if they aimed to, not a man in your job."

Luther had no comment. His thoughts obviously had turned inward again.

The physician cleared his throat. "Folks are going to want to know what happened. Not to mention Carl Norris."

"I know they are," the mayor frowned, "and they're going to be told what happened. Luther's going to tell them. You're the coroner, Doc; I reckon you're bound to have a hearing."

"And for Luther's sake the sooner the better I'd say."

The marshal nodded backward from the region where his thoughts had gone.

"Like tomorrow," Doc said officially.

CHAPTER 28

The ardent, wary draft of Mattie's breath warmed Mark's ear and wafted the disparity into his brain: fervor and restraint, principle and charity. Her coupled pleas stabbed his dreaming: "Love me and don't leave me!"

Later the night lay down with Bancroft as Luther did with Carrie: half-drunkenly, desperately, aching with passion, wearily, hiding fears with exertions. The moonrays through her Drovers open window paled Carrie's face and arms and breasts and Luther's hand moving down her belly and his arm and shoulder raised on an elbow and his long thigh and lean hairy calf. Far beyond the unscreened opening a great horned owl asked faintly its old question, lamenting its and Carrie's and Luther's quandaries. Who was this man, who was this marshal of Bancroft, who was this killer of other men? Was killing an incident of his calling or itself his calling? Legality aside was he law-abiding or lawless? On the other hand wasn't "legality aside" inconsistent with his oath to uphold and enforce the law? Could a sworn lawman abide any form or degree of lawlessness? Could he live in twilight and see his duty clearly? Was he a lover of humankind as he was of his parents and cousin and Noble Buck and Carrie Shaw or was he a hater as of Jack Bennett and Frenchy Lesueur and Herman Strauss or rather Indian Jesse? Or was he both? Was he one man of two halves or two men? Was he a boon or a bane to Bancroft?

He had thrown back their sheet and blanket. "I want you," he whispered hoarsely.

"Yes, Dear."

"Goddammit, what am I supposed to do?"

"Take me."

"I mean what the hell do they want?"

"Isn't what you want and I want the important thing this minute? Please don't swear, Luther, don't be mad right now."

"I ain't mad at you, I want you."

"Then kiss me, love me." She half-laughed. "Dammit, before we freeze."

When their loving had drained and renewed and drained and

renewed and exhausted and fulfilled them completely at last Carrie pulled their covers over them and they lay entwined and breathed deeply and calmly now of the night's loving essence. Luther seemed to Carrie to have poured out of himself into her—thankfully better than into some indifferent or hostile vessel like aloneness or censure—the sourest bile of his confusion. He was a long way from serenity, given today's turmoil and tomorrow's hearing, but his discomfort seemed less for the time; and she took the moment to offer some quiet advice as her fingers lay gently against his cheek. She spoke very slowly and very softly.

"Dear, when you're dealing with different folks ain't it a good idea to treat them thataway? Like they really was different I mean? Because that's the truth. There's bad folks and good folks. Ain't the law supposed to tie the bad ones down and help the good ones up?"

Her question scorched his mind as the cup of Teddy Quillin's cooking brandy had his throat when he'd gulped it on his way upstairs. He shook his head on the feather-filled pillow in the dimness. "Sounds like taking account who the folks is instead of what they done. That what the hell you trying to say?"

"More like taking account of the fix they're in. It's not all or nothing, Luther."

"Goddammit that's like turning up a bucket and telling half the water to run out and half to stay."

"Yes, Dear," she said after a moment's silence. "We'll talk about it another time. Just kiss me now. Before we sleep. Now, Luther. Please."

CHAPTER 29

. . . *The good parson's agitation mirrored what seems to be sergeant's main occupational hazards: the impossibility of pleasing everybody.*

As our interview progressed, the reverend's voice heightened as his flush deepened. He was complaining, not as much about Sergeant Keller arresting in the downtown mission an alleged child molester and wife beater, as standing by while others there pulled down the accused's pants and kicked him around the room to let him relive some of his child's and wife's humiliation. The minister was really charged up. I was glad my tape recorder was.

"I'm not excusing those crimes, if the man committed them. I'm saying a policeman oughtn't to take the law into his own hands. And he ought to take some account of why people act the way they do. They say an abuser has been abused himself as a child. People are human beings with human frailties; they're not always bad because they've done bad things."

When we ventured, in the absent sergeant's defense, that we'd ridden a few squad cars into what seemed like an all-day, all-night free-for-all, and that crooks don't have rules and there's no referee, the pastor wasn't slowed much.

"The aggravations of police work don't change the rule that a man's innocent until proved guilty. A police badge isn't a license to assume the worst of everybody, to ignore discretion. Sergeant Keller has a reputation

*as a hard-nose. I've told him I hope he's not
gotten hard-hearted in the process, that he
can see the difference between crimes and
mistakes."
We risked commenting that the policeman probably had a response.
"Oh, sure. The sergeant said he didn't
make either people or laws, he was paid to
arrest people who broke laws. Was I telling
him to judge which people to arrest for breaking which laws? I said of course not, I was
only telling him to have some humility and
use some common sense doing the job he was
paid for. To clean up his act, for his own sake
as well as others'. Before the curtain rings
down on it . . .*

"Well here we go again," Roy Bowman said seemingly to
himself but loudly enough for some of the courtroom's spectators
to overhear. He hitched himself forward in his chair against the
presiding end of the council table, cleared his throat and raised
his voice above the room's conversation. "If you'll settle down we'll
get this inquest under way and over with."

"'Here we go again' is right," somebody said. "This week's
wake."

Doc reflected parenthetically that the commentary wasn't
Carl Norris's despite the alliteration. "As coroner I'm going to
hear evidence this morning on how three people died yesterday:
Roscoe Light, Herman Strauss, and Injun Jesse. Then I'm going
to decide how. After I do that it'll be up to Jim Watts whether
there's anybody to bring to the law. And believe me if there is he
will." He looked about the room. "Any questions?"

There were none, only some rustling of clothes and scuffing
of boots and a cough or two.

"All right," the coroner said. He turned to Luther Cain who
was standing at one side of the room with his dog at his feet as
he had during the inquests into the deaths of Jack Bennett and
Frenchy Lesueur and for most of the time during council meetings
and mayor's courts since he had come to Bancroft. "Marshal, Billy

216

here's going to swear you in. Then I want you to tell us what you know about these killings."

While the local government's all-purpose Clerk Custer was carrying its all-purpose Bible toward the lawman to perform his official duty over the dog's bared fangs the county attorney on the front row raised his hand. "Now wait a minute, Doc. For the record the deaths have to be established first. Dale here can do that."

"Right," the coroner acknowledged. He nodded to Undertaker Darling seated next to Watts. "You can tell us from there, Dale. Just stand up—" he waved the clerk from the marshal to the alternate witness—"and after Billy swears you in let's hear what you know about the corpses."

The administration of his oath accomplished Dale Darling stated his findings with splendid awareness of his momentary prominence although he should have preferred speaking from farther up front beside the table. "Sheriff Light's corpse had a .44 caliber bullet from I'm sure a pistol that entered under his sternum and got stuck between a couple dorsal vertebras mashing them and the spinal cord. Herman Strauss's corpse had two bullet holes clean through the torso by a rifle I'd judge from nothing stopping them; and seeing the damage they done one went in the chest and out between the scapulas and the other in the back lower down and out the belly. Injun Jesse's corpse had a surely rifle bullet in the face that blew out the back of the cranium. If it took anything else to kill any one of them I don't know what it'd be. Glad to answer any questions," he added hopefully.

The physician looked at the county attorney. "Sounds like they're dead all right. With bullet holes."

Jim supressed any hint of a smile.

Doc's gaze returned to the undertaker—"You can sit down"—and shifted to the clerk. "Now you can swear in the marshal, Billy." When that had been done the coroner nodded to Luther. "Marshal, can you tell us how the bullet holes got in the people?"

The room breathed very quietly.

Luther's voice also was quiet but firm and clearly audible. "Three shots was mine. Two at Herman and one at Jesse. He shot Roscoe."

"Who shot Roscoe?"

"Jesse."

"Naturally before you shot Jesse."

"That's why I done it—that and I was going to be next."

Jim Watts raised his hand again. "Doc, you're getting away from the business of the inquest. Like I told you before all you got to do here is find out what caused the deaths, whether accident or suicide or by some third party, not who or why."

"I know dammit but it won't hurt to let Luther talk some more. The people in this room and this town are interested. And so am I." The coroner returned his attention to the witness. "Did Roscoe shoot at Jesse first?"

"I don't 'low so. But my mind was on Herman. Things was noisy. And we didn't know the goddam half-breed was there 'til he started shooting at us."

"Where was 'there?'"

"Herman's dugout. We was outside it."

"Why were you there?"

"We'd rode out looking for the man robbed the Schmidts and hurt Fritz."

"Why Herman's?"

"We figured he maybe done it. I figured so."

"'Maybe' or likely? Didn't you have a reason to believe Herman was the robber?"

"Turned out I was wrong. Turned out to be Injun Jesse. Must have heard or figured out about the money."

This time the county attorney half-arose. "Now wait a minute. I'm telling you again . . ."

"All right," Doc interrupted him, "just one more question, Marshal."

Jim lowered himself into his seat with a despairing glance at the ceiling.

The coroner leaned forward. "Luther, was your shooting Herman maybe accidental?"

The lawman didn't reply at once. As the spectators waited in what Carl Norris later was to describe as spooky silence he stared over their heads seemingly outward into confusing space and backward down some trail of time. Then he looked at his questioner and spoke with care. "No it wasn't accidental if you're asking did I pull the trigger a-purpose. Yes it was if you're asking did I mean shooting a law-abiding man." He took a deep breath and exhaled slowly. "It was a mistake to shoot Herman. But I didn't know it was. He dove and rolled at me grabbing his shirt for what I took was his gun. Then it was him or me like always; like over and over again here and in them other places you hired me to come here from." He leaned down and in a gesture which seemed to surprise him too—a strange and almost bizarre gesture—he gathered his dog into his arms, straightened and squinted at the coroner. "Reckon you folks is the ones got to decide what it was I done. Now if you don't need me for nothing better I got my job to do." He walked along the room's wall and out its door, Spot's tail dangling from beneath his arm.

Roy Bowman's frown was half-disconcerted and half-amused. Carrie Shaw's eyes brimmed with tears. Preacher Smith stared at the floor but didn't see it for mental images of human fallibility. Johnny Newlin shook his head in evident disgust for everyone to see; Harry Guttman shook his head privately. Colonel Evans' face was inscrutable. Lila Haniford's expression was philosophical. Billy Plunkett and David Berg sitting with David's father looked puzzled, Ruth Blaine looked sad and Laverne Strauss, summoned earlier from Dodge City by telegraph, looked out the window. Enos Dowling grunted an obscenity and shifted his loose shirt on his bandaged shoulder. Carl Norris scribbled on a sheet of newsprint.

"Well," Doc said, "being there's no more witnesses—living witnesses—looks like it's up to me again." His unhurried gaze swept the audience. "Everybody here heard everything I heard and it's damn certain all three men died by shooting. And none of them committed suicide unless you could say Injun Jesse did by going against . . ." He abandoned that interpretation wishing he hadn't started it; clinching his regret nobody smiled, the room was too tense. "And as far as an accident's concerned there plain wasn't any in the sheriff's or Jesse's case; and in Herman's the marshal didn't deny pulling the trigger for whatever his reason, the why of that not being for this inquest." He looked at the county attorney. "Right?"

"I've got some thinking yet ahead of me, Doc, but you're right for today here."

The coroner looked back at the audience. "Then my finding is Roscoe Light, Herman Strauss, and Injun Jesse died of gunshot wounds inflicted by a third party."

"Or parties."

"'Or parties,' Jim. And all you folks: Carl Norris told me their funeral times will be in tonight's paper. Adjourned."

Enos Dowling's voice bullwhipped in the air. "Watts, you better do your thinking goddam hard!"

The county attorney and the coroner and most but not all of the spectators ignored—for the time—the limping, shoulder-maimed cowboy as they shuffled from the room.

CHAPTER 30

On the afternoon following the triple-death inquest Howard Smith stood in the high grass dividing the cemetery's sickled better section from its less-trimmed poorer one, which is to say dividing Roscoe Light's and Heman Strauss' graves from Indian Jesse's, and spoke to God and the silent crowd about their souls with undivided concern. After pausing for the lowering of their caskets at the same time into their identical pits he gazed over the assemblage and lifted his voice again. "Lord, as we go now from this funeral we pray You remind us we all live together on earth and we better live peaceable with each other because we're all we got here. And have us remember our salvation is not by ourselves, it's by You. You don't need help doing right but we do. You're the one can get along alone, not us; we can't make it on our own. Bless every one of us, Lord. And thanks. Amen."

Standing a little apart from the rear of the crowd listening to Preacher Smith's closing words Luther winced at a spasm of pain suddenly clutching his stomach. Laverne Strauss who had walked to the graveyard with the Lacys and Allgoods winced at the funeral's waste of scarce lumber; she had paid Lester Blaine for Herman's casket. Hale Meese hurried back to the jail at Howard's "Amen" because his job as turnkey wasn't as secure now as before his brother-in-law Roscoe's death; it wasn't that Deputy Sheriff Bones Baker disliked Hale but that Bones had a brother-in-law, too. As the mourners dispersed Clarence Tilden took orders for prints of his photographs of the occasion from the mayor and other members of the town and county governments who had attended the service in a body out of respect for the sheriff. Fritz Schmidt's bandaged head throbbed from his walking and standing for the hour. Carrie's heart and body both ached as she looked at Luther, one from commiseration and the other from abruptly surging love. Enos Dowling spat in the afternoon's dust and on its testimonial to injustice; and on his way back into town the limping cowboy with his flapping shirt caught up with Jim Watts and spewed more of his bile: "You know goddam well Cain shot Jesse and Strauss out of pure goddam meanness and maybe the sheriff so he couldn't tell. Undertaker said Strauss was shot in the back and . . ."

Jim jerked his elbow from Dowling's grasp. "Once in front, once in back. Herman was scrambling and rolling at the marshal. Looked like he was after his gun. And Roscoe . . ."

" 'Looked like' enough reason to murder a man laying on the ground? You sonsofbitches in this camp string together like unweaned calves and their mammies; your whole goddam town sucks the marshal's teats; you're either scared of him or don't know what to do about him. He's God Almighty. But one of these days he's going to the Devil like he sent Herman and Jesse. You'll see that, bygod."

"I'll have to pass your threat along to the marshal." Jim turned on his way. "He's bound to be scared."

The cowboy's lip corners seeped saliva of frustration. "I ain't threatening nobody goddammit! I'm saying the truth and you'll see it."

A half-hour later in the Portugese its proprietor made a rare gesture: he stood for a round of drinks on the house. With a sardonic grin he raised his glass and his voice above the appreciative clamor. "Boys, I'm back from burying Herman Strauss and Injun Jesse and Roscoe Light and along with them the answer to everybody's question. Coroner found no blame—Doc said that ain't his job—and looks like the ones it is their job ain't in a big hurry to do it. So here's to a man you got to admire his riding a daylight trail and never mind what's in the shade alongside it, a man knows his way and got it again this week bygod and the hell with the rest of us: Luther Cain."

The catcalls and boos were drowned quickly in the Portugese's best. No not its best, Johnny admitted to himself; he was saving that bottle for what he hoped was to be Carrie Shaw's visit before long. He had sent word to her by Hortense Bass of all people— thereby reassuring both women of his forgiveness—that he wanted to talk over old times and other things with his former employee who now was in the sewing business. Their longtime friendship pretty much guaranteed her coming in; she was a woman who didn't forget old friends and favors. God knew he hadn't forgotten her. Not anything about her. She had swallowed some loco weed, not as much by leaving the Portugese as taking up with that out-

222

law meaner than Injun Jesse; but maybe he could make her puke her mistake as Doc Bowman once had Nola's mouthful of varmint-poisoning meat.

Several afternoons later sitting with them on the sunlit train-station bench a half-hour ahead of the west-bound's scheduled belching, clattering, hissing arrival agent-postmaster-councilman (and ice house owner) Ed Sarver illumined his view of Marshal Cain for the benefit of equally interested Councilman Bert Oliver of Oliver's Hardware and Councilman Solly Berg of Berg's Dry Goods and less interested or at least less officially involved Herman Northcutt of his homestead north of town and very interested if unimportant Billy Plunkett of the *Republican*'s two-man printing and one-man distribution departments. Bert had borrowed a wagon from Bell Mare Livery to haul to his hardware store the hopefully incoming kegs of nails he'd ordered from Kansas City Supply; Solly had come down to the station to pick up the cloth bolts he'd been expecting from St. Louis by way of Kansas City and had accepted Bert's offer to drop him and those off at his store if they arrived; Herman was there to see whether the mail-order proposition of the new Montgomery Ward outfit paid off with the goods, in this instance a banjo for his boy; and Billy was waiting for the newspaper's weekly insides.

"Way I figure," Ed laid it out, "he ain't working for the money. He's . . ."

"Couldn't pay me enough," Bert said.

Ed hadn't finished his thought but he accepted Bert's interjection gracefully. "That's what I'm saying, got to be something else. Something more important to him."

"Than money?" Herman Northcutt's tone was clearly skeptical but not to the point of disrespect.

Again Ed was forgiving. "Something like for the good of humans, specially ones here in Bancroft; maybe these folks is more important to him than dollars."

"That's pretty highfalutin," the homesteader said.

"And maybe bragging on ourselves," Bert added.

Solly raised a defensive finger. "It's a nice sentiment, Ed."

"I try to look at all sides," Ed said comfortably. Then he frowned and pursed his lips. "Could be even he don't know why he does the job, he just does it."

223

"Or could be he plain likes it," Herman allowed. "Some men even looks for trouble."

Solly shook his head. "Not Luther; trouble looks for him."

"I got to agree with Solly." Ed spoke thoughtfully. "But you know some way Luther don't have the face of a man enjoys his work."

"Nosir, he don't," Bert said. "I noticed that. He ain't got a happy face, not on his job anyhow."

"Closest I ever seen it," Ed recalled, "was with that woman at the fire brigade dance. Carrie what's-her-name."

"Shaw," Solly supplied. "Nice lady. Seamstress. Luther likes her."

"I was there," Herman said. "Thought I remembered her from the Portugese once."

Solly's expression was bland. "Sews nowadays for the nicest ladies in town."

"That's right," Ed testified for the defense. "Couldn't think of her last name."

"What I hear too," Bert agreed.

Herman accepted their verdict with a shrug. "I don't get in town much. But I remember I did see her at the church too." He refocused his thoughts on Luther's face. "Wonder if a man ain't happy in his job he don't goddam quit it."

"Sometimes it's all a man knows," Solly said. "And does best."

"Maybe there's more'n one reason," Billy had the temerity to offer, "for the marshal doing what he does and being way he is. But he sure does good what you hired him for. And he's a good man for me and my friends' way of thinking."

After a moment's general silence Ed cleared his throat and returned to his initial premise. "Well whatever's the reason it ain't the money. And that's a fact."

CHAPTER 31

Luther Cain had finished his late noon dinner at the Drovers and was starting to walk toward the courthouse with Spot at his heels when David Berg hailed him from the ice wagon's high seat. "Wait up, Marshal." Shag was pulling the wagon from Bolinger's stable next to Mother Swain's on West Pacific Street eastward into the plaza. As the lawman waited in the dust for the rig to draw abreast of him its driver's slightly hunched young form seemed for a flicker of time to be Noble Buck's. Abruptly Noble's image fell from the wagon and Frenchy Lesueur leered at it in the light of a terrible igniting lamp. Mentally Luther waved off the vision but in the instant before its return to David's reality the wagon driver's face became the marshal's own young one.

What the hell? Luther rebuked his unbidden imagining. Lack of sleep must be getting to him; he was up at six after going to bed at three because of Johnny Newlin's inability or unwillingness to keep the lid on the Portugese. All of the Texas cowboys had gone back south except the three or four who had holed up in Bancroft for the winter or had filed for homesteads to start their own ranches in the normally fine grass country; but there still were enough whiskey-loving human varmints in and through town—bullwhackers, railroaders, trappers, hunters, gamblers, drifters, ornery locals—to give him and his deputies enough trouble to see they earned their pay. He'd been obliged last night to come down hard on a couple of those disturbers of the peace including laying his pistol barrel under the ear of a belligerent stranger in Johnny's saloon. That maverick's jail-cell rantings after he'd come to had identified him as a Kentuckian who'd seen action at Shiloh and Vicksburg; and judging by his frenzy those agonies must have unhinged him to some extent. As strangely Luther had heard again Carrie's soft words in recent darkness about taking account of the fix folks were in and had remembered his own Civil War ordeal he impulsively—daftly—had told Big John to run the troublemaker on out of town early this morning instead of bringing him before the mayor's court. He had rationalized such an irregularity to his deputy on the grounds of saving time presently and no doubt in the future. His deputy had grinned a little.

David Berg reined up Shag beside the officer of the law. The wagon's wheels stopped creaking but the old horse's ribs in their slow rising and falling seemed not to and drops of water from the melting ice continued to stitch an outline of the wagon's bed in the dust. "Howdy, Marshal."

"Howdy to you, Son. What can I do for you?"

"Not a thing, Marshal." The boy lowered his gaze to the dog which had taken the moment to bring a frantic hind leg to bear on one ear. David swallowed before he spoke. "Looks like old Spot's after a flea there."

Luther glanced briefly at the dog. "Does at that."

The youngster's eyes met the man's again. "Just wanted to say 'Howdy.'" He cleared his throat and nodded northeastward. "Headed up to them houses and seen you come out of the hotel and . . ." He broke off and shrugged.

Luther laid his left hand on Shag's bony rump. "Heard you been doing good with the ice and water barrels. Stepping in Noble's boots has took some learning I reckon with the different places and pounds and days. And the lifting."

"First week or so was kind of hard but I got it figured out. And wasn't so stiff after that either. And folks been real nice about mistakes."

"You're lucky there," the lawman felt able to vouch.

"Just do the best I can for them and they mostly give me leeway when I need it. That's what my father says: do your best for folks and they'll do the same for you."

Luther's very faint smile was invisible under his moustache. "Solly's right about most things."

"Job's eased up as the weather's got cooler but when the real winter comes then'll be the hardest part of all. Noble used to tell Billy and me that. People either won't need ice or else they'll freeze their own in buckets and such; but I'll have to cut it from Owl Creek and store it up for summer. And that'll be a back-buster. But Mister Sarver thinks I can do it. Father, too." He squinted at the man. "You think I can, Marshal?"

The lawman appeared to ponder the question. He took a swipe with his cupped palm at a fly on Shag's rump and after a moment looked up at the boy again. "Seeing it's you, David, you're damn right I do."

There was pride in the youngster's quick nod. "Same as I think you do your job damn good."

This time Luther's smile was visible.

Across the larger desk of the Stockmen and Farmers Bank the establishment's owner Clay Gibson accepted Mack Heckel's check with one hand and returned the butcher's promissory note with the other, thus bearing out Doc Bowman's dubbing him a two-fisted banker. "Paid in full, Mack, principal and interest . . ."

"Which I ciphered careful," Bookkeeper Midas Hinkle warranted from the Bank's smaller desk ten feet away. Doc Bowman once had cautioned Clay about a bookkeeper named Midas possibly ending up as owner himself.

The banker ignored his employee's interruption. ". . . and I thank you for your business. Been good for us both. Banking helps a business grow and vicey versey. Anyone pays the way you do welcome back anytime. Some haven't last year or two."

"I was lucky with them Texas steers this year. Bought cheap off a good trail boss drove them up here slow and easy. Had some meat left on them. But they wasn't going to keep that way waiting their train turn on what pasture them goddam grasshoppers hadn't et. Got to say they slaughtered out right good considering. And I been peddling their cuts and hide and soap right good ever since too. Yep, I been mighty lucky."

"Maybe you'll buy a few again next year." The banker's tone became facetious. "That is if Luther Cain don't run all the shippers farther out the railroad."

"One man ain't likely going to do that."

Clay frowned. "One man can make a town look unfriendly, anyhow if he's marshal and acts like the town's his own herd and visitors are a gang of rustlers."

"Maybe some of them is, judging what I seen a few times this summer."

"It's a matter of sorting out which is which. Big difference between meanness and mischief don't forget, Mack."

"Maybe so." The butcher started to his feet. "Well thanks again to you."

"Anytime. Like I said I'm glad to have your business. You come back anytime."

The Bank's door had opened with a bell's tinkling as the men were rising and shaking hands across its larger desk. Midas's face just above its smaller one was contorted with what struck his employer's turning glance as either loathing or lust as the bookkeeper gaped frontward where Clay's gaze also landed.

"I'm counting that goes for me too, Mister Gibson." The grin of the woman who stepped toward them was wide enough to include the butcher along with the banker and even to sweep in the bookkeeper. Its possessor never wrote off a man until he was hopelessly broke; not good banking practice maybe but time-proven in her line of work. "I mean about being glad to have the business and to come back anytime. Because here I am again for another loan." She extended her right hand to the banker— "Howdy, Mister Gibson"—and after he'd shaken it and said "Afternoon, Nell" she gave it to the butcher—"Ain't run into you lately, Mack"—but she didn't confront Midas with it for fear he'd faint from the looks of him. "Don't want to horn in on your parley you fellows."

"Just leaving, Nell," Mack said. "Your turn to try prying money out of him."

"You vouch for me?"

The banker answered for the butcher. "You don't need his vouching, Nell, just pay in full again."

"Then I'll take my leave." Mack tossed them a ham-handed salute and left.

"How much you need?" Clay waved toward the chair across his desk and when she'd taken it he sat down opposite her. "And what for?"

"Enough for some new brass beds from back East. This summer was hell on my old wood ones; cowboys play damn rough. Brass'll last longer and be prettier too. And some new chairs. And a couple or so nice bureaus. With mirrors. And two door jambs."

"Goddam—excuse me, Nell—they sure play rough at that."

Midas Hinkle at his desk had flinched and bent forward to peer intently at some papers before him as the woman had commenced her loss inventory and now redness was creeping up the back of his neck, whether from mortification or excitement it should have been hard even for Nell to say, had she noticed it.

"I 'low it'll take six hundred dollars. Clarence says that, too."

"Tilden going to sign the note with you again like when you two bought the house on mortgage?"

"Not if you don't need him on it. Or a mortgage on his gallery. He deeded his part of the house to me after I paid you off; he only held that to help me get my loan. I'd like to cut this one on my own."

"Seeing how you paid last time don't reckon I'll need more'n your own note for six hundred." The banker squinted at her. "Those cowboys and all this summer like you said, haven't you got some cash so you can save the interest?"

Her grin returned. "Thanks for asking but all the cash above the girls' and me's keep went for your final house mortgage payment. Right back to the Bank."

He joined her in a chuckle. "Kind of like riding in a circle."

"Place ain't so busy in the winter but I'll likely have cash next summer to pay this back and be in the clear from then on. Least if the Ladies Welfare League just minds . . ."

"Betterment League."

"All right, Betterment League, whatever the hell they call it, if they just mind their own goddam business and let me mind mine everybody'll be happy. I don't do them no harm, none of their men comes down to my place—well, none to speak of—and I don't know why they'd want to sic the marshal on me." Her tone grew fierce. "Speaking of bettering the town you tell me one sick cowboy they ever tended, one broke sodbuster they ever lent a few dollars to, a hungry kid they give eating money. And the nature of my business cools down hell raising instead of heats it up."

"Whoa, Nell. I didn't say the League was God's gift to Bancroft. Nor that you don't do good. You do." He continued before she caught her breath. "But going back there a minute: you say they sicced the marshal on you?"

"Guess you're wondering about me paying if there's trouble."

"Not that exactly . . ."

"I understand and don't blame you. But I feel like it ain't going to come to nothing too bad; just a damn nuisance."

"What was it about the marshal?"

"Just come by last week and said a couple them women was in to see the mayor and was going after the council hot and heavy.

Like I was a smallpox epidemic, for godssake. Said he and the mayor figured to let things lie because I wasn't causing them no trouble. But that could change. If the League got to singeing their men's and the council's asses they might pass a ordinance against my place. Then that'd be the law, and the marshal'd enforce it. Ever goddam body knows he's hell on enforcing the law."

"They can't pass an ordinace against one place, have to be all like it. Jim Watts'll tell you that. And Johnny Newlin owns the Portugese and he's on the council. He won't want it." Clay's eyes narrowed for a moment. "If I heard right Luther Cain's lady friend used to work there, friend of Johnny's, so I'd have to guess she won't want it either and then maybe Luther won't."

"The Portugese ain't . . . well ain't out and out you might say like my place. Sure those four girls supposed to be friendly, humor the boys into drinking and gambling, but they got their own choice after that. Least that's what one of mine used to work for Johnny told me. So I reckon his place being different they could pass a ordinance against mine but not his." Nell was determined to be optimistic or anyhow seem that way to the banker. "But like I said, Mister Gibson, it's in my bones nothing worse'n a nuisance is going to come out of it. And I ain't one for setting around waiting for the sky to fall on me or the council to crap a law or Cain to wipe their asses. Else nothing ever'd get done."

Clay blew out his breath softly with an admiring smile. Ten feet away Midas's ears had turned crimson. The banker opened a drawer of his desk and pulled out a blank promissory note form and smoothed it on the desk's top. Pushing the drawer shut with his belly he picked up a quill pen, dipped it in an ink bottle and began scribbling on the paper. "I'll fill in the six hundred and the year's ten percent interest so you can sign this and be on your way. You want the money on account here or cash?" He turned the paper around and pushed it toward her and handed her the re-dipped pen.

"On account. You been good to me and your bank's sure good enough for me." Laboriously she printed her signature. "Made it through two years ago's panic. Not all of them did."

"You did, Nell."

"And I had to foreclose on a few of my customers, too."

"Don't know whether your or my doing that was painful'r
To us and them both."

She shrugged, arising. " 'Bye to you, Mister Gibson."

" 'Bye, Miss Nell."

When the front door had closed behind the woman the banker looked at the bookkeeper. "She and I do business the same way: quick but satisfying."

Midas was cautious about questioning his employer's judgment. "Unusual line of work, Mister Gibson."

"Unusual woman." Clay's tone didn't have the humorous glint his eyes did. "Might be good for you to learn more about her business. For the bank. Part of riding herd on our loans."

The bookkeeper's shifting in his seat came close to squirming. He opened his mouth presumably to comment about loan auditing; but his erupting words obviously bushwhacked him. "Might be at that, Mister Gibson." The quick clamp of his jaws below his widened eyes cut off further unorthodoxy. After an instant he licked his lips and veered the subject's precise direction. "Hope for the loan's sake the marshal doesn't have to close down her . . . business."

The banker felt better about the bookkeeper than he had previously. And he continued feeling good about his vocation; a banker encountered many interesting people and their doings and ways. He almost got to be a kind of half-ass philosopher. "The council knows the town's cash-heavy visitors favor Nell's Place same as the Portugese and Eastern and the Longhorn and the rest. The ladies aren't hardly going to change that. 'Specially seeing they can't vote against any councilmen. So I doubt if Nell has to fret about being closed down nor us about her loan."

"Couldn't the marshal close her down on his own if he was a mind to; disturbing the peace or something?"

"Why would a man kill his eggs-laying goose for the sake of its liver? No matter how hell-bent he is for goose liver? He's got a pretty good job in this town and from what I hear a pretty good-looking woman." The banker paused and looked speculatively beyond the bookkeeper. "I'd hope he's got enough sense not to wear out his welcome."

CHAPTER 32

The voices across Mark Keller's obscenely gaping chest continued to be unheard by him; instead he heard the echoes of a muffled shot and a shout for help from his partner sprawling wounded onto the sidewalk in front of the arcade beyond the hood of their squad car. He watched himself dive from the car and run around it, drawing his revolver, to confront a familiar young troublemaker and an older one he didn't recognize racing in tandem from the arcade, one waving a Saturday Night Special and the other a sawed-off shotgun. In the instant's chaos the shotgun appeared the more immediately threatening given its waver's sudden shocked "Keller!" Mark heard a roar and by the jerk in his palm knew it had been his own gun firing, confirmed by the older hood's doubled-over collapse. Again he heard his downed partner shout and whirled to see the younger gunman raising the Special, eyes wild and glazed. Mark's revolver roared a second time as a panicked, scrambling teenage girl plunged across his line of fire and spun into the gutter and as the young hood's arcing hand finished ridding itself of the Special. In his avenging rage Mark heard and felt his gun roar a third time. And the young hood then ceased troublemaking forever.

"Never heard such a mumbler as this one, Doctor."

"Likely a good deal to mumble about, Nurse."

Four buildings down the plaza's west side Lester Blaine's scissors put the finishing snips on what hair Everett Lane had left. In Everett's seventieth year that wasn't a great deal—mostly a chaplet of yellowish white above his ears and nape—but as he always told the barber-carpenter his "late wife fancied a man's hair looking new-cut neat." He was one of Lester's few every-two-weeks haircut customers; those were outnumbered ten to one by the every-month and longer ones. The moustache-beard boys were a different proposition; they came into his layout anywhere from weekly to monthly. Of course his total number of customers wasn't overwhelming exactly. And a number of male citizens didn't come in at all; their wives or partners did the honors on their hair and they trimmed their moustaches or beards themselves. Naturally there were no female haircutees.

"That about does it, Everett." Lester eased the hair cloth from

232

between a two-month-old *Police Gazette* and his customer's belly and made a show of shaking out the cloth as though his ministrations had been unquestionably worthwhile. "Don't take any wooden nickels now."

Everett got out of the barber chair, tossed the magazine onto its seat for the next man and glanced briefly and self-consciously into the mirror Lester handed him. "Looks all right considering what you were up against." He returned the mirror. "I'll take any kind of nickels I can get but what I need's dollars. Been talking to Clay Gibson about a loan to build the rooming house again. Think I'm going to get it. Got a little land other side of the loading pens to mortgage besides the lot on Jimson." He waited until the barber looked back at him from stepping off his milk stool, laying the mirror on a shelf and getting a new bottle of bay rum out of a cabinet. "If I get my loan I'd thank you to rebuild the damn thing with me, Lester. Pay whatever's fair. You carpenter and I'll do the grunting and groaning, the dummy parts. Like to get started right soon, get her framed and floored and sided anyhow before cold so then we can finish inside."

Lester didn't take long deciding to accept this out-of-season windfall. He could barber longer mornings, starting at sunup if necessary, and carpenter afternoons until sunset. Ruth coveted a bigger stove but he wanted to buy her the second piano in town after the Portugese's. The extra income should help toward its three-hundred-fifty-dollar cost. She had loved playing her family's old Chickering upright in Crawfordsville but a series of freighters had manhandled it on the couple's trail over the years to Springfield and then to St. Louis where finally it had been ruined by a fall from a railroad car while being loaded for Bancroft. A new one should be a partial reward for all the running she'd done in his wake since their marriage. "Sure, Everett. You got yourself a deal." He shook his customer's grateful hand. "Lumber yard last week got a good-size board-foot shipment before next summer's price raise. When you want to commence?"

"Tomorrow too soon?"

Lester looked thoughtful. "Afraid so. Got to get my tools ready and we got to plan and figure lumber and all the rest." Then he grinned at Everett's disappointment. "But how about the day after?"

"Say now, Lester. And I'll not be the only one glad to see her

233

going up. Hotels are too damn expensive for long. My by-the-weeks like Carrie Shaw been asking if I was going to build again. And Johnny Newlin and Max Coleman want to keep overnights with their gambling down below the track. Portugese and Eastern both been losing some of them they used to get to the Longhorn and Shawnee up here." He nodded happily. "Yessir, going to be good getting back in business."

"For you and the town both. Speaking of Carrie Shaw, Everett, want to tell you again that sure was fine the way you got her out of the fire."

The rooming house—currently the vacant lot—proprietor felt the reminiscent warm agitated spasm in his gut. Nobody had mentioned the rescue for a week or so. It was both satisfying and disturbing to hear of it again. The farther it had receded in time the scarier it had loomed in his mind; he was glad it already had happened and wasn't something yet to be done. In the first days after the event he'd settled on what he had hoped was a seemly shelter in the rain of congratulations; he fell back on that now. "She was a lady worth saving."

"You're right there, Everett. Friend of mine and the missus."

"Luther Cain's, too." Everett's addition of the marshal's endorsement betrayed his glimpse into the mirror of that night; its reflection of the stoic man's fear was stark. "Friend of you folks and Luther Cain too got to be worth it. Now I like the marshal; I ain't one of them been bad-mouthing him lately. Too bad he shot the old hermit but I reckon that half-breed needed killing for gunning the sheriff if that's what happened. Mostly just been doing his job. Doing it a mite hard some say but not me. Got plenty hard rocks to hammer around here."

"This where the goddam shearing's did?" The door had clattered open ahead of a shaggy-headed, bearded, bullnecked man whose small eyes glittered like wet anthracite under his rank eyebrows. He was dressed in greasy buckskin and carrying a rifle in a greasy buckskin scabbard; and his abrupt spectacle along with his whiskey-smoke-sweat fume tended to validate Everett's last remark.

" 'Plenty hard rocks' all right," Lester muttered so the newcomer wouldn't hear—and just as well didn't, Everett thought as he edged to the door.

"Ain't had a shearing nor a bath outside a goddam creek nor a woman in six months," the buckskinned man announced loudly, staggering toward the barber chair and sagging into it and onto the magazine with his rifle across his lap, "but I aim to get me all three goddam quick."

"Nor a drink maybe 'til a bit ago," Lester grinned affably.

The man's head jerked around, his eyes focusing on the barber's expression for a moment. Evidently satisfied with what he saw he turned back again. "No they's a dab of whiskey in the couple hundred miles twixt here and there but sure as hell ain't none in them bear-piss mountains. And I aim to make up for that goddam womanless, dried out, lonesome baching and any sonofabitch wants to get in my road better lie down dead before he starts."

Without thinking Lester touched the collar of the mountain man's leather shirt and suddenly found his fingers in his customer's grip and as quickly flung away and replaced by a knife snaked from its nape sheath. "Whoa there," the barber apologized, backing off a step. "Didn't mean a thing; just going to tuck in the hair cloth."

The man in the chair grunted and re-sheathed the knife with both hands, elbows overhead, absurdly looking as a woman does fastening her necklace. "Ain't a good place to tuck, Mister."

Lester couldn't think of another place so he simply flipped the cloth over his customer's lap including the rifle, hung its upper folds on a pair of the thickest shoulders he'd seen in a good while and returned to the previous subject. "Don't 'low anybody has it in mind to get in your road." He was aware of the frontier's customary avoidance and sometimes unhealthy consequences of personal inquiries; but barbers generally were permitted a little leeway here if clearly they were passing the time of day, even in which case guts helped. "Headed on East or going to stay with us a spell?"

This barber apparently had passed muster; his customer didn't give him a glance this time, merely hoiked up a glob of phlegm, leaned sideways to splatter it into the spittoon Lester quickly kicked into its way, and growled an answer and a question. "Depends on the play. They got some good play around here?"

"Longhorn a couple doors down, Shawnee up on the corner, three or four games below the track. They got the play if you got the money."

"What the hell you think I been doing in them mountains, whittling? What about women? And good eats?"

"Both."

"And rooms without no varmints. Had my fill of shit-fur varmints." He grinned. "But not them yellow pebbles."

"Plenty rooms in the winter."

"This here looks like a pitiful-poor winter camp but might stay a spell. Headed for Kansas City and maybe St. Louis but might stay a spell first. 'Less'n your shoot-itch marshal is the timber wolf I hear. I been chewed on by hungry wolves and ornery grizzlies and had my fill of bedevilment. Don't mean no harm to no one don't mean it to me but I'll claw any sonofabitch's balls off wants to crimp my joy." He let out an exuberant whoop just for the hell of it.

"Don't know who'd want to do that, Friend. Only me if you don't set back and let me work."

Now the customer stared at the barber for an instant before he burst into a guffaw. "You a reckless bastard, ain't you?"

"A haircutting one. You want a shave while I'm cutting it?"

"Let her rip, Barber."

CHAPTER 33

On his afternoon rounds Luther had encountered Little John Brock in front of the stage station where again they'd watched Hearts Ferris climb out of Nick Caldwell's rattling conveyance and had recalled they'd first met in August at the same place watching the same happening. "Life's a lot of the same things over and over," the deputy had philosophized. "Hope not," the marshal had said with some fervor. "While I think of it Big John told me you had in mind moving on for fear the town ain't got the money to winter us all four. Talked to Bill Crum; you forget moving 'less you got another reason." Little John had grinned. "Got a reason to stay. Kind of liked a Nola Priest woman I met here." An hour later after walking with Spot back along East Pacific Street past the *Republican* and Jim Watts' law office on one side and the Plains Hotel, Gopher Hole, funeral parlor, and corner firehouse on the other and turning diagonally down across the plaza Luther had stopped in the Schmidt Bros. Cigar Factory. He'd viewed Fritz's week-old scar in company with Gus and two interested customers and had conversed about the Democrats' national resurgence and bought and vest-pocketed four Lola Montezes. Then he'd gone on southward past Oliver's Hardware and between the train station and the Bell Mare Livery Stable and across the track into the upper end of South Street where he'd run into Big John McAlister talking about Indians with Jake Barlow—Jake's favorite topic these days—in front of the smithy. Again he'd joined sparingly in the conversation until Jake's return to shoeing had offered him a chance to ask Big John how the deputy had fared with a differing kind of shooing that morning: the belligerent Kentuckian out of town. "He was hostile as hell," the lawman had said; "couldn't get it through his sore head"—Big John had grinned at his own chance jest—"that you was doing him a favor not taking him to court. Hollered he had some unfinished business in this town. Including you. Didn't say what besides you but I told him all his business in Bancroft just went broke and there wasn't no grub-stakers anywheres around. Quirted his mule for him—he was riding a goddam Army mule—and loped him on out of here." The deputy had chuckled. "Saw one thing: he took a trail different from the fort. Likely stole that animal from some remount depot."

Doc Bowman at that moment had turned from Jimson Street below them and started up South Street scuffing along in the dust with his saddlebags over one shoulder. "Doc, you look like you need a good doctor," Big John had said when the physician had paused opposite them; "too bad we ain't got one." Doc had grunted, "Go to hell, you and Mary Baker Eddie both; I'm not in a good mood. Think the Thelma girl at Nell's might have a fatal belly. Told me about it last week, too damn late, listening to this damn mind-over-matter . . . " His bitter condemnation had sputtered into a calmer appraisal. "I believe in prayer, in miracles bygod, but not in purging the science of medicine." He had turned away to resume his office-ward trek. "You boys keep smiling." Briefly he had stared back at the marshal. "Somebody sure better; town's getting downright melancholy lately."

Assured by Big John that for the time the below-track mood had been peaceable Luther had decided to do some personal buying he'd been putting off. Returning to Oliver's Hardware on the west side of the plaza he'd acquired a small screwdriver to keep his Colt's screws tightened, had accepted for Spot from Mack's Butcher Shop a large bone wrapped in last week's *Republican* and had ordered in O.K. Outfitters a pair of angora chaps for the coming winter. As he'd stepped from the Outfitters he nearly had collided with Lila Haniford and Ruth Blaine on the board sidewalk; and although mostly he'd listened and later should have found it awkward to retrace its path their ten minutes' conversation had ranged the terrain of current events from the frustration of women's suffrage to the publication of Mark Twain's "Life on the Mississippi."

These had been at least most of the mainly forgettable happenings on Luther's afternoon rounds preceding Lafe Jackman's shouting at him across the plaza from in front of the barber shop. At that moment the rest of the afternoon turned unforgettable for those participants and witnesses who were to survive its chaos.

"Use help over here," Lafe yelled hoarsely.

Within a space of twenty seconds a muffled shot boomed inside the shop mingled with the shattering of a pane followed by a less muffled shot, Lafe dropped to his knees and scrambled crab-like away from the shop's doorway trying to grip one arm and his pistol simultaneously, Luther ran across the plaza bent over with his Colt drawn, gusting over his shoulder to the women—"Get in the store!"—and gimpy, flapping-shirted Enos Dowling plunged from the building with the mountain man raging on his trail.

The tempest was half spent. During the ensuing twenty seconds Enos's ominous, pleading howl as he ran toward Luther was ground to an echo by the roaring curses of the buckskinned specter suddenly embodied in the turmoil, rifle pointed in the marshal's and cowboy's direction, one or the other or both of the two manifestly in deadly peril. "Look out, Luther!" his deputy shouted, struggling on his knees in the dust to raise his own weapon with a bloody hand. The marshal's shot, its crash burying Lafe's "No!" was not deflected enough by Enos's passing elbow to prevent its sprawling the mountain man and cartwheeling the rifle. The cowboy now rearward of Luther kicked at Spot's snarling jaws ineffectually, off balance with his bound shoulder. As he scrabbled out his pistol with his left hand and shot the dog his eye corner reflected Lafe's struggle and his head swiveled his glare in that direction and seeing the deputy's shakily upraised gun he started to drop his in panic. Whirling at the deafening explosion the marshal saw the cowboy's outheld pistol and squeezed his trigger too soon to choke its lead venom at the instant Ruth Blaine burst into his consciousness and across his line of fire toward her husband's shop. Her yelp like Spot's and the debacle of her spin into a heap with the dead dog at Enos's feet pounded Luther's reason into a shambles of fury and hate; squinting through a red haze he killed the staggering cowboy with a bullet in the chest.

As Lester ran from his shop and dropped at his wife's side next to the dead dog and took Ruth in his arms to kiss her fluttering lids and faint smile the mountain man a few yards away spoke to the sky before he died. "This sure ain't the particular joy I had in mind."

CHAPTER 34

"REPUBLICAN

"Founded 1870   Vol. 6, No. 42   Oct. 17, 1875   Bancroft, Kansas

"BANCROFT BLOOD BATH

"★★ Three Dead — Two Wounded ★★

"(High Price of a Haircut)

"At approximately 4:00 P.M. Wednesday, gunplay echoed again in the streets of our community, shattering the comparative peace that has held sway hereabouts since clear back to a week ago yesterday when we lost our county sheriff, a homesteader and Texas cowboy who hadn't headed for home soon enough.

"This Wednesday we said our goodbyes to a couple of strangers we hadn't yet had time to say hello to and another Texan we'd got to know slightly through a horse-stealing charge; and luckily for everybody we didn't have to say goodbye, only 'Sorry, hurry and get well,' to our fine citizens, Mrs. Lester (Ruth) Blaine and Deputy Marshal Lafe Jackman.

"Your editor has made every effort to sort out the facts surrounding the fracas. The following account comes as close to the unvarnished truth as a lot of digging and a few deductions make possible.

"Because of his rowdyism last Tuesday evening at one of our pleasure palaces below the railroad, a non-local identified only as hailing from Kentucky was jailed by Marshal Luther Cain overnight to sober him up and on Wednesday morning was shown the road out of town by Deputy Marshal John McAlister on Marshal Cain's order. When asked why the offender was thus 'tried' by the peace officers instead of the mayor's court, in view of Marshal Cain's well-known and respected letter-of-the-law way of doing things, the latter said his letting sentiment about the man's war service overrule his law-enforcement standards had 'added to the day's hell raising' and wasn't likely to happen again.

"In fairness to our good marshal, it must be noted that the Kentuckian, according to Deputy McAlister, was 'just natural aggravated and wouldn't been less so for going to court.' Councilman John Newlin, proprietor of the establishment where the Kentuckian was arrested Tuesday evening, told your editor that in his opinion the man's aggravation was justified by Marshal Cain's '--- ---- mean treatment' of him during his arrest, saying he saw the marshal 'drop my paying customer with his pistol barrel like an axed steer.' Questioned as to this, the marshal answered that 'Johnny Newlin likes it both ways; he wants his place not busted up by a drunk, but the drunk not busted up out of paying.'

"Deputy John McAlister has told us that after he had pointed our Kentucky visitor out of town Wednesday morning, the latter circled out of sight and headed back again, ending up in the same Jimson St. establishment where he'd got into trouble the night before.

"The Kentuckian's maneuver has been confirmed by Deputy Jackman, whose forearm wound we're glad to report is responding well to Dr. Roy Bowman's capable treatment.

"Deputy Jackman received his wound later in that afternoon's Battle of the Barber Shop when he walked into Lester Blaine's place for a haircut and 'smack into a drunken argument' involving accused horse thief Enos Dowling, the Kentuckian, and the other unidentified non-local who was 'buckskinned out like a half-wild mountain man,' all three of whom shortly thereafter were deceased. The deputy says they referred to Dowling and the Kentuckian having joined forces when they found out in the saloon they both had bones to pick with Marshal Cain for alleged—your editor emphasizes 'alleged'—past manhandling of them by that peace officer. Also, Dowling agreed to show the Kentuckian where Lester Blaine could be found, the visitor claiming some unfinished business with the barber. (Incidentally, Mr. Blaine has told us he has no idea what that business might have been, or, after viewing the corpse, who the Kentucky man was. Maybe the man only wanted a haircut, too.)

"Deputy Jackman said the argument in progress when he entered the shop appeared to be mainly between the Kentuckian and the buckskinned stranger, the latter demanding that the barber's attentions to him not be distracted, and the Kentuckian demanding to talk immediately with Mr. Blaine. The buckskinned man was yelling that nobody was going to interfere with his 'joy.' Dowling was loud in backing the Kentuckian. And Mr Blaine was trying to mediate what was fast heading toward a shooting war. In fact, it was at this point that the war broke out, according to Deputy Jackman and Mr. Blaine. What happened next, as so often with such brouhahas, was like a blur, our reliable raconteurs tell us. Nevertheless, the deputy, the barber, Marshal Cain, Mrs. Blaine, Miss Lila Haniford, Dr. Roy Bowman, and other conscientious witnesses of part or all of the action whom we've interviewed agree it went about as follows from that point on.

"In his rage, no doubt heated up further by whiskey, the 'mountain man' un-scabbarded his rifle and pointed it and shouted curses at the intruders. Considering the latter to be in pretty serious but maybe not deadly jeopardy, and also realizing that drawing his own pistol likely would start the shooting for sure, our brave deputy stepped up to the rifleman and asked him to put his gun away, intending afterward to run the other two out of the place. Luckily, Deputy Jackman's calm request evidently delayed the man's firing; instead, he gripped the deputy's arm, and with amazing strength, dragged him a couple of steps to the door and gave him a forceful shove outdoors. The deputy saw Marshal Cain across the plaza in front of O.K. Outfitters talking with Mrs. Blaine and Miss Haniford, and called to him about the trouble.

"Inside the shop at that moment, the Kentuckian took advantage of the rifleman's turned back and grabbed for the rifle, a move he probably didn't have time to regret before he died with a bullet in his stomach. At about the same moment, Mr. Blaine knocked Enos Dowling's drawn pistol aside, deflecting its seemingly defensive shot from the intended 'mountain man' outward through the window and happily only through the flesh of Deputy Jackman's forearm, jerking the deputy down.

"As Marshal Cain ran to help Jackman, he was met by Dowling (whose pistol was now holstered) and the irate stranger charging toward him out of the shop, and in the moment's riot he judged the rifle-toter to be the biggest danger to himself or Dowling and shot that man as Dowling ran past. Then, hearing a shot close behind him, he turned to see his faithful dog stretched on the ground and Dowling's pistol out of its holster again and

242

rising in Deputy Jackman's direction, and he fired at the alleged horse thief, but unfortunately hit Mrs. Blaine (although, 'happily' again, only in her shoulder) as she ran in front of him to see if her husband was all right in his shop, which it turned out he was.

"Your editor has to say honestly he's not sure exactly what happened next. Marshal Cain hasn't seen fit to talk about it more than seeming to indicate he's not sure himself in all the commotion; and witnesses differ somewhat in their accounts. One thing is sure: the marshal shot at Dowling a second time, striking him in the chest fatally.

"Some say the lawman shot the cowboy unlawfully, that the young man acted like he didn't want to fight at that point; others say the marshal shot him in upholding the law, which was what a town hires a lawman to do.

"Your editor feels constrained to withhold further comment at this time, and hopes the good people of Bancroft will not go off half-cocked either. We've got too much rumpus already."

CHAPTER 35

*. . . After hearing all the testimony back then,
the Firearms Review Board, charged with in-
vestigating such shootings, condoned Sergeant Keller's self-defense killing of the shot-
gun-waving arcade robber (who incidentally
had wounded his partner) and only a bit less
quickly vindicated the sergeant's inadvertent
and fortunately non-fatal wounding of the
teenage girl. The Board, however, took longer
to absolve him of blame for the death of the
robber's accomplice; although the accomplice
also was armed, a witness said the young man
had thrown away his "Saturday Night Special" before Sergeant Keller shot him, maybe
implying that the officer had panicked and
fired unnecessarily. In view of the sergeant's
outstanding record of courage, the Board re-
jected the idea of his panicking.*

*As to last night's fracas, resulting
among other things in the killing of an alleged
drug dealer allegedly by Sergeant Keller, who
himself is lying near death in a hospital, a
couple of witnesses have told us that the two
men grew up as neighborhood pals, that their
wives had become friends also, that the sergeant often lamented his friend's wayward-
ness as the latter did the sergeant's strictness,
that the alleged dealer had been tipped off
about the tough cop's search for him and must
have become terrified of arrest or worse, because he fired at Keller from ambush before
the policeman spotted him and defensively—
even with an instant's reluctance, it seemed
to one witness—returned the fire.*

It has occurred to us from the accounts

of both shootings, separated as they were by
time, that nevertheless there may be one factor
which ties them together. Begging the reader's
indulgence of our own temerity here, might
that common element be fear of Sergeant
Keller's touted inflexibility . . . ?

For an instant Luther wasn't sure whether he was still asleep or had awakened to a vivid memory of his nightmare. His head swirled and clanged with images and echoes of strife. Either his heart or bear paws pounded his ears. He realized his eyes were open and therefore he must be awake but the unreality of recent days clinging stubbornly in his mind like a cobweb after a cloudburst seemed to deny his wakefulness. Staring up from his bed at room 14's ceiling, almost dark in the day's first light, he cleared his throat and heard the sound of that distinctly and felt it scraping his larnyx and knew surely he was awake; but his confusion persisted.

His impressions and memories since Wednesday's blow-up which last evening's *Republican* had dubbed the "Battle of the Barber Shop" were dangerous distractions; as a marshal he couldn't afford to be deafened by their reverberations in his head; as a man he was compelled to listen to their muddling din.

He winced almost physically at his hazy recollection of his lover Carrie's scream as she had run from somewhere into the maelstrom's aftermath and fallen to her knees beside his friends Ruth and Lester—all three victims of his public trust—and looked at him across the Blaines' huddled forms with eyes as anguished and questioning as any he had seen in his life. Her gaze somehow had seemed shaded with the same fright as her ardent response that night to his own strangely urgent lovemaking. It had seemed they both had been afraid without knowing of what, making love with sad, puzzled desperation. That had been three nights ago in this same room—he'd spent the second on the jail's cot, Turnkey Meese having been drunk and Acting Sheriff Baker in Dodge— and the room, his soul, his loins, his moustache, his arms still smelled of the woman who so swiftly and with such power had bewitched him. Imagining her hurt now, not to mention her disapproval, tautened his stress.

In the past few years he had waded through a stinking morass of disorder and blood and excrement and rot but he also had breathed rain-wet sage, mountain snow, sunny pines; he'd seen mostly bad but some good; he'd visited Hell often but had passed by the door to Heaven once in a while on his way. None of the dismal windings had been of his choosing, rather happenstance. His own choice had been to find order and direction for his daily existence; and it had been in the law's conformity and symmetry where he'd found these. Fate had not dealt him an attorney's hand but he'd sat into the game as a law enforcer. Helping preserve the system's stability had become his life.

Now his life's footing seemed to be feeling tremors of instability. Besides Carrie's slight frown before her nod yesterday when he'd asked her if Ruth were well enough yet for him to pay her an apologetic call—didn't Ruth understand the accident?—there'd been other bodings: the chalked "Killer Cain" on the courthouse wall; Lafe's deep uneasiness in reporting the buckskinned stranger's and maybe even Dowling's innocence of aggression; the *Republican*'s unnecessarily defensive tone and at the same time perplexed undertones; Doc asking him if he felt all right nowadays, hurriedly adding "in the belly"; Bill Crum saying he and Doc and Jim Watts judged it was best this particular time to put off the inquest another week "to let the town simmer down a mite"; Lila Haniford stopping him on the street with a gentle but earnest hand to say "empathy" might be the language's wisest word (which he hadn't yet looked up somewhere); his unexpected twinge of regret at the struggle of a drunken chider's tongue with "Enos Dowling"; Dale Darling saying drolly if the marshal ran for mayor he'd have the undertaker's vote even without further favors; in the same asinine vein Uncle Vince Simpson's advice: "You ain't never going to get elected, Luther, shooting all the voters."

It was a hell of a prospect that folk's passing huff might stay around longer and grow from wrong-headedness about a lawman's duty to disrespect for law itself. Why the hell should people buck law enforcement when that was the trail to no law? They want hawks in their goddam chickens? Enforcing the law half-way or half-time was the same as keeping half of the hawks out of the flock half of the time: a passel of dead chickens anyhow. Trembling in his arms Wednesday night in this bed Carrie had quoted Preacher Smith to him. " 'There could come a time when unforgiveness in a man might make him unforgiveable, " she'd whis-

246

pered. But forgiveness was a judge s and a jury's job, not a peace officer's; his was to enforce the peace as and when he saw it violated, to halt its violation, to arrest its violator, and if resisted to overcome the resistence with the means and skills he commanded.

Was his loved one also getting mixed up about the importance of law and order? Had her trembling in the darkness been partly from doubt of some kind? When he'd asked why she had been trembling she'd whispered again before damming his mouth with hers, "I'll try not to be, Dear; but I'm afraid." She hadn't filed any claim on fear, that was there for all folks to stake out for themselves; but a body had to stand up for what was right regardless. And decent folks had to stand up with him. At least his friends did. For sure his loved-loving one. How could they and she rightly expect less of him than loyalty to his job which was their protection for godssake? The hell with it. Not with Carrie. With what was turning into a goddam riddle and with starting another bellyache trying to figure it out. He threw back the blanket, put on his hat, pulled on his socks and longjohns and boots, got out of bed, took swigs from both of the bureau's laudanum and Hostetter's Bitters bottles, and watered them down directly from the pitcher. As he put on his pants he thought about Lafe's and Ruth's wounds likely hurting even more than his belly did. And in the painful moment strangely he thought about some of his own much older wounds, not only his cousin's death but his father's and mother's within a month afterward of smallpox and Elijah's at Shiloh. Successively, self-defensively he had cried less at each of those. Inside. No one had seen his tears those times and now his sadness at Ruth's injury and regret at Lafe's were to be borne inwardly also.

At this early Saturday-morning moment Lafe Jackman's cauterized forearm jabbed him awake like a spur rowel because he'd rolled onto it. Doc Bowman had told him his creased muscle was bound to be angrily swollen and sore for a good while and so far Doc had drawn aces. "Sonofabitch," Lafe muttered aloud, not even in the privacy of his Plains Hotel bunk voicing—merely thinking—his dismay over Wednesday's botch.

Ever since she'd been shot Ruth Blaine's shoulder had hurt like the devil, too. Sleep had been possible only in fits and starts because of the pain and she was exhausted. Doc had said it was

247

no wonder with her broken collar bone and mangled flesh—trapezius muscle he'd called it. He had given her morphine to ease the hurt some and had bled her even further for her fever, told her the marshal's bullet had gone on through although probably had been deflected and convinced her she wasn't going to end up with a crippled arm. Lester had told her he was glad to hear about her continuing hugging ability and that had helped; but all in all she was about as uncomfortable lying on her uninjured side in her Buffalo Street bed as a turkey on Thanksgiving eve.

A diversion from Ruth's ordeal was in the offing however: the man who'd shot her was coming for a visit. Carrie had said Luther wanted to have a talk with her, that he was sorry about hurting her. She of course was willing to talk with him and had sent him word he might stop by that morning. She was obliged to admit to herself a vague, almost queasy sense of apprehension about his visit, a feeling absurdly verging on fear of him. Sensibly she knew it might be the other way around: he might be fearful of her resentment. And her disquiet was an understandable reaction to Wednesday's carnage over which he had loomed so terrifyingly if surely by necessity. As she'd told her husband when Lester had been awakened a few minutes ago by her involuntary groan she was determined not to let their friend the marshal glimpse her uneasiness; the lawman hadn't meant to shoot her, it hadn't been his fault she'd run blindly into his way. Her husband, coming fully awake at the mention of Luther Cain, had said softly something about the benefits of staying out of their friend's way and had got up and begun to dress.

An hour and a half later Lester had milked the cow and fixed Ruth and himself and the children breakfast and sandwiches for her and them to eat at noon and was ready to leave for his split day's work at the barber shop and on Lane's rooming house which he and Everett had started rebuilding the previous day. As he was heading for the front door a firm knock rattled it and he pulled it open upon Luther's lintel-grazing frame topped by the round-crowned black hat; and even though he was expecting the visitor Lester felt a qualm at sight of him.

"Howdy, Lester. Hope I ain't too early but Carrie Shaw said . . ."

"Not a bit of it, not a bit, Luther, we were just talking about you; Ruth wants to see you, come in." The barber-carpenter motioned the visitor inside and closed the door behind him. "She's in bed. The young'uns have gone somewhere. We didn't tell them you were coming or they'd never left. Follow me if you want."

By the time the men stepped into her bedroom Ruth had managed to sit partly upright against her pillow and overcome flinching from the torture of the effort and set her lips in a cheerful smile. It occurred to her briefly that Luther Cain was the only man other than her father, her husband and two or three doctors ever to enter any bedroom of hers. Looking up at him as he stood a head taller than her husband in the small space she realized he felt as awkward as she; his long fingers which curled the brim of his swept-off hat seemed as uncertain as hers clutching the collar of her flannel nightgown. She couldn't offer him that hand without letting go of the collar and her other was strapped down with her arm under her gown. She made up for it with a widened smile. He smiled back and took hold of his hat brim also with his free hand.

"Please sit down in that chair, Marshal," she nodded toward the room's only one, "and you sit here on the foot of the bed, Lester."

"Thank you, M'am," the lawman said, doing her bidding.

Her husband eased himself onto the patchwork quilt. "Don't want to jounce you." He cleared his throat in seeming nervousness. "Got to get to work soon."

"Can't stay but a bit myself." Luther's gaze met the lady's squarely. "I thank you for letting me come to see you, Ruth. I only wanted to tell you I'm sorry for what happened—" he frowned, motioning with his hat—"your shoulder there. I'd never in the world hurt you a-purpose." He glanced at her husband. "Either one."

"We know you wouldn't, Luther. Like I told Lester it was my fault running in your way." She shuddered at the recollection, hoping her pang was invisible.

"No, it wasn't your fault; Dowling's maybe, but not yours for sure." Once again he felt a melancholy twinge at the cowboy's name.

The wife and husband exchanged quick glances. Dowling's?

"It was my bullet done the damage." The marshal's expression became quizzical. "I reckon you're two of my best friends left in this town and I had to hurt both of you in different ways. I'm

249

surely sorry." His frown returned and he shook his head and got to his feet. "Hell with them. Pardon, M'am. I best . . ."

The Blaines were fleetingly confused.

". . . be moving like the cowboys say before the sun gets higher and the broncs spookier. Hope you're feeling a whole lot better right soon, Ruth."

Lester stood up after him. "And this being Saturday maybe some haircuts are already waiting for me. Got the place cleaned up and the window fixed and ready to go again."

As her visitor stepped across the room's threshold ahead of her husband Ruth called after him—"Luther"—and when he paused to look back at her she smiled the best she could. "Thank you. And for your own and Carrie's and the good Lord's sake watch out for yourself." After the barest hesitation she added, "In every way, Luther."

He stared at her for a moment without returning her smile. "Yes, M'am." Then he continued down the hall, a trace of his earlier frown hovering above his eyes.

Walking eastward along Pacific Street toward the plaza neither man spoke for a few minutes, Luther engrossed in his own thoughts, Lester wondering what Luther was thinking.

Presently the barber-carpenter broke the silence. "Ruth was grateful for you coming by. So was I "

The marshal nodded. "Needed to say what I said. Grateful she let me. You too."

Lester's tongue was slightly thick. "Headed for the courthouse?"

"Got to see Carl Norris first."

Another minute of silence passed before Lester spoke again. "Haven't had a chance for much talk since all that ruckus Wednesday. Making caskets and fixing my window and all. But I'll say now—I know it's not much but I'll say it—any time you want a free haircut, Luther, stop in."

In spite of his depression Luther managed to summon a brief smile. "That go for a shave and moustache trim?"

The barber-carpenter softly exhaled his relief and nodded. "No question about it."

They entered the plaza and continued along its north side. As they arrived at the forking of their ways Luther lifted a restraining hand, squinting at his friend without any other expression. "Got to ask you again, Lester: like Lafe told me and you too and the newspaper printed about that Kentucky jaybird claiming business with you, what the hell's fire you reckon could the sonofabitch had in his craw?"

Lester's swallow was visible although his voice was unstrained. "Like I said only thing I can think of he got me mixed up with somebody else. Never saw him before."

Luther shook his head. "Mayor hoped we'd find some kin of him and the mountain man both. Save the town paying Dale and you." Having opened the subject he felt obliged to close it. "Dowling's cow outfit is good for his."

"Bill running out of burying money?" Instantly Lester regretted his question. "Not like I'm worried, don't mean that."

The marshal's tone was as flat as the plains. "The cost ain't my job, Lester. Only the law."

They reached the plaza's northeast corner not far above Pete Rice's small building on the east side as the dentist was opening up for the day's tooth-pullings and abscess-lancings. In his usual heavy-handed way he slammed the door several times to get its latch working and kicked a loose board from the edge of the wooden sidewalk into the street and practiced some curses ahead of the coming hours' boredom. He wasn't happy in his work as could be attested by hundreds of mouth-sprung cowboys, mule-skinners and buffalo-hunters from the Rio Grande to the Missouri. But he'd been all they'd had at their times.

"Painless Pete," his neighboring barber called down to him, "trying to wreck your damn place?" Lester felt easier for the digression.

"Go to hell!" The dentist turned his eighty-feet-away dolor on Luther. "You don't give a damn who trails after you now I see. Your dog was a credit to the coyote you got there; Dowling ought to shot him instead."

Another thing about Pete, Lester recalled too late: he talked and then thought. The barber spoke before either of the others could although the marshal didn't seem inclined to comment. "Luther, don't forget what I said about that free haircut."

The lawman nodded as he continued eastward toward the newspaper's building.

" 'Free haircut?' " the dentist echoed the barber, his gold in-

251

cisors gleaming. "What you got to do to get one of them, gun somebody?"

Fiercely Lester waved down the loudmouth, hissing "Brainless!" and hoping Luther hadn't heard.

Luther's ears hadn't been plugged since his last Civil War barrage.

CHAPTER 36

Boss:

Here's a quick transcription of what little we got of your and the mayor's phone talk this morning. Our recorder went bad again—now maybe you'll spring for a new one—and I'm rushing, but this has the gist. I'll retype, date, catalog, etc., later for the file. Hope this dab helps. (Also hope the sergeant makes it! I want to meet him.)

C.N.. . . . *appreciate your talking to me . . . piece about Detective Sergeant Mark Keller, badly wounded last night by a drug dealing suspect. Sergeant killed him in the shooting . . . maybe you'd be willing . . . people of the city . . .*

MAYOR: *Always glad to talk to you, Cal. Just sorry . . . like this. Fine man. Outstanding officer. Always put his duty . . .*

C.N.: *. . . give me some insights from both your official and personal standpoints. Understand you knew him . . . know him personally.*

MAYOR: *The public couldn't ask . . . dedicated, braver policemen . . . not closely acquainted, but . . . to pin medals on his chest . . . proud also to shake his hand . . . friends in the public service, you could say . . . more men like him.*

C.N.: *. . . heard some people . . . a little over-dedicated, maybe; too tough, maybe.*

MAYOR: *They don't . . . talking about, how frustrating the job is. Takes a tough man to face . . . day out.*

C.N.: *. . . serious complaints about him?*

MAYOR: *Commissioner was looking down in the mouth one day . . . bellyachers go with a cop's job. Mine, too, matter of fact.*

C.N.: *I guess there'll be a Firearms Board review . . . survives or not.*

MAYOR: *I assume so. Cal, I'm interested . . . this story on this particular officer?*

C.N.:   . . . *fascinates me, he's special, has a special way of looking*
          at things. I only hope . . .
MAYOR: *So do I, Cal. So do I. And I wonder . . .*
Damn recorder quit for good here. Sorry, Boss.
                              TH

    Striding along the East Pacific Street block from the plaza
to the *Republican* the marshal for once regretted not being stalked
by somebody. He didn't know what it had been about Spot he
presently missed unless it was the plain company. Although their
effects on him certainly had differed the dog and Carrie separately
and together in some inexplicable way had filled an emptiness
he couldn't explain either. Now Spot had vanished from the trail
leaving only the woman; and the thought of her disappearing too
seemed to pour some of Doc's acid onto his raw vexation. It stung
like hell and made his bellyache worse along with his day generally.
    Pushing into Carl's office he collided with the editor who was
coming out of it and who immediately turned back and motioned
the marshal inward. "Sorry, Luther. What can I do for you?"
    "Don't want to hold you up. In a manner of speaking."
    The editor grinned. "Glad you've not lost your sense of humor."
He waved toward the bench. "Have a seat. I'm in no hurry."
    "Thanks but got to be down in the mayor's court in a little
bit." He glanced toward the pressroom. "Just wanted to ask a
question. No damn humor in it," he added wryly.
    "I'll be down there myself." Carl had noticed Luther's glance.
"Billy's out back gathering eggs and Fred doesn't work on Saturdays. Go ahead and ask."
    "You think I do my job good?"
    Carl sensed it was the first time Luther ever had asked that
question of anyone. Including of himself. The editor wasn't sure
whether or not to be pleased by his own insight. He wasn't sure
how to answer the question either.
    The marshal reprieved him. "What the hell's 'empathy' mean,
Carl?"
    "Well I guess feeling what the other fellow feels. Kind of put-
ting yourself in his shoes."
    "Most everybody can do that can't they?"

Carl hesitated for an instant. "If they try. I'd say some don't try very hard."

"Me for one?"

"I didn't say you, Luther. What the devil's bothering you this morning?"

"It's other folks that's acting bothered. And not only this morning; quite a while now. Not all at once. Gradual. Things wrote on walls . . ."

"I saw that," the editor interrupted; "don't let that kid stuff bother you."

"It ain't kids that's been asking if I feel all right, not meeting my eye square, talking about gunning for a haircut and shooting voters and the like. Putting off the inquest." He squinted at another recollection: "Acting scared and quoting preachers at me, bygod."

The editor tried to keep his voice casual. "I suppose all peace officers have to put up with complaining."

"Maybe folks quit hankering for peace hereabouts."

"You want to hear complaining you just put out a newspaper. No they want peace all right, Luther, the good citizens. Others you don't have to mind."

The marshal's frown looked irritated and perplexed at the same time. "Some of the others I reckon is 'good citizens.' If that means doing a day's work and not killing and thieving and bullying and raising holy hell." Abruptly his perplexity seemed to deepen. "Killing ain't always murdering. Goddam murdering to hell. And thieving and bullying. Except when the sonofabitch is a bully hisself." Luther's discomfort suddenly had become obvious. "You think I marshal too hard, Carl, like Colonel Cole told the goddam mayor?"

The editor wanted to help this surprisingly sensitive man for whom he had respect and admiration and indeed, as far as Luther seemed to allow it, affection. "Of course not. You've got to marshal hard with some of the hard customers you go against." Again he took pains to speak casually. "But I expect you've found some are harder than others. Maybe a good many aren't even as hard as they act; just get drunk for the fun of it; or maybe put on for one reason or another, like to impress somebody. But a savvy peace officer like you can pick those out and send them somewhere to sleep it off. Keep them from harming anybody and out of harm's way themselves. Maybe have to tap them on the head now and then to get their attention but naturally not waste ammunition on them."

Luther had stared at Carl intently as the editor had spoken. He took a slow, deep breath and exhaled it in a whisper of concentration. "Hope you ain't backing off from keeping the peace like you said."

"My article yesterday sound like it?"

The marshal's faint shrug wasn't altogether assured.

"My law and order editorials before you got to town helped bring you here. One of their titles was 'Bancroft's Future Depends on Peace.'" He grinned. "First I had it 'Pursue Peace for Perpetual Progress' but Lila Haniford saw Fred setting that in type and laughed so hard we changed it." His grin disappeared. "Law enforcement isn't a laughing matter to the *Republican*. We stand for just laws justly enforced. Say I kind of like that, might use it. Heard Jim Watts tell a jury once 'There's no justice without law and no law without justice.'"

Luther pulled his hat brim lower without comment except "Best be on my way after I use your privy if that's all right."

"Why sure, Marshal, help yourself. And glad you stopped by."

The lawman nodded, turned to the outdoors and walked around a side of the building. Wading through several dozen squawking chickens and passing the henhouse—noticing a basketful of eggs on the ground beside it—he came to the outhouse and entered its half-open doorway. It was a two-holer. Billy Plunkett, his back to the doorway, was standing before one of the holes and Luther stepped up to the other.

"Morning, Billy." The man hitched up his gun belt and unbuttoned his trousers. The boy's trousers already were unbuttoned. Involuntarily Billy amost stopped what he was doing but nature was persistent. "Yessir, good morning; yessir, Marshal."

They each stared at the plank wall two feet ahead, Luther in his pondering barely aware of his surroundings let alone his companion in necessity, Billy exquisitely aware of where he was and what he was doing and with whom he was doing it. A grin spread slowly across the boy's face as great pride suffused him. There was no doubt about it, there couldn't be. He absolutely had

256

to be the only one: the only boy maybe in the whole world and for sure in Bancroft, Kansas who was able truthfully to say he had stood beside the great Luther Cain while both of them had peed. And then the memorable moment was finished but not the memory.

The marshal blinked his mind back to reality. His voice was solemn. "You ever noticed, Son, no matter how many times you shake it, it always drips in your pants?"

CHAPTER 37

Two mornings later Mother Swain's boarders were eating their week's first breakfast. The kitchen and the food both were hot, the kitchen from the hay-burning cook stove and the food "as much from Mother's heart as from the hay-cats" in Preacher Smith's words.

"Pshaw," the landlady set him down cheerfully, "eat your flapjacks and be glad somebody cares about your belly like the Lord does your soul."

Wyoming Nye spoke through a mouthful of the cornmeal beatitude. "The Lord must have give you His recipe. These is the goddamdest—damdest—the best flapjacks I ever et. And that's the goddam truth."

"Glad they pleasure you, Wyoming," she said; "learned making them from a mammy back home. Only don't cuss at my table; you know my rule."

His embarrassment was obvious. "Yes, M'am."

"Save cussing for the Shawnee."

"Sorry, M'am," he said earnestly. "No offense?"

"Hell no," she smiled.

His own wide smile measured his liking. Howard Smith laughed heartily. Fred Martin chuckled.

Jeb Hill grunted. "Ain't nothing funny about this here article." He was re-reading Friday's *Republican* for the half-dozenth time in the three days since its publication. "And I'm telling you again it's just the terrible way I seen it happen through the Hardware window." His morbid fascination with the details of the previous Wednesday's gun battle seemed even to have outstripped the town's generally; and the town's certainly wasn't mild. "Terriblest thing I ever hope to see. Everbody shooting and shouting and running and falling down. And when they quit I went over there with Mister Tinsley and a customer I was waiting on. But I wish I didn't, all that blood and corruption. You never smelled such a stink in that barber shop with the one there getting a load of buckshot in his gut. Like a shithouse in August . . ." He clapped his hand over his mouth but Mother Swain appeared to be busy

258

at the stove and he accomodated her sham by not apologizing. "And I'll tell you what was just maybe the worst thing I seen of all." He lowered his voice and almost seemed to glance over his shoulder as though there might be eavesdroppers in the room. "I know sure as I'm setting here Luther Cain killed that Dowling kid without needing to. If you want to call it by name it'd have to be . . ." he whispered the word hoarsely "murder."

The landlady turned from the stove. "Now hold your horses, Jeb, I don't know why you'd want to say that, how you could prove anything of the sort. You better be careful going around saying such things."

"And shooting that rifle-toting stranger was awful free with the lead too," Jeb said defiantly. "Besides I ain't going around, I'm saying it here where I live. I reckon you folks ain't apt to pass it to the marshal."

"You better hope not," Wyoming said.

Fred Martin pointed at the newspaper. "Carl Norris's advice about not going off half-cocked is good."

"I know what I seen with my own eyes," the Tinsley Hardware clerk defended himself. "I ain't saying the young lobo didn't deserve shooting, he likely did; I'm saying he didn't want no part of Luther Cain there in the street when Cain threw down on him."

"How can you know what was in his mind," Howard said; "in either one's for that matter?"

"I seen Dowling trying to drop his pistol, Preacher."

Fred raised a rebutting finger. "Fellow who saw it told me it looked like Dowling was aiming to shoot Deputy Jackman. That'd be reason enough for the marshal."

Jeb shook his head. "I'm only telling what I seen." He looked now as though he wanted to change the subject. "I'd thank you for the molasses, Wyoming."

The saloonkeeper passed along the pitcher. "Dowling was in the Shawnee time or two. May been up for stealing a horse but I didn't figure him for bad, only wild. And a fool to cross Luther Cain again after once in the Portugese over the horse. But he wasn't no killer like that Injun Jesse half-breed killed the sheriff."

"The one Luther killed in the same fight," Fred pointed out in the marshal's favor.

Jeb couldn't resist a final citation. "Same fight as the marshal killed Herman Strauss . . . accidental."

"Talk about women gossips." Mother Swain had raised her voice sternly. "You boys beat all. Luther Cain's a hard man maybe, but he's got good in him." She brandished her spatula. "You better remember our young friend Noble at this table before he was took from us, how the marshal set him down here amongst us out of a leaking shack. Maybe this lawman's quick with his gun sometimes but he's for the law and you better remember how it was when Charlie Tucker was here—meaning no disrespect to that poor soul wherever he is. I'm saying just eat your flapjacks."

The preacher made a slight bow to her from his seat. "We stand corrected, as the saying goes. Everbody's got good in him and this one's got his share." Howard spoke to the group generally. "Not a real happy man I'll grant you. Maybe he had some bad times along somewheres, maybe as a young'un. But like with Noble and some other kids—going fishing with them and the like— he's square with honest men and gentle with good ladies."

Jeb nodded solemnly enough but his conversion wasn't complete. "And even some not so good like that women from the Portugese."

"Including Miss Carrie Shaw," the preacher frowned at him, "who left the Portugese behind and makes fine dresses for other good ladies and is a church-going friend of mine."

"And of the marshal's," the landlady said pointedly to the store clerk before turning back to the stove. "They make a handsome couple," she added partly to herself, "and I'm glad."

Jeb's nature—all too human Howard reflected—required one final jab. "He's sweet on her all right. Heard they visit in the Drover where they're living."

"Where else would they visit," Mother said without deigning to turn around again, "in the middle of the plaza? You too old to remember, Jeb?"

The other flapjack eaters had to grin.

CHAPTER 38

From far away Mark saw himself standing naked beside his naked wife, staring at her image in the windowpane of the hotel's high bedroom. Mattie's body seemed to sink into the vast, darkening bed of Central Park beyond and at the same time into the reflection of the dimly lit bed behind them, rumpled by their lovemaking. He saw the two of them watching the dusk tuck the night's blanket under the tiny, yellow-windowed buildings edging the Park; he felt the heat of her waist against his encircling arm; his trance was filled with her nearness. And he heard the chord of her joy and her concern: "Oh, Mark, what a happy twentieth anniversary, a wonderful surprise, a beautiful second honeymoon. And the Plaza—of course I've never been here before—my, it's so elegant. And expensive. Can we afford it? Will it hurt your getting that new coat? I don't want to hurt anything for you, Mark, or hurt you in any way. I never want anyone else to hurt you either. Ever!"

He heard himself chuckle. "With your loving who needs a coat? And 'way up here who can hurt me?" He felt more than heard his chuckle stifled; but he clearly heard his returning ire, forgotten in the hour's enchantment: "The creeps can't reach above the gutter. And most of the time the others out there," his specter waved at the city, "don't give a damn. But goddammit I'm not feeling sorry for myself, I only want to do the job they pay me for!"

"Hush, Mark; I got us sidetracked. This is love time, not mad time. The only job you've got right now, my darling, is making love to me again. Please? We need it; we need it very much. Love. I need it and you do. To give it as well as receive it. Don't forget that."

As sometimes when he was awake and again now, in his unconsciousness, he felt the thought dart across his mind: we need a child, too. Had that blessing been lost to them, as his beloved sister had to him, in punishment for forgetfulness?

A week and a day after the "Battle of the Barber Shop" and five prairie miles north of the plaza Luther's tall roan gelding followed Carrie's black mare through a stunted cottonwood grove, across a tributary of Owl Creek and up the bank on its far side. The sunlight dripping through the yellow fall leaves spattered the rumps of the horses and their riders' hats with the day's unseasonable warmth.

The outing had been Carrie's idea. Yesterday she had finished a dress for Missus Wagner whose pleased whimpers as the seamstress had pulled it over the lady's grotesquely arthritic body had made the four hours of close work worth eight. Today she felt the need of long vistas and fresh air and pursuit of her lover's recently, strangely receding presence. For his part Luther wanted to be out of Bancroft's ambiguities, alone except for two rented horses and the pledged woman who had seemed to understand or at least to accept him until very lately for whatever the hell he was, and to vent on Carrie his frustration and gloomy passion; and watching her smoothly denimed buttocks ahead of him rise in her saddle as she leaned forward to urge her horse up the bank he felt his own desire rise like the hackles of a pit dog. He wanted very much to make love to her at the same time that he wanted her to understand and accept his hate of disorder. He wanted her to grasp both his dislike of violence and his use of it. He wanted her to be entirely female and to share his male convictions. He wanted her wild ardor and tame concurrence and he wanted to own her present and disown her past. His brain as well as his body buzzed with his goddam wanting.

"Hold up, Carrie." He cleared his throat of some nonexistent dust as they topped a hill to which the stream's bank ascended abruptly. Being in Kansas it wasn't much of a hill except comparatively speaking but at least it was higher than the encircling plains and even than the scrub cottonwood grove they'd just threaded. They could see for miles in every direction, only Bancroft's tiny blotch southward and the toy fort's speck near it giving scale to the horizons' sky-hung distances. "Worth looking around from here," he explained as she reined in her mare and as his roan brought him up beside her. "Ever ride out to this rise before?"

She stood in her stirrups for a moment. Her brown hair glistening downward from under her hat brim fondled her shoulders as she turned her head slowly to gaze about. "Never did, Luther. Surely a sight to see."

"Noble Buck and them boys brung me here one day. Scouting fishing holes. Said some old-timer told them the Injuns looked for buffalo herds from here. Up to three-four years ago. And for wagon trains not too long before then."

"I can believe it. See the whole world from here seems like."
She shuddered minutely at thought of the wagon trains. "Glad
the Injuns ain't hostile now."

"Most of them," he nodded. "Maybe some up north going to
be soon according to Jake Barlow."

She had lowered her body into the saddle again. His wayward
sidelong glance at her spread thighs ricocheted nearly painful lust
through him; he had to catch his breath and swallow; he wet his
lips with his tongue before continuing to speak.

"Not hereabouts Jake says."

She returned the marshal's stare unblinkingly. Her tone was
soft but assured. "That's good."

"Carrie?" He rubbed his chin. He reminded himself of a
chuckleheaded school kid.

"Yes, Luther?"

"Want to get off a spell, goddammit?"

"Not if you're going to cuss," she grinned. It may not have
been as clear to all or even most ladies as it was to Carrie what
he was up to. She was one however whose instincts in this regard
were sound; and those were rooted as much in the warm soil of
her love he'd tilled as in experience. "But I'd surely like that."

He hauled a shaky smile from the well of his grace as he
dismounted and held up his arms for her to slide into with her
own blithe flush. She was too wise a woman to trifle further now,
to babble irrelevantly, to ask questions about his marshaling or
anything beyond his moment's needs. Later there should be time
for asking, now it was giving and receiving time. When a man
and woman loved each other and had some troubles unrelated to
their love and needed escape from those into each other's bodies
Carrie knew the troubles had to bide for a while. At this instant
on this sunny morning atop this remote hillock her lover's inner
tumult had to be enveloped by her womanhood and quelled by it
before anything helpful could come of talking about anything else.
Within less than a hundred quick breaths their horses were hob-
bled and they were undressed lying on their clothes spread on the
grass, glistening arms and legs turning and clasping in an urgent
tangle, suntanned hands finding the peaks and hollows of alkali-
white, tufted bodies, lips searching and devouring and murmuring
and grunting, damp backs arching and hips thrusting until with
stifled wails the lovers drowned in their love's cataract.

After a while Carrie was sitting blissfully on Luther's shirt pulling on her pants over her gartered cotton stockings and underdrawers when she heard him chuckle. Glancing up at him standing on one foot beside her pulling on his own pants she saw that he was grinning down at her pink-ivory breasts. She winked inwardly at her dependable intuition. In the midst of her self-congratulation he took a sideways hop with one of his feet in a pants' leg, lost his balance, fell onto the grass, and scrambled up laughing.

"Well, hallelujah," she laughed with him; "first time I seen you half-way cheery in a coon's age."

"Feel right cheery." His tone sounded as though he meant it but his grin already had begun fading into the long shadows of reality. "Wish we didn't have to get back."

He hadn't said "ever" but Carrie wished she might add the word for him; with an eerie sense of foreboding she wished it very much; then her uneasiness dissipated. "So do I. Thank you, Dear." She pulled her muslin chemise over her head, slipped her feet into her boots, stood up, retrieved their shirts and handed him his and put on hers as he did, and stretched on her tiptoes to kiss his lips with all the tenderness of her contentment at that moment. Taking his hand she led him slowly toward their horses. "I'm glad we come out here today."

"Makes two of us," he said.

"You love me like you just said?"

"Wouldn't said it otherwise."

She trailed a finger across his back smiling as he bent down to unstrap her animal's hobbles. "I'm glad of that too, Luther."

"Likely I'll be saying it right often." His moustache tilted under his almost humorous eyes as he handed her the mare's reins and stepped to his roan. "Long as you behave yourself."

Her gaze clouded faintly as she watched him un-hobble the big gelding. "I'll behave if you do the same by watching out for yourself. In every way. Can't help fretting about you. That goddam job."

He straightened and looked at her. "Now you're the one cussing." Neither of them smiled. His eyes narrowed. "Ruth Blaine said exactly them same words to me Saturday."

She waved down his recollection as inconsequential. "I reckon we talked about you after you was there. She was glad you visited.

Lester too, he said later. We talked about the ornery critters comes around this town."

"This ain't the only town. Sonsofbitches ain't particular where."

"This is the town you're at. That's what keeps me from sleeping."

He reached for her elbow to help her mount the mare but she kicked a foot into the stirrup, raised her other leg across the saddle and settled into it.

He turned and swung onto his roan. "You ride pretty good."

"My daddy taught me. We rode together some when I was a kid." She leaned across the space between their horses. "Kiss me once more before we start back, Luther."

As he kissed her he touched one of her breasts lightly. Their horses began moving off the hill as though aware that the day's dream-like respite had ended.

"Carrie, why'd you say 'In every way' back there?" he asked quietly without looking at her. "What you mean? What the hell did Ruth mean by that?"

She frowned thoughtfully and pinched the bridge of her nose. "Well maybe just don't let them sonsofbitches we spoke of rile you too much." She lowered her hand and raised her eyes. "Nor other folks that ain't sonsofbitches but only maybe wild or drunk or stupid."

"Goddammit. 'Wild' and 'drunk' and 'stupid' don't change the law."

She sighed quietly. "I know, Dear, I know. But I don't want them to change you neither from the way you was to me this morning. Back there. I want you a man first—my man—then a lawman if you got to be one."

"I'm either a lawman or I ain't. You're my girl all right and I'll watch out for myself along with you and everybody else the best I can." He was staring ahead toward Bancroft. "I just got to do what I swore to do the best I can."

She reached toward him with an encouraging hand which didn't quite span the gap between them.

CHAPTER 39

Niagara Falls' thunder drowned Mattie's giggling, the suicidal deluge washing the open joy from her twenty-year-old face, draining even its smile, leaving through the spray a worried, more mature face. Her present one. And through the mist of Mark's dream he found himself staring uncomfortably back at other faces frowning with varying concern: his police captain's, the offended clergyman's, the assistant D.A.'s who recently and too casually had decried lawsuits against cities for police "firmness," a stinking street drunk's who had offered him a cool drink to "cool him down," a reporter who had asked him at a shooting scene six months ago whether he'd had to kill the goddam hopped-up hood, even his buddy's face as she'd muttered in their car one busy night lately how hard it was not to let the sonsofbitches turn yourself into one.

The earth under the Keller's honeymooning feet and bed and precious long week end those years ago had seemed to tremble under the hammer of the Falls but it had been sexually provocative then rather than perplexing and even oddly sinister as it was now. At present, as they walked beside the rapids above the great demonic plunging cliff, their path's vibration increased and the ground started crumbling. Mattie began to fall toward the water and screamed and he gripped her arm, jerking her back, fighting for his own balance. The fright in her voice turned into pain: "You're hurting me, Mark; too hard!" She didn't look exactly like Mattie; in her thirties all right but her brown hair was longer and her makeup heavier. Then her instant's strangeness melted into her familiar repetition nowadays: "Too hard!" His reproach was squeezed from his soul by his effort: "I'm trying to help you, goddammit, and everybody else!" Having rescued her he dropped her arm, almost threw it down. "You got to understand I'm helping you, I'm doing my job!" He winced as he saw the tears well in her eyes. "I'm sorry, I didn't mean to hurt you, only help." And as her tears overflowed he clutched her to himself and she sank eagerly, nakedly with him to the ground from where they could have seen a great distance but stared only into each other's eyes, their arms entwining, bodies pressing, lips wrenching apart enough for her gasp: "You are the best a man can be; stay with me, stay with me always!" and his reaffirmation: "I'll do the best I can."

Suddenly the trembling of the earth became a quaking and they were

heaved from the bank into the torrent on its perilous way towara the cat-
astrophic brink.

"Don't drop him for godssake." The surgeon had slackened the op-
erating room's stress. "Lift him onto the gurney easy-like; that was too
damn much work to waste."

During a considerable number of the twenty-four hours since
returning from their horseback ride Carrie had thought about
Luther. Images of him and their lovemaking and autumn vistas
still mingled in her memory with echoes of his distraction by recent events and with her own incidental puzzlement.

As had happened several times during the past year when
she'd needed special private advice her friend Johnny Newlin's
name had come to her mind. She'd recalled his invitation relayed
by Hortense Bass to visit him and had decided to take him up on
it. With an inward smile she'd recognized the hope implicit in his
request—maybe even the expectation, being the stallion he liked
to think he was—and had regretted his eventual disappointment;
but also she had recognized his unique awareness of what made
Bancroft tick and his gambler's acceptance of any honest game's
outcome. She'd felt he might have a helpful eye for the cards of
her confusion different from Preacher Smith's, for instance. Not
keener. Different.

Luther Cain certainly was a different man from any other
she'd met. She could use all the help she could unearth in figuring
him out, not to mention in helping him figure himself out. She
didn't want him not to be different; his difference was one of the
reasons she'd fallen in love with him. She simply wanted him to
be happier in his difference, more relaxed in it, more forgiving of
himself and others as the preacher had put it during a talk with
her last week. And it was because of her love for her rare man
that now she was pushing through the newly hung winter doors
of the Portugese into the saloon's noon-drab interior.

"Well bygod, if it ain't Carrie Shaw." Uncle Vince Simpson
motioned her toward the table where he was sitting with Nola
Priest. " 'Light and set."

"Hello, Honey," Nola smiled her welcome. "Come over and
have a seat. Just talking about you."

The day bartender greeted her with a cocked forefinger and

267

thumb like a pistol. She fired back at him, winking as she crossed to the table. Nicodemus Endicott, the only other person in the musty room, paused in sweeping the floor to raise his broom toward her—" 'Day, Miss Carrie"—and she returned his smile— "Good day to you, Mister Endicott"—and sat down in the chair Uncle Vince shoved out for her with his foot. She'd forgotten how stale the air of the Portugese could become without summer's openness. Nothing about her former workplace kindled nostalgia in her; in fact she was depressed by it until Nola spoke again.

"You're looking the best yet, Carrie; better ever time I catch sight of you. That ain't too often nowadays so I can tell the difference." The woman's tone was genuinely warm. "Must be your man. Which I understand."

"Thank you, Nola. That and more sleep maybe."

Uncle Vince looked as though he might comment on her surmise's possible contradiction but Nola's glare turned him onto another trail. "Reckon sewing's more restful than fighting off these yahoos down here at that." He wasn't quite finished with the subject of Luther. "Speaking of Marshal Cain and fighting off yahoos, I hope he don't have no trouble at the inquest coming up whenever it is. I ain't got no more patience than him with outsiders making bad medicine for us Bancroft folks. Maybe that young waddie didn't want all he got but them other two asked for it the way I hear. Leastways that Kentucky hardass."

Nola kicked him under the table and he winced. Carrie pretended not to notice. Sadly she realized Uncle Vince was reflecting some of the town's gossip, not gossip in the mean sense altogether but exchanges of varying attitudes and opinions and conjectures. And of uncertainties of course. Not entirely unlike her own.

"Nola, is Johnny around?"

"Just got here myself, Honey, but I think he's in one of his rooms there."

"He is," Nicodemus said from his work.

Uncle Vince raised an admonishing finger briefly. "You know I feel kindly toward the marshal, Carrie. He was good to Noble Buck, getting the boy moved from that shack to Mother Swain's and seeing he got a fine rifle to take the place of a busted Spencer I give him." The man tilted his head toward Johnny's closed door. "But other folks ain't so kindly, for one your friend in yonder." He raised his finger again to point at her. "You best see the marshal watches out for hisself. Including at the inquest. Wouldn't want nobody blind-siding him." He lowered his finger. "Nor you neither far as that goes."

She was startled. "Me?"

"A body's knowed by company kept, they say."

"That's crazy," Nola scoffed and kicked his shin harder. "Folks ain't blaming Carrie for what he does."

"Goddammit, woman," the man glared back at his censor, "I'm only handing her a cut of friendly advice."

Carrie knew she was hearing fragments of answers to the riddle of Marshal Luther Cain, anyhow of its public image, and they were as sharp and hurtful and difficult to gather into pieces as a shattered mirror. It wasn't going to take Johnny Newlin to tell her Luther had got himself into some trouble with some townsfolks. How much trouble and how many townsfolks remained to be asked of the universally acquainted saloonkeeper. And she might be able for old times' sake to defuse at least the worst of Johnny's hostility toward her man although she recognized there was barbed wire against her claim of possession. Johnny's fence. Not Luther's she assumed. Hoped.

As she arose from the friendly table to walk across and knock on Johnny's office door she said to Nola, "What was you saying about me when I come in?"

"How I was glad you and the marshal like each other."

Carrie smiled. "Thank you. I'm glad Little John Brock likes you."

"He does?"

"Ask him sometime. Least give him a chance to tell you. '

Nola grinned. "Well I'll be damned."

"I'd say he's got his warrant out for you."

Uncle Vince guffawed but the women ignored him.

"I ain't going to fight the little bastard off I reckon."

"Wouldn't do you much good, Nola. Luther says he's a hell of a fighter."

"Well . . . the little bastard. He never said."

"Don't tell him I did."

A moment later the Portugese's proprietor answered Carrie's tapping with a muffled "Who the hell is it?"

"Me. Carrie."

The sound of boot heels approached the door's opposite side. She recalled his affectation of hand-stitched, high-heeled boots despite his galling fear of horses. The door swung inward toward his suddenly pleased, faintly calculating expression as he stepped back with a welcoming flourish of the towel in his hand. There were flecks of suds about his ears.

"Come right in, Chestnut." He'd celebrated her hair with the nickname on her first day at work last year. "A sight for sore eyes, prettier ever time I see you." When she'd entered his small office he closed its door casually but quickly behind her and gestured toward the other one beyond his desk into his even smaller bedroom. "Go on and have a seat while I put up my shaving gear so we can talk." He followed her into the bedroom, closing its door also—"Don't want nobody interrupting when we do get a damn chance to talk"—and strode to the mirrored bureau with its porcelain pitcher and washbowl half-filled with soapy water. As he wiped his straight razor carefully on a scrap of newsprint and folded it and laid it gently on the bureau's top beside his rinsed shaving brush like the prized possession it was she sat down in the horsehair-upholstered chair next to the unmade bed, smoothed her dress over her knees and contemplated his graceful movements.

There was no doubt Johnny had a certain rustic elegance about him. Although he wasn't a rugged man by any means he exuded vitality. She'd had occasion long ago and emotionally far away to feel the impact of what had come damn close to being his charm. Or maybe just his sexual appeal. Anyhow it had seemed to pass for whatever it was she'd needed in those pre-Luther days, indeed in even still more ancient days wherever she'd started being whatever she'd become. Watching him now she admitted to herself feeling warm but it was a wry warmth tinged with humor and tolerance and without regret; it wasn't kindled by recalling the past but by rejoicing in the present and hopefully, please, God!, the future. In her mind she patted his back fondly as he stepped to the window, raised it, emptied the washbowl out of it, lowered it, and replaced the bowl beside the pitcher.

She returned his intently artless smile as he wiped the remnants of suds from his face and tossed the towel onto the bureau "Johnny, you're handsomer than ever yourself. That ain't what I come to talk about, but it's true."

He walked to her chair and stood looking down at her. "Can't say I mind hearing it. But I was the one asked you to come." His smile changed subtly to an investment in optimism. "Not that we got to do my talking first. We'll do yours and then mine." He lowered himself onto the bed and reached across to finger the calico over her knees, being sure not to touch them yet. "That's a real pretty dress."

Because of his delicacy, although she didn't believe it, she felt she couldn't brush away his hand abruptly. She could give him a signal however. "Be careful. There's hemming pins in it."

Either missing her point or ignoring it he continued slowly rubbing the material between his thumb and forefinger. "Yes indeed. Real pretty." He looked up then straight into her eyes and narrowed his lids slightly and clarified the ambiguity. "Just as pretty as what's always under it." Now his hand fell to her stockinged calf and began sliding upward beneath her hem. "And still is I bet."

Pretense no longer being the game but wanting to stay in it a while longer for the sake of her errand she chuckled and crossed her legs tightly and tucked her dress under her knees. "Still the same Johnny." Seeing the resentment spring into his eyes she qualified her veto. "Always in a hurry."

Apparently it worked. Hope returned to his gaze although he did withdraw his hand to scratch his head in feigned incomprehension. "You damn women don't know what you want." He pursued his optimism one bid further. "But I do." Then tactically he let it ride for the moment and leaned back on his elbow on the bed. "What else you come to talk about?"

She saw her opening. "The truth."

" 'Truth' about what?"

"Something you figure to know and I need to find out. What folks is saying about somebody."

Indulgently he gestured for her to explain.

"Luther Cain."

His indulgence drained like a water barrel hit by lightning. He sat up. His mouth was clamped but his eyes commanded her to continue.

"I know he can take care of hisself in a fight but backbiting ain't fighting. And it's chewing at him; he ain't said that but I know it's so. And it makes me sad." Her demeanor was earnestly open as though she were oblivious of Johnny's reddening face and twitching jaw muscles. "Is many of them talking against him? What are they saying?"

"Is he humping you regular these days?" the man on the bed asked through stiff lips.

"Johnny, stop it; they ain't saying that. I'm serious. What are they . . . ?"

"I'm saying it; and something else: you think he's better than I'd be right about this minute?" He reached for her leg again, her nearest thigh.

She didn't hesitate to slap away his hand this time although lightly to preserve a semblance of friendliness. "Are they trying to bushwhack him, Johnny?"

"Like he bushwhacked the sheriff to make one less mayor candidate? And Injun Jesse and Herman Strauss because they witnessed it?"

The woman was shocked speechless.

"And Enos Dowling and the mountain man last week because they heard that dumb Kentucky bastard talking about a friend of Cain's and yours? You notice the Kentuckian didn't live through that barber shop hurrahing either."

Carrie managed to regain her voice. She heard herself talking as though through a hollow log. "Lies. The inquest told about the sheriff and them. And Lafe Jackman was in the shop."

"Jackman works for your humping partner."

"The newspaper . . ."

"Norris thinks Cain shits daisies."

She shook her head like a stunned prizefighter, her fingers clutching her knees. "I don't want to hear any more of this, I want to leave now."

He prevented her firmly but not roughly from arising by his arm across the chair's two arms. "You come asking questions and I'm giving you answers. For old times' sake. You and me could make it, you know. But you're so hot for that sonofabitch Cain you can't do nothing but squirm your pretty ass and shut your eyes and ears to what's going on. The things I just told you is some of them I heard. Others I'm going to tell you like you asked. For your own damn good. You going to listen to me goddammit?"

She shook her head but otherwise didn't move.

"I got to hog-tie you?"

272

She glared at him fiercely but mutely. Her arms and legs felt as heavy as a New Orleans hypnotist had made them feel once.

Gradually he withdrew his arm and straightened where he sat, clearly ready to bar her again if she started from the chair. "All right here it is." His glare was locked with hers. "Cain fancies hisself a hidebound law enforcer and he's got some folks bamboozled and some riled over that. But I notice he enforces it different with different ones."

She couldn't let that go by. "If there's one thing gets him in trouble more than any other it's playing no favorites. He comes down tough sometimes but everbody is the same to him."

"Not when it's a friend of his and yours to boot."

Unreasoningly she was seized by a sense of dismay. "What you talking about?"

"That drunken Kentuckian bragging how close he was to the end of a twenty-year trail, to catching up with somebody killed his wife while feuding with his old man."

Carrie felt her heart constrict; breathing suddenly became a labor.

Johnny's stare held hers pinioned. "Didn't say it first time he was in here, night he hit town, only got a little rowdy that night and Cain just happened," the proprietor snorting his disbelief, "to come in here and buffaloed him unnecessary and hauled him up to jail."

Her defiance wasn't extinguished. "If Luther buffaloed him he needed it."

Johnny ignored her denial. "But next day after Cain got Big John to run him out of town so he'd be easy to bushwhack in some creek bed . . ."

"That's another lie," she gasped.

". . . he circled back here and got drunk with Dowling this time, both of them grudging Cain. They got me cornered at the bar and that's when the Kentuckian told us he'd tracked off and on since fifty-five through three states and the army after the man he had unfinished business with about his wife. That's what he called it: 'unfinished business.' Like Lafe Jackman said in the *Republican*."

Carrie's eyes were glazed as though their life had retreated inward a step or two. Maybe to reconnoiter. She didn't appear aware of her tongue wetting her lips. Johnny was aware of it; his stare had shifted momentarily to its pink moist tip; he leaned forward and patted her cheek casually and then straightened, confident she shouldn't be lunging out of the chair now. "I got nothing against Lester Blaine. Acts like a gentleman. And his wife acts like a lady. Too bad Cain shot her."

"That was accidental and you know it."

"Not his only accident." The saloonkeeper smiled sarcastically at 'accident.' "Herman Strauss for another. But I grant you most of his shooting sure is on purpose. Just what purpose ain't so sure. Anyhow whenever the hell they set the inquest I got to say what that Kentucky jaybird told me."

She felt lightheaded. Red flecks sifted across her vision. "The man was lying."

"Only got to say what I heard. Up to folks what they believe."

"You can't."

"Can't do nothing else, Carrie. I like Lester Blaine same as you do. And if he's on the run from a killing warrant," Johnny shrugged, "maybe folks won't believe it or they'll figure it's too long ago." His voice turned hard again. "But if Cain knows bygod that's different. He claims to be a goddam hard-ass lawman . . ."

"Who said 'warrant?' " She swallowed at her rising nausea. "If there's a warrant Luther would know."

"If he knows from a warrant or Lester or any other damn way and didn't call him on it no matter how long ago, the town's got a right to hear, bygod."

She shuddered at the grotesqueness of the conversation. Lester Blaine's amiable, calm, competent manner, his pleasant face, Ruth's obvious loving pride in him clashed in Carrie's shaken brain with the trash Johnny was hurling against those. The spunk which had seen her this far in her thirty-three years jabbed through her daze. "The man lied. How could he track Lester twenty years? What three states? What army?"

"You can bet it wasn't easy. That's why it took such a time. Kept his ears open he said, moving on to another job when he'd hear the hounds up ahead, sniffing around towns and farms and rivers and backwoods. Had a couple women leave him for his wandering. Down the Ohio, up the Wabash, Terre Haute, Indiana . . ."

"Mygod," she blurted, "I been there."

". . . cross country to Springfield, Illinois, St. Louis. Getting places when his man was long gone. Turned a little crazy after a while, I reckon, and the Union Army didn't hinder that. Wounded bad at Vicksburg right when he almost caught up. He got to slobbering while he told us drunk like he was but we could make out enough. He was telling the truth all right." Tiny beads of rancor sprayed from Johnny's lips. "Like I'm going to tell the truth about your goddam humper."

"Spite;" she gusted, "spiting Luther because you ain't the man he is."

"Pretty little bitch!" He jackknifed toward her and clawed her shoulders and jerked her out of the chair against himself, twisting them both as he sprawled backward onto the bed with her so she was spread-eagled half-under him. "I'll show you a man."

Rage seized her overpoweringly and plunged its red blade into her vitals, wrenching a muffled wail from her as she heaved at his weight. "Quit it damn you!"

CHAPTER 40

The room's door slammed open. "What's going on here?" Luther Cain's question sliced across the bed's struggle like a bullwhip. His eyes were slitted under his hat brim and above his moustache. "What the hell you doing?" Two strides brought him looming above the couple. He bent and grabbed Johnny's booted ankles and hauled him from atop the woman onto the floor, smashing the man's face against the planks so his nose and bitten tongue gushed a red puddle and his voice gurgled for either mercy or Luther's ruin, it should have been hard to say. Indeed it was going to be hard for Johnny to say anything for several days. The marshal stepped over to Carrie, reached down for the woman's arm and pulled her to her feet neither roughly nor gently but with an inconsistent detachment given his previous moment's ferocity. His eyes were not cold or warm, simply open. There were men in his past who might have called this seeming mood his most dangerous in augury like the greenish stillness ahead of a tornado. Carrie's immediate concern with danger was protection from it, not from its guise Johnny Newlin just had enacted but his personification of ghosts of her earlier times which hadn't haunted her especially until Luther had come along but now must be laid. She wanted sheltering arms and sympathetic eyes, not inscrutable aloofness. She wanted more than "What the hell you doing?" and then apparent withdrawal from hearing her answer. Her hands began to shake as she tried to straighten her skirt with Luther still gripping her elbow. Tears budded in her eyes and her knees felt weak. Surely he didn't believe she was in Johnny's bedroom for any purpose but helping her beloved, forgodssake!

"Thank you, Dear. I was . . . " She broke off awkwardly. How was she to say he unnecessarily was earning dislike and suspicion of double dealing and worse without his nettled reaction maybe lumping her with his defamers and doubters? How could her mouth yet hold, much less speak, a word about Lester like "murderer?"

"Let's go," the marshal said flatly as he should have to a prisoner. Without other words he guided her past the crouching man

276

through the bedroom and office doorways, across the barroom and outside into Jimson Street.

"Luther, please let go of my arm. I'm fine now. It's embarrassing."

He dropped his hand as though her arm had scorched it.

"I meant you were squeezing too hard. I went to see Johnny . . ."

"So I seen." He turned toward South Street and continued walking without a sign for her to follow.

She chose to assume it was implied. As they passed the gun shop next door he pulled her from collision with the backing rump of a rein-trailing horse, dropped her arm again, gathered up and retied the animal's reins to the hitching rack, and resumed striding toward the corner.

She skipped for a couple of steps to catch up with him. "Goddammit, Dear, we just made love yesterday out on that hill," waving northward, "and you can't act like I'm somebody else today. Slow down. People will think you're mad at me."

"What do you think?"

"I ain't done nothing for you to be mad about. If it's Johnny back yonder he's the one you ought . . . "

"Me yesterday. Newlin today. Who tomorrow?"

The impact of his words stopped her in her tracks. The day's shocks were beginning to overwhelm her. She flung out a hand and snared his shirt sleeve and pulled him to a halt. "What are you saying? You can't be saying that to me."

"I just did." He had heard the slander come out of his own mouth but he couldn't have stifled it. The anarchy of the past two weeks welled in his throat like vomit and spewed over her and the tethered horse and the Portugese and Johnny Newlin and Jimson Street and all of Bancroft. And over himself. "What you want me to say with you wiggling around underneath him on that bed?"

She sucked in a lungful of air. She tried to make her voice steady in spite of her trembling chin. "I was fighting him off."

"What the hell was he doing on?"

"He forced me. You're talking like a kid."

"Being there was like a goddamn kid."

"I went to visit him, talk to him. We're . . . we used to be friends. I didn't know he'd give me trouble."

The marshal almost snorted. "Trouble's that bastard's ace." In Luther's ferment her visit, aside from its agonizing sexual questions, struck him as mirroring the town's revolt lately against order, its shortsighted repudiation of him and his job. Anyhow the lawless and wrong-headed parts of the town. The thought of her joining such a betrayal sharpened the pain already knifing him. "Can't figure you wouldn't know all about him, seeing as how you're old friends."

She pinched her lip with her teeth and tried once more. "Didn't you ever have a friend fool you?"

He stared at her and nodded slowly. "I sure as hell did." Then he swung on his way along the windowless side wall of the Wholesale Exchange.

The dam of her patience burst abruptly and she felt herself awash in a flood of sorrow and resentment. She was harrowed by awful revelation and exhausted by fending off assault followed by accusation; and now the final affront of his retreating back momentarily drowned her caring what he thought about her. At least until he came to his senses. If he did. Right now she was too sad and tired to care whether or not he did. Almost.

She burst into tears.

An elderly rider passing her reined up his horse. His smile was kindly. "What you bawling about, Carrie?"

She shook her head without speaking, waving him on his way with one hand and wiping her eyes with the back of the other.

He touched his mount's flank with his spur and his hat brim with a finger. "Don't you mind, Girl. Found out long time ago there's always another day."

"Counting on it," she scarcely was able to call after him.

CHAPTER 41

Around the corner on South Street Luther was heading northward toward the railroad depot and the plaza beyond. His mind writhed with confusion; and confusion was something he hadn't suffered until recently and he wasn't getting used to it worth a damn. He wasn't even sure of its make-up. There was the underground stream of defiance he sensed was eroding not only Bancroft's legal underpinnings but obscurely his will if not authority to keep shoring them up. And now he'd found himself charging into a belly-stabbing set-to with the second female in his life for whom he should give that life without a second thought but whose shenanigans on a bed with a sonofabitch had fired him with enough rage to take hers. No not take her life for chrissake; jealousy couldn't make him cut her out of his life by taking hers. And also there was too much of her under his skin and he didn't want to kill himself. There could come a day if this cowshit kept up, he thought derisively, when he might feel like it but sure as hell not today. Today if he wasn't going to kill her he maybe ought to beat her into understanding his mix-up, his need, what it was like to find somebody you need rassling on a bed with a sonofabitch. But had he already cut her out of his life? He'd just turned his back on her, walked away from her. Maybe instead of beating her he ought to love her into understanding and helping him understand whatever the hell it was she talked as though he didn't understand. Her and Preacher Smith's "forgiveness" and Lila Haniford's "empathy." Carrie had claimed innocence with Newlin. If what she'd said was true she didn't need forgiveness. If she needed loving she'd gone to the wrong sonofabitch today. Yesterday she'd gone to the right one. Man, not sonofabitch. Or had he too been a sonofabitch today? He shook his head in disgust. "Kid" was right. A goddam muddled mess. He was abreast of the smithy when a familiar voice hammered through his misery.

"Talking to yourself these days, Luther?" Jake Barlow's

laughter rang like the horseshoe on his anvil. "First sign of getting old."

The marshal couldn't come close to smiling. "Second sign."

"That right? What's the first?"

"Set in your goddam ways, Jake, getting set in your goddam ways."

CHAPTER 42

Back at the Portugese Johnny Newlin's bloodied fury had whipped Nola into a race up across the saloon's rear lot and the railroad track to the courthouse and to Doc Bowman's and Jim Watts' offices. Not being in the best shape with his oozing, swollen nose and tongue to do it himself he'd ordered her to take an identical message to the mayor, the coroner, and the county attorney. At the top of his fuming, garbled voice he'd made her repeat its words to him twice to minimize her misquoting him: "I don't want the inquest on Cain's killing Dowling and the Kentuckian and the mountain man put off no longer. I know things about Cain and his stinking murders the town needs knowing. Same as I know things about you the town's going to know wide open if you don't set the inquest pronto."

She was embarrassed about having to say that last part to three men she liked. Liking them was another reason besides her personal style for not having told anyone about her occasional, private visits with each of them during the four years she'd worked for Johnny. She might have figured on the saloonkeeper with his squad of spies finding out about the visits even though they'd occurred early mornings at the men's rooms on her way to her own after work. Johnny likely hadn't demanded a share of any presents she'd got from the men because he'd valued the information more. Those visits had been pleasant ones despite her weariness; the gentlemen hadn't been weary; and the term "gentlemen" fit all of them like a glove—or like herself, she reflected with a quick grin.

Her grin didn't last long because her enforced errand not only was distasteful to her but loaded with gunpowder for the marshal and therefore her friend, Carrie.

She was going to have to alert Carrie to the danger if she could sneak away from Johnny's frenzy long enough. She couldn't let him catch her at it because his rage might slip into craziness obliging her to use her rifle on him as she had on mad dogs a couple of times. She hoped it wasn't going to come to that and allowed there was a chance it wasn't even if he did catch her; the

281

Portugese proprietor was more a crafty than a violent man and he'd never hurt her intentionally although once he'd bitten her shoulder in the clutches of passion—again her grin was quick—but she didn't count that. He'd been fair with her and she valued fairness as her dad had. But whatever the consequences were she was going to have to report Luther Cain's jeopardy to the girl who loved him and for whom she and the marshal and the Blaines and Hortense Bass and Johnny and seemingly half the town had come to have a high regard. Besides she hadn't liked the way the saloonkeeper, although she couldn't say she disliked him, had belittled her with this errand, yelling at her just now like one of Nell's common whores. And she didn't see why a few visits with her—if that's all Johnny was talking about—were such clubs over Bill Crum's and Doc Bowman's and Jim Watts' heads, "respectable, big-gun officials" or not as Johnny had sneered about them even though he was a councilman himself. They were human beings, for godssake. Same as she was. And they weren't even married for whatever that counted. The past few years especially she'd had a good deal to do with men but she couldn't say she understood all about how their minds worked. The thing was these three friends of hers were kind. That's what did count. She put a lot of store in kindness. That's why on her hunting trips with her dad he'd taught her to be a fine rifle shot; he'd wanted her game dead, not crawling off wounded to suffer and die. She didn't want Luther Cain to suffer either, not only because looking at him heated her up—after all, she did seem to have smoldering Little John Brock on her tail now—but because Carrie's resulting hurt was bound to be neither fair nor kind.

Hell, Nola gusted to herself; it was a downright rattlesnake of a day.

282

CHAPTER 43

Late in the memorably dismal afternoon Carrie was seated by herself at one of the long painted tables in the Drovers dining room half-listening to Teddy Quillin. Other diners hadn't begun to arrive. The former trail cook spoke proudly of the "Friday Special" he'd been working on for three hours: "Fresh-killed rabbits browned in the pan and then baked in Cal Hubbard's blackberry wine, Carrie. Stewed tomatoes with nary a taste of the keeping brine, I promise you. Turnips boiled soft. Hominy with molasses. And right good coffee even if it be partly shelled peas. Close to out of coffee, so damn high and hard to come by." Realizing it was called for she forced a smile—"Sounds mighty tasty"—although her throat suddenly tightened—"but I ain't feeling very good, just come down for maybe some soup to take to my room"—prompting his stopgap for lack of soup—"Maybe a bowl of rabbit broth, Carrie? You just set there and I'll fetch you one."

While he was gone her weary psyche slid deeper into the morass from which she'd been struggling for hours. Her straining to make sense out of the day's nonsense seemed to have sucked her farther into its melancholy. She'd thought talking to somebody might help and had tossed aside her sewing and dried her tears and come downstairs as much for the company as for soup; but Teddy and his rabbits and turnips and hominy weren't the answer.

When Nola had knocked on her door several hours ago to report Johnny was pushing for the inquest so he could tell things "the town needs knowing" her friend from the Portugese had noticed her distress instantly and had demanded "What's the matter, Honey?" which had brought Carrie's silly, wadded kerchief to her stiffened lips again and her embarrassed "I'm sorry, Nola, Luther and me had a squabble." She hadn't said she'd heard already of Johnny's aim from the man himself because she hadn't been ready to go into that noon's crazy-wild actions and accusations in case Nola had wanted details. The woman had wondered aloud what things the saloonkeeper believed "the town needs knowing" but had taken Carrie's shrug as either not knowing or not wanting

283

to say, both being acceptable to a friend, and had swallowed her curiosity.

After Nola had gone and as the day had crept toward mid-afternoon Carrie's earlier shocked numbness had worn off. She had almost been immobilized at first by the angry pain of her fracases with Johnny and Luther. Then her torment had returned wearing different masks: the bone-weary, discouraged face of Luther and Lester's sad, apprehensive profile gazing backward and forward and backward again, each man looking haunted. These visages had racked her. The anguish of her loneliness at thought of losing both men and inevitably the wife of one—Luther her lover, Lester her friend and the husband of dearest Ruth—seemed unbearable. For years she had been surrounded by men and women, "lovers" and "friends" among them, but not in the priceless way of these people. Or was the price of finding these losing them? Her head throbbed with its buffeting. Were she to ram through Luther's sulkiness and tell him about Lester what chaos might result? Were she not to tell him what chaos again?

"Damnation!" she said aloud.

"Sunday's a couple days off but we could take that subject up now," Howard Smith offered. He had entered the room quietly under cover of her preoccupation. "Want some company?"

She tried to return his smile, motioning toward the chair beside her. He hung his hat on the back of it and sat down.

"You look like a thirsty critter at a dried-up water hole. Else lost your last friend, Carrie. Got trouble?"

Her tone was rueful. "Say that 'friends' and 'troubles.' "

"If I can help any . . . " He left the bid unfinished.

For a moment she stared wordlessly at her hands folded on the table, then moved them so the cook could set a bowl of broth in front of her. "Much obliged, Teddy. I'll eat it here."

"Betchy. Eat the whole of it; get you to perking."

Before picking up the tin spoon at her place she raised her gaze to the man's seated beside her. "Obliged too for you wanting to help, Preacher."

He nodded without speaking, his eyes waiting affectionately.

"Damnation," she muttered again.

"You said that. But the Good Book says it don't have to happen."

She waved down her hesitancy. "All right, being you asked." She sniffed and frowned. "No use dragging in the whole wrangle but maybe you can answer me one question." She hadn't formed it carefully in her mind so she mulled it over before clearing her throat and leaning toward him. "Preacher Smith?"

"Yes, Sister Shaw?" he encouraged her with the faintest twinkle in his eyes but earnestly.

"Must I tell to somebody I like a thing about another one I also like that'll bring trouble to both of them?"

Howard considered the riddle for a moment before replying. "You left out a part. Maybe you meant to," he said gently, "so you could hear me put it in: what'll happen to them if you don't tell your first friend?"

She sighed. "Likely still trouble."

"Way Jim Watts would say it this is 'irrelevant' but any of the trouble your fault?"

She shook her head. "Not in truth. Only caught in the middle."

He twisted in his chair to pat her on the shoulder approvingly; had she been a man it should have been on the knee. " 'Low you answered your own question, Carrie."

She looked surprised. "How'd I do that?"

"If it's trouble either way for both then the truth is all you got left I reckon. Tell him the truth."

She stared for a while at Bancroft's visionary who'd been known to hit reality on the nose.

Then she nodded and turned to her bowl of perking rabbit broth.

285

CHAPTER 44

It was in the very early darkness of the next morning when her first chance came to follow Howard Smith's advice.

After tolerating increasingly two bowls of Teddy's antidote to down-heartedness the previous late afternoon she had told him and the preacher goodnight and had nodded to a couple of arriving diners and to the desk clerk and a drummer in the small lobby, each reading the *Republican*—each had suspended reading as she'd walked across to the stairs—and had climbed to her room. By then the half-hour's daylight remaining before the fall sunset and its pell-mell dusk had precluded her sewing even if she'd felt like it and needlework by lamplight was equally eye-pinching and already she'd had a headache since noon. She hadn't wanted yet to confront Luther; she'd needed a little more time for thinking out and remembering and forgetting and regaining strength. And plain deep breathing. She had judged he shouldn't be coming to the Drovers to eat his own supper for another hour so she'd gone back downstairs—the clerk and the drummer smiling at her again over their papers—and had taken a nervous walk around the block behind the hotel, including a stop in its outhouse, and returned to her room without feeling any more hopeful. Then she'd decided a full bath might help. Although it had been Friday evening and Hortense's Saturday help-yourself hot-water vat out back hadn't been fired she'd accepted her friend's swap (with Teddy's sufferance) of six bucketsful of stove-heated water for the "favor" of carrying them two at a time to the second floor's iron tub. "Honey," the woman had grinned as she'd left Carrie to undress and bathe in the cubicle down the hall from her bedroom, "I'm the one getting the favor like I said because you're the nearest thing I got to a daughter. I like doing for you. And I'm partial to your man that's latched onto you, too." Carrie barely had avoided wincing at that; Luther hadn't been latched onto her the last she'd seen of him. Before closing the door Hortense had added "When you're done there don't mess with the water, I'll scoop it down the sluice after while."

Padding to her room barefooted from her bath wearing her

286

dress and carrying the rest of her clothes Carrie had passed two evidently new guests. The one carrying a large straw traveling case undoubtedly had been another drummer. The other she'd taken from his soot-blackened face for a railroader. They both had staggered a bit, she assumed from patronizing one or more saloons since alighting from the west-bound. The drummer had stared at her wide-eyed as though the last vision he'd expected this Bancroft call had been a barefooted lady with clearly nothing on under her dress. The railroader had stared at her with such exhaustion she'd wondered whether he'd seen her.

In her room she had closed the window curtains, lighted the coal oil lamp by the bed, pulled her dress over her head and hung it beside her two others and her jeans in the pine clothes press Lester had made for her after Everett's burn-out, set her shoes next to her boots and moccasins on its floor and put her underclothes in one of the bureau's drawers. Then she'd lain down on the bed and pulled the muslin sheet and army blanket over her nakedness in the hope that by delving and probing and pondering and craving enough she might conceive a way to exorcise the day's evil, to banish Luther's doubts about her, to convince him of his need to grasp his own vulnerability as well as Lester Blaine's, to draw him and Lester and Ruth and herself from the shadows she'd sensed even before today had moved over them like her lamp's on the ceiling. She hadn't meant to fall asleep. She'd meant to lie in bed a while before getting up again and putting on her jeans and moccasins and flannel shirt to wait for the sound of Luther's boots in the hall passing her room toward his.

A squadron of tornadoes bearing the sky as an enormous black flag had rumbled distantly and then roared across the prairie toward Bancroft hurling random lightning spears ahead of its charge into the town's ambush. Carrie had screamed a warning; Luther's face had been stony but his eyes had flickered; Lester in his jeopardy had stood apart waiting for the storm; Ruth had stared at Luther unbelievingly; Johnny Newlin had raised a vindicated fist; Bill Crum had sighed with the tired patience of a veteran officeholder; Doc Bowman had stanched a gushing artery; Teddy Quillin had offered everybody bowls of rabbit broth.

Carrie lurched awake with a gasp as the door which she knew was room 14's clicked shut behind its roomer. A few minutes later

287

wearing jeans, moccasins and shirt and breathing a little faster than normally she tapped on it. It was the second man's door she'd tapped on within the past fourteen hours; fervently she hoped it shouldn't open on another fourteen as wretched as those. At least this voice wasn't surly; if memory served her it omitted the "hell" in "Who is it?"

"It's Carrie, Luther." She was afraid he mightn't have heard her through the wood. She swallowed and rose on tiptoe as though that should heighten her audibility too. "It's Carrie." Suddenly she wanted to hurry back to her own room although not as urgently as she felt obliged to talk to him. "I need to tell you something. It's important."

"This time of night it's got to be." His words as he opened the door didn't clear away the storm of her dream but his gaze somehow made it less forbidding. His eyes seemed to hold a glimmer very faintly akin to warmth; anyhow they weren't as bleak as when they'd last gripped hers before they'd jerked away to stare at his inner riot. "Can't talk about nothing important in the hall. Might as well step in." He had taken off his gun belt and boots and pants and now was standing back from the room's doorway in his socks, longjohns, open shirt and round-crowned black hat. He removed the hat and waved her inward with it in one gesture. Then he tossed it onto the bed.

An almost maternal throb at his dishelved dignity flushed a smile from her lips in spite of her unease. It has been an involuntary smile and faded quickly under his stare. She stepped into the room and he closed the door and motioned her toward the single straight-back chair and when she'd lowered herself onto it he sat down on the edge of the bed. Since she was the bearer of the important tidings he waited for her to speak.

She wondered what was going through his mind as he sat in his long underwear and not much else in the chilly hotel room's wee-hour lamplight looking at the woman for whom he'd declared reciprocated love and with whom he'd made love on a hill a day and a half ago and whom he'd accused of making love to an enemy less than a day ago and from whom he'd turned away coldly as though she too were his enemy. She might have guessed his mind hadn't vented wholly the stinks of disillusionment and anger although the bittersweet scent of regret may have begun wafting through it. She didn't have to wonder what was going through her own mind; her images and recollections of the past day and night made it a caldron of emotions, if less acute now than sadly aching. Her anger had waned into a desolate, wasted feeling that a hopeful trail she'd been following had come to the edge of a cliff and had been washed out behind her as well. No way to go now seemed left to her unless remotely but hopefully the regret in him she'd fancied might turn into something like reality, unless somehow his tautness should slacken, not to betray his creed but validate it, unless her one more appeal to him— even indirectly through the evident tragedy of Lester Blaine— should let him see clemency as a strategy rather than surrender. If she could bring him to be lenient with her (although she hadn't done wrong) maybe he could bring himself to be lenient with others. As he sat mutely looking at her, his eyes clogged with misery, she felt compelled to say something. She wasn't so blanketed by weariness that all her resentment was smothered; she still was wounded; but she had to speak first not only because she'd come to speak but because in some strange way he was the worse wounded of the two of them.

"Ain't you getting cold setting there in your underwear. Luther?"

"Don't trouble yourself about me." He didn't sound as though he meant it.

She took courage from the trace of uncertainty she sensed in him. "Trouble is what we got. Both of us."

"I don't like our trouble no better than you."

She was caught off guard for an instant. "I don't mean our trouble."

"Ours ain't enough?" At his question she felt an illogical surge of elation which ebbed when his next words seemed to confirm its illogic. "But I wasn't broke in to let trouble ride me."

She took a deep breath. "Our trouble's been riding me right hard since noon. But the trouble . . ."

"Just so it don't ride you off my range."

His range? This seesawing of her perceptions was almost dizzying. She shied from it. "The trouble I'm talking about is Lester Blaine."

He frowned but didn't say anything.

She dreaded the words she had to speak. She sidestepped the

Portugese owner's name for the moment but couldn't the others. "That Kentucky stranger, the one last week, said he was looking for Lester—been trailing him twenty years—for Lester killing the man's wife. Back in Kentucky. There was some kind of trouble between Lester's and the Kentuckian's kin. In a shooting she got killed. He claimed Lester shot her." Carrie put out her hand, reaching for Luther's reassurance and his forbearance. "It could have been not on purpose. Accidental." The rush in her memory of Johnny's sarcasm knocked her hand back into her lap. "I had to tell you, you had to know."

For an instant his expression was half-incredulous and half-astonished and before a familiar curtain lowered over it she saw that he never had heard of Lester's trouble. "Who told you all this?"

"That's why you had to know." She cleared her throat. Her hands crept together like coyote-threatened sheep. "Johnny Newlin told me. The stranger told him and Enos Dowling. Got drunk in the Portugese . . ."

"I know he got drunk." The marshal's interruption snapped like a trap, his eyes cold as its steel. "I throwed him in jail."

"Not that night, Luther. Next day after he snuck back in town. The day he . . . got shot." She plunged on while her resolve lasted. "Johnny's going to tell about Lester at the inquest on them three that got shot, he's going to tell it like   "

"Nobody's going to believe the bastard." Again his interruption was uncompromising.

"Luther, listen to me. Johnny's going to tell it like you knowed all along that Lester," forcing the word past her teeth, "murdered a woman back East and you ain't done nothing about it." She loathed adding: "Because Lester's your friend." She scarcely whispered: "And mine."

"That's a goddam lie and you know it."

"I ain't the one has to know it's a lie. Nor only the coroner nor the county attorney nor the mayor. It's ever one of the folks you live with that has to. For all your days."

He squinted at her through his head's mounting uproar. "Not your days?"

Her spirit took flight before other drifts of his question like skepticism and apartness and bitterness brought it to roost again. "I got to figuring our days was the same," she heard herself say nevertheless. In her startlement at her own words she hurried on. "He's going to say the stranger told him. And you and Lester can't prove he didn't because the man's dead."

"Other way around: because the man's dead he can't say Lester done nothing. I know from marshaling. Maybe inquests ain't as strict as trials but that's the law. Anyhow, what's Lester got to do with last week's shootings?"

Although she knew frustration had wrung the question from him her hand half-rose once more toward him, her eyes clouding with concern. "Luther, you're not thinking when you say that. The fight started in Lester's shop. Folks read where the Kentuckian said he had business with him. 'What business?' Lester says he don't know but Johnny's got an answer for them. It surely ain't the answer they want to hear even if it's true; everybody likes Lester. But Johnny ain't taking aim on Lester." In her anguish she got up and stepped to the bed and sat down beside him. "It's you he's after. Your job. More than that: your name. He wants to dirty your name. I don't know what all he wants."

"The sonofabitch."

"That ain't the point, Luther. Not to get mad at Johnny." She quailed at the thought of putting her conviction into words. "He ain't the only one. Not everbody is back of you, not even all them that wants to like you." She had said it. She watched his profile for what she was terrified she'd see, which was one of two calamities now: unrelenting anger or warping prejudice. Despite her qualms she kept on talking as though it should help both of them through this ordeal "Luther . . . Dear," the word trembled only faintly, "you're a good marshal, you do good keeping gun-toting lobos from treeing the town, nobody claims you don't. It's a better town more ways than one for you keeping it law-abiding." She felt as though she were easing past a crouching catamount. "But if you've lost some friends along the way it's maybe from not giving folks a little elbowroom, maybe from not looking at both sides."

His swiveling head reminded her now of an eagle's. His stare was fierce but somehow not threatening toward her. "Goddammit, you talked like this before, you and the preacher and that schoolteacher."

"And maybe others, maybe more than a few."

He either ignored her interjection or absorbed it. "You saying there's more than one side to doing right? You want me giving

291

elbowroom to wrong? You saying you don't believe right's right and wrong's wrong?"

"I didn't say I didn't. I'm saying and they're saying sometimes there's reasons why folks do wrong that bears looking into. They don't have to be bad to do wrong. Maybe they made a mistake. Maybe they're sorry."

"Ain't they got to pay for their mistakes? Bad or good, sorry don't pay for nothing wrong."

Impatience pinched her tongue for an instant. "Yes they got to pay. No being sorry don't make wrong right. But it's a different way of looking at things. It could even make a difference in them that does wrong." Her rashness amazed her. "And in you."

She couldn't imagine his gaze ever being forlorn but it was far from happy at this moment. "My game is enforcing the law but remember I ain't the dealer I got to play my cards the way I get them dealt me."

"I come to tell you you're going to be dealt one you don't want—we don't want. How you going to play it, Luther?"

His eyes, sad as they were, didn't waver. "What choice I got?"

She shrugged sadly too for all of them—him, Lester, Ruth, herself. As much as anyone herself. "Maybe it's past choosing. But anyhow you know now what the card is." She looked down at her lap, sensing that his gaze still lingered on the side of her face, her forehead, her hair. Her fatigue and discouragement didn't prevent warmth from crawling up through her neck into her cheeks. But it seemed unwarranted. "Luther, I want to tell you something else before I go. You can believe it or not but it's true." She raised her eyes to his. "I didn't do nothing wrong with Johnny and it wasn't a mistake going there. I found out what I went for, what some of the townsfolks anyhow is saying about you so you can look out for yourself. And lucky I found out Johnny was fixing to blind-side you with Lester's trouble. Maybe 'lucky' ain't the word but it's better knowing than not." She looked away from him and leaned forward to arise. "That's all. I'm going to bed now and let you do the same."

"Hold up." He reached out and pulled her back firmly. "I want to tell you something myself." The fingers of his right hand which she'd seen move with dreadful swiftness turned her chin slowly toward him; his sometimes stony voice was soft. "You said a bit ago our trouble down at the Portugese has rode you hard. I want to tell you it has me, too. Goddam hard. You said you'd come to figuring your days and mine was the same. Well I'm telling you I done likewise, Carrie." He lowered his hand to gather her folded ones into it. "You said there's a card about to be dealt we ain't going to like, neither of us; you wanted to know how I'm going to play it." He leaned toward her and kissed her lips briefly with a tenderness incongruous in him except to her and perhaps to someone long ago with whom he'd shared a love almost as sweet but not as deep and passionate and lasting as theirs surely could be. She heard his answer through her heart's swelling music. "I'm going to play it the only way I know. I heard everthing you said tonight and I truly thank you for ever bit of it. As Judge Hooper says once in a while when he rides through here"—Luther's short grin was not facetious—" 'I'll take it under advisement.' The way I got to play our card is the way I always done. I'll tell Lester what Newlin claims and ask him if it's true. Reckon I won't even take his word for it, seeing folks ain't sure to take that," the marshal's jaws clenching fleetingly, "nor mine now. I'll telegraph back East. If they want him for killing a woman I'll arrest him. If they don't Lester can sue that . . . can sue Newlin for slander and likely end up owning the Portugese."

Carrie smiled. "You don't have to stop calling Johnny a son-ofabitch. All I want is you to stop cussing yourself inside. You don't have to like everbody, Luther, only yourself. And liking yourself bars taking on blame for something happened once you couldn't help."

"I ain't so sure I know what you're talking about," he frowned; "I like myself fair to middling." His moustache tilted slightly. "Ain't complained to myself lately." Abruptly his eyes sobered. "Excepting since noon. Been complaining about me like hell since noon."

She couldn't tell whether or not he'd understood her reference to his cousin. She abandoned the subject.

"I only want you to—" she groped with a freed hand for the words— "ride yourself gentler. Other folks too but mostly yourself, that'll take care of others." She returned her slender hand to the nest of his big one. "Our argument, fight, whatever it was at noon growed partly out of the way things looked but partly out of you being riled at Johnny already."

"I hadn't ought to let that . . ."

Her urgency overrode his self-reproach. "Sure his cussedness riles you but maybe he acts that way from figuring in your mind he's green scum on a pond for not dancing to ever law tune you fiddle. Maybe some others feel that way." She couldn't know Luther's wince was at his memory of Mayor Crum's reference in another place and time to fiddling. "I'm sorry, Dear." She lifted his hand to her mouth and pressed it there while she thought for a moment, staring across the shadowy room. Then her eyes returned to his. "I ain't meant to find fault. I only been telling you what you had to know about Lester. And how I found out, everthing about how. And some good things I want for you." She whispered three more words: "And for us."

He let go of her hands and put his own on her shoulders and turned her squarely to face him sitting on the bed. "I ain't sure I'm worth the trouble. I don't know if I could change."

Her fingers flew to his lips. "I don't want you to change from the man you are, only from the one I know you truly ain't, the one that ain't happy, the one scares me because his unhappiness might get him," her fingers going to her own lips, "hurt."

"I ain't going to get killed if that's what you're thinking. I been marshaling too damn long, I know all their plays." He leaned forward not very far this time and kissed her not as briefly. "I'll tell you something else I ain't going to do: fight nor argue with you no more."

"Oh, Luther, I'm so glad."

"Because I love you, bygod."

"I love you too, Luther."

"I get my fill of fighting in my job. And I ain't as good at arguing as making love."

"Setting here in the cold? In your longjohns on top of the blanket?"

"Better underneath it."

Her smile was splendid. "Then I'm for getting underneath it, dear Luther."

CHAPTER 45

Everett Lane lifted his cap and coat from the nail he had hammered part-way into a stud of the rooming house's skeleton when he'd begun the day's work early that morning ahead of Lester Blaine's noontime arrival. As he put on the rumpled Confederate headgear and the short woolen garment he peered through the dusk at the carpenter who had put on his weathered felt Union hat and fraying coat and was boxing up his tools. "Getting chilly of an evening now, Lester. Figure we're going to be inside by first snow?"

"Well let's see. This is Saturday; started eight days ago. With those three days' help of all the boys you rounded up the job is already foundationed and floored and mostly studded. Another ten days ought to see it raftered and sided if we keep working Sundays. Then another week for roofing and that'll put us toward the middle of November. That ought to be good enough." He closed his toolbox, hooked its lid and straightened with it, smiling at his thought: "I don't think Howard will mind me missing church Sunday mornings long as I make it up Sunday and Wednesday nights." His smile seemed to become preoccupied. "But I'm not saying I don't need all the church-going I can work in."

Everett wasn't entirely comfortable with such ruminations but he was a polite man. "Reckon most of us could say that. I could go once in a while myself."

Lester hadn't intended to evangelize not to mention embarrass his friend. "Just rambling, Everett." They had begun walking eastward on Jimson toward South Street. "I'm going to fix Ruth and the boys a batch of white-flour biscuits for supper. They're partial to those with bees' honey. Those are one thing I make good if I do say so."

"Who the hell ain't partial to white-flour biscuits? Don't know how long since I et some." Everett hastened to forestall an invitation; a laid-up wife and two youngsters were plenty at a working man's table. "I run into Marshal Cain while ago at the lumber yard when I went for the nails. Told him I'd eat supper at the Drovers with him. Wish I roomed there myself but the Plains is cheaper. Missed out on Teddy Quillin's 'Friday Special' last night but maybe he'll have some of his rabbit left. Heard it was mighty good." The rooming house proprietor-to-be again grinned, apparently oblivious of the carpenter's stiffened cheeks. "Course not as good as your biscuits. Where the hell you find white flour?"

Lester sought to compose himself quickly. "Wagner's Grocery got it and more baking soda in yesterday." He needed to talk a little further while thinking. "At home I got the lard and sour milk and salt and a damn spavined stove with a buck-shinned oven I can still get to pulling slow anyhow. Sure got to buy Ruth a new one of them. But not 'til after the surprise I'm working on."

Since something was to be a surprise Everett didn't feel obliged to ask for particulars. "Speaking of your missus, I sure hope she's feeling better."

"Thank you. Still mighty sore but better. Hard to keep her down. Walks around a little bit."

"How old you say your young'uns is now?"

"George is six-and-a-half and Tim's five."

"Ain't Tim the one . . .?" Everett looked as though he not only could kick himself but hit himself in the mouth. "Time goes fast."

"It's all right, Everett. Tim was born deaf and can't talk regular but he's smart as a buggy whip. Doc Bowman and Lila Haniford both say being deaf kept him from talking for he can't hear other folks talk and learn from them." It was very important to Lester for Everett and others to understand about Tim. If the boy should have to grow up in Bancroft without a father as well as a mother to explain his problem his life should be even harder. "Understand that?"

"Well I'll be damned. Never knowed it. Never even thought about it to tell you the truth."

"Everett," Lester's tone was over-casual, "when you talked to the marshal this afternoon I reckon he asked how the house was coming along?"

"Told him we was making right good time." They had reached the corner and turned up South Street toward the railroad depot. "And we still figured on finishing outside before winter sets in."

"Mention me did he?" The question hadn't sounded as offhand as Lester had intended. He lightened his voice and attempted a smile. "Like whether I was doing a good job for you or needed official jogging up?"

"Only what time you mostly quit work of an evening lately. I said we worked long as there was light to drive a nail by and you drove a hell of a good nail "

Why did a marshal want to know a carpenter's quitting time? With a start Lester thought for an instant he had asked the question aloud. "Right generous of you."

"Likely Carrie Shaw wondered how soon she can move back. My rates beats the Drovers'."

Everett's seeming answer to Lester's silent question gave the carpenter another start. He sucked saliva from his tongue. "Carrie could have asked me or you instead of Luther Cain when we'll be done." Immediately he regretted his comment; it drew attention to the marshal's curiosity about such things as his quitting time. He was curious himself about the marshal's curiosity but Everett wasn't the one with whom to discuss that. Maybe no one was. Unless it was the marshal. "Tomorrow I'll be down at sunup. Milk the cow and fix them all breakfast and dinner before light so they can heat it up. Cow's not happy about it but the family don't mind. Give you and me better than ten hours' work."

"You're making money and I'm making a new start and we're both having a damn good time." Everett gave his friend's back a slap. "Least I am and I hope you are, Lester. Something about building does a man good. And alongside a good man makes it better yet. I'm enjoying working with you."

Everett's effusion of sentiment threw Lester off balance. He appreciated it but it came at a bad time. In his disconcertion he didn't know what to say and his expression showed it.

"I didn't mean to shove that down your throat, Lester. Just feeling good this evening."

"No, no. Thank you for your kind words. I'm just . . ."

Everett interrupted him with another backslap, a gentler one. "Likely wore out. Barber all morning, carpenter all afternoon, all day Sunday. Take care of the missus and young'uns nights. On top of that only about ten days ago in the middle of a goddam gunfight in your shop and seen your wife near killed. Ain't no wonder you look a mite peaked right now. Maybe tomorrow off is a better idea than working."

"Don't fret about me, I'll be raring to go tomorrow. Ruth mostly sleeps through nights now and you couldn't wake the boys with a cannon. I'll get a good eight hours "

"If that's your druthers."

They had walked up the middle of South Street past the side of the Billiard Hall and the front of the Wholesale Exchange and the Eastern Saloon and the Square Deal Poker Parlor, sidestepping horse droppings and early drunks and dodging a few riders and barn-bound wagons, and had arrived at the railroad right-of-way with the darkened smithy to their left and freight house to their right. "Speaking of last week's hullabaloo, Lester, I noticed the *Republican* yesterday said the inquest ain't been set yet. The one on them three killed. But maybe soon. Reckon you'll have to be there."

The carpenter nodded wordlessly as the two of them stepped across the track through the falling darkness. Lester's thoughts merged with the gloom between him and the lightings of coal-oil lamps in stores and saloons around the plaza ahead. Abruptly he longed to see a personal sort of light before him.

Everett wasn't finished with the inquest. "You'll have to tell about knocking Dowling's aim off the mountain man and saving his life there in your shop like last week's paper said. Sort of a funny thing the mountain man had to get killed outdoors a minute later. Both of them. Sort of wasted your time you might say." The men skirted the loading platform and the shadowy depot and started up across the plaza. "Course I didn't know neither of them from Adam but somebody did I reckon. Someplace."

The black-powder and death and excrement stench of that savage moment seared Lester's nostrils again. He tried to exhale it but it clung in his head like a monstrous perversion of newly mowed clover. He couldn't speak and he didn't want to and he didn't.

Everett did: "It sure couldn't been no picnic."

Lester at least was able to shrug in agreement.

His friend seemed to construe agreement as encouragement. "Reckon for another thing Doc's going to ask you again about that Kentucky hombre claiming business with you. Way Lafe Jackman said he done. Already answered once: you never seen him before. Read that in the paper. But Doc's got to ask something to earn his coroner's pay you know. And he'll likely ask Jake what he heard and seen, beings you and the deputy was the only ones in there that's still alive."

Painfully the barber-carpenter admitted to himself Everett's questions were likely to be asked, strictly relevant or not to the inquest. He might as well start practicing his answers to them including the most important and dangerous one. "I never saw him before Enos Dowling brought him in my shop when I was haircutting the mountain man. I don't know whether he was from Kentucky or not; he didn't tell me. He bellied up to me saying he wanted to talk. I told him to wait his turn, I had a customer. He commenced acting hard but he sure met his match in the mountain man. That was when Lafe walked in and heard the Kentuckian or whatever yelling he had business with me and for my customer to quit waving a rifle around and sit back in the chair. I was trying to make peace between them. Lafe walked over and calm-like told the mountain man to put down his rifle. Instead the man grabbed Jake's arm—I never seen such power in a human—and shoved him to the door and tossed him outdoors like a bean bag. Right then the Kentuckian grabbed the rifle barrel and it went off into his gut. I saw Dowling aim his pistol at the mountain man and I pushed that sideways and the bullet must have shot through my window and hit Lafe. The rest happened outdoors and I only heard the shooting." Lester took a deep breath and snorted it out at the night the way a spooked horse does.

"Yessir, a hell of a time," Everett muttered, now more fully aware of his friend's discomfort. "But I think you done fine."

Lester wondered what Everett's thinking should be if he were to learn the whole truth. Most of the story was true but its one lie held seeds of disaster not only for Lester but for the three people about whom he cared most in the world: gentle, loyal, patient Ruth; sweet, earnest George; bravest Tim. But those seeds never were to sprout because nobody was going to cultivate them; nobody knew of them except himself and the man from Kentucky who was beyond knowing not to mention telling.

Why did a marshal want to know a carpenter's quitting time?

In the dimly yellow-punctuated darkness they stood in the middle of the plaza at their place of parting, Lester to head north-westward past the Drovers and out Pacific Street toward his house on the corner of Buffalo, Everett northeastward past the firehouse and out Pacific Street's opposite direction toward the Plains Hotel. They stood almost exactly where Noble Buck had fallen dead from his wagon four weeks ago less one day The railroad depot was directly back of them, Berg's Dry Goods straight ahead, the Lone Star Cafe in the middle of the west side, Lester's barber shop halfway up the east; the men were in the epicenter of Bancroft and thus of their world as it presently was apportioned to them. Had Everett thought of that fact he most likely should have shrugged at its inconsequence. Its geographical essence hadn't occurred to Lester either but the animate implications for him and his family of everything physical and temporal around him had brought bile surging to his throat half a dozen times since the worst hour of his life—on a week ago Wednesday—except two. One of those two had been on the wretched day twenty years ago when his pistol's fire had been crossed inadvertently for a terrible instant by a childlike face which he almost had given up trying to forget. The other had been on the night ten days later when he'd last glimpsed another lovely face through another kind of fire.

"Well, Lester, if you're set on it I'll see you in the morning."

"I'm set on it."

"Hasta manāna."

The barber-carpenter flicked the brim of his hat with two fingers and stepped away in the shadows.

"Give the missus my respect," Everett called after his friend. Strangely he felt a twinge of the melancholy he'd sensed in Lester lately. "And the young'uns "

CHAPTER 46

Walking through the gloom toward home Lester tried not to think of anything before the day's labor with Everett or after the evening's refuge with his family; but his mind wouldn't side with his aim; his memories and misgivings wouldn't be caged. His killing of a bride against whom or whose groom he'd borne no ill will with a bullet meant for her feuding family's sire who'd been trying to kill him had been a devastating mistake. It had been spawned by senseless familial hate and nurtured by youthful recklessness; its offspring had grown through twenty years into the monster now threatening everything penitent and merciful and productive those years had yielded.

In his youth Lester's wild, headstrong nature had seemed to invite violence despite his small stature or maybe partly because of it. His retreat from hostility and his rebellion against scrounging tobacco and cotton from Kentucky's hill-hemmed patches had prodded his increasing absences from his parents' farm to roam the woods and creeks and villages of the larger world beyond it. He had lived on berries and nuts and roots and the prey of his rifle and pistol. Through natural talent and practice he'd become expert with his weapons. He'd entered shooting matches on holidays and election days and at family reunions and important weddings; and his skill with his pistol especially had become well known among the mainly rifle-toting hill people. It had been a matter of pride with him until later his errant bullet had shattered a young girl's brain.

Inevitably perhaps, at least in fact, as he'd become longer and more widely acquainted with regions beyond his home valley he also had become acquainted with what once he'd heard a tree-stump preacher call "man's triple tormenters: whiskey, wenches, and cards." (That sky pilot's definition was his only memory tonight allowing him a real smile; he should pass it on to Carl Norris. God willing.) It was while courting these acquaintances in some Ohio River towns that he'd heard first of an Indiana place called Terre Haute, a former land-office community well up the Wabash River from Vincennes. A Gypsy with evil breath had told him his fate's ferryman awaited him there like a hopefully kindlier Charon. At the time he hadn't gone hunting down the Ohio and up the Wabash for the bizarre soothsayer's prophecy. When he'd become the hunted however instead of the hunter after the bride's death he had remembered the remote Indiana town where opportunity and adventure allegedly had mingled and more crucially for him where the girl's father and husband and possible Kentucky officials hadn't been apt to seek him.

It had taken a week of grueling forest and river travel, several times a day and night at a stretch, living off the land as he went, for him to reach Terre Haute. There he'd fallen exhausted into a twenty-four-hour sleep in a saloon's back room, unable to care during those hours whether or not his pursuers had been closing on him or had been outdistanced or at least temporarily outwitted by him. When he had emerged from his near-coma he'd found the saloonkeeper willing to let him sleep there a few more nights without charge and to pay him to boot fifty cents a day eating money in return for cleaning out the stable behind the establishment. The proprietor had wanted to rent out the building. What had made the job well worth the daily fifty cents and room, Lester recalled, had been neglect of its reeking urgency for the two weeks before and a month after the owner's sale of his three horses. It was another smothering stench in his memory's slough tonight.

During his several days of shoveling, he had paused frequently, heart pounding, to listen to passing voices and glance out of the stable's door or windows about the neighborhood, absurdly alert to any sound or sign of swooping or creeping vengence. But had it been absurd? How could he have known for sure? He had counted on his pursuers guessing he'd gone on down the Ohio River to the Mississippi and its limitless choices of sanctuary instead of up a tributary of the Ohio flowing from obscure Indiana creeks. Indeed his own first impulse had been to light out for the Mississippi but it had been then he'd recalled the Gypsy's words and had felt eerily in his bones that his recollection had been a beckoning up the path he'd taken. Yet in his panic after the bride's death he may have traded superstition for reason.

Despite the December's cold he had been in a sweat all of the short time he'd been in Terre Haute, not because of the stable work but from prickling, random apprehension. He had been seized by a compulsion to move on farther up-river, putting still more distance between himself and Kentucky, and had overheard in the saloon mention of a thriving smaller community named Crawfordsville as not being on the Wabash itself but about twenty-five miles up a creek entering the river thirty or so miles north of Terre Haute. The town had sounded good to him: remote but with opportunities to put to gainful work his vigor and initiative and a few skills he already had acquired on the farm besides farming, things like barn and even house building and the more than primary-grade arithmetic his former schoolmaster father had found time to teach him.

With the same fearfulness tonight as on that night twenty years ago but now with infinitely greater regret he recalled overhearing also in the saloon a drunken man brag to a group of his friends about his harvest's golden return in an iron kettle under the floor of his farmhouse. To say the rest had been easy was to say going to Hell was easy.

Lester's jeopardy then not only had made him desperate but had made having some money seem mightily handy if not imperative. He had learned that the hoarder's farm had been only two miles east of town on the plank National Road and had made his way there on foot through the woods and clearings bordering the Road and had watched the house from a thicket until after dark. He had seen a couple leave in a buggy followed a bit later by a horseman who had called in answer to a female voice from indoors about returning in two hours. After another half-hour's wait he had stolen across the clearing in the moonlight and determined by quick glances into the house's windows that its only occupant had been a girl lying in bed, her hair a dark cascade on the lamplit pillow, her eyes glistening with tears. He had walked through the house's unlocked front door and into her room, hoping not to terrify her, wondering himself what in God's name he was doing there, inevitably frightening her, demanding in a guiltily loud voice where the money was hidden, struggling with her brave, crippled, unsuccessful defense of it when her glance had given away its cache under the floorboard where he'd found it, seeing the upset lamp's coal-oil flames leap onto her nightgown and the

303

bed and across the room, fleeing from the fire's terrible heat and its grasping for him and from her screams and from the house and farm and Terre Haute.

On the trail to Crawfordsville his fear of madness as much as pursuit had kept him fighting his nightmare of flaming nightgowns and blood-drenched wedding dresses and had kept him plunging through the winter's forests and across its hills and along the Wabash River and Sugar Creek. Gradually over the years since then, finding succor in Ruth's steadfast love, burying himself in demanding enterprises in four successive towns despite seizures of dread which had prompted their several moves, pondering and eventually praying over the New Testament's tenet of repentence and forgiveness, he had pushed his nightmarish memories to the back of his mind although not utterly out of it and had gained comparative peace.

Now surely his peace of body and mind and his recreated world weren't in peril compelling his defense of them. Surely God!

Lester was walking past the Drovers when Luther Cain's voice wrenched him to a halt in the dimness. Quelling his reluctance he turned to face the lawman who was stepping toward him off the hotel's porch. "Evening, Marshal." His mouth felt sticky. "Didn't see you."

The shadows concealed it but Luther's reluctance was almost as discomforting as his friend's. "Waiting for you to come by."

The carpenter-barber now knew why the marshal had inquired about his quitting time. "What can I do for you?"

"Mind if I walk along a piece?"

Lester felt bad about minding his friend walking with him; he wished Luther were anything nowadays but marshal of Bancroft. "Suit yourself."

They turned from the plaza westward on Pacific past the dark side of O.K. Outfitters and the nearly dark fronts of Mother Swain's boarding house and Bolinger's Stable and three houses across from those toward the Blaine's home on the corner of Buffalo Street. Luther knew what he wanted to have said once he'd said it but he didn't know how to put it into words. Lester didn't know what the lawman was about to say but he had the feeling he wasn't going to like hearing it. At the moment they both could think of a hell of lot better places to be and things to say. Sunlight couldn't have accounted for Luther's squint or the lack of a coat for Lester's slight shiver. It was a bad moment for friends.

"Goddammit, Lester, the paper said it last night: the inquest on Dowling and them is coming up one of these days."

Lester nodded as though his concurrence were visible in the darkness. He waited for the lawman to continue, staring ahead a short block at a glowing window of his house.

"Mayor told me the same thing today, Lester. Him and Doc and Jim Watts talked about it at noontime."

"Does there have to be the inquest, Luther? Seems like enough folks watched what happened so the whole town knows." It had been a rattled man's shot in the dark. "Reckon that's a lame-brained question."

"No, it ain't. Jim told me once a coroner don't have to hold one. County attorney can decide hisself if the law's been broke. But there's time it saves him a trial or plain vexation by folks wanting him to bring someone to book. That's kind of the way Bill said them three is thinking now, him and Doc and Jim."

"What way's that?"

"Bill said them stalling, waiting for the talk to die down or plumb out wasn't working, said there's one sonofabitch in particular keeps it going."

Lester's tone was regretful. "Carl Norris?"

"Hell, no. He's a long way from a sonofabitch." The marshal spat the name into the darkness: "Johnny Newlin." The sour taste hadn't left his mouth along with the spit. "The way them boys figures it the inquest is going to air the town out, going to blow Newlin's cowshit off the veranda." Luther gritted his teeth in the instant's silence. "The boys don't know this, Lester, but I got to tell it to you: even if Newlin don't belong in the inquest he'll have his say there; and what he'll say ain't going to do you no good."

"Me?" The word was like a single beat on a soggy drum.

"Goddammit, yes."

"Far as I know Johnny wasn't around during the trouble." Lester's tone was edging toward anxiety. "How could he see anything to talk about?"

"Ain't what he seen. He heard something. Figured he could make it into trouble for me. Not doing my goddam job. Only thing is it's trouble for you too; only that don't fret him."

"Heard what?"

305

The darkness had hidden the barber-carpenter's swallow but the marshal had sensed his alarm. He felt bad. "Lester, you recollect a week ago today I called on your missus about being sorry she got shot?" He didn't expect or wait for an answer. "And you and me walked along this street back to the plaza?" Again he assumed his friend's assent. "And you told me I had a free haircut when I wanted it?" This time he waited until Lester had muttered an assent. "Then I reckon you'll recollect telling me you never seen that Kentucky stranger in your life." It had been a statement, not a question; and Luther wasn't finished making statements. "Same as you told me after the fight. Same as you told Carl and he put in the *Republican* last Friday. And you didn't have no idea what 'business' Lafe heard the stranger say he had with you."

Lester didn't speak. It was as though he couldn't for the moment. Either that or he could only bellow in frustration. Goodgod he'd come a long way to have everything and everybody he had worked for and loved blown away by an inquest into deaths he hadn't caused. Surely for godssake not. Anger began to throb in his temples at such unfairness. At the turn's perversity. Its lunacy. Villainy. At Johnny Newlin. At Bill Crum and Jim Watts and Doc Bowman.

Luther was doing the speaking again. "Lester, I'm going to tell you one more thing. And I'm going to ask you one more time. Yesterday Newlin told Carrie Shaw what the stranger said his 'business' with you was: that you shot his wife twenty years ago in Kentucky and he's been on the lookout for you ever since." They had arrived at the corner. The barber-carpenter stumbled in a rut and the marshal caught his arm to steady him and dropped it after turning his friend half-around to look at him in the glow of the Blaines' window. "You'll likely be answering this again at the inquest but I'm asking you for my last time. You know who the man from Kentucky was and did he claim the truth?"

The throbbing of Lester's anger mounted to pounding; it echoed Carrie's name now.

And abruptly, even more loudly Luther Cain's name.

What right did this hired killer in the shadows before him have to glower over killing? None worth a damn. The hell with him.

Now wait. Luther was his friend; if a marshal killed it was his job.

But Cain sure as hell wasn't acting like a friend.

Hell was right. Hell was closing in. On both of them

"Go to hell, Luther."

"Where I'm going is scouting back East in the morning."

Lester forced derision into his voice. "You riding the morning train East?" The derision was tinged with dismay. "What the hell you doing that for?"

"Not the train. Telegraph line. Runs plumb back there and all over nowadays. And I'll likely have a visit with Colonel Evans at the fort. Reckon the army can find out most everything. Most everwhere."

The springing redness of Lester's face looked black in the dimness. "Goddam you, Luther, you oughtn't be doing this to me. We been friends."

"That's part of why I'm doing it. You ain't answered my question so I'll be asking it of others. Reckon I'd do that even if you did answer. It's my job. But I'm doing my job for me and you both."

"Not for me you're sure not." Lester's bitterness was stinging raw.

"If you're going to catch hell, Lester—even if you already know why—I figured you'd best know when. I know when I'm going to but I best find out why; I aim to do that. I ain't got no choice."

Luther had sounded almost apologetic which Lester even in his agitation realized wasn't the marshal's style. Luther could regret happenstances while not being apologetic about them. Maybe instead of apologetic he'd sounded unsure. No. The marshal's sureness about things was a constant of his own and therefore of Bancroft's daily equations.

Fear was beginning to mingle with the frustration and anger in Lester's gut. "You're damn sure of yourself bygod." He lowered his voice to a hoarse whisper, glancing toward the lighted window. "Dammit, Luther, my Ruth don't . . ." his hesitation like the night not veiling his struggle, "know about my life before I went to Indiana and fell in love and we got married. That's when I started living. Not only for me. For her. In Crawfordsville, Indiana, not Kentucky. For godssake leave it thataway. Can't you leave us to live in peace, me and Ruth and George and Tim? Where's the skin off you? What kind of man are you?"

The marshal shook his head in growing frustration of his own. "A man that's swore to do a job. Keep the peace. There won't be no peace for any of us now 'til things is cleared up. You ought to know that."

"I'll keep my own peace; nobody's going to take it from me. All you got to do is keep yours."

"How can either of us live peaceable after Newlin has his say at the inquest?"

"Call him a liar. Who's to prove he's telling the truth? If he is who's to prove the Kentuckian was?"

Luther let his unspoken reply float in the night air between them.

Agonizingly Lester seized it "You're wondering how they're going to answer your telegram.'

"And what reason Newlin has to lie against you You and him ain't been on the outs."

"To make trouble for you; you already said that goddammit."

"And what reason the stranger had for lying why he was after you."

The barber-carpenter's throat tightened as though a hand had gripped it. "When your answer comes back, Luther, what you going to do?"

"From now 'til then I'm hamstringing the inquest if that takes a week. I'm counting on the answer saying nobody wants you for nothing, never heard of you." The marshal's tone was rueful but calm. "But if they want you, Lester, I got to come for you." He touched his friend's arm briefly. "Even so I figure nothing's going to happen. Too long ago. And far as folks around here goes you already said it: that was another life. Ain't likely they'll stand for the governor sending you back."

"But you'll come for me. Why for godssake? For Jesus' sake why?"

"I already told you. I got no choice."

"This is Bancroft, Kansas, not Daviess County, Kentucky, not Terre Haute . . ." He broke off; his mouth suddenly was gorged with bile. He hoiked the sourness onto the black dirt at their feet.

"Lester?" Ruth had opened the house's door and was peering

into the shadows. One sleeve of her dressing gown hung empty. "That you out there?" Her voice smiled. "And Marshal Cain I see. Why don't you both come in?"

"What you doing up again?" her husband demanded gently but with an irritated echo of his commotion.

"Now don't be upset with me, Lester, I'm not an invalid. Marshal, will you eat with us? Venison tonight courtesy of Cal Hubbard. And it's a big cut. He soaked it in some brew of his for two days and the boys and I roasted it all of today." She forestalled her husband's further complaint with her raised good arm. "I sat and told them how and they did it."

Luther touched his hat brim. "Thank you, M'am, I just finished at the hotel. Starting my night rounds."

"That's too bad. Wish I'd thought of it sooner."

A lamp-glint of teeth showed under his moustache. "So do I."

"Next time," she laughed. "Well, whenever you're ready, Lester. Goodnight, Marshal." She closed the door against the evening's chill.

"Can't you see for godssake?" Lester gusted. "How the hell could I tell her?"

"Better tell that woman soon, Lester. Awful damn fine woman. Earned hearing it from you, not some jackass in a public hall." The marshal hitched his gun belt forward a potent inch and started turning away. "She said she ain't no invalid. Reckon you believed that when you married her; and her the same of you. Reckon a little trouble ain't going to whip neither of you nor both together."

" 'Little?' " Lester choked over the word. He coughed his throat clear. "Sonofabitch."

The marshal chose to consider the curse aimed at the barber-carpenter's personal devil and not at him as its embodiment and he strode off into his own frequently hellish darkness.

"Don't come for me," Lester hissed after the tall figure blending into the night, "I'll not let you take me back there. Don't come for me, Luther!"

CHAPTER 47

The pressroom behind the building's loading cavern next to the idling squad car rumbled its streams of dailies through tying machines into trucks waiting in the night to throw bundles onto thousands of City sidewalks before dawn. It was a subterranean, clandestine operation full of anxiety, mortification and dread. There were shouts of "Watch it!" and "Coming through!" and "Heads up!" interspersed with gusted "secondary hemorrhage," "whole blood," "respiratory rate," "critical."

A headline on a piece of tire-smudged newsprint swept up by a wind from the gutter and plastered against Marks' eyeballs blazoned the riddle: when is a cop not a cop? It never had been a riddle to him; a cop always is a cop. As it seemed he had to keep saying, his job was collaring criminals; judgments about why they had become criminals weren't part of it. And things like discretion, moderation, compassion, remorse, and reform were the stocks in trade of judges and parole officers and preachers, not of cops. But his nightmare's vision was warped and its hearing rattled by the persistence of the dilemma. His chest was pressed down by it as though a monster were standing on him. Sonofabitch! Life should be pretty good these days if it hadn't been for a snitch tipping him that his ex-friend had returned to using and incidentally dealing after several years of being straight and living in a decent Manhattan neighborhood with a good wife and a good kid and a busy appliance shop. It wasn't so much having to upset the dumb bastard's apple cart even though he may have been strung out and maybe blackmailed into backsliding—Mark hadn't seen there was a choice except arrest—it was the sergeant's mistake telling Mattie about it. Gently she had asked him twice in two days whether he absolutely were convinced there weren't a choice.

The universal newsboy stuck his head and arm brandishing a newspaper into the squad-car window. "Hey, Sergeant, you fucked up, didn't you?" But the kid was grinning; he was a great admirer of his friend the policeman. "Bet you'd give me a break, though, wouldn't you?" The young face turned quizzical as he added softly. "Right?"

The tolling of the church bell the morning after Luther's talk with Lester admonished the town's denizens indiscriminately, awake or thereby awakened, sober or drunk, that it was Sunday whether or not, as Preacher Smith liked to substitute for hoot, they gave a toll. Actually "clang" should have been the apter word but Howard was defensive about the bell, having endured the eastbound's seemingly endless smokey hours to Kansas City last spring and found a second-hand one off a locomotive and ridden herd on it back to Bancroft in a dead-heading cattle car, arriving in what Carl Norris had termed a state of "groggy grace."

Carrie Shaw smiled up at her escort under whose left arm her right hand curled lightly as they walked from the Drovers along the plaza's north side toward the East Street corner. "I thank you for coming to church with me this morning, Luther." She lowered her gaze to the wooden sidewalk not self-consciously but in earnest thought. "I wanted us to do this after our set-to Friday. And for our love that night. Not just our loving. Our love. We got a thing to be forgive and one to give thanks for. Forgive us not understanding, fighting. Thanks for love to make us understand and be together again."

Luther wasn't used to this kind of talk: about things a man sometimes thought, maybe more than sometimes, but didn't say outright. It didn't trouble him exactly; it even felt like something agreeable that maybe needed saying, anyhow by somebody like Carrie whom he didn't have to look out for. He just wasn't used to it. He thought he ought to say something provided he meant it. "I'm sorry about our fighting and glad about our love."

She squeezed his arm and smiled up at him again briefly. "That's awful nice, Luther." She looked back down, watching her step on the rough boards, her tone becoming wistful. "The only other thing I could want this beautiful morning is Lester and Ruth being all right."

"Like I told Lester last night, Carrie, Ruth'll be fine. And I 'low he will too whatever answer Colonel Evans gets back. For sure there's no use fretting about it before then."

She sighed. "If the answer comes back bad you're going to arrest him. I can't help fretting about our best friends. Leastways, mine." She frowned at the sunny fall morning. "How long you say the colonel said it'll take him to hear?"

"Maybe a week. His West Point friend in the War Department knows the way. Army has trails in states and territories it rides alongside lawmen. Same as the colonel and me. If he was after a deserter I'd help out."

311

Carrie spoke more to herself than to Luther. "Lester could desert Bancroft."

"He knows I could run him down. And he wouldn't leave Ruth and his boys; he ain't that kind."

"I'm glad you know he ain't."

"Hell yes. He's a good man."

"Yes. No matter if he done something bad as a boy. He didn't grow into a Jack Bennett. Or a Kid Owen." She obviously hadn't noticed the slight, quick tightening of the marshal's jaws. "He growed into one of the finest husbands and fathers and law-abiding citizens of this town."

"I'll agree to that," Luther nodded solemnly. "I'll say something else: he wouldn't do to another man what's being did to him; made into a scalping knife after somebody he didn't have no war with."

"And I'll agree Johnny is a sonofabitch for using him." She tugged Luther's arm. "Look at me. Johnny Newlin is a sonofabitch for more reasons than that. You understand?"

The marshal gazed obediently down at her, his moustache tilting a little. "I understand."

"I'll say something else too: you still ain't got a war with Lester. And no sonofabitch has a right to start one. Does he?"

Luther wasn't sure what she meant. "There ain't no war. Lester don't want one and I sure as hell don't. I'm a marshal waiting for a telegram. And Lester is whoever he is if he ain't who we think, setting tight in his saddle the next few days, I hope." They had passed Allgood's and Berg's stores and the Farmer's Restaurant and Tinsley's and were rounding the Shawnee and heading up East Street toward the church on the corner of Cottonwood. The board sidewalk had ended with the plaza; they were walking in the street's dust now. Other couples and families were converging on Howard Smith's earthly headquarters. "We got to talk low, Carrie. You and me and Lester and Colonel Evans and maybe Ruth is the only ones knows. Not counting Newlin. If Newlin ain't told some others."

She sounded fairly confident. "I don't figure he has. He wants to catch everbody unawares at the inquest as much as he can."

"Don't he figure you're going to tell me?"

"Sure and you'll likely tell Lester. But are you two likely to put an ad in the paper saying Lester didn't kill somebody's wife twenty years ago and you didn't know about it even if he did?"

"Lester could run off," Luther muttered mostly for something to make her feel better, "like you said. Another reason for Newlin not talking now." He wished the whole goddam calamity could run off. He wished he could make himself feel better along with her.

Her tone made it clear he hadn't succeeded. "And like you said you'd catch him."

Luther's stomach hurt. He knew his next words were absurd before he spoke them. "I could leave town, too."

"That'd be just dandy with Johnny. That's what he's aiming for."

"It sure would spoil his play if I arrested Lester right now."

She shook her head, gazing at the church's belfry without seeing it. "He'd only say you done it because you found out he was onto you." She glanced at Luther with another thought. "There's someone else knows by now ain't there? Ed Sarver. He's the only telegraph man."

"No, not Ed, but there is two I forgot to say: Corporal Black and Private Blue. Colonel sent them to ride the twelve miles back up the line to Clark's Station. Put the telegram on the wire there instead of through Ed. Left about daybreak, back this afternoon. I've worked with both of them enough; trust Black and Blue same as the colonel does."

The marshal's closer acquaintance let him yoke the troopers' names without noticing it. Carrie still was tickled by it, however. The past few minutes not having been loaded with tickles she welcomed the diversion although it was short-lived.

"Carrie, something else I forgot." Luther squinted at recalling it. "Last night when Lester and me was talking, when I told him about the trouble he's got, we all got, and he was bucking like hell over it, well he half-hollered he was living in Bancroft now and 'not Terre Haute' and then stopped sudden, damn near gagged. It was too dark to see but I had a hunch he turned red like when folks say something they wished they didn't. I reckon it's because I was raised near there but it stuck in my mind. Ruth come out then and we talked about something else." They were a half-block from the church and he realized time was short to finish their conversation but he was bound to do that if they had to stop in the middle of the street. "Ruth ever say anything to you about Terre Haute?"

"I recall her saying something about Lester being there before he went to Crawfordsville."

"He lived there?"

"If I recall right he went up to Indiana from Kentucky with money he got from selling a farm his daddy willed him. Looking for a good deal to stake. Passed through Terre Haute and heard chances was good in Crawfordsville so he lit out for it. Ended up partner in Ruth's daddy's store and marrying her." Carrie laughed softly. "Ruth says he traded gold coins for gold hair, her being blonde, and got a store throwed in."

Since she wasn't looking at him Carrie didn't see Luther's wince. It was so slight she mightn't have seen it anyhow. His words were audible only slightly too but she heard those: " 'Gold coins?' " They seemed remote from her as though he hadn't intended her to respond to their question.

She felt red in the face like the folks he'd mentioned. Damn such a deep and terrible wound that still bled even a little at commonplace, unemotional words with sore meaning only for the wounded. She was discouraged and resentful for an instant before her good sense pushed away such nonsense. She was sure her love was salving his old cut and eventually was going to heal it completely. She was almost sure his clinging so long to the image of a girl—granted, a lovely girl—was how he handled his loneliness, was his way of not having to walk his life alone as he did the streets of towns which hired him to be maybe their loneliest man. She was going to see he traded all that for her loving. Right now she was going to pull him out of his momentary bog. "Ruth was just making a joke. She told me when Lester got to Crawfordsville he had his farm money in gold coins. Her daddy saw him start a bank account with them. Lester said he was lucky to get them all the way up from Kentucky."

"When was they married?" The marshal's attention to their conversation had returned.

"She said a year after he come to town; close to twenty years ago."

Luther's voice was reflective. "You know, him and me must have been in that country the same time. I likely was living on

314

our farm outside Terre Haute when he come through that town. Things takes peculiar twists sometimes. We passed each other and never knowed it. Maybe he was running from a bad life to a good one. Now maybe he's headed back again. Only this time him and me knows we're passing and I wish to hell we wasn't."

"Oh, Luther, I feel so sorry for him."

"How you think I do, goddammit?"

"I know, dear." She didn't know exactly but at least she wasn't alone in her distress. Maybe Lester wasn't either.

CHAPTER 48

They had reached the church's few steps at the foot of which Howard Smith stood welcoming his flock as he always did except in bad weather. He was grinning at the lawman. "Take it to the Lord in prayer, Luther, instead of His name in vain. Works a hitch better." He winked at Carrie. "Don't it, Pretty Girl?" With an affectionate bow he shook hands with each of them. "Best of the morning to the marshal and his lady. As I was saying to Clay Gibson there you're just in time for my sermon on evils of loving money. Causes more trouble than near to anything. Loving it, not loaning it at interest. Fair interest naturally."

Preacher Smith was developing his theme a half-hour later from the pulpit with enthusiasm. Doke Ledbetter already was asleep in his customary seat at the far end of a pew where he could rest his head against the wall. The squirming children scattered among their elders throughout the dozen-row room with a stove beside its rear door weren't engrossed in the sermon either. The rest of Howard's listeners were attentive, including the marshal with his hat on his lap and his gun in his boot and Carrie with one hand's fingertips tucked unobtrusively under the outside of her escort's thigh. "Gold makes pretty teeth and pretty wedding rings and they're good. But don't forget the Isrealites' calf was made of gold. And gold fever makes well men sick and good men bad. They tell me up in the Black Hills right now some men's coming down with gold fever and shooting and robbing and burning out each other's camps."

Carrie visualized red firelight in the night flickering on low pine branches drawing back in shock from the heat of flaming tents and cabins and wagonloads of picks, shovels, pans, food, clothes, cooking pots, even mined gold. (She wished today's sermon hadn't so much to do with gold.)

" . . . at the end of the rainbow," the preacher was saying with heightening excitement, "is more likely to be a pot of fool's gold instead, shining with lies of escape from trouble but leading men into more trouble than they ever bargained for including spilling the blood of their fellow man."

Or girl!

Carrie almost had cried it aloud instead of within her quailing psyche. Her fingers had jerked involuntarily from the pew to her mouth. Peripherally she saw Luther's head turn toward her and she avoided his questioning glance; as an answer she pretended to cough behind her hand, nodding to reassure him and anyone else who might have noticed her abrupt motion. She couldn't think momentarily much less whisper a spurious explanation. Frowning she stared intently at the preacher as though concentrating on his words and suggesting the marshal do the same. From her eye-corner she watched Luther look back toward the pulpit; and with outward calmness she withdrew inside herself to fight off her rising panic.

Her mind clamored with sounds of the past, of months and minutes ago: Luther's bitter voice telling her in a private hour of his cousin's death, of the distant red sky, the smoldering black house-heap, the ash-covered iron pot empty of gold coins; Howard Smith saying the marshal's terrible cussing then may have been at the pain of Carrie's conjuring his past by warming him but certainly hadn't been directed at her; Luther dismally repeating Ruth's words "gold coins" on their walk to church this morning and saying about Lester "I was likely living on our farm outside Terre Haute when he come through. . . ."

Her lightning thought had seared and terrified her. Goodgod, NO, it wasn't conceivable, it couldn't be true; yet somehow—God forbid—it could be true that her good friend Lester, husband of her dear friend Ruth, appallingly was the night-stalker, the fugitive from a Kentucky tragedy to whom tragedy had dealt a second deadly hand to play out in the darkness of an Indiana farm. He had reached Crawfordsville with gold coins after passing through Terre Haute from near where gold coins had been stolen. Had those which he'd brought there come from a Kentucky farm sale or from an iron pot under an Indiana farmhouse floor? Rather than roaming Indiana in search of a deal to stake had he been fleeing Kentucky vengeance which after twenty years may have almost have caught up with him a week and a half ago in Bancroft and still might? No it couldn't be true, not his part in two deaths. Yes, it could be true, but it wasn't. It just couldn't be. Yes, it could, but it wasn't. Even though it could. It wasn't. Whom was she or anyone to believe about the bride's death: her friend Lester

317

or a stranger from Kentucky; her trust or her imagination; sense or supposition? Even if he had caused the bride's death by an awful mistake—for which then surely he'd died since over and over—what sane reason should Carrie have for suspecting his part in the robbery-death of Luther's cousin? She may be the daft one.

Reason? Because Lester had been in the vicinity; because he likely had needed money to aid his flight; because he could have been among those who Luther had said had heard his father brag about the cache; because the Cains' gold coins had been stolen at the time of the fire and Lester soon afterward had turned up in Crawfordsville with gold coins; because as law-abiding as he seemed now it was claimed Lester had killed one girl in Kentucky and either may have been angered or panicked at unexpected resistance by the Indiana robbery victim.

His second victim?

No. No. No. It could be true dammit but it wasn't.

Surely.

Vaguely she realized her back was damp. Her forehead felt beaded. She was sweating. 'Glowing' she'd learned in New Orleans to say Inside her head there was a buzzing like a prodded hive.

Outside Carrie's head Howard Smith's voice was ringing, "If the wages of sin is death the price of loving gold is lack of peace. If you put too much store in money you'll never get all you want and you'll hate not having it all. And hate and peace don't mix. Just be sure in this world you want what counts whether it's peace or love or health or knowledge or all of them. If you want peace of mind help others, if you want love give it, if you want health don't hurt it, if you want knowledge go after it. Knowing where you're headed is the first step in getting there. Be sure you know because after you get there it's too late to be somewhere else. Knowing the truth takes looking hard for it but it's worth finding so don't settle for no less and look hard for it. Right now."

It was as though he were speaking to her. He was right for Heaven's sake. She wanted to know something so it was up to her to go after the answer. "Right now." When Luther leaned slightly toward her she became aware she'd whispered aloud; she took it back outwardly with a flutter of her hand but not inwardly. She knew what she was going to do. Coming into church she'd overheard Rosella Guttman telling Louella Allgood in a voice Carrie had deemed overly loud—she'd winced for Luther—that Ruth's being shot by the marshal was keeping her housebound another week, and, incidentally, Lester was carpentering dawn to dusk on Lane's boarding house. That meant Carrie could talk to Lester outside Ruth's or anybody else's presence by catching him going to or from his work; and if anybody asked (as her experience led her to allow possible if not probable) what they'd been talking about either one of them could say her new room there. What she was going to do in order to find out what she wanted to know was to ask Lester, the one man who could answer her if he would. If he wouldn't maybe that itself should be a kind of answer. Silently now she tried out some of her questions based on Ruth's past stories and Johnny's harangue day before yesterday of which Lester had learned from the marshal: How did the Kentucky man know you lived there, Lester, twenty years ago? What reason would he have coming here claiming you killed his woman? Why don't you write back there for a copy of your deed selling the farm for the gold you brung to Crawfordsville? Did you know another girl, a dearly loved one of Luther's near Terre Haute, got robbed of gold coins and killed the same time you was through there? Did you maybe accidental kill her, Lester, accidental not being murder?

Trying to imagine Lester's reactions to her questions scared her. She believed she knew him but who knew anybody for sure including himself or herself? She believed he wasn't violent. She trembled at such a vagary. One thing she knew: she wasn't going to tell Luther ahead of time about asking Lester anything. If it turned out not to amount to a hill of beans Luther was apt to be mad at her butting in although not harmed by it. If it turned out very bad—if Lester (dear God, no) had been mixed up in that long-ago burning—the end of the world should be like kindergarten compared to the ensuing tempest if Luther found out. And he might be hurt bad by the storm. So bad.

She had to overcome some qualms about not telling Luther; in her heart she had made a commitment to herself and him never to be untrue in any way. She found sense however in the thought it wasn't untrue to try helping him and maybe Lester too without telling Luther unless of course that became necessary to prevent his being harmed. He was more likely to be harmed one way or another seeking vengeance for his cousin's death if it turned out Lester had played a part in it. Nothing could bring back the girl herself, only memories of her which were torturing him less and less but then should hemorrhage again. And the fire truly may have been accidental; there was no reason to burn down a house in order to rob it. Accident or not Lester was bound to have suffered over the years between then and now as he had married sweet, pure Ruth and sired two innocent children and helped save the Union and moved time and again to better his family's lot.

Ohgod, she was scared.

Oh, God, please help me do right, she prayed in her mind under the preacher's resounding benediction. "God love us all!" Help me help Luther. And Lester and Ruth. "Help us find truth and love and health." Help me protect Luther from himself. "And help us find peace." And protect Lester from Luther for the sake of peace for them both. "In Thy name we ask it." In Thy name I ask it. "Amen." Amen.

She was scared.

OH, YES.

CHAPTER 49

The night's distant siren, like a wolf's howl, underscored the drama of Mark's tracking, reminding him of the importance of keeping his own counsel, of putting down each step precisely as he skirted the waterfront toward the uncertainty ahead. His hand was on his revolver, eyes squinting into the gloom. Abruptly, astonishingly a semblance of himself floated upward to stare down at his strangely black-hatted, booted figure as it rounded a dock shed into a flashing roar which he was unsure had been his own revolver's until a running form sprawled in the shadows. Quick strides brought him to his knees beside the skirted heap. In the dimness of a nearby warehouse's light the female's face, framed by brown hair, horrendously was Mattie's; and before she died she whispered into his ear, lowered against her lips, "Forgive him, he didn't mean it."

The mutter of one recovery room nurse to another was preoccupied. "Hand me the catheter and pay close attention here." After a moment she added, "Maybe the 'Mattie' he's asking for is his wife. Nuts about her whoever she is."

The trainee held out the tube. "She's been watching through that viewing window."

"You forgot to draw the curtain, Simpson. And how'd she get there anyway?"

"Sorry. Don't know. Does his talking like this mean he's coming to?"

"They go in and out. He won't remember. Sometimes just as well."

The patient's eyelids had fluttered minutely, barely enough for his wife's living image to stab through his unconsciousness for an instant. He hadn't killed her and thereby himself thanks be to God! But who was dead—or was yet to die? In the half-light he saw the shadows of the tracker being tracked, the lawman periled by the lawman's relentless stalking. The grotesque circling had to be broken off, the whirling current sluiced from the brink of death.

"All the signs seem to be stabilizing, Simpson. Beautiful surgery. But we'll have to keep a careful watch."

For a week that had started off so agonizingly Carrie's had brightened in a hurry. Compared to their Sunday's abysmal gloom her Thursday's spirits were as radiant as the afternoon sunlight when she stepped from Doc Bowman's office onto the plaza's boardwalk. Emphasizing that it was still a month too early to be more than damn suspicious he had added her morning nausea and sore breasts and lack of usually punishing cramps to a month's skipping of her typically clock-like period—her reason for visiting him—and had come up with a happy sum: "You just might, Young Lady, be pregnant. Anyhow there's nothing else wrong with you. If you can call having a baby wrong which I reckon neither of us can. If you're having a baby."

As she relished the prospect of motherhood—tentative but relishable—she was sure the only thing unhappy or wrong about it might be Luther's feeling trapped. Maybe she oughtn't to tell him until she were certain. On the other hand she already had chafed during the week about withholding something ugly from him and now she could tell him something beautiful although chancy yet. He could deal with the chance as well as she. Her main concern was that if there were to be a baby it have a father by law as well as by nature. And he was a lawman. She grinned at the little joke. Her relief from the week's grimness let her make a game of skipping over loose boards in the walk, head down, humming. Luther's work-bound frowning most of the week presumably over Lester's trouble hadn't given her much to hum about.

Her own encounter with their mutual friend last Sunday afternoon had made her feel more like screaming. As her thoughts were dragged back to that time now a cloud drifted across the sun like a bad-medicine sign and she shivered although the next-to-last day of October was merely chilly, not quite cold yet. After Sunday's church she had headed by herself for the Lone Star to eat and visit with the Lacys after Big John McAlister apologetically had snared Luther from her side on marshaling business; and as she'd approached the cafe Lester and Everett had emerged from gulping their noon meal. She hadn't expected the opportunity so soon after her resolve to ask Lester her morning's questions but she'd found herself seizing it. Everett obviously had sensed she'd wanted to talk to his partner alone and had told her goodbye and had told Lester he'd see him on their job and had vamoosed.

She remembered every anguished word and gesture and look of their talk which couldn't have lasted more than ten minutes but had seemed to go on for hours probably because her pain from it had. It had been the most harrowing experience of her life, even worse than her defilement by the Indiana preacher and beating by her mother when she'd been fifteen, worse than seeing Luther kill Jack Bennett in the Portugese while she'd watched through the window fifteen feet away. After her talk with Lester she'd felt as she had when she'd told Luther following Bennett's slaughter "Tomorrow I'll be awful glad today will be yesterday." She remembered Lester's first surprise at her questions before his surprise had frozen into shock and had begun thawing with scoffing denial and had turned into resentment and flowed into anger which she'd seen tinged with panic and finally glazed with desperately hidden terror. She had been flooded with pity for him and impatience with him and ire at him and unfeelingness about him and love toward him.

She had told him her reasons for wondering whether he'd played a part in Luther's beloved cousin's death and that she had to know the truth because "I'd rather know you did it and try to keep loving you than suspect you did and be afraid I couldn't. Maybe that's a woman but that's the way it is." She'd told him she hadn't wanted to lose him or Ruth or the boys if there were any way at all she needn't. She'd said even if he had been involved she was sure, knowing him, the tragedy had been accidental. Suddenly he had become sick at his stomach, vomiting in the street, damning Oscar's tainted food through gritting teeth, and had lurched away from her toward the railroad track and beyond into his undoubtedly tortured afternoon and four days since. And she'd realized his answers had been simply overwrought denials without explanations. Miserably she'd felt her suspicion had been justified. Just as miserably she'd felt her not telling Luther had been justified. She'd felt miserable all around.

On this sunny Thursday afternoon however returning thought of Doc's guess brought back her smile.

"You look like you just been proposed to."

She glanced up in startlement which reverted instantly to her gladness. "Oh, Luther, you scared me. I was thinking . . ."

"I scared myself shaving this morning; got to get a new mirror."

"I was thinking about something else." Her eyes focused more closely on him. "You look right contented for a scared man."

"Had some good news. I was on the lookout for you, Carrie. Colonel Evans come over from the fort with the answer about

Lester. Ed Sarver told him at daylight there was a telegram waiting at Clark's Station. He sent Black and Blue hightailing back there and they just brung it."

Because she'd absorbed his words "good news" her heart hadn't skipped more than one beat. "Tell me, Luther."

"He showed it to me. A lawman working that country then remembers the killing but any kin left is scattered to hell and gone. The girl's daddy got killed later in a gunfight and nobody back there knows what become of her man." Luther glanced briefly beyond Carrie. "Reckon he got killed here couple weeks ago you'll recollect. Anyhow they said being it was so far back and no witnesses now there ain't no use trying nobody." He looked at her with a grin of his own. "They ain't interested in whoever we got here. And if it comes up at the inquest the colonel's going to say that."

Where Lester was concerned Carrie's capacity for enjoyment wasn't as roomy as prior to last Sunday; but respecting the father of her possible child it was limitless. A wave of gratification almost inundated her. She touched a dampening lash quickly. "Luther, I'm awful glad. For both of you Oh I'm so awful glad. Have you told him yet?"

"Aim to right soon. Got to stop by the courthouse on the way, tell the mayor in case Newlin's been cowshitting him too."

Swimming upward through the slime of his boyhood's East River toward today's still crummy Manhattan waterfront, Mark saw Mattie's face sinking past him; he grabbed her hair to pull her up from drowning because if she died he wanted to die with her but if she lived he'd take her back to the rest of both their lives, for the fulfillment of those. Lives which could be fulfilled doubly, God even yet willing.

She opened her eyes in the gloom, nodded, touched her belly and smiled brightly at him.

The cold water became warm about him, like a bed—a whimsically elevated one. Somehow he felt cleansed by the River's wetness, as also by hers. He smelled an elegant, expensive aroma, like the Plaza's.

Everett Lane had come out of the bank on the corner; and as he approached them along the board sidewalk he touched his Confederate cap to the woman. "Howdy, Carrie. Marshal." He smiled at her. "Had to see Clay Gibson but heading right back for the job now. Don't worry, we'll get her done for you soon all right, Lester poorly today or not. It's going like a house afire—goddam, didn't mean that." All three of them chuckled, Everett with the least amusement. "Like a damn antelope," he amended. "So best put my feet where my mouth is." He turned on his way and bumped into Doctor Rice who'd stepped from the plaza's dust onto the walk.

"Just try not to put your feet where my mouth is." The dentist rearranged his coat, smiled goldly at the group and crossed the boards to his office door. "Feet on the ground, teeth in the mouth. That's the Rice way." He closed the door behind himself.

Carrie glanced at the sky. " 'Painless Pete,' " she whispered; "he wouldn't leave a tooth in anybody's head if he could help it. 'Pull for Profit' is his motto." Her own teeth glistened in the sunlight. "Carl Norris would love that." She got the giggles, bending partly over, hand covering her mouth.

Luther looked at her ginghamed back. He felt possessive as he patted it for her attention. "Meet you at the hotel for supper."

She straightened. "No, wait. You ain't the only one with good news." She stifled her laughter to a half-smile of happiness mingled with timidity. She figured lightness was her best bet. "Minute ago you said I looked like I just been proposed to. Well you can ease your mind, I ain't been." She heard herself add, "You still got a chance." She was mortified but excited by her rashness.

"That's good news all right, Carrie."

She was thrown off for a moment and his uncommunicative gaze didn't help. She worked at keeping her voice bantering. "Not that you'd want to take the chance."

"I been wondering about that. Likely that's why you being proposed to come to mind when I seen you here."

His gaze still told her nothing so she decided wordlessly to let his tongue have a further go at it.

"Got to thinking: why would I want to propose to Carrie Shaw?"

Her heart didn't exactly sink; it floundered as her power of speech seemed to. She finally managed, "That right?"

"All she's did is make me see things better maybe. In my job and other ways. Her and that damn preacher. Then I come up with the best reason there is." His face softened and his eyes warmed like Kansas in spring instead of fall. "Because I love her, bygod, like I keep telling her."

In what might as well have been and very nearly was the middle of Bancroft they hugged and kissed; as Uncle Vince Simpson told Opal Vollie the next day, "They just up and hugged and kissed right there in the plaza, God bless the both of them."

A cowboy riding past whooped Two men in front of the Longhorn clapped before stepping into the saloon. A lady stepping out of Wagner's Grocery blushed scarlet but smiled. A freighter cracked his bullwhip from his wagon seat like a rifle.

"Oh, Luther, Luther," Carrie gasped when she'd caught her breath, "I know another awful good reason. Might be, anyhow."

His was the confused glance now. "That right?"

She motioned toward the next little building. "I been to visit Doc. What he said could be awful nice."

Luther never had seen her smile so beautifully. Suddenly the thought hit him: "You ain't . . . ?" He let her nod finish his question and give its answer at the same time. "Now wait a minute, here." His forehead creased. "We got to do things in the right order. I ain't proposed yet." Then his forehead smoothed. "So that's what I'm about to do." He hitched up his gun belt. "Carrie Shaw, reckon you'd marry an old rawhide like me?"

She nodded again, "I'd even marry you," her eyes brimming.

"All right then." He was an orderly-minded man. "Now what was you saying about another reason?"

She took a deep breath. "Maybe—just maybe now remember—Luther Cain, Junior."

He stared at her for a moment solemnly. His voice was almost harsh. But not quite. "Nothing wrong with Carrie, Junior is they?"

She shook her head with a joyous swirl of hair.

The cowboy's whoop had been a croak compared to the marshal's.

After Luther had strode off toward the courthouse and as Carrie resumed her way to the afternoon's unfinished sewing in her Drovers room his exuberance still rang in her being like a bell. It was a brand new bell in Bancroft's being as well as hers, even newer than Preacher Smith's herald of good news. She couldn't remember Luther ever having been so unbent, in such a sprightly mood as to grab and kiss her and let go a Rebel yell in the middle of the plaza. It had seemed then to her filled with buoyant prophecy and it still did. She almost was afraid of making too much of it especially not knowing for sure about the baby. Hopefully his mood wasn't a passing one and wasn't dependent on the baby's sureness.

Maybe at last the marshal of Bancroft was on his way to respite from his self-chastisement, to amnesty for himself, reconciliation with himself. Of course only a few others—the noisy cowboy, the men outside the Longhorn, the freighter, likely Pete Rice through his window, maybe some folks she hadn't noticed—had been aware of the drama if not of its possible meaning; but somehow she felt everybody was going to learn the truth of it. And not too far in the future.

Nola Priest already knew of Luther's proposal. On Carrie's way around the plaza to the hotel she'd met her friend and had gushed it as a starry-eyed schoolgirl might. Nola, encumbered by a rifle she'd been taking to the gun shop, nevertheless had hugged her and wondered whether "the fever is catching with his deputies" and had asked where Luther was so she could hug him, too. When Carrie had replied he might be headed down to find Lester Blaine for some reason which she hadn't particularized Nola had frowned, likely at his head start, half-said something about seeing Lester herself and hurried southward with a kiss blown over her shoulder.

In her room, fingers dipping and pushing and pulling her needle and thread, Carrie judged she was closer than she'd been so far in her life to complete happiness. Luther and she were going to be married, they were going to have babies, if not starting now not long from now, and Lester and Ruth and their boys were safe from incidental devastation by Johnny's attack on Luther which itself abruptly had become baseless. There was only one reason her happiness wasn't complete, if anyone's in this life could be as Howard Smith cheerfully denied, and that was Lester's failure to have cleansed her mind of his Indiana guilt. Even that shadow across her bright day was shortened by Luther's unawareness of it and by her reckoning now of peace for him—especially him— and for her and the baby (please God) as well as for the Blaines. Despite what she'd said to Lester she intended trying her damnedest to bury her suspicion under an earnest belief he was incapable of murder. Both the Indiana killing and the Kentucky one had been accidental. That was all there was to it. That was all there was going to be to it.

327

CHAPTER 50

Luther's walk from the courthouse across the track and down South Street and westward on Jimson was one of deep thought. There was no doubt his thoughts were happier than they'd been in a long time. A very long time. A feeling of well-being crept into them. He almost had forgotten what contentment felt like but he recalled it now from his childhood, from his mother's loving wink around some pious dictum of his father, from the feel in those days of the first spring breeze over his eyelids and beside his ears. As he passed the corner's Billiard Hall and the vacant lot between it and the Maverick Saloon with Everett's house in view beyond another house and a couple of other lots he savored the prospect of having a son. Or a daughter. And ahead of either of those of course a wife. A particular wife. Carrie. He thought how life should be different then. It should be different not only because of them but also, compatible with their presence in his, because of the unfamiliar amity he'd felt nudging his outlook lately. He was aware of Carrie's gentle elbow in that nudging. And of Howard Smith's. But he'd done some thinking on his own, including and maybe especially during the past week of his and Carrie's set-to and their deep making up and his friend Lester's jeopardy.

It was agreeable to cogitate on a kind of truce with others and with himself, on the quarter he was closer maybe than previously to giving others and asking for himself. The thought did take some getting used to but it was indeed an agreeable surprise. In fact it was in the nature of a small miracle that he felt himself moving toward a less wary, more sociable tomorrow in which he could enjoy friendships without wondering how long his job was going to let those last. He sure didn't allow the world and the folks in it were going to change tomorrow; he reckoned lawmen were going to be needed right along. It wasn't he didn't think his job wasn't worth doing or he didn't like doing it. Most of the time. But when he came right down to it he was getting tired of being treated like a goddam lone wolf. He'd got Carrie's drift that maybe he was treated that way because it was how folks judged he acted.

Well maybe he had to act hard because he dealt with hard people. Most of the time. At least a good bit of it. Some of it. Today he owned with a half-grin there was a chance she might be half-right. But he had a job to do which he'd been trying to do the best he could and Carrie herself had said he'd kept Bancroft from being treed by rowdies. He was paid to enforce the law and he'd enforced it. On the other hand he admitted to himself she'd been talking about the ornery rowdies, not the skylarking ones. She never had let on he ought to ease up with the truly bad varmints, only maybe on young cowboys like Raymond Davis and on the town's braying asses and assorted drunks and such; and even at that she'd seemed to mean more what was in his mind when he went about his job than exactly what he did on it. She wasn't against enforcing the law, she was more for dealing it out in a game everybody understood.

His racing thoughts paused for an instant. Maybe all these damn cheerful notions were partly his own from stepping into the light of some new kind of understanding instead of altogether Carrie's. He grinned inwardly again. Of course she'd lit the lamp, he'd have to say. He hadn't yet got a hold on all her ideas but they seemed like they'd not be too hard to handle. A man had to get used to figuring folks were likely to disappoint him because he forgot their shortcomings which, bygod, was his own shortcoming after all. He might say trying to make angels out of hogs ended up proving a man's own hogness. Not that humans were hogs, most of them. They were humans. The same as he was. And as Carrie was—even though she seemed closer to an angel right now. And Lester Blaine. A little leeway might not hurt either taker or giver.

Abruptly he was gripped in a vice of absurd realization pinching his gut and brain; its reproach made him wince visibly as though his chronic bellyache had returned along with a pounding head. Momentarily his afternoon's light dimmed and its harmony turned discordant as he imagined himself yesterday or earlier today or tomorrow heading out Jimson Street to arrest Lester instead of reassure him, to jail instead of free him.

For godssake his friend was a man who'd made a bad mistake as a boy but surely had paid for that in his nightmares and who'd grown for the twenty years since then into a respected citizen with a fine family and had fought to save the Union and who now helped his friends and neighbors like Carrie Shaw and Everett Lane. And Luther might have been heading out to ruin the man's life if the telegram from a stranger hundreds of miles away had decreed the law required it. What the hell kind of monkey-on-a-string marshal was that? And what kind of law didn't count humans for more than flunkies? Well he was a goddam good marshal!—who did an honest day's peace-keeping every day; and the waddies still were herding the cows instead of the other way around. Every ranch needed a foreman but not a deaf one who couldn't listen to his cowhands. Maybe he hadn't mulled such things a lot until lately when his mind had begun reaching out to touch them but just now his image of himself striding toward Lester's downfall made him grab them hard. He'd just scraped past doing injustice to a friend in the name of bringing him to justice.

Of course if the telegram had read the other way and Luther hadn't brought Lester to justice folks might have said he'd set himself up as judge and jury. He reckoned simply not sending the telegram might have been one way to justice, maybe a better one. Then he remembered he'd done that to prove he was an honest lawman.

As cheerful as he was this afternoon his mind still buzzed with a few uncertainties. One thing for certain though: things weren't always goddam black and white on a closer look. Now where the hell had he heard that? The image of Carrie's knowing, comely face smiled across his mind and he grinned to himself for the third time on his clement walk.

The third time wasn't the charm.

CHAPTER 51

When he had cleared the front porch of the small house before Everett's skeletal one he had left the street and started diagonally across the lot separating them because he'd caught a glimpse through some studding of Lester hurrying toward a rear room of Everett's. The sound of hammering had stopped. "Hold up, Lester," he called, raising his left arm by habit with his right hanging at his side; "I come to . . ."

If a black-crimson bullet should shatter one's heart, how should the next instant be? On the far side of dying should one see, hear, feel anything without living senses; should one seem to be saying something; what; to whom? In death should one understand misery, accept disappointment, endure punishment, calm panic, forgive another's unforgiveness and thereby conquer dread of that? These rushing questions almost were fascinating enough to invite their answers by another moment's hesitation. Most likely a fatal moment, however. Hesitation's probable fatality therefore precluded the invitation.

"Goddammit, Marshal Cain!" Nola Priest's voice rang from behind the smaller house which the lawman just had passed. The echo of her cry was lost in two almost simultaneous explosions, one closer than the other to Luther. The woman was running toward him with her rifle held outward but she wasn't looking at him, she was looking across the lot at Everett's house. She dropped to her knees beside the lawman who was gasping with his attempt to sit up and draw his Colt. "Jesus, Marshal, Lester's gone crazy; acting spooky in the Lone Star this morning." She sucked in a deep breath. "Carrie said you was headed here and I come a-running. Figured you mightn't know. But I think I got the sonofabitch." She stared for an instant at Luther's reddening shirt and then at the house again. "If I ain't because of the damn studding, I will get him."
"No," Luther gritted; "help me up."
Another explosion roared out of Lane's and its fury gouged

a furrow in the dirt beside the lawman's elbow and ricocheted off a buried rock.

"Bygod, looks like I ain't," Nola muttered. "Yet." She stood and raised her rifle toward Lester's asylum.

Luther managed to seize her arm, using it to pull himself nearly upright and at the same time prevent her firing. "No I said!" He squeezed her arm so hard she winced. "No!"

"He'll kill us both thisaway." She jerked her arm from his grip, staggering him. In her concentration on the house she didn't see his struggle to keep his feet. "Least I'll run him outside." She yelled in the house's direction, rifle leveled at it. "Lester, your head's in my sight. Don't move or I'll blow it off. You can't duck fast enough!" She waited a few seconds. There was no response, verbal or active. "All right, throw your gun over that lumber real easy-like." Peripherally from her bead she saw his arm fling sideways and his rifle bounce over the nearby stack of planks. "Now step outside the damn easiest you ever stepped anywheres."

Death's unexpected reprieve, got and given, reopened the sluices of fear, swamping awe of its mystery; fear bore desperation on its tide; desperation gushed escape; and this day's escape had to be from a killer of sinners, an executioner who from every sign understood neither sinning nor repentence but only retribution. There might be one last chance. In his convulsion the fugitive had no choice but to grasp that.

"Don't shoot him, Nola." Luther's teeth ground on his pain and shock, his words scarcely audible. "Ain't acting right."

She spoke from the side of her mouth, squint not leaving her sights. "Like I said." She couldn't see the marshal a yard behind at one side of her swaying slightly.

"He don't understand. Neither would Carrie or Ruth. Don't hurt him. Ain't his fault. Remember!"

"He's coming out!"

"I holstered my gun so he can see." The lawman coughed rawly.

"You hurt bad?"

Luther's breath rasped inward. "Left shoulder some."

"Here he comes," she said as though the marshal couldn't see the barber-carpenter stalking toward them across the lot's dry buffalo grass. "You reckon he's drunk?" She lowered her rifle.

"Scared. And riled." Luther's tone became dully quizzical for an instant. "Sad." He shook his head. "No matter, Nola. Don't shoot him." The ordeal of raising his voice a little to Lester made it quaver. "Lester, listen. I come to . . . ."

Ruth Blaine's wail added its grief to the day only a second before the crack of Lester's derringer did. She had run half-blinded by her anguish across the lot from Jimson Street as he covertly had palmed his weapon from his coat sleeve. Her cry hadn't defended Luther's belly from the small pistol's bullet, but her lunge against her husband's chest had deterred Nola's finger—that and somehow the echo of Luther's "Don't shoot him! . . . Don't hurt him. . . . Remember!" Ruth's momentum sprawled Lester and herself into the dusty grass and Luther, bent double, blood gushing from his mouth and nose, lurched backward one step and incredibly forward two and plunged to his knees and then full-length across the gasping couple, his long frame jerking once and becoming still.

"God, God!" Nola stumbled to the grotesque heap and sank beside it as she had done beside Luther a couple of minutes previously. "Get up get up get up!" Clawing at his clothes she pulled him partly off the man and wife. As they rolled from under him and scrambled to their feet Lester's derringer fell from his slack hand to the ground beside Luther's gun, scraped out of its holster in the moment's melee. Nola twisted the lawman's face toward her and gazed at it. Tears sprang down her blanched cheeks and a whimper leaked from her jaws.

The eyes of the marshal of Bancroft were open and stiff and unseeing.

Oh, Jesus Christ. Oh, God.

CHAPTER 52

In his dream Sergeant Mark Keller reached out to the dim tombstone squatting on the prairie like a black-hatted man beside a campfire. His fingers sought to trace its chiseled words:

> *MARSHAL*
> *LUTHER CAIN*
> *1835–1875*
> *"HE BROUGHT US*

The inscription's final line had been weathered or worn or chipped away. Mark muttered "LAW AND ORDER." The faraway thunder muttered "TROUBLE." Another distant ligthening bolt illumined, as a flaring ember might, the squatting marshal's stony face; his eyes were staring unblinkingly into the sergeant's; and the eyes of both were one pair, gazing inward at one soul.

"Sorry it had to happen, Marshal," Mark said loudly.

The recovery-room trainee's hand jerked, dropping the pressure cuff's bulb. "Heavens! He scared me."

"Calm down, Simpson."

"No, M'am; I mean yes, M'am. But it's like he's telling someone else and himself too . . ."

"I'm sure a man in his job has lots to tell. Maybe even be told."

Marshal Cain nodded his thanks to Sergeant Keller but their indistinguishable selves remained unsmiling. "It didn't have to happen. Best not let it any more."

Holygod! people like Carl Norris and David Berg and Bill Crum and Lila Haniford lamented.

Horray and good riddance! the Portugese-Eastern-Maverick crowd exulted—not loudly because Luther Cain still might be alive, at least spectrally patroling the streets of the town.

Nobody whom Luther had known or who had known him had been a historian. The history of Bancroft, however had been embellished by Luther according to Howard Smith as he was to arise to the pulpit and to the occasion the next afternoon at four o'clock.

Since there still was some ice in town, thanks to the late Noble Buck's industry, Luther's body could be viewed in an open casket at the church starting at two even though Dale Darling's order of the new embalming fluid from a Michigan undertaker hadn't arrived. It was understood Lester Blaine had worked behind the jail most of the night building the marshal's casket under the cold squint of Big John McAlister. And indeed the casket was handsome. The same couldn't be said for the carpenter; his grayness was dismaying. Truthfully Nola didn't give a damn how Lester looked or what became of him although at the later inquest into Luther's death she was to give a try toward exonerating the killer on grounds of self-defense, being the only close witness. "Luther was the best lawman a town ever had," she was to testify, "only maybe a mite hard, you might say." (Even if giving Lester a little hand didn't make sense she liked to honor a dead man's last request when she could.)

Deep in the night, while Lester agonized over the casket and Ruth over her husband, Carrie lay on Luther's Drovers bed writhing with grief and remorse, knuckles of one hand chewed red and throat hoarse from sobbing, moaning over and over the dirge: "Luther's dead, I loved him, I killed him, I didn't warn him, Luther's dead. . . ." because she hadn't told him his killer might fear his vengeance more than dying. The only thing alive for her now in the world was pain. Save maybe one thing. "Please please, dear God, at least let his baby live."

Sitting beside Carrie holding her other hand Howard Smith repeated her prayer confidently and said to her over the softer sound of her moaning "It won't lighten the burden of your grief tonight, Carrie, but someday it will to know Luther is happier right now than we can ever be in this world. And right now he wishes he could tell us that." Dimly but surely she heard the preacher also say, "Instead of killing him your love brought him to life, from aloneness into the company of folks including ones that makes mistakes too. You give him the finest thing you ever could: his deep-buried self. And he loved you for it and so do I and so does God . . . though naturally I'm not putting myself in a class with God."

Although she had told Carrie last Friday about the Portugese proprietor taking aim on Luther's job Nola hadn't got to tell her friend how Johnny planned to do it. She hadn't known herself

335

until his half-drunken brag to her the night before last about spilling Lester's startling Kentucky trouble in public. His ornery idea was to make Luther out a goddam crooked-stick hypocrite not fit to be marshal of anything, and the hell with Lester standing in the way of the town hearing what it needed to know. She liked Johnny all right but lately he'd been hitting at folks, not only the marshal and the barber-carpenter but folks like the mayor and the doctor-coroner and the prosecutor almost as though he were taking coup to make them respect him or maybe pay for past slights. She didn't know whether Carrie and Luther had learned about Johnny's idea of cutting the barber-carpenter's throat to butcher the marshal but Lester's rabid eyes in the Lone Star had convinced her he'd got onto it somehow and had gone wild inside. She wasn't as smart as Miss Haniford but it didn't take a school-marm to figure how Lester could go spooked crazy with a lawman looking for him likely to squash the rest of his rebuilt life. That had sent her running to head off Luther from Lane's when Carrie had said in the plaza he'd gone to find the unhappy bastard. A rattler had been waiting down there to strike a newly happy, un-aware man.

Doc Bowman for once was stunned enough to keep his inter-pretation of current events to himself. He wasn't sure enough anyhow of what he thought to talk about why what had happened had happened. Secretly and with unaccustomed meekness he wondered if his friend, without realizing it but perhaps with char-ity at last, had purged himself of the cancer of anger—as baleful as the malignancy Doc had begun suspecting Luther's belly held. The physician was pretty damn sure of one thing: nobody no mat-ter how brave or scared could have drawn a pistol faster than Luther Cain.

Lila Haniford remembered once commending empathy to the marshal and being unsure he knew what the word meant. Maybe he had asked somebody.

In Luther's hotel room Little John Brock found a very small volume entitled "Military Maxims of Napoleon." Colonel Marcus H. Evans' name was inscribed on its flyleaf. When the deputy returned it to its owner the colonel found a tiny corner of its first page turned down and some words of Maxim II underlined lightly in pencil: ".... it is requisite to foresee everything the enemy may do, and to be prepared with the necessary means to counteract it." Leafing further through the book he found a marked phrase of Maxim VII: ".... flanks should be well covered...." He put the volume back on its shelf in the fort without upturning the page corners or rubbing out the pencil lines. And he stood looking out of the window for a while at Sergeant Sullivan's continuing, futile battle with the sorrel stallion without either enjoying or being annoyed at it this time, simply muttering quietly "Marshal ought to have remembered."

CHAPTER 53

Howard Smith spoke across the casket after Dale had closed it with a subdued but proud flourish and retired one step to the front row beside Jake Barlow. The church was full which wasn't saying a great deal because its dozen rows held only about a hundred people between its unlighted stove in back and pulpit in front. Body heat made stove heat superfluous; indeed the windows had been opened to October's late-afternoon air. Throughout the room most eyes were dry if varyingly solemn. Some however like Ruth Blaine's and Esther Berg's and Hortense Bass's and Louella Allgood's and Widder Shultz's and Mother Swain's were varyingly wet. Carrie Shaw's eyes, as she sagged against Nola Priest, were drowned by wretchedness. Maybe another hundred respectful or admiring or gratified or curious townspeople (permanent and transient) stood outside with their elbows on the windowsills or craning over the elbow-leaners or, in the case of children, squeezed tiptoe between them. As Carl Norris was to editorialize the next afternoon in the *Republican,* having delayed Friday's issue a day to cover the important event, Preacher Smith's quoted words were untypically brief but to the point:

"Folks, we're gathered here to bury a man.

"Sometimes some of us didn't know what kind of man. And sometimes I reckon he didn't either.

"But there's no mistaking he was a man.

"We're saying goodbye to him for a spell. While the rest of us stay behind for now we're going to meet folks on earth like the way he was maybe I heard 'til yesterday: unhappy. When we get up to Heaven—those makes it—we'll meet folks the way he is now anyhow: happy. But I don't know if anyone can be plumb happy down here and I'll tell you why: to be thataway everthing and everbody including yourself has got to be perfect and nothing or nobody is going to be perfect for you. The surer a man figures he can heave his own self out of his living bog the deeper he'll sink and unhappier he'll be. He just plain can't save himself."

(At this point Preacher Smith held up his Bible briefly: Ed.)

"And I've got the verses to prove it. Only right now we're

going out to the graveyard and put Luther Cain's body back where it come from and turn his spirit loose on the wind as the Injuns say. The pallbearers will bring him. The rest of you follow on out.

"Amen."

(Amen! Ed.)

CHAPTER 54

Beside the freshly filled grave after the crowd had gone quietly, except for some very young boys playing tag, Carrie sank gradually onto her long-skirted, side-folded legs, one arm around Howard's calves, head against one of his knees; and he lowered his hand gently to the top of her head; and they stayed that way for a while in the quick, red dusk crying mutely for Luther and for themselves and for each other. Presently she spoke.

"Will it be the same again ever?"

"Not the same, Carrie, but it will *BE*. You and me and his other loved ones and friends, we'll be; we'll go on living who knows how long or short. And he'll always live in our lives."

"What will become of Lester? And poor Ruth?"

"Ruth will keep being Lester's loving, loyal wife. And Lester— well Doc said he's going to hold an inquest on Luther's death right after Dowling's and those others' come Monday; and if Lester's not in jail 'til then he'll sure have the deputies for steady company. You know Lester's and Luther's guns in the fracas ended side by side on the ground don't you? Reckon it depends on who was after who. I figure though nobody Luther was ever after got away." Howard seemed to be talking to himself now. "Nobody faster than him. Sure not Lester. But Lester's not the important one. Luther is. And Luther found out—never mind with five minutes or fifty years to live—beyond a man's self is where he's going to find himself. You might say there's a terrible beauty in all this ugliness."

She looked slowly up at him, whispering. "Not terrible, Preacher; just beauty." After a moment with his supporting hand she arose. "I'm cold and it's getting night and I know, too, I can't stay here." She looked down once more at Luther's grave and took a deep, tremulous breath and exhaled with a gasp and turned in the direction of Bancroft. "You been good to stay with me."

Standing bareheaded and silent, he gazed after her as she walked across the Kansas plain toward the dark but not ominous eastern sky arching above the town's faint glow.

In Carl Norris's lamp-lit office the editor closed his journal of Bancroft with a sigh but not without hope.

Never.

340

Far beyond the Hudson River and the Wabash and the Mississippi and before the turn of the century Mark watched the sun stroke the day from the plains with red fingers. In the dusk a man and a woman stood silhouetted beside a grave looking at a range cow across the cemetery fence as it gave birth to its calf. Another dozen rods away a cow's skull lay in the brown grass. The woman took the man's hand. "Life. Living. I guess it hangs on, even when it ends. Just goes on and on, over and over again without end."

Mark heard his wife's voice and felt her hand squeeze his on the coverlet. He opened his eyes. She was standing close to his intensive-care bed staring at him shakenly. He felt as though she were standing on him rather than beside him; his chest was iron-bound against his breathing. He licked his lips and forced them to loose a whisper. "You haven't seen the end of me, either."

"Oh, Mark, now I know you're going to be fine. Like your doctor just told me. And we all are because my doctor said I'm going to have a baby at last." He could feel her smile. "It could have been from our twentieth's loving! We've got to think of a name, Mark. Oh, darling, I'm so glad you didn't leave us. But you've got to never come this close again, to find a way of fighting wrong without wronging yourself. You understand that?"

He spent the last of his temporary energy on a nod and a grin and a prophecy. "Beginning to . . . with the marshal's help." He was almost asleep. "Baby named 'Luther' or 'Carrie.' " He was asleep.

" 'Marshal?' ", she murmured; "Luther?' 'Carrie?' " He was dreaming again. She became aware of a gentle hand on her elbow. "Yes, Nurse. But I'll be back." She was speaking mostly to herself. "He needs me now more than ever before, you know."

"M'am, all good men need a good woman."

The cataract had sucked him within a gasp of its devouring brink and her with him. His ears roared with its threat. Its momentum seemed irresistible and in another instant should have been absolute except for the rope which the tall, shadowy man threw to them from his vantage point. Mark had the presence or luck or blessing to seize it and, clutching Mattie tightly, to hold onto it as their rescuer hauled his salvage to solid footing.

The man dropped the rope and swept off his round-crowned black hat toward the distant radiance of a brown-haired woman and saluted the nearer man and the nearer brown-haired woman; and his exultant whoop echoed across the space and time between their guises and his hymn out-rang all hate.
    "Hoorayandhallelujah!"

By Cal Nolan

New York—Nine months ago, when we wrote about the City's detective Sergeant Mark Keller and his wife, Mattie, we didn't have a finish for the story. His grievous wound threatened to end his life and theirs together and the career of truly one of "New York's Finest." Today, I can report the happy ending: the officer has recovered completely, is back on duty, in his words "for as much longer as they'll let me—as a kind of reborn man, you might say." And last night, Mattie gave birth to their first-born. . .